Praise for

DEATH IN A PROMISED LAND

THE TOWERS

ROBERT ANDREWS

POCKET BOOKS

New York   London   Toronto   Sydney   Tokyo   Singapore

For

Lansing Bennett	*Steve Knapp*
Frank Darling	*William Macko*
John Digiovanni	*Wilfredo Mercado*
Robert Kirkpatrick	*Monica Smith*

An *Original* Publication of POCKET BOOKS

POCKET BOOKS, a division of Simon & Schuster Inc.
1230 Avenue of the Americas, New York, NY 10020

ISBN: 0-671-86652-4

First Pocket Books printing May 1996

10 9 8 7 6 5 4 3 2 1

Cover design by Steven Ferlauto

Printed in the U.S.A.

Acknowledgments

No book is solely the creation of its author. This one owes much to a friend of many years, George Weigel. He was a trusted and imaginative sounding board throughout the writing. He then read the first manuscript with industry and thoroughness and commented with grace and tact. But even more than this, he has always been a refuge from the craziness that periodically afflicts Washington.

Thanks too, to J. J. Gertler, Al Srnka, Tom Ferrando, John Wilhelm, Tony Fainberg, Al Galiani, and Creid Johnson. Without their help, advice, and commentary, I would have stumbled far more often.

As is frequently the case with stories that involve the mirror-house of international espionage and terrorism, there are those who must remain nameless who provided details and insights along the way.

And my admiration and affection for my editor, Dana Isaacson, whose insights and perspective cleared out distracting thickets to bring a sharper focus on Bradford Sims and the horror that could wait just around the corner for all of us.

—Robert Andrews
Washington, D.C.

There are strong reasons to doubt that deterrence will be effective against a terrorist driven by extreme ideology, ethnic hatred or self-destructive behavior. Intelligence must urgently address the problem that there are those seeking to acquire and use weapons *in ways that we have up until now dismissed as irrational and not credible.*

> —David Kay, Chief nuclear weapons inspector for the United Nations in Iraq during 1991. *Wall Street Journal,* March 18, 1993

. . . this world . . . is a world very different than the one we have dealt with before. We may well find that the last forty-five years have been easy.

> —R. James Woolsey, Director, Central Intelligence Agency, December 2, 1992

Rockville, Maryland
January 25, 1993

. . . a dark, sunless world . . . never ending wind . . . a life-less plain broken by jagged cliffs . . . eternal night filled with nameless evil . . .

Shackled spread-eagled to the granite wall of a sheer precipice, Isaac Felton twisted against his chains to escape the blood-drenched talons ripping at his eyes. Helpless, sick with fear, he knew that in the next pass his face would be shredded, his eyes torn from their sockets. All around him the icy air shuddered with the frenzied beating of leathery wings. Felton struggled to scream but no sound came. The wings beat closer . . . the talons reaching . . .

Gasping for air, Felton awoke. Sobbing in relief, he waited for reality to wash away the obscene traces of the nightmare. He turned his head to stare at the green glow of his bedside clock. Monday, early morning—3:28 A.M.

Cold fingers probed the core of his body and Felton felt the nightmare returning, its tentacles reaching to reclaim him. Rolling himself in the blankets, his teeth began an uncontrollable chattering. Like a wave growing in a night sea, the nightmare swelled and now the cold fingers reached into his guts and twisted as he curled, fetuslike, trying vainly to escape the excruciating cramps.

Suddenly, from Felton's right leg, a pulsing pain, no more than a pinprick at first, ballooned into an immense living thing, speeding upward to join the agony in his stomach.

1

His body became a swirling vortex of pain. He pulled the blankets more tightly around himself, but the shivering worsened. Time raced in a crazy, dizzying spiral toward infinity, yet the green numbers on the clock still said 3:28.

Felton struggled to sit up, but his body refused to work. He got only a fraction of an inch before he fell back, paralyzed. Suddenly, the pain leaped into his chest, stabbing with a rapier intensity. His heart hammering, he tried to call out, but managed only a choking, gurgling sound.

A bedside light snapped on. The glare scalded his eyes.

"Isaac!"

His wife, up on one elbow, was over him, her face etched with fear.

Her face was the last thing Isaac Felton ever saw.

Northern Virginia
January 25, 1993

Michael Gribbins backed out of his driveway at his customary time of 7:45 A.M. Staff meeting started at 8:30, and he'd made it a habit to get to the office for at least one cup of coffee before. Traffic was unusually sparse on Route 123, and he drove quickly through the strip suburb of Vienna and past the huge mall at Tyson's Corner. Four miles farther east, however, he came to the usual stack-up at Langley, where two lanes of commuters waited at the light to make the turn into CIA headquarters.

Exhaust plumes clouded the chill air and the light seemed especially slow this morning. He rolled to a stop at the back of the line, looked at the dash clock and sighed; he was going to miss his coffee. He turned on the radio: WRC drive time call-in, the talk show host refereeing calls on the topic of the day, the Clinton presidency, now all of five days old.

Gribbins escaped into an increasingly frequent daydream: retirement and the trout stream in Idaho, both nineteen months away. Staring absentmindedly straight ahead, he felt his wrist flick into the first cast of the morning. The yellow leader carried the fly—a White Irresistible—tracing a lazy S-shaped path to drop softly through the mist that hung just above the stream's tumbling surface. Above, a red-tailed hawk hung in a rose and cobalt sky.

An insistent noise broke into the dreamworld of Idaho, bringing Gribbins bolt upright. Outside his passenger window, a bearded young man stood, a smile on his face.

Gribbins shook his head to clear away the traces of Idaho. He couldn't make sense of it—people didn't walk between cars, not in the middle of rush hour traffic, not at that intersection. Gribbins felt the horror claw at his throat when, in the last second of his life, he realized that the bearded man had rapped on his window with the muzzle of an AK-47 assault rifle.

1

And he shall set engines of war against thy walls,
and with his axes he shall break down thy towers.
—Ezekiel 26:9

The deaths of two CIA officers in the opening days of the Clinton administration triggered a chain of deadly events that led to an American awakening.

It was a reluctant awakening—the America that had vanquished the mighty Soviet Union would laugh at the notion that ragged bands of religious fanatics could seriously threaten the world's only remaining superpower. Even less did Washington's wise men imagine that those believers would bring their holy war to the United States itself.

This was not a war for land, or wealth, or to force a change of policy. This was a war of total death, a war to destroy the Great Satan. And Bradford Sims was to be the next link of this chain—a link that would be forged in the medieval hill town of San Gimignano, Italy, just hours after Mike Gribbins was killed.

Before they threw him out of the CIA, Bradford Sims, thirty-seven, had spent the last years of the Cold War running agents out of Prague, Czechoslovakia. He'd had a promising career in the Agency: the youngest chief of Berlin base, mentions in dispatches for helping capture the *Achille Lauro* hijackers, and the Intelligence Star for wounds received in the abortive coup against Mikhail Gorbachev in August 1991. Some had said he'd be the first black man to be the CIA's director.

The trouble came when he refused to ignore what others

5

before him had swept under the carpet. Outraged by official stonewalling and armed with new information from a KGB defector, Sims had taken off on a one-man crusade to prove that James Earl Ray had not been Martin Luther King's sole assassin.

There had been a lot of killing and the cleanup crews had had to work overtime. And when it was all over, the Judge had asked him to come back to the Agency. Sims had thought about it then turned the offer down. He wanted to find a quiet place where he could put his head back together and figure out what was next in his life. The quiet place turned out to be a farm near San Gimignano, just south of Florence.

For the first several months, Sims crammed each day with the hard work of making the farmhouse livable and shaking out his dusty Italian.

Inevitably, time began to drag. He didn't see spending his afternoons and evenings gossiping and drinking red wine with the regulars in the *caffès* on the piazza. Instead, Sims's interest in history led to a small article that he submitted to the *International Herald Tribune*—two thousand words on the stone towers of San Gimignano that made the walled village resemble a miniature of Manhattan's skyline.

To his surprise, the *Trib* had published the piece and a month later, an associate editor had sent Sims a letter of inquiry about a series of articles on Tuscany. Sims took just a day to consider the offer—new careers for old spies were hard to come by, and writing had always come easily to him—so now he was back in harness, meeting deadlines. Different deadlines than the reporting he'd done for the Agency, but deadlines nonetheless. And, Sims had to admit to himself, he'd gotten infected with the Hemingway bug at too young an age to fight it off. Since *For Whom the Bell Tolls,* he'd thought that the life of a writer would be incredibly romantic and exciting.

It was just after two in the morning, and Sims bent over a large thirteenth century folio, trying to make sense of the journal of the Salvucci, one of the two great families of San Gimignano. San Gimignano's towers had come about because of the obsession of the Salvucci and their competitors, the Ardinghelli, in building square stone towers, some as high as fifteen stories. The towers served two purposes: as icons of wealth, and as refuges if the city walls were breached, which periodically happened with bloody consequences as roaming mercenary armies pillaged northern Italy.

He had checked the dates again and again. The puzzle remained: if, as the standard Italian histories had it, the Salvucci had been slaughtering the lords of lower Tuscany in 1293, then it didn't follow that they would have been at home in San Gimignano, overseeing the building of yet another tower. Day after tomorrow he had to have the copy to the *Trib*'s Paris offices. He could finesse the question, but he knew he wouldn't—he knew he'd stay up until he either found an answer or decided it couldn't be found.

Sims rubbed his eyes, then rose to work the stiffness out of his back and legs, pacing the large storeroom off the kitchen he had turned into a study. Windowless, it gave him the sense of isolation he needed for translating and writing, but tonight it felt cramped and confining. Flexing his legs, he found his way in the dark up the familiar stairs. At the top of the stairs, a long passageway extended right and left. To the right and toward the back of the house, a low flight of steps led up to a door which in turn led to the attached barn. To the left was the large master bedroom with its terrace that overlooked the valley with its vineyards and, in the spring and summer, fields of sunflowers.

He stood in the doorway, and in the glow of a dim nightlight, admired Lourdes, a woman whose tawny skin smelled of oranges. Her raven black hair fanned across the pillow, and her generous mouth that hinted of a wide sensuous smile even in sleep. A thick feather comforter covered her, but he could picture the delicate curve of the small of her back and how, downward, it flared out over her hips and her firm buttocks, and how, up and around, the same curve led to her full breasts.

Lourdes's father had been a *pied noir*, a penniless French farmer who'd left the Alsace for Algeria, married a local

7

woman, and carved out a farm near Sétif. Lourdes had left Algeria to come to paint San Gimignano in the light of late summer.

They had met on her third day in the town. She had set up a folding chair in the Piazza della Cisterna and had been working on a preliminary sketch of the towers. He had been at a long lunch with the town's registrar, negotiating the loan of the town's oldest records.

That afternoon, he had shown her around San Gimignano. Later in the day they had talked and drunk too much wine and then had a very late dinner at La Griglia's on the Via San Matteo. He had invited her for dinner the next evening at his old farmhouse just outside town. She had driven up in her battered Citroën and they had made love that night and she had simply stayed.

Watching her sleep, Sims realized, not for the first time, that she had made the past six months far richer than he'd thought possible when they'd met. Neither felt ready to ask the question of how long. There was an unspoken agreement between them that it was enough for now to say that there would be a tomorrow. Suddenly wanting to be beside her, Sims took a step toward the bed then remembered the lights and computer in the study.

Downstairs, as he passed through the kitchen, he heard a familiar scratching at the courtyard door. Thinking of Lourdes upstairs and the warmth of her, he sighed and opened the door.

"*Ciao,* Orso," Sims said with exaggerated formality. "You're out late."

A large buff-colored cat made an entrance, fussily kicking its feet to rid them of the outside dampness.

Orso was Giovanni's cat, and Giovanni tended to the vines and Giovanni's wife saw to the marketing and house-keeping. Giovanni was also a retired security officer of *Servizio Informazioni Generale e Sicurézza Interni*—SIGSI, Italian intelligence.

When Sims had decided to come to San Gimignano, the Judge had persuaded him to accept what the Agency called "discreet protection." At first, Sims had said no, but when Giovanni, his wife, and Orso had shown up, he'd agreed to a month's trial. The Italian couple had moved into the cottage that, with the barn, the main house, and the connecting walls, made a compound that surrounded a cobblestoned courtyard. They were still here almost a year later, and Sims had come to enjoy their company and, in particular, Giovanni's operatic tales of deceit, deception, and bravery in the Italian service.

Orso rubbed against Sims's legs, and Sims went to the cupboard where he kept an emergency supply of dried cat food. He set a ceramic bowl on the floor and stood back. Orso paid no attention, but kept winding around Sims's legs.

Sims addressed the cat with mock severity. "Goddamnit, Orso, I don't have all night. Now eat or get."

He bent and ruffled the big cat's back fur and ran his fingertips down the cat's spine. Orso arched his back, looked up at Sims, and ignored the food. It wasn't until Sims straightened up that he realized that his hand was wet. He stretched out the hand, angling it to catch the dim light from the study, and rubbed his thumb across his fingertips. The wet was blood.

He picked up Orso. The cat seemed unharmed. The blood drenched Orso's hindquarters and legs and now Sims saw the bloody tracks on the terra-cotta tile floor near the door. Then, from out in the courtyard, he heard the slightest grinding sound: the sound heavy boots would make on the paving stones.

Still holding the cat, Sims shut his eyes for a moment and tried not to think about what the noise and Giovanni's bloody cat meant late on a cold winter night. He couldn't stop the thinking and opened his eyes and saw the blood again. Oh, shit, the words formed, and then he knew what had happened and what would happen. He put the cat down gently on the floor and walked quickly to the study.

Seconds later, Sims slipped into bed. Lourdes, still asleep, but sensing him near, rolled toward him, fitting her body to his. Bringing a hand to her cheek, he kissed her. As she started to respond, he pulled away, putting his lips to her ear. He let the air out of his lungs so his whisper wouldn't hiss on the esses.

9

"Somebody's here. Maybe to break in the house. We've got to get up."

She started to say something, but he slid his hand around to cover her mouth.

"Don't talk. Get dressed." He whispered other instructions, watching her eyes widen, seeing how the whites of her eyes had a bluish purple undertinge in the dim light.

"You understand? No talking," he whispered to her. When she nodded, he rolled off his side of the bed and stood by the doorway. He watched her pull on the canvas painter's trousers she'd flung over the arm of a nearby chair, the heavy Georgetown University sweatshirt she'd appropriated from him months ago, then slip her feet into a pair of worn sneakers.

The sneakers on, Lourdes looked up and for the first time noticed the weapon. He saw her mouth open in surprise and he shook his head and waved a warning hand. Then he made a follow-me sign and slipped out the door and into the passageway.

Sims lay belly down on the landing at the top of the stairs leading to the barn. From here, he covered the length of the passageway leading to the bedroom. To his left, at middistance down the passageway, was the stairway from the first floor. Lourdes lay close beside him on his left, a hand wrapped around his biceps, her face buried in the crook of her elbow. She's not trembling, Sims thought, and wondered if he was. Sometimes you didn't know—you knew what everybody was doing except yourself.

From reflex, Sims began counting. He'd learned to count on a night surveillance long ago. You count because if you don't, time becomes everything and nothing at all and soon you start to see and hear all kinds of shit.

Sims started with a-thousand-one, a-thousand-two, counting and watching the stairs and the passageway. He cradled the stubby Bullpup shotgun in the hollow of his right shoulder. Just over two feet long, the weapon carried six twelve-gauge shot shells. Each shell contained nine double-aught lead shot, each about the size of a pencil eraser. In the distance to the bedroom, Sims figured that the shot pattern would spread to about a foot in diameter. A large enough hole to take down a grizzly, or a man.

He counted. He finished his first hundred and was up to twenty-eight again when he saw the first figure. Little more than a darker dark against the top of the stairs, it took form as it moved toward the partially open bedroom door and the night-light within. Several feet behind, another shadow. Behind that, a third.

They were good, Sims observed. The lead shadow crouched lower as it approached the doorway, the second kept its distance and the third stopped to guard the top of the stairs. Now the first two shadows flattened themselves against the wall on either side of the bedroom door.

Beside him, Sims felt Lourdes move and out of the corner of his eye he could see that she'd raised her head slightly. She, too, was watching the shadows. He let go of the weapon's pistol grip and squeezed her hand, willing her to remain silent, if only for the next second, the next two seconds—

Lightning flashed and thunder exploded in the passageway. The two shadows kicked the bedroom door wide open and sprayed the room with submachine gun fire. Muzzle flashes glared in a continuous jittery light. The hail of bullets tore at the room, shredding furniture, drapes, their bed, shattering glass. Feathers, bits of cloth, clouds of gunsmoke filled the air.

The shooting kept on, relentless, merciless, all consuming.

The noise climbed in pitch and the vibration hammered Sims's ears and chest and he felt Lourdes struggle beside him, writhing in the unstopping terror of it.

Silence and darkness came, the suddenness as shocking as the cutting off of a scream in full voice.

His night vision ruined by the muzzle flashes, Sims saw only blackness until one of the shadows switched on a flashlight. The beam raced around the room then came to focus on the bed.

"Vuoto!" one of the shadows screamed—empty!

Sims killed him first. Compared to the rattling of the submachine guns, Sims's shotgun thundered like a booming cannon. Slamming the slide back, then forward, Sims chambered another shell before the sound of the first shot died away. Swinging the muzzle slightly to his right, he fired again, and again the passageway became daylight.

Sims saw the second shadow become a man in a black jumpsuit. The man was turning his submachine gun toward Sims as the flight of double-aught shot struck. A large portion of the man's lower body disappeared into a dark red spray.

In the shot's after-flash, Sims retained a retina-image of the third shadow at the head of the stairs—the man's face—and the kill-lust on the face. He swung the shotgun toward the image and fired and saw in the light that no one was there. All that remained were Lourdes's screams.

Dawn came as a gray mist drifting from the glaciers to the north. In spite of the damp cold, Sims stood in the open doorway of the kitchen, staring into the courtyard at Lourdes's dented blue Citroën, its doors and trunk open. Beyond the Citroën, at the far corner of the courtyard was the cottage where Giovanni and his wife had lived and died. A green and white police ambulance and the small black Fiat of the medical examiner were parked in front.

Lourdes brushed by, arms full. She hadn't spoken since the killings. She had painstakingly cleaned the blood from the cat. Then, for almost an hour, she'd sat in Sims's study, holding Orso in her lap, rocking back and forth. Then she began packing her car. He'd offered to help, but she'd only shaken her head.

An ambulance attendant emerged from Giovanni's cottage, opened the rear of the vehicle and pulled out a folded gurney. It made a crashing noise as it hit the courtyard cobblestones.

Sims had found Giovanni and his wife in bed, their throats cut. He had sat by the bed until they weren't Giovanni and his wife anymore, but only two bodies, and then he'd called the trouble number at Florence base.

The duty officer had woken the chief of base who'd had Sims tell the story twice more. He then told Sims to sit tight. The police came forty minutes later. There had been the prescribed taping off of the scene, the photographing, the fingerprinting.

The police *tenente,* a lean, wolfish-looking man, had wanted to take statements, starting with Lourdes. Sims had refused to let him and there had been a heated, nearly violent argument.

Then the SIGSI representative arrived by helicopter, the helicopter making much noise and causing the police to look meaningfully at each other, then at Sims. The SIGSI man was a patrician Roman with exquisitely styled silver hair who had a brief, one-sided conversation with the police *tenente.* The *tenente* had looked angrily at Sims, then back at the SIGSI man and finally nodded.

The SIGSI official had walked over to Sims. A straightforward case of banditry and murder, he had explained. *La violenza* was shameful, the official shook his head as if suffering much pain. It used to be in this country . . . The *signorina?* The SIGSI official had looked up at Sims's question and shrugged. Of course she is free to go. Why should she not be free to go?

Lourdes shut the Citroën's trunk, making a hollow thunking sound that echoed in the courtyard. A dove on the barn roof took flight in a noisy flapping of wings. Suddenly forlorn and fragile, Lourdes stood by the back of her car, a hand still on the trunk. She looked at Sims.

With a growing empty feeling, he started across the courtyard toward her. She had on a bright yellow slicker and Orso was rubbing against her legs. Behind her, two white-jacketed attendants wheeled a gurney out of Giovanni's house to the waiting hearse. The gurney carried a body bag and Sims wondered whether it was Giovanni or his wife. He stopped close enough to Lourdes to take her in his arms, but kept his hands at his side.

Her eyes, puffed and red-rimmed, stared dully at him. It was not a look of accusation or even of pain, merely one of defeat and emptiness. She stooped and picked up the cat, cradling it in her arms. She rubbed her cheek against the animal. Orso mewed softly and she put the cat in the back of the car where it worked itself into a nest atop a tangled pile of clothes.

Lourdes looked at the cat for a moment, then looked up at Sims. "I'm not coming back," she said.

"Where'll you go?"

Her dark brown eyes fastened for an instant on something past him, then she focused on him. "We are through," she said simply. "It doesn't matter where I go."

Sims made a futile gesture, a small wave of a hand around the courtyard. "I'm sorry—"

She cut him off, motioning with her head to the house. "What happened . . . it was part of you . . . something you were."

"I thought it was over."

"You never told me . . ."

"Because I thought it was over."

She stared at him a long time, her eyes wounds of betrayal. "It's not."

Sims remembered the face of the third shadow, the one at the top of the stairs, and he shook his head. "No," he said, "it's not over."

And he stood in the center of the courtyard as she drove away. He watched her car disappear down the road to Florence.

Sims walked back to the house. When he'd come here, he'd made plans. More out of habit and training than in any expectation that something like this might actually occur. That's why there'd been the shotgun. He hadn't thought he'd need it, but he was thankful for it now. And thankful for the plan that, for a little while, would keep his mind off what he'd lost. Passing through the kitchen, he entered his study.

In the cabinet where he'd kept the shotgun, he reached into a compartment and came out with a zippered canvas pouch. He took the pouch to a plain wooden table where he pulled up a chair and sat down to inventory the contents. A flashlight, a Swiss army knife. Large battle bandage in a foil wrapper. Waterproof match container with a small compass set in its top. Lock picks in a flat plastic case. A wad of mixed currency held by a rubber band. He riffled through it—three thousand dollars more or less in dollars, lira, and francs. Last, he came to two sturdy manila envelopes.

He pinched together the metal wings of the clasp and opened the first envelope: inside, a dark blue U.S. passport, an expired District of Columbia voter registration card, a D.C. driver's license, all in his name. He inspected the passport, saw it was still valid, then opened the second envelope. Inside, another passport, this one Nigerian, and a small gray booklet, an international driver's license. Both the passport and the license carried Sims's photo over the name of Otmar Schelleng.

He methodically stuffed everything back in the pouch. He'd finished the inventory. He couldn't avoid thinking any longer and he felt his anger returning, impatient and demanding.

He shut his eyes and tried to make sense of the night. The face on the stairway came back to him—Emil Schmar. Schmar had tried to kill him once before—a lifetime ago, it seemed to Sims. Now he was back. Was it something old? Or something new? Sims thought about Schmar for a while, then shrugged. Whatever brought Schmar here, it had something to do with the Agency.

Like many Agency officers, Sims had come aboard without realizing at first that he was, indeed, coming aboard. The recruitment had begun in Sims's junior year at Georgetown. Just after football season, his history professor had told him about a well paying part-time job. Sims found the address, a frayed mansion on Massachusetts Avenue. There he'd met Riddle. A large round man of indeterminate age who spoke with what Sims later found out was a Cambridge English accent, Riddle ran a government office that ostensibly cataloged foreign broadcast transcripts. During Sims's junior and senior years, Riddle deftly steered Sims into serious chess and into the arms of the Agency's clandestine service.

As is often the case for many hinge-of-life decisions, when Sims looked back from the perspective of a few years, sorting the motives that caused him to go into the Agency resembled peeling an onion.

To do something that's more than filling up a bank account, he first answered himself.

To keep the feeling that he only got in football, when he was running out front with no one ahead of him.

And, too, Bradford Sims wanted to be something other than what everyone expects a smart black man to be.

But, Sims found later, when things got truly binding, when he got down to the very heart of himself, he knew he'd done it for the simplest, most unsophisticated reason of all—he truly thought he was doing something good for his country.

The Agency had picked Sims apart. In a sparsely furnished room in a Rosslyn apartment, he passed the polygraph tests designed to uncover any falsehoods in his forty-page biographical history form. He impressed the doctors with his strength, endurance, and coordination. The shrinks probed every detail of his life: his father the D.C. cop, his mother the nurse, his uncle the preacher, the women, school, and football. They particularly noted his high scores in cognitive skills, especially in deductive reasoning and problem solving.

Five days after the testing, a map arrived in the mail. No return address on the envelope. The map and a four-hour drive south had put him at the gates of Camp Peary, near Williamsburg. Generations of American spies, however, had known it as their boot camp and called it the Farm.

In his first three months, he breezed through intensive classroom work in recruiting, reporting, communications, surveillance, and operational security. His instructors were the best of the old hands. What they taught, they had practiced. That they were alive proved that they had been good at their craft. It was in a Farm session on the history of intelligence that Sims learned that Riddle, who had recruited him, had been one of the more serious spies in both the British and American intelligence services, with a career that began in Hitler's Germany.

In his fieldwork in the following five months, Sims did especially well in unarmed combat, demolitions, and the darker skills such as SE (surreptitious entry—locks and picks) and surveillance (bugs, taps, and cameras). The trainers uncovered and developed an aptitude for languages and exceptional proficiency with a variety of weapons from *shuriken,* the star-shaped Ninja throwing blades, to Stinger antiaircraft missiles.

Christmas 1978 had been his first away from Washington, posted to Prague station as a junior-level case officer. The next four years had been tumultuous: the Iranian hostage crisis, Ronald Reagan elected president, Leonid Brezhnev dying after miring the Soviet Union in Afghanistan, and Anwar Sadat assassinated in Egypt after making peace with Israel.

Sims had played a part in all these events—recruiting an Iranian student to carry a radio in to the hostages in the American Embassy in Tehran, establishing a covert pipeline for weapons for Afghan *mujaheddin* fighting the Red Army, eavesdropping on Czech intelligence's escapades in the Middle East on behalf of its protectors in Moscow.

Sims had done well in Prague, and so the talent scouts at headquarters sent him to Berlin as deputy chief of base. There, the Cold War had settled into a humdrum standoff until a wave of bombings swept over Europe. In October 1985, Sims had a firsthand taste of counterterrorism tactics when Kamäl Zohdi's fanatics hijacked the *Achille Lauro,* an Italian cruise ship, and murdered a wheelchair-confined American tourist. Later, Sims's sources inside the Turkish foreign worker community paid off after a popular West Berlin discotheque blew up, killing several American GIs. Within hours, Sims's agent handed over tapes of conversations that convincingly pointed to Qaddafi's Libya, tapes that led to the U.S. bombing raids on Tripoli the following week.

After a year back in the States, Sims returned to Prague, this time as deputy chief of station. There, he worked to hasten the crumbling of the Soviet empire—quiet support for East German demonstrations in Leipzig and Dresden and the uprisings in East Berlin. Payoff came in November 1989, when the Wall came down to the accompaniment of Beethoven's Ninth Symphony as if choreographed especially for CNN. A month later, Czechoslovakia threw off Communist rule, although the Soviet army stayed on, an intimidating and unwelcome visitor who had outworn its welcome.

The finale came in 1991—the Soviet Union's unraveling began with the August coup against Gorbachev in Moscow. Sims had helped Gorbachev climb back on top of the heap, but in doing so, he'd gotten the short end of a running gun battle with the KGB's border guards.

Patched up in Prague, he'd been evacuated to Bethesda Naval Hospital aboard an unmarked jet. There, two operations on his shoulder and medals awarded in a secret ceremony. And then he'd found the forgotten files on the King assassination, and then . . .

Sims put everything back in the pouch except for the money, which he stuffed in his jacket pocket. He zipped the pouch shut and put it and the Salvucci journals in a worn knapsack. Leaving the study, he looked up the stairs for a moment, then shrugged to himself and climbed them slowly. Reaching the top, he stopped and stood still, looking down the hall to the bedroom. Taking care to avoid the blood on the tiles, he walked to the bedroom door.

As if meeting an invisible barrier, Sims stopped in the doorway and leaned his head wearily against the wood of the door frame. The violence that had been done to the room—*their* room—ate away like acid at the memories of what he and Lourdes had had here. She'd been right, what had happened had happened because of what he had been.

Like a sudden storm, Sims's anger broke, and he pounded his hand against the door frame, giving way to a swirling rage, dark and murderous. Deep inside, the injustice of it boiled and erupted. Anger at Schmar and whoever had sent him. Anger at a future that had been destroyed before it had even begun. Anger at Lourdes for deserting him. His fist hammered the rough wood and Sims knew that he was really angry at himself. He should have known that he couldn't walk away from his own history so easily.

Dulled from the outburst, Sims stared for another moment at the ravaged room, then straightened up, turned his back on it, and made his way back down the stairs. Whatever it was that brought this about, it wouldn't stop here, and there damn sure wasn't any walking away from that. And he couldn't wait here. He might not be so lucky in a return engagement with Schmar.

Locking the house, Sims shouldered the knapsack and took the shortcut across the fields to San Gimignano three miles away. There, he woke the registrar and returned the Salvucci journals. His second stop was at the home of D'Antouno, the banker who had served as the agent for the farm's owner. Sims left a thousand dollars for rent and damages, and a forwarding address at a post office box he had kept in Washington.

Outside the town wall at the Porta San Matteo, he hired a cab and forty-five minutes later, he was in Florence. At the flea market on the Via Pietraplana, he bought a cheap overnight bag, then found a coffee shop filled with working-men and the rich smells of baking bread and roasted coffee. After rolls and a *caffè ristrétto,* he entered the toilet, where, in a stall, he operated on the bag. In the bottom liner along a welted seam, he cut an unobtrusive slit. Into this pocket, he slipped half his money, his American passport, and the lock picks.

Using the Nigerian passport and international driver's license, he rented an Alfa Romeo from a sleepy clerk at the Hertz counter at the Continental Hotel down by the river and made for A-1 north. Holding the sleek Alfa at a steady 150 kilometers per hour, he bypassed Milan, and before eleven, he crossed into Switzerland north of Lugano. At the rest stop at Bellinzona, he found that snow had closed the pass at San Gottardo, and so he took N13 north. Soon he was seven thousand feet above sea level in the Lepontine Alps, his headlights boring through the long tunnel of the San Bernardino Pass.

Shortly after two-thirty, Sims, as Otmar Schelleng, said to hell with the cost and splurged for the last seat in first class on a SwissAir 747 at Zurich's Kloten airport. Before pulling away from the gate, a flight attendant came by taking drink orders. Sims waved her away, then said to hell with that, too, and called her back and ordered a double Stolichnaya and rocks.

On its way to cruising altitude, the big plane broke

through the gray overcast. Sims ordered another double Stoly and sat staring morosely out the window at a deceptively simple world, nothing but a clear blue dome over a tufted field of cotton that stretched out to the horizon in every direction.

Somewhere in the grayness below, Giovanni's sons and daughters would be hearing the news about their father and mother. And somewhere down there, Lourdes would be driving the beat-up Citroën. She'd be driving too fast and, without him there, she'd be talking to the cat. He felt the vodka hitting him like a velvet hammer. She'd be heading toward Strasbourg, he guessed, where her grandmother lived. Then he remembered how she had put it in the courtyard that morning—it was over, and it didn't matter where she was going. As he thought about Lourdes, the anger and slow burn of resentment returned. It wouldn't do any good to think about her, Sims told himself. What was important now was Schmar.

2

As Bradford Sims finished his second drink, a green and white Airbus A310, Alitalia's Flight 2908 from Florence, touched down on runway Two-Eight at Paris's Charles de Gaulle Airport. Among the first passengers off the plane was a tall man in a dark raincoat who walked with a slight but noticeable limp. His black hair and the raincoat framed a thin face, pale almost to the point of luminescence. The face, someone once remarked, of a fallen angel.

Emil Schmar felt no frustration at having missed the assignment on the black American in San Gimignano; he would have felt no flush of victory had he succeeded. Killing was an art, not a science; it sometimes took many brush strokes to fill a canvas. He passed quickly through customs and took a cab to an address in the third *arrondissement*.

A steady rain was falling and cars and delivery trucks choked the center of Paris, and so it was more than an hour before the cab turned onto Rue Picardie. Schmar paid the driver and got out in front of a small cafe. Standing under the cafe's dripping awning, he smoked a cigarette while surveying the narrow street.

He located Zohdi's bodyguards almost immediately—one was sitting in his car almost directly across from the Hotel Vieux Saule. On the second floor of a cheap *pension* a few doors down from the car, he saw the flutter of a curtain being pulled aside and the arm of a man who'd been standing too close to the window.

Pitching his cigarette into the gutter, Schmar crossed the street and approached the rear of the car, keeping close to the buildings' awnings and overhangs.

The man inside the car was sipping tea, blowing across the top of a Styrofoam cup as he bent down to watch the hotel entrance out the far window.

Schmar walked up to the car and stood for a moment studying the watcher's vulnerable neck, inches away. He calculated how the glass might deflect a bullet, then, satisfied, he reached out and tapped a fingernail on the aiming point.

Inside the car, the startled man spun, spilling his tea, but Schmar had already crossed the street. Before he entered the hotel, he turned, aimed a trigger finger at the watcher in the *pension* window, and squeezed off two imaginary shots.

The lone clerk on duty behind the desk looked up from a book.

"Chambre deux cent vingt," Schmar told him as he crossed the small lobby.

The clerk made as if to ask Schmar's business. Then, looking at the man's face, he apparently thought better of it and pointed wordlessly toward the elevator before ducking back into his book.

Room 220 was at the end of the corridor, guarded by two men with short dark beards. Both wore ill-fitting suits. No ties—their white collarless shirts were buttoned at the neck. One stood by the door, the other, a short distance away, sat in a straight wood chair, its back against the hallway wall.

Schmar gave them better marks than the watcher in the car. At least they were alert and covered their backs. He walked toward them, taking care to keep his hands out from his side and to make no quick movements.

The one standing stepped to partially block the door and frowned at Schmar. "You are late."

Schmar paused in front of the man and shrugged. He brushed by and opened the door.

The two men in the small suite sat in easy chairs well away from the window. A low table between them held a tray with glasses and bottles of mineral water and orange juice. Schmar stood at a semblance of military attention before the men. They were only men, and he could kill them as easily as any men, but these two—for now—were his . . . clients.

Clients. Schmar liked the word. A straightforward businesslike word, *client*. Clients sought a service. He provided it. They paid. That was that.

No more of this romantic shit about killing for the revolution. No one gave a shit about causes anymore. The Americans were selling franchised hamburgers and pastel condoms in Red Square and there was talk of putting Lenin's corpse on a world tour—perhaps with a rock group? No, now it was a different world. Now money was everything, and in a market economy you sold what you could sell, and Schmar sold killing.

"You are late," said Kamāl Zohdi. Zohdi was a neat, compact man. Like his goons in the hall, Zohdi wore a thick, well-trimmed beard. Unlike the goons, his taste in clothes was impeccable and ran to Italian conservative. Today he wore a dark charcoal double-breasted suit with a pale salmon shirt and a tightly knotted burgundy tie.

"The traffic," Schmar grudgingly gave the explanation. He disliked Zohdi. Not because he was an Arab—Schmar had no use for racial distinctions. He disliked Zohdi because the man was incomprehensible. And Zohdi was incomprehensible because of the way he looked at death. Schmar understood killing people because they got in your way. Or you were paid to do so. But Zohdi . . . this man killed for his *god?* Schmar would get that far then shrug to himself. No skin off his ass. Fine. As long as Zohdi paid the tab. And Zohdi, so far, had paid.

The other man, a man with a long brooding face and a thick mane of silver hair, motioned Schmar to a third chair.

That was Sergei Fedorovich Okolovich, the last chairman of the KGB. Okolovich had tried to make the jump from KGB to the new Russian Intelligence Service, but that had been too much of a stretch. The long knives had been out for the privileged of the *nomenklatura* and Okolovich had been one of the most privileged.

Schmar took his seat.

"You failed," Zohdi hurled the accusation.

"Failed!" Schmar felt his face tighten. "There can't be guarantees—"

Zohdi cut him off with a slashing hand gesture. "You failed."

Okolovich interrupted, trying to smooth things over. "Perhaps," he said soothingly, "the attempt in Italy could have gone better had we more time for planning."

Eyes wide, Zohdi sprang from his chair and shook an angry fist at Okolovich.

"Do not attempt to shift blame!" he screamed at the Russian, "I won't have it! I forbid it! Remember, Okolovich, you were the one who let Valek defect! You were the one who let him escape with the files!"

"But we've gotten rid of two of those who could have the files."

"Two! But the third remains! If he has the files, and if he turns them over"—Zohdi stopped and took a deep breath, as if by saying what he feared, he'd cause it to happen—"if he turns the files over, then everything I have worked for could be destroyed."

"A lot of *if*s, Kamāl."

Zohdi got even angrier. "I am where I am *because* I think of the *if*s, Russian. Remember, Okolovich, who are the winners and who are the losers. Your empire lies in ruins because we destroyed you in Afghanistan. We, the *mujaheddin,* brought you lords of Moscow to your knees."

Zohdi, face flushed, paused to gather his breath. His voice grew heavy and dramatic, as if swearing an oath. "And, Russian, we are going to do the same with the Americans."

Schmar shot Okolovich a questioning look. In return, Okolovich made a small hand gesture that said later.

"I have set events in motion," Zohdi rasped, paying no attention to the silent exchange between Schmar and Okolovich. Zohdi's eyes took on the glistening frenetic energy of a ravenous wolf. "Momentous events! I am going to bring death to America! In a month—*thirty days!*—America will no longer pollute the wellspring of Islam. America will cease to exist!"

The shining eyes danced from Okolovich to Schmar and back to Okolovich. *"Cease to exist!"* he repeated, his voice rising. But suddenly he stopped, as if a last, fraying strand of rationality held him in check, preventing him from saying more. He sat back in his chair, breathing deeply as though recovering from a great exertion. Slowly his face lost its angry flush and his eyes grew calm.

"A month from now, the world will know what I have done." A cool calculating tone replaced the passionate heat in Zohdi's voice. "But until then, I must have secrecy. I cannot have our preparations upset by this man . . ." —Zohdi snapped his fingers at Schmar—"this man, his name . . . ?"

"Sims," Schmar supplied.

"Yes, yes." Zohdi turned toward Okolovich. "Where is he?"

"We suspect he's gone back to America," Okolovich said. "We believe he will go to Washington."

Zohdi took this in. "You have information about this man?"

Okolovich nodded.

"Stay after him, Okolovich." Zohdi stared at Okolovich until he got an answering nod, then picked his overcoat off a chair and walked to the door.

Zohdi stopped at the door and turned to Okolovich and Schmar. "You realize we both have a stake in this man Sims?" Again the demanding stare until Okolovich obediently nodded. Zohdi then left, taking the room's energy with him.

Schmar and Okolovich sat in their chairs, listening to the sounds of Zohdi outside the door with his bodyguards, then, moments later, the more distant grinding of the elevator.

"Bastard," Okolovich breathed. He said it warily, as though he feared Zohdi might fling open the door and catch him at his treason.

"Do you need his money?"

Okolovich stared glumly at the door through which Zohdi had disappeared. The look on his face was that of a trapped

25

man. "That's what got me into this mess. Now I can't get out," he said more to himself than to Schmar.

"You owe me an explanation, Sergei," said Schmar.

"Explanation?"

"Explanation. You called me with your hair on fire. You wanted Sims dead. A chance to even an old score and make some good money, you said. You said nothing about files."

"Isn't the money good enough?"

"It was, before today. But it looks like the value of Sims has gone up. So has my price for killing him." Schmar watched as Okolovich, without hesitation, nodded agreement. "Now," said Schmar, "what about these files?"

Okolovich was silent for a moment, as if weighing how much to tell Schmar. With a shrug of resignation, he threw open his hands. "Miloslav Valek defected in December 1991—"

"I remember Valek's defection, Sergei," Schmar said impatiently. "What's that got to do with this?"

"Before Valek left the KGB, he copied certain files."

"Of what?"

"All my dealings with Zohdi—everything."

"But you killed Valek."

Okolovich nodded. "And for over a year, we thought that the secret of where he'd hidden the files died with him. But someone, somehow, got the files."

"How do you know?"

"Ten days ago, we got a demand for money. The demand was accompanied by samples from the files. There is no doubt—someone has Valek's files. If those files surface, everything will be exposed—"

"Including the Arab's crazy scheme?"

Face ashen, Okolovich paused, then, "Whether Zohdi's scheme is crazy or not doesn't matter. He *thinks* it will work, and he thinks that he is doing the will of his god. He has the money and he has the talent. And he has the single-mindedness to crush anything that he believes stands in his way."

Okolovich thrust his head forward and caught Schmar in a piercing look. "Anything that stands in his way, Emil. That means Sims and it means you and me."

"What makes you think Sims has the files?"

"I don't *know* that he has them. But we narrowed it down to three CIA officers who had access to Valek. Sims was one of them. We killed the other two."

"What's the Arab got planned?"

Okolovich didn't answer, but stared off into the distance, as if still coping with the mysterious way that things had come down to this, still unable to understand why he was no longer one of the most powerful men in the Soviet Union and why the Soviet Union itself was no more. "Planned?" Okolovich asked absently.

"Planned for the Americans."

Okolovich snapped out of it and focused on Schmar. "I don't know exactly . . . and I don't want to know. Whatever it is, we can't be connected with it. If Sims has those files and if they surface, it won't only be Zohdi's ass, it'll be ours as well."

"Ours? You mean yours."

Okolovich's lips pressed to a thin line. "Oh no, Emil. If it is my ass, it will be yours, too. We've got to keep those files from surfacing for thirty days."

Without expression, Schmar regarded the Russian. "And so Sims?"

"And so Sims."

3

At four-thirty, Eastern Standard time, Sims passed effortlessly through U.S. customs at New York's Kennedy Airport using the Otmar Schelleng alias. Otmar Schelleng then disappeared as Sims slipped the Nigerian passport and driver's license into the slit in the bottom of his overnight bag. At Avis, he rented a blue Buick, and by seven-thirty, he called Riddle from a pay phone near Havre de Grace, Maryland, ninety miles north of Washington.

Just after nine, Sims parked the Buick in a garage at Sixteenth and H. For a moment he stood at the garage entrance, surveying the streets and sidewalks. This was the western fringe of political Washington, where Pennsylvania Avenue connected the Capitol to the White House. If Capitol Hill with its crazy quilt town houses, run-down parks, and raucous bars represented the Democrats, this part of town was definitely Republican, with its pricey hotels, gilt-edge office buildings, and expense account restaurants.

He turned his collar up against the chill and started off down Sixteenth toward Lafayette Park. At the Hay Adams hotel, he got his first view of the White House, floating almost dreamlike in the winter mist and the glow of hidden floodlights. He had grown up among Washington's monuments, yet no matter how often he saw it, the White House brought on a stirring sense of pride. There was nothing to bitch about, he told himself. He was home and he was alive.

He walked into the park, straight for the White House, then, halfway in, took a path off to his right, toward the stately redbrick Federal row houses where Stephen Decatur and Henry James had once lived. Behind him, the brick pathways were empty. Nonetheless, he continued a roughly circular route that took him out of the park and up Seventeenth back toward I Street.

Still not satisfied he hadn't picked up a tail, he stepped past a derelict at Farragut West and took the down escalator to the subway.

The platform was nearly empty. A middle-aged white commuter in a tan raincoat leaned against a railing, dividing his attention between his newspaper and four black teenagers in a rowdy conversation on a nearby bench. Sims waited near the escalator. Flashing lights along the platform edge announced an approaching train. With a rush of air and clattering wheels, an Orange Line train pulled in, swallowed the anxious commuter and the teenagers, and left. Seeing both platforms were empty, Sims left by the Eighteenth Street entrance.

Five minutes later, he tried the service door behind Riddle's building. The door was locked. Slipping the lock pick case from his jacket pocket, Sims selected two spring-steel instruments resembling dental probes. Both about three inches long, the tension tool ending in an L-shaped rod, the pick's end had a rounded tip with a slight upward curve.

After a quick glance up and down the alley, Sims slipped the L-shaped tension tool into the lock, twisting it counterclockwise. Keeping pressure on the lock cylinder, he inserted the curved pick as far as possible into the lock. Then he raised the pick, wiggling it slightly until he felt the first lock pin push up. He drew the pick out rapidly, trying to tell through his fingertips if he was raking all the pins. The tension tool refused to turn. Sims pressed harder on the tension tool and repeated the raking maneuver. He was rewarded with a neat ticking sensation as he felt the pick skipping across the pins. With a metallic *snick,* the tension tool suddenly turned freely, and the door opened into a dimly lit hallway.

At the end of the hallway, Sims came to another door, this one with a simple spring-bolt lock. Sliding a playing-card-size piece of thin metal shim through the crack, he pushed back the bolt and stepped out into a plushly carpeted corridor. Taking the elevator to the seventh floor, he took the fire stairs down one floor.

A third of the way down the corridor, he came to a door painted in glossy black enamel. An engraved antique brass plaque read TABARD BOOKS. Visitors stepping through the door found themselves in a brightly lit anteroom the size of a small closet and under the eye of a closed circuit video scanner. Even expecting it, Sims got a momentary touch of claustrophobia.

Before he could push the buzzer, an electric lock rattled and released, and Riddle opened the door.

"Come in, young man." Riddle, a frown of concern pulling at his mouth, examined Sims. "You are all right?"

"Yeah, Riddle, I'm all right." For the first time since leaving San Gimignano, Sims felt the tension within him ease. The rich English accent, the round ruddy face with its grave hazel eyes that despite the years still looked out on the world with marvel at the ingenuity of humanity's persistent search for evil and intrigue. The meticulously tailored Saville Row suit sagging under the burden of Riddle's substantial body and the pockets stuffed with pens, clippings, and the notes he incessantly scribbled on pale blue index cards. All of this was uniquely Riddle, and Riddle a rock of consistency in an inconsistent world.

You never learned Riddle in one sitting. His history was too rich, his personality too complex. What Sims knew, he'd collected in small pieces during the seventeen years he'd known the man.

Riddle had been introduced into the world of espionage in his native Britain in the winter of 1938, when he'd been recruited at Cambridge by MI-6. The youngest son of an English father and a German mother, Riddle was equally at home in London or Berlin. And so it was only natural that he was targeted toward Germany. In June 1939, three months before Hitler and Stalin dismembered hapless Poland, Riddle, under cover of Swedish citizenship, established a bogus trading company in Stockholm. A month later, Riddle took on a partner, Ibrahim Bazdarkian, a displaced Armenian with a Turkish passport. Bazdarkian was truly an Armenian, but the passport had been manufactured by U.S. naval intelligence which had the foresight to send Bazdarkian to Europe, even though America's official policy was to ignore the gathering war clouds.

Riddle and Bazdarkian had taken to their work with exuberance and flair. Although London and Washington had sent them to build agent nets inside Germany, both decided that the times demanded a more active role. Without higher approval, they set up an underground escape route to Palestine along which they funneled thousands of Jews who were fleeing Hitler's growing holocaust. When Sims had asked about it, Riddle said little except to mutter, "Constructive disobedience," with a small, prideful smile.

After America entered the war, MI-6 and America's new intelligence service, the Office of Strategic Services, cut cards for spheres of influence. The Americans won, and Riddle and the Stockholm operation passed into Washington's orbit. Riddle stayed with the OSS through the war and after, took up the offer of the newly formed Central Intelligence Agency to become an American citizen and the Agency's first chief of base in Berlin.

Riddle checked the lock, activated the alarm system, and motioned Sims into the bookshop. Everything in the shop spoke of Riddle's England, from the rolling ladders against the eighteen foot mahogany shelves to the brass lamps with their green glass shades to the smells—a rich spicy mixture of leather, Turkish coffee, and aromatic pipe tobacco.

Tabard Books dealt only in espionage. Entire sections were devoted to arcane subjects such as honey traps, agents of influence, national networks, black, gray, and white propaganda. Riddle's fiction collections ranged from contemporary masters like McCarry and Ignatius to classicists such as Greene and Conrad. Even the shop's name was a code word for spying; Tabard came from Chaucer, who had served Edward III as a secret agent in France and Italy.

Bazdarkian had been the first owner of the bookshop, having retired from the Agency in 1974 while still in his early fifties. Then, in the fall of 1991, Bazdarkian had been reported killed in a plane crash while visiting Kars, his ancestral home in eastern Turkey. Although search teams combed the area, no bodies were ever recovered. Riddle, then CIA's deputy director for special projects, abruptly retired and took over the shop.

Agency talk in the small bars around McLean had an explanation for Riddle, Bazdarkian, and the bookshop. It went like this: From its founding in 1947, the Agency had been prohibited from spying on American citizens. (Apologists mark that down as proof of altruism; critics say it was only because J. Edgar Hoover had already cornered the domestic market and wasn't about to put up with any competition from the oh-so-social spies from the Ivy League fool factories.)

Despite the legal niceties, the bar talk continued, Agency operations against foreigners also pulled in an enormous take on Americans. You bug a KGB love nest, and before the German industrialist drops by, you get a tape of a prominent American senator or TV personality literally letting it all hang out. That kind of stuff, illegal to keep, was too damn good to get rid of. Special vaults were set aside and, from 1947 on, filled up with all manner of reports, tapes, photographs. Even infrared images of goings-on in darkened rooms.

And the Agency kept it all. Until 1974.

In 1974 an Idaho senator named Frank Church began a probe into the Agency's domestic activities.

Now—here the bar talk generally dropped to a whisper—this is where Riddle, Bazdarkian, and the bookshop came in. The Agency, wanting to hang on to the family jewels, set up a repository. Bazdarkian retired and the Agency turned the keys over to him. Now the Agency had plausible denial. When the Church committee's process servers came, everybody could, under oath, shake their heads. Why no! We wouldn't keep such information! When we come upon it, Senator, it goes straight to the attorney general. Honest.

Bazdarkian, of course, always had instant access to all succeeding Directors of Central Intelligence. That access and the repository passed on to Riddle when Bazdarkian disappeared. The bar talkers even gave Riddle a title. They called him The Keeper.

Sims had dared to lay the story he'd heard out to Riddle. Just once. Even now, Sims winced, thinking about it. He'd never do that again. Riddle had looked at him like he was something the dog had dragged in. Riddle had dismissed it with his ultimate expletive—*silly*. Riddle's world had room for many things, but there damned sure wasn't any for "silly."

Riddle led the way into the shop and motioned to his office in the loft. "The Judge is here."

Sims wanted to ask why, but Riddle was already heading to the stairs. Three sides of Riddle's office overlooked the shop, giving it a flying bridge effect. The one wall, painted a deep antique green, was covered with framed etchings from *Punch*. On the floor, a dark burgundy Azerbaijani carpet, a gift, Sims knew, from the late Shah of Iran. A Sheraton sofa in red Moroccan leather backed along the wall, facing two Queen Anne chairs.

The Judge stood in front of one of the chairs, resplendent in tuxedo and studded shirt. A deserter from some benefit, Sims guessed. Maybe one for old spies? The Judge offered his hand, a tentative welcoming smile on his face.

Richard John McClelland, CIA's fourteenth director, was known simply as "the Judge." McClelland (Yale '55, Harvard Law '61) had touched all the bases: three years commissioned naval service (destroyer duty, Atlantic Fleet), clerk for Earl Warren on the Supreme Court, partner at Williams and Connolly, nominated by Jimmy Carter to the Third District Circuit Court. On the bench, McClelland had upset roughly equal proportions of liberals and conservatives, in the process building a following among Democratic and Republican moderates. And since CIA was, above all else, a lawyers' intelligence agency (Britain's MI-6 tended to go for military officers), no one in Washington had been greatly surprised when Ronald Reagan asked McClelland to take over the Agency after the death of Bill Casey.

McClelland was a Washington rarity, a man given to introspection and a penchant for rational analysis. Lean and balding, McClelland contributed to a Presbyterian deacon's appearance with gold-stemmed rimless glasses, conservative ties, and impeccable dark suits. And McClelland was indeed a Presbyterian deacon, a man whose only closet skeletons were a passion for scuba diving and a secret pride in his ability to do the electric slide.

Sims took the Judge's outstretched hand. "Didn't expect to see you here."

The Judge arched an eyebrow. "I didn't expect to be here." He measured Sims up and down for several moments. "You have a talent, Bradford. If anyone ever seems to attract trouble . . ." He let it die with a wry smile and pointed to the chair opposite his. "Florence base sent someone down to San Gimignano. You had already left."

"Wasn't good odds, waiting around."

"Mr. Sims," Riddle suggested, "perhaps you will tell us what happened." Riddle settled himself on the sofa, rummaged through his pockets and came up with a small deck of blue index cards.

Sims took the chair, and in quick professional strokes, outlined the night in San Gimignano and his journey to Washington. Finished, he sat back in the chair and looked expectantly at Riddle, then the Judge.

The Judge began, "You're certain of this Czech?"

"Schmar."

"Absolutely certain?"

"Emil Schmar." Sims nodded. The Judge obviously didn't like what he was hearing. "He tried before. About a year ago in Prague. Just after Valek defected."

"At the time, I recall, he was working for Josef Broz," Riddle interjected.

"But Broz is dead," the Judge said.

The Judge's manner struck Sims as uneasy, but he couldn't put his finger on it.

"It *was* Schmar," Sims said. "I saw him full face. Coming

up the stairs." He was tired and impatient and purposely let it show. "Now, why're you here?" he asked the Judge.

"You haven't read the papers."

"Not much time to." He really doesn't want to get into it, Sims told himself. As if he once says it, it'll never go away.

The Judge paused, then, "Yesterday, in the morning rush hour, a Pakistani with an AK-47 shot up a row of cars on Chain Bridge Road waiting to get into the Agency. He killed Michael Gribbins."

"Mike?" Sims remembered the thick dark hair streaked with gray, the square cop's face with the measuring blue eyes. A deadly gin player. A place in Montana . . . Idaho . . . someplace. Whether it was Montana or Idaho was somehow important to Sims and he reproached himself for not remembering. You spend time with a genuinely good guy like Gribbins and you think you'll always remember.

"Any make on the shooter?"

Riddle shook his head. "The FBI is investigating."

"The Bureau? I won't hold my breath."

"Gribbins's killing got in the paper," said the Judge.

Sims could tell from the Judge's face there was more. "And—?"

"There was another one that didn't." The Judge reached into his jacket pocket, withdrew an envelope and passed it to Sims. Sims slid out a photograph.

The graininess told him that it was an enlargement. The camera had centered on a sphere with a silvery metallic finish. Two dark dimpled holes resembled eyes. The background was a uniform gray. Sims studied it for a moment while he riffled through his memory. He'd seen this before. Not exactly this, but close enough. And that had been a photograph too. He turned the photograph slightly, and the image matched that in his memory.

"Georgi Markov," Sims recited, remembering the class at the Farm and Bodnant, the weapons instructor. "London, 1976—no—'78. KGB assassination." He waved the photo at the Judge. "The killer fired a pellet like this from an air gun concealed in an umbrella. It carried a poison—ricin, I think—a toxin made from castor beans. No known antidote."

35

"Splendid, Mr. Sims," Riddle murmured with obvious pride. Then, somberly, "And Isaac Felton died in the same manner as did Georgi Markov—fever, chills, intense pain."

"Felton?" Sims watched Riddle nod. "Isaac Felton . . . Gribbins . . . me. A Pakistani and Schmar." Riddle and the Judge were looking at him expectantly. It was like an orals board exam: Find the connection.

"Miloslav Valek," Sims said, certain he'd hit it.

"Valek?" The Judge shook his head in frustration. "The details escape me."

"A summary, young man," Riddle suggested.

Sims took a last glance at the photograph of the poison pellet and handed it back to the Judge. "Miloslav Valek was Czech who worked for the KGB until December '91. Then he defected to us. I picked him up at the Rosslyn metro station. Mike Gribbins was his baby-sitter. Isaac Felton ran the psyche exams and the polygraph. Valek's story smelled. The rotten part seemed to be Valek's relationship with Josef Broz, who had been head of Czech intelligence before the Communist government fell. Valek had worked for Broz before shifting over to the Soviets. Houghton and I went to Prague to talk with Broz. Broz didn't want to talk. Schmar was Broz's muscle. Schmar and a couple of his buddies tried to whack Houghton and me one night."

"But you did talk to Broz?" asked the Judge.

"Yeah, finally. The KGB killed him that same night and at the same time they killed Valek in a men's store in Georgetown."

The Judge nodded. "Then the rest—"

"Look, Judge," Sims explained, "from the time Valek defected to the time he was assassinated was just over a month. That was the only time that Felton, Gribbins, and I worked together. From there on, it was just Houghton and me."

"And so whatever this is, you think it had something to do with that month. That connects Schmar, but what about the Pakistani who shot Gribbins? And who fired the pellet into Felton?"

"That's part of the new equation," said Sims with growing certainty. "But whatever that is, it's linked to Valek's defection."

The Judge sat wooden-faced for a moment, then nodded, obviously unhappy. The three men, absorbed in their own thoughts, sat motionlessly, as if captured in amber.

"I shall get coffee." Riddle broke the spell as he heaved himself up from the sofa. A moment later he was back with a silver tray with three cups of pungent *turska kava*.

As Sims sipped the thick coffee, he noticed the small tremor in his hand. You're tired, he tried to convince himself. That's what it is, you're tired. He put the cup down too quickly, spilling some into the saucer. He looked up, his eyes meeting Riddle's.

Sims said what he'd been thinking. "It wasn't revenge."

"Oh?" challenged Riddle. "You broke a lot of rice bowls."

"That's right, Riddle, *I* did the breaking. If it was revenge, getting me would have been enough. Mike and Felton were just doing their jobs. They weren't in on what happened later. Felton and Gribbins had nothing to do with that."

The Judge cracked his knuckles with a bony popping sound. "What then?"

"Somebody thinks we got something from Valek, something that's still dangerous to them."

"But Valek was almost a year ago," the Judge said, shaking his head. "If the three of you had gotten something from Valek, others would know it too. No sense in trying to kill—"

"Somebody *thinks* it makes sense," Sims disagreed. "Look . . . Valek had access to the KGB registry. He defected just before the Soviet Union fell apart. I always thought he might have grabbed something to go into business with."

"Files?"

Sims shrugged. "Locations of drug caches, secret bank account numbers, names of KGB agents he could blackmail. There was no end to the shit he could've gotten his hands on."

The Judge's unhappiness noticeably deepened.

"You don't like this," Sims said.

"Like it?" the Judge picked up sharply, "What's there to like? Two men killed, you—"

"I didn't mean it that way. I meant, you don't seem to want to go after it."

A mask slid over the Judge's face. "They worked me over at the White House today," he said in a neutral voice.

"Worked you over?" Sims repeated. "Why?" he asked.

The Judge started slowly and deliberately, picking his words the way a man did who was trying to keep his anger down. "Ah . . . President Clinton's new national security adviser is Ralston Dean. Mr. Dean has . . . an . . . agenda for the Middle East."

"Agenda?" *Here it comes,* a voice said inside Sims's head, *you hear that word and you know you're back in Washington. You hear "agenda" and your bullshit detector pegs the meter.*

"For peace," the Judge explained levelly. "First, a resolution of the Palestinian issue, which means getting the Israelis to a sit-down with Yasir Arafat."

Sims pictured the unshaven terrorist who always reminded him of a hyena, and got a sour taste in his mouth. "Then?"

"Then an accommodation with Jordan, and finally, with Syria."

Despondency, like a deadening fatigue, engulfed Sims. He'd been around Washington long enough to know where the Judge was heading.

"And so we—Gribbins and Felton and me—we're . . . inconvenient? We might get in the way of all this peaceful accommodation?" Sims asked.

The Judge looked at Sims, taking care to neither confirm nor deny. "I sent the president a memo on Gribbins and Felton. I laid out the possibility that the killings were terrorist related. After all, Gribbins's shooter was a Pakistani; that we suspected Syrian backing for the venture—"

"And Mr. Dean in the White House didn't like that," Sims interjected.

"Mr. Dean's words: 'I'm not going to have *this* president start out by scaring the shit out of the American people.'" The Judge gave Sims and Riddle a look he'd learned on the bench, a somber look that conveyed a depth in his summary. "In short, Bradford, Riddle, the new people in the White House don't want to start out with a bang."

"What, then?"

The Judge stared at his shoes for a long while, then looked up to Sims. "I don't see any other choice. We have to find out why."

Sims looked at the Judge, then Riddle, then the Judge again. They were eyeing him like a biology specimen on a pin.

"And me?"

"Do you know anybody better?" the Judge came back. "If the connection had something to do with Valek, you're the only person left on our side who'd know."

Riddle regarded Sims sympathetically. "You don't have to come back to the Agency. If you want to hide, arrangements could be made. New identity, plastic surgery, resettlement somewhere—"

Sims shook his head. "I'd run in a minute, if it'd do any good. But you know it wouldn't." He remembered Schmar in San Gimignano and before that in Prague. "I don't think they'll stop looking."

"You're going to need cover—" the Judge began.

"I'll put something together until you can figure some way to keep me out of sight."

The Judge's eyes went off in thought, then came back to Sims. "I'll set up a cutout for you. Someone to take care of communications and funding. They'll be working blind, won't know who you are." He pulled a calling card from an inside pocket, scribbled on the back of it, and handed it to Sims.

"Call that number tomorrow."

Sims memorized the number and handed the card back to the Judge.

The Judge looked at his watch, then stood. "I'd better be getting back," he said, making a sweeping gesture over his tuxedo jacket as if that explained everything. Riddle walked him to the top of the stairs.

"Judge," Sims called out.

The Judge stopped and turned back to Sims.

"Can I have Alberich?"

The Judge nodded, then took Riddle's arm above the elbow. "I'm certain Riddle can arrange it."

Sims heard sounds of Riddle letting the Judge out. He walked to the window. Below, on K Street, a black Buick. Out of long habit, he picked out the nearly invisible strands of the security net around the Judge. Fore and aft, the chase cars, engines running. Two men in overcoats just across the street. Under the overcoats, Sims guessed, were the small arsenals: 9-mm Beretta in shoulder holster, Uzi submachine gun slung on a quick-use harness, a couple of stun grenades hung in straps on Kevlar vests. Probably two more guys on this side of the street as well.

"More coffee?"

Startled, Sims turned. Riddle was at the top of the stairs. "I didn't hear you."

"You were standing there, thinking."

Sims glanced out the window again. The Judge was getting in his car, one of the overcoats held the door for him, the other continued to scan the street. Not bad, Sims thought. Not bad at all. And he realized that a small germ of excitement was working on him deep inside.

Sims looked down on the rain-slicked street and knew he would always see streets and shadows differently than other men. And he knew Lourdes had been right—it wasn't over. And he knew now that part of him didn't really want it to be over.

"In Italy," he tried to explain to Riddle and to himself as well, "there were times, sometimes weeks, when I forgot about this kind of thing. I almost convinced myself that I'd found something else. I thought I could make a different life for myself. But"—he paused, seeing Lourdes's face again as she stood before him in the courtyard—"but there weren't any goals. And"—he turned to face Riddle—"if you don't have a goal, where does a fullback run?"

Riddle gave him a thoughtful look. "Where to start, Mr. Sims?"

Sims felt a naturalness about getting back in harness. "Meet with Alberich. Look at the files, especially the two-oh-ones on Schmar."

Riddle nodded. "I shall see to it. Also to a meeting place."

Riddle went to a Hepplewhite sideboard, rummaged in a drawer, and came back to Sims with an imitation leather case. The outside carried a Waterman's logo. "The latest from the toy shop."

Sims opened the case. Inside, the fountain pen glowed with a rich ebony finish. Sims took it out.

"Unscrew the cap, then the ink reservoir."

Cap off, the pen still looked ordinary enough. When Sims unscrewed the nib, however, a small spring-driven clip popped out of the pen recess.

"A miniature scrambler. Attach the clip to the cord of your telephone. There are two tiny lights. The green one tells you the scrambler is working; the red one that your telephone is being tapped."

Sims studied the workmanship. Exquisite. No patchy splice work, everything clean, neat, and functional. He looked up. Riddle held out what appeared to be a telephone pager.

"It works worldwide," Riddle explained. He handed Sims a small plastic laminated card. Sims recognized Virginia, Maryland, and District area codes. "These are your trouble numbers. They are safe; however, I advise that you always use the scrambler."

Sims put the pen back together and stowed it in an inside pocket. He looked up to see Riddle studying him, an owlish appraising look in the hazel eyes.

"You need documents, a place to stay."

Sims picked up his overnight bag and leather jacket. "That's next. I'll take care of that."

4

Leaving Riddle, Sims made his way east on K Street. At Eighteenth, he crossed K Street, checking for a tail. A block later, at Connecticut Avenue, he crossed back again and near Trover's found a sidewalk pay phone. A brief call, and he hung up and walked out to the curb.

The rain that had followed him from New York finally caught up with him, and the mist had become a cold drizzle. What cabs there were weren't stopping. He stepped out into the street. More cabs passed. "Shit," he muttered. A block away, the lights of the Sheraton-Carlton cut through the night. Shoes soaked and squishing, he set off for the bright lights and the hotel cab stand.

The lead cab had been painted a robin's egg blue and the hand-lettered legend on the doors read PARADISE TAXI. The paint had sagged and dripped, and the sprung door made a popping sound as Sims opened it to get in. The cabby, a lanky black man with thick glasses, took in Sims, the wet leather jacket, and the cheap overnight bag. He waved a hand palm out at Sims and said something that Sims missed because of the door noise.

"What?"

"This's for the hotel."

"Say what?" Sims gave the man what he thought of as his iced-snot look.

The cabby looked past Sims to the uniformed doorman,

42

standing under the hotel marquee. The doorman wasn't paying any attention. The cabby tried it again. Weakly. "This cab's for the hotel."

"Hunh!" Sims came back. "Eighth and I—southeast."

"*Southeast?*" The cabby's voice cracked in disbelief, eyes big behind the glasses. "You know what time it is?"

Sims thrust his hand over into the front seat area. He gestured, palm up, making it seem a reasonable and at the same time faintly menacing gesture. "I know what time it is, brother," he said, putting a hard edge on *brother*. "And I know," he added, giving the man a look that'd peel paint, "that this's a public conveyance vehicle."

The cabby's face and shoulders sagged in surrender. "You said Eighth and I?"

Fifteen minutes later, the cab turned off Pennsylvania Avenue onto Eighth. Sims knew Eighth well. He'd lived one block over until college. A Popeye's Chicken, an auto parts store, two video rental shops, your standard Korean-run 7-Eleven, and five liquor stores that cashed checks and sold lottery tickets. Steel shutters and bulletproof glass topped off with neon. Mom and Pop, fully armored, the bunker entrepreneurs of the combat zone.

Sims pointed to the right, halfway down the block. "There's good." He paid the cabby and had barely closed the door when the car lurched forward.

He stood for a moment in the drizzle and watched the Paradise Taxi disappear into the night. Across the street, a high brick wall connected a series of three story brick buildings that stretched down the entire block—the Marine Corps barracks and the home of the commandant. When the British burned Washington in 1812, they'd left the barracks standing. Out of respect, Sims had read, for the fight the outnumbered American marines had put up at nearby Bladensburg. You could be safe here, Sims reflected, but it took one helluva lot of firepower to do it. Checking the streets, he turned and entered a restaurant.

Faded Mexican flags and red, white, and green crepe paper streamers, dusty and drooping with age, festooned Casa Miguel's ceiling and the usual bullfight posters hung on cracked plaster walls. The dining room stretched back

43

for several rows of tables, then jogged off to an alcove on the left to the kitchen and rest rooms. And, Sims reminded himself, the kitchen doors opened onto an alley that ran the length of the block. The place was empty, and smelled of cumin, chili peppers, and stale beer. Off to his right, several tables had been pulled together for a party. A teenage busboy noisily loaded dishes and glasses onto a huge tray. The busboy looked up.

"We closed."

"Yeah," Sims acknowledged. "Somebody's waiting for me."

"Maybe back there." The boy pointed a dirty fork toward the alcove and went back to his work.

Sims rounded the corner into the alcove. Two black men, heavyset and irritable looking, sat at a small table drinking coffee. A third man, thin and wiry, stood beside the kitchen's double doors. All three wore dark suits, white shirts, and conservative ties. The thin man took several steps towards Sims, then stopped. Sims saw he stayed out of reach and out of the way of the two men at the table.

"May I be of assistance?" The thin man asked with a sneering overpolite manner.

"I'm here to see somebody."

"*Some*body?" The thin man raised his eyebrows with exaggerated energy. "Somebody *who?*" The thin man made a show of unbuttoning his coat and one of the coffee drinkers had slipped his hand from his cup to the edge of the table.

"Rollo. I'm Bradford Sims."

A look that could have been disappointment flashed over the thin man's face. He jerked a thumb toward the wall. "Spread."

Sim's immediate impulse was to tell the thin man to fuck off. He stifled it and walked to the wall.

"There. Stop."

He was three, three and a half feet from the wall.

"Go ahead. You know the rest."

Hands above his head, Sims leaned forward into a fall that stopped when his palms slapped flat against the wall.

44

He was now at an angle that made it impossible to threaten anyone behind him. He heard footsteps and in the corner of his vision, he saw the thin man's shoe rest itself just inside his right foot. One kick and the thin man could bring him down to the floor. It was a two hand search, rough, thorough, and professional. The thin man's shoe disappeared.

"Okay."

Sims pushed away from the wall and turned around. The thin man motioned with his head through the kitchen double doors. "Through there."

Brushing by the thin man, Sims gave him a touch of hard elbow. Sims pushed the double doors open and took in the restaurant kitchen: tile floors, aluminum cookware hanging from pipe racks, the scullery sounds of exhaust fans, scraping and cleaning, and muttering complaints of tired men eager to close up and go home. The smell of spicy food reminded Sims how hungry he was and how long it'd been since he'd eaten.

"Belly up, Bradford." It was a familiar voice, a bourbon bass that rumbled like distant thunder.

Sims spun around. Off to his right and partially hidden by a floor-to-ceiling cupboard, a doorway opened into a small office. Rollo Moss had a chair pulled up to an overflowing desk. Papers and ledger books had been shoved aside to clear a space for a huge platter of tacos and refried beans. Rollo had a can of Tecate in one big hand, the rest of the six-pack sat on the floor near his feet.

A year hadn't made any difference that Sims could tell. There was, of course, the first impression—big. Big in the way of mass and gravity; big in the way of strength and awesome muscle. The massive blue-black face carried its full roundness without sagging, and the thick shoulders hinted of a crushing bearlike power. Rollo wore an impeccably tailored double-breasted charcoal gray suit, burgundy pindot tie, and a creamy shirt of double-weight silk. The shoes were meticulously buffed cordovan wing tips, and from his right hand, a huge diamond pinky ring flashed magnesium-bright.

Sims had been eight when his policeman father had brought Rollo Moss home to dinner. Rollo, his father's new partner, had become a once-a-week regular until April 1968, when Sims's father had been shot in the riots that followed Martin Luther King's assassination. Rollo lost a kidney to a sniper blast, trying to save Thomas Sims's life. After the hospital, Rollo left the force.

Over the following twenty-five years, Rollo built a lucrative business in bodyguards and security. Like any new venture, the first years had been the toughest. The black leaders of Washington's only profit-making growth industry—organized crime—had wanted in on the action. Characteristically, Rollo had taken the direct approach. Taylor Franklin, generally acknowledged to be Washington's crime boss, woke up one morning, not to find a horse's head beside him, but Rollo Moss sitting on the edge of his bed.

This, in a way, was more disconcerting than a horse's head. Particularly when Rollo had Franklin's personal SWAT team hustled in. All twelve, disarmed and handcuffed, showed signs of wanting to move into less demanding lines of work. Ten minutes later, Taylor Franklin had signed the multiyear contract Rollo tossed on the bed.

The rest of the Washington underworld got the message, and Rollo Moss, for his part, kept Franklin alive and well without involving Moss Protective Services in Franklin's criminal activities. "You heard of equal opportunity employers?" Rollo had explained it to Franklin. "Well, we're equal opportunity protectors."

The FBI (the Rollo Moss take: "*F*amous *B*ut *I*ncompetent") didn't make the distinction between Rollo's protection of Taylor Franklin and Taylor Franklin's illegal enterprises, and so, when they got Franklin in 1987, they threw Rollo into the same bag. The resulting twenty-three months in the federal penitentiary in Atlanta were, in Rollo's words, "most instructive." After he got out, he made certain that the next addition to Moss Protective Services was a phalanx of lawyers.

Over all those years, Rollo Moss had been Bradford Sims's protector. Rollo's protection had been simple enough; he had been there when a growing-up Bradford Sims had needed him.

Rollo pointed to the platter. He had a plate in front of him with the remains of a taco and refried beans. "Thought you'd be hungry. You late though. Gettin' cold." Thick fingers closed over a paper napkin wrapped around silverware and slapped it onto the desk.

"Had trouble with a cab."

"Didn't want to come down here?"

Sims nodded. "Driver was black too."

"Black don't mean bulletproof. Not around here. Sit." Rollo reached back and found another chair and pulled it alongside him at the desk.

Sims sat down and freed up the silverware. Rollo popped open two cans of Tecate and pushed one to Sims. With his fingers, he picked up two tacos, put them on Sims's plate, then ladled several spoonfuls of beans and rice on, tapping the edge of the spoon on the plate. Sims went after the tacos first. For a moment, the two men sat side by side at the big desk, eating and occasionally taking a swig of beer. Sims was on the second taco when Rollo started.

"You get tired of Italy?"

San Gimignano came back to Sims, a memory of Lourdes, the narrow sunlit lanes, white market umbrellas in the piazza. Sims shook his head. "Somebody tried to kill me this morning."

Rollo went after some more beans. "Jealous husband?"

"Wish," Sims said through a mouthful of taco.

Rollo worked on the beans and rice as Sims told him about the morning in San Gimignano. When Sims finished, Rollo put his fork down and turned to Sims. Rollo's left eyelid drooped slightly, giving him a permanently skeptical look. "Unfinished business of yours?" He asked it with a wary undertone in his voice.

Sims nodded. "Something to do with Valek—"

"The commie defector?"

"There were three Agency guys close to Valek. Me, a guy named Isaac Felton, a guy named Mike Gribbins. When Valek came over, I was his case officer. Felton worked for the Office of Medicine. He ran the psychological profile—"

47

"Valek—I didn't know he was a nut case."

"He wasn't. Psych profile was standard with defectors. Felton did the testing and then the polygraph on Valek." Sims paused, and seeing Rollo nod, continued: "Mike Gribbins was Valek's baby-sitter. There were other security people, but they were shift work. Mike was permanent. He ended up spending more time with Valek than I did."

"So you and these two guys and Valek."

"Gribbins and Felton are dead. Gribbins was shot—"

"That shit yesterday?" Rollo put it together. "Outside the CIA—"

"—and somebody shot Felton with a poison pellet."

"Same bunch tried to kill you?"

"I recognized one of them. A Czech. I ran into him before in Prague. He likes to use a knife."

Rollo waved a dismissing hand. "A bunch of pissed-off commies."

"They think the guy who shot Gribbins was a Pakistani."

"A commie an' a Arab?" Rollo Moss pursed his lips, studying Sims, then shook his head. "Shit, Bradford." He looked at Sims some more, then wadded up his paper napkin and tossed it on his plate.

Rollo eyed Sims for a long time and just when Sims was getting uncomfortable about it, Rollo asked, "You goin' back?"

"Back?"

"Back into the Agency?"

Something was behind the question, but Sims was too tired to work at it so he shrugged. "I gotta find out who's after me. I can't do it by myself."

Rollo nodded. The drooping eyelid dropped a notch lower. "You goin' back," he declared. "You'd be goin' back even if the commies and Arabs wasn't havin' at you."

"Why you say that?"

Rollo grinned. "Shit, Bradford. You are your father's son. Tom Sims always thought he was the Lone Ranger. Had a mission to set it all right. Good *will* pre-*vail!* Hi-ho, Silver!"

Rollo brought his face closer to Sims's. The grin went away and his voice got somber. "An' you just like him,

48

Bradford. This hadn't a happened, you'd a been back here anyway. You're not made to sit on your ass eatin' pasta. There'd be a dogfight somewhere and you'd figure you got to go stop it."

Sims didn't argue. He knew when Rollo had closed out an argument. Instead, he reached over to Rollo's plate and scooped up the last of the beans. He put down his fork. "Whatever, Rollo. I'm back."

"Well, what you need?"

"Left a rental car in a garage. Buick, New York plates."

"Got the stub?"

Sims handed it over. The food and the beer made Sims realize how bone-tired he was. "I need cover . . . some ID . . . place to stay."

Rollo looked him up and down. "You need some clothes too." He turned the parking stub over and scrabbled around the desk for a ballpoint. "Give me your sizes."

Moments later, as if summoned by a secret signal, the thin man pushed through the kitchen doors. Over one arm he carried a black fur-trimmed cashmere overcoat. In his hand he held what Sims recognized as Rollo Moss's trademark black homburg hat.

Rollo got up. As he did so, he hooked a hand under Sims's arm and pulled him up with him. "Place to stay comes first. Hot shower, fresh sheets. Tomorrow, you wake up, you goin' to be a new man."

Rollo gestured to the thin man, the one who'd searched Sims and who'd brought Rollo's coat.

"This's Payton."

Payton, expressionless, nodded and went out to fetch the car.

Rollo Moss's dark blue Chrysler was parked out front on Eighth, engine running, Payton at the wheel. One of the heavysets partially shielded an opened back door. Rollo climbed in, then Sims.

Payton pulled away from the curb and made a smooth U-turn that headed them back toward Pennsylvania Avenue. Close behind, a car with the two irritable heavyweights. At

Pennsylvania, Payton turned right, heading for Anacostia. Behind them the white dome of the Capitol glowed a crystalline white.

At Eighteenth, the small convoy turned right. Once off Pennsylvania, the Capitol dome disappeared and the reality of the war-torn projects closed in. Long-broken streetlights stood useless guard over block after block of two-story redbrick garden apartments with treeless front yards of hard packed dirt. Many of the apartments were boarded up, their windows covered with sheets of graffiti-covered plywood. Dumpsters overflowed, and here and there off the buckled sidewalks, the wreckage of children's cheap toys. Cars lined both sides of the street: rusting tireless hulks next to new BMWs, Nissan 300Zs, and Mercedes.

They were coming up on a glistening red Cadillac. Rollo regarded it through the window then pointed it out to Sims. "Mayor's always whinin' about bustin' crack dealers." He looked back at the Cadillac. "Shit!" He drew the word out. "All's they gotta do is collar the muthafuckers who drive cars like that."

"They wouldn't get your clients?"

"Don't need that kind a business." Rollo ducked his head forward, searching the street ahead.

They passed through the projects and came to a block of two and three story row houses. Toward the end of the block, Payton slowed. The car following them passed and pulled over to the curb some twenty yards ahead. Payton pulled in just behind. In a smoothly choreographed sequence, the two heavyweights were out of their car at Rollo's door. At the same time, Payton slipped from behind the wheel to stand on the other side of the car, scanning the street and the houses opposite.

"Let's go."

Rollo opened his door and got out. Sims followed, finding Rollo and himself in a tight cluster on the sidewalk, the two heavyweights in front of them, Payton close behind.

Rollo swept a hand down the block at the row houses. "Bought all these. Real estate's only depressed if you're sellin'. Always good to be buyin'—God isn't makin' any more."

A jungle gym of tubular steel scaffolding hid the two end houses. Windowpanes bore paper labels. Wheelbarrow ramps led through the doorways of the houses and lumber scraps and construction debris filled the small front yards. "Fixin' these up," Rollo explained. "Rent them to people who work for me. They pay off for a year, we convert the lease to a mortgage, then they own their own house." He pointed to the rest of the block. Sims counted eight more homes. "We finished those last summer." He gestured toward one of the houses. "Let's go."

The heavyweights led the way to a cream-colored stucco house where a short flight of steps ran up to a wide covered porch. With Payton leading the way, Rollo and Sims climbed the steps, the heavyweights stayed at the bottom, scanning the street. On the porch, four cane-bottom rocking chairs had been neatly reversed and tilted against the front of the house. Next to the chairs was a round wicker table. Over each, a carefully taped shroud of sheet plastic protected them from the winter weather. You could sit on the porch in the summer, Sims imagined, and drink iced tea and watch the street in the evening and talk to neighbors.

Two solid oak doors opened onto the porch. Payton went to one, and worked the lock with keys on a large metal ring.

"This's a duplex," Rollo explained, pointing to the two doors. "You're upstairs."

"Downstairs?"

Rollo motioned to one of the heavyweights, the one standing in the yard to the left of the steps.

The closer of the two big men turned away from the street and looked up to Rollo. Apparently deciding it was all right, he gave Sims a small smile and a nod. A thick irregular scar furrowed his right cheek, running from the corner of his mouth nearly to his ear.

Payton unlocked the door, reached inside, and switched on the stairwell light. Rollo pushed Sims ahead and brought up the rear. In passing, Sims noted the six-tumbler Schlage dead bolt lock and the heavy-gauge steel door frame.

At the top of the stairs, another door, also set in a steel frame, also equipped with a dead bolt. Payton unlocked the door, swung it open, and stood aside. Sims stepped into a small foyer that was no more than a landing with a rack with hooks for coats.

Sims smelled new paint and recently sawn wood. He followed Rollo into the living room, whose principal furniture was a blue three-cushion sofa, a deep red leather club chair, and beside it, a brass floor lamp. A large multicolored rag rug covered the well-polished dark oak floors. The sofa and chair were drawn up to a coffee table whose top was a rectangle of thick green glass that reminded Sims of the bulletproof windows in Rollo's Chrysler.

"Stand over here." Rollo pointed.

Puzzled, Sims moved to stand against a stretch of cream-colored wall. Payton produced a small flash camera.

"Need this for the IDs," Rollo explained. "Look mean."

Payton snapped four pictures, the flash making silent explosions of light that reminded Sims of the gunfire in the night in San Gimignano.

Sims reached inside his jacket and came up with his U.S. passport.

"Get me one of these too?"

Rollo looked as if he wanted to ask a question, then decided not to and nodded at Sims, then at Payton. Rollo took Sims by the elbow and led him through the rest of the apartment: the small eat-in kitchen and the bedroom with its bathroom and glass shower stall. Sims threw his overnight bag on the floor by the double bed.

"Alarm system." Rollo pointed to the keypad panel and blinking red light set into the wall near the bed, then walked to the window and gestured outside. "Fire escape here."

Sims went to Rollo's side and raised the window. The frigid air brought with it the late-night sounds of the city. He leaned out. The steel slat landing outside had steps leading upward, a ladder going down.

He heard Rollo's voice from inside. "Go up, you go to the roof. You can take the rooftops all the way down the block. Down takes you to the alley. Open at both ends." Sims could see to the next block and the beginning of the projects. On a flat roof of the nearest project apartment, two, maybe three people clustered around the rapid on-and-off flaring of what appeared to be a cigarette lighter. He pulled back in and shut the window.

"Might want this under your pillow." Rollo reached in his coat, came up with a pistol, and handed it to Sims.

Sims automatically catalogued it. Colt Model 2000: 9mm parabellum, double action, sleekly blued steel. Fifteen-shot staggered box magazine. Effective range seventy-five yards. With a smooth, practiced motion, he pressed the button release, slid the magazine from the grip, then pulled back the slide. A stubby brass cartridge sailed out of the pistol chamber and skittered along the floor. Rollo bent easily, scooped the cartridge up, and tossed it back to Sims.

Pistol still gripped in one hand, Sims walked with Rollo to the door.

Rollo buttoned his coat and adjusted his homburg, cocking it jauntily down toward his right eyebrow. "Call me when you get up." He looked Sims up and down. "We gotta new man to put together tomorrow."

Doors locked and alarm set, Sims took the Colt into the bathroom and put it on the toilet seat. Then he stripped and stepped into the shower and adjusted the water until he felt the hot spray dissolving the tightness between his shoulder blades. Moments later, he slid naked between the sheets. The mattress was firm and he groaned with the pleasure of simply lying down. The last thing before he went to sleep, his hand crept under the pillow and wrapped around the hard grip of the Colt.

5

Exhausted, Sims slept through the night as if drugged, waking stiff and gummy mouthed just after eight. An hour later, showered and dressed, he called Rollo. Rummaging through the cupboards, he found a jar of instant coffee. Moments later, he stood in the kitchen, blowing across the top of a steaming mug and staring absentmindedly at the small countertop television, trying to put the coming day in order.

On CNN, a reporter in an artillery-ravaged town described the latest act of bloody self-consumption in Bosnia. Behind the reporter, an old woman in a kerchief knelt on a gray cobblestone street, moaning and rocking in grief over a child's sprawled corpse. Sims flicked the remote.

On "Donahue," a bearded man plugged his book about the wonders of cultural diversity.

"Shit," Sims said. Elvis used to blast TVs with a shotgun when he didn't like the program, Sims recalled. Something to that, he thought as he thumbed the set off.

He had just finished the coffee when the telephone rang. It was Rollo, calling from his car. He was several blocks away and would be there in a few minutes.

Sims went into the bedroom, set the alarm system, and shouldered into his leather jacket. He noticed the Colt automatic on the night table. For an instant he had a disjointed feeling. It was like a needle on an old LP had skipped a groove and he suddenly found himself in a new time and place. Just two days ago, he'd been in his farmhouse with Lourdes at her easel in the room with the north light. And now Lourdes and San Gimignano were no more. A door had slammed shut and Sims knew it'd never open again. With a furious motion, he picked the pistol up, jammed it under his belt, and jerked his jacket closed over it.

Outside, Sims closed the wrought iron gate behind him and walked to the corner to wait for Rollo. The winter clouds lay low and heavy with a slate gray expectant-snow look and the air had a rawness to it that Sims knew came just above freezing. Down the street to his right, he saw the glint of a windshield a half block away—Rollo's blue Chrysler.

An hour later, Sims and Rollo were finishing breakfast at a back booth at Kinney's: sausage, ham, biscuits and red-eye gravy, four fried eggs, grits with butter, double orders of scrapple, and a small ocean of coffee.

Rollo delicately touched a napkin to his lips, belched, and, from an inside coat pocket, produced a thick envelope and slid it across the Formica tabletop to Sims.

"The new you—Reginald Williamson."

"I've never been a Reg," Sims muttered. He casually dropped the envelope into his lap, then thumbed it open. The D.C. driver's license was suitably wallet-worn and featured the photograph of Sims that Payton had taken the night before. Another photo appeared on a corporate ID card of Moss Protective Services.

"I work for you?"

"Gives you good backstop, in case anybody calls to check," Rollo explained.

Reginald Williamson, six feet two inches, 210 pounds, was also a registered D.C. voter, a United Airlines frequent flier, and a member of the downtown Y.

Sims held up a Visa card. "Any good?"

Rollo nodded. "Corporate account. Just don't buy no Rolexs or fur coats with it."

"Passport?"

"Some things take longer—tomorrow."

Last was a set of keys on a ring.

"Gray Pontiac, parked out back." Rollo motioned over his shoulder. "Clothes in the trunk. Couple suits, shirts, shoes, that kinda shit. See that gizmo?" He pointed to the small black plastic tag on the key ring. "Push that button on the end and hold it for five seconds. It starts your car from a safe distance."

Sims looked at the key ring and suddenly became aware of the Colt, jammed in his belt, the barrel of it metallic and angular against his belly. "You're a real belt and suspenders guy, Rollo."

Rollo tilted his coffee mug, glancing into it, as if hoping there'd be some left. He shook his head, then gave Sims a warning look. "You don't have belt and suspenders, Bradford, you likely to lose your ass."

It was almost eleven when Sims parked the Pontiac in a loading zone on North Capitol near Union Station and found a pay phone. He dialed the number the Judge had given him.

A woman answered after two rings. "Hello." The voice carried a straightforward sensuality, a smoky contralto, and for a wild moment, he had the crazy thought that it was Lourdes.

Sims found himself trying to picture her, wondering if the voice really sounded like Lourdes or if he were only imagining it. "I . . . ah . . . I was told to call this number," he managed to get out.

"Oh, you were?"

It was there, all right, the faint trace of the throaty pulsation that—

"What?"

"I said, what was your badge number?"

"HX-five-eight-six." The line fell quiet. Sims imagined a pencil underlining his former Agency badge number on a checklist.

"Date of bir—"

"Twelve May 'fifty-six."

Another pause, then: "I've been told you need funds."

Sims listened carefully to the instructions.

Fifteen minutes later, he entered the Map Store on Farragut Square. Inside, he browsed among the display racks while checking out the store and its customers. Satisfied, he walked back to the reference section where a long counter carried atlases, gazetteers, and geographical dictionaries. He found the Hammond World Atlas. A young Asian couple with knapsacks bent over it, pointing, chattering, making notes.

Chinese, Sims decided, catching the soft slurring of Canton dialect. For several minutes, he paged through a European gazetteer until the Chinese couple moved on. Moving over to the atlas, he pretended to search the index while he ran his fingertips under the counter. He found the stiff plastic card, peeled it away from its paper backing, and palmed it into his trouser pocket.

Outside, the temperature had dropped and it was beginning to snow. He walked north several blocks to an ATM machine at Connecticut and L. There, he inserted the card, and punched in the PIN number the woman on the phone had given him. To his surprise, the machine didn't turn down the request for a thousand dollars. He found a pay phone in the lobby of a nearby office building. Standing so he shielded the phone, he hooked up the fountain pen-scrambler and called Riddle.

The phone rang three times, then Sims heard the pickup and Riddle's voice. Usually reserved, it now carried with it a hidden excitement.

"You've taken care of your logistics?" Riddle asked.

"I'm a new man."

"We got the files. Five o'clock?"

Sims glanced at his watch. It was now one-fifteen. "Where?"

"The *USA Today* building in Rosslyn. Twenty-three-oh-four."

Sims repeated the room number, and, as he hung up, felt cold needles prickling along his forearms and the back of his neck. Suddenly the streets around him were no longer home and sanctuary, but foreign and menacing. He walked west on L at a pace close to a jog, and in several blocks felt better.

Turning north on Nineteenth, he found a place at the bar at Sam and Harry's and ordered a rare hamburger, fries, and an ice-cold long-neck Bud. Half an hour later at a theater around the corner, he settled into a seat in the last row to watch Michael Douglas blast his way across the freeways and barrios of Los Angeles.

During the afternoon, the temperature continued to plunge. When he left the theater at four, Sims had to make his way to his car through thickening curtains of snow. It took him almost half an hour to get through Georgetown in the snarled afternoon traffic. Finally, he crossed Key Bridge into Rosslyn, Virginia.

Rosslyn's explosive growth into a minicity had been fueled by nearby Washington's irresistible urge to strangle geese laying golden eggs. First, the D.C. city government had levied massive taxes on pawnshops. Naturally, the pawnbrokers fled the district. They traveled no farther than Rosslyn, then a barren spit of land on the Virginia side of the Potomac. There, pawnshops prospered and multiplied. In a second act of shortsightedness, the D.C. government, desperate for revenue, aimed its tax cannons at commercial real estate. The predictable result: office buildings emptied in Washington and Rosslyn came quickly to resemble a massive geometric cluster of crystals as glittering glass and aluminum high rises squeezed out the loan sharks. By the '90s, the only pawnshop left was an oak and brass and fern bar by that name where office workers ate salads at lunch and downed designer water and wine spritzers after work.

Sims found a parking place on Kent Street. Half a block away, Kent ran into Wilson Boulevard, with the *USA Today* building standing at the intersection. The building was a shimmering, thirty-story electric-silver airfoil whose top was lost tonight in the thickening snow. On his right, a portion of Kent Street lifted upward, branching off into an elevated roadway which passed by the *USA Today* building at the tenth floor, then curved west, a cloverleaf to hook in with the clogged commuter arteries of Northern Virginia.

Switching off the ignition, Sims watched the street and the entrance to the building. There were few pedestrians, and what little automobile traffic there was came from office workers leaving the huge building's indoor garage. He watched until snowflakes covered the windshield. It was now four forty-five.

He pulled the Colt from under his belt and pressed the magazine release button. The magazine jumped out from the grip just enough for him to be able to pull it out the rest of the way. He examined the top cartridge. The rounded stubby bullet somehow reminded him of a wingless bee, the blunt slug a coppery color, the cartridge case a yellower brass. Experimentally, he pushed his thumb down on the cartridge, testing the slight give of the follower spring. Satisfied, he slid the magazine back into the pistol, making certain it was firmly seated, then flicked the safety off, then back on again. Securing the pistol under his belt, he pulled his jacket down, got out of the car, and made his way to the building.

On the sidewalk, the snow crunched, then gave way to a compressed slipperiness. When you were a kid, Sims remembered, this was the right kind of snow for snowballs and sledding. Ahead, rows of lighted office windows climbed into the overhead darkness. As he crossed Wilson Boulevard, he looked up at the elevated roadway, and saw that it was still under construction, supported by a jackstraw tangle of massive steel support beams.

Moments later, he pushed through the doors of the *USA Today* building. The lobby resembled a modernistic Southwest cliff dwelling, a vast four-story space of earth-colored granite complete with outcroppings and rising angles that captured the eye and carried it upward. Offset flights of escalators, bright chrome slashes, connected staggered levels on the cliff's face, with towering ficus trees and falling water softening the effect.

Sims took the elevator to the twenty-fourth floor, then found a stairway and walked down to the twenty-third. Up the elevator and down the stairs, he'd been alone. He passed 2304. The brushed aluminum sign outside read TRENCHARD AND ASSOCIATES, EXPORT LICENSING AND CONSULTING. The gently curving corridor ended on a glass wall. Outside, the snow was falling even heavier. He could barely make out the

Key Bridge and lights of Georgetown University across the river. Below, he found Kent Street and his car. From here, he couldn't see the rusted steel support beams, and the snow-covered elevated roadway traced an elegant white arc outward from the building.

Back at the Trenchard office, he stood outside the door for a moment, listening but hearing nothing but the muted incidental sounds of the building keeping itself alive. He opened the door. Trenchard and his (her?) associates did well enough at whatever they did to have a plush waiting room with thick carpets, indirect lighting, and two blond receptionists. The nearer blonde was on the phone. On her desk, television monitors showed the hallway outside. The other blonde looked at Sims for a long time, then pointed to a door on her right.

"Through there. First on the left."

Sims stepped into a carpeted corridor. The first door on the left had a metal sign similar to that in the outer corridor, this one reading CONFERENCE. The door swung easily, but even so, Sims felt the heavy mass of it. The first thing that struck him was the large square of light as a slide disappeared from a projection screen. The second thing was the chair behind the projector. Electric servomotors whining, the chair swiveled in a rapid precise motion.

"Just can't stay away, can you?"

The voice had a high constricted tone. Matthias Alberich's vocal cords had been deformed with the rest of his body when his mother's doctor had prescribed thalidomide for her morning sickness. He had been born legless, and tiny flipper hands spouted directly from his shoulders.

"Didn't want to miss out on all the fun," Sims replied.

Like Sims, Alberich was a Riddle recruit. While passing through New York in 1974, Riddle had heard about a boy chess master who at fourteen was destroying all comers in a Bronx ice-cream parlor. Riddle investigated the ice-cream parlor and found Alberich, like a prince, enthroned on his wheelchair and wearing a T-shirt emblazoned "Master of the Long Diagonal." He had challenged the kid in the wheelchair. Riddle lasted longer than most opponents, but in forty-three moves, Alberich had lured him into a variant of the Tomenkin Maneuver, and that had been that.

Riddle had used his connections and within weeks, Alberich had been accepted at MIT. At first, Alberich had been known as "the kid in the wheelchair," then he'd become "the kid," when the wheelchair simply seemed to disappear into irrelevance. And five years later, when he'd graduated with a Ph.D in computer engineering, awestruck students and faculty alike talked about "The Kid," and everyone knew who that was. Along the way to the Ph.D, Alberich had composed and commercially recorded eight piano concertos, playing them on a special electronic keyboard he had designed and built in a marathon session in which he had gone without sleep for forty-seven hours. At Langley, thanks to the Agency's deep pockets, he put together the most advanced computer center, as he put it, "this side of Mr. Spock and the Horsehead Nebula."

Sims walked toward Alberich. If you didn't pay attention to the missing legs and arms—which Sims no longer did—the rest of Alberich was standard white male. Thick thatch of blond hair, deep brown hell-to-pay eyes in a square, almost handsome face. The usual greeting routine was a squeeze of Alberich's flipper hand.

"Wait," Alberich said with a slight grin.

Sims stopped. A black matte boom swiveled smoothly toward him from the wheelchair frame. Perhaps a yard long, the metal arm had an articulation joint where an elbow would be, and at the end, a hand. A hand with only three fingers and an opposable thumb, a hand with exposed metal hinges and varicolored spaghetti wiring, but a hand nonetheless.

"I can't do high-fives, but high-fours work pretty good." Alberich waggled the hand.

Feeling foolish, Sims took it. Even minus a finger, even with the metal and all, it felt like a hand. He squeezed. The hand—Alberich—squeezed back.

"It's the feedback that makes it," Alberich explained. "It tells me what I'm doing out there at the end of the arm and what you're doing. Anybody can make a mechanical hand,

61

but without feedback, the hand does a shitty job with delicate stuff—"

"—like shaking hands." Sims gave a final squeeze then let go.

"Or picking up eggs." Alberich turned the hand, and held it up before him, examining it. He looked over the fingers to Sims. "Legs next. No limits to this stuff, not like skin and bones. Maybe when I get the legs, I'll take up pro basketball." Alberich flexed the hand again and rested it along the armrest of his chair.

Sims surveyed the conference room. It had been darkened for the slide projector; only a few ceiling spots threw cones of light onto a richly polished rosewood table that ran much of the length of the room. Each place at the table was marked by a high-backed leather chair and a tooled leather desk pad. By each pad, a telephone handset had been built into the tabletop. The projection screen hung from the ceiling at one end of the table, and a slide projector sat on a small stand beside Alberich. On the stand, Sims recognized an Agency-issue gray canvas case, the kind with the built-in incendiary device that could turn the bag and its contents into ash in a fraction of a second.

"Whose's this?" He waved his hand across the room.

Alberich gave a small shrug. "Trenchard's real; I met him once. Tokyo station. Handled economics. Retired and set this up."

"The 'and Associates'?"

"Silent partners." Alberich gave him a tight, between-us-guys grin.

"Oh." Another retired spy running another Agency proprietary. You see enough, Sims told himself, and you begin to wonder if there's anything Langley *doesn't* run.

Alberich's face got serious. "Welcome back. I hear Italy was the shits."

Sims slumped into a cushioned chair at the long conference table. He slapped the tabletop with the palm of his hand. "All of a sudden some Czech psychopath's after me and a Pakistani's turning Chain Bridge Road into a shooting gallery. For what, Matthias?"

Alberich didn't try to answer but sat looking sympathetically at Sims.

"It scared me at first," continued Sims. "I'm still scared. But mostly, I'm pissed off."

Alberich sat quietly for a moment. Finally, he asked, "You sorta missed it—the Agency—didn't you? Being off in Italy and all?"

Sims allowed himself a pause to think about it some more, then nodded. "Yeah," he admitted.

A cricket-chime chirped softly from the telephone before him.

"That's reception. It's probably Riddle." Alberich turned his chair slightly toward the opening door.

"Gentlemen." Riddle made his entrance, his bulk filling the doorway from reception, his face red from the outside cold, flakes of snow still clinging to his black fur Cossack hat and dusting the shoulders of his Burberry coat. He pointed his cane at the corner of the conference room where, for the first time, Sims saw the brushed glint of stainless steel. "A cup of coffee," Riddle said, "and we're off to the races."

Finally settled, his hands laced around a huge white porcelain mug, Riddle nodded to Alberich. "Let us proceed with your cavalcade of charmers, Mr. Alberich."

Alberich played with a remote device. The overhead lights dimmed and the projector came on. "Emil Schmar," Alberich announced. "This was taken in December of '89, just after the fall of the Communist government in Prague. The police rounded up as many of the old school intelligence apparatus as they could, photoed and fingerprinted them, then turned most loose."

Full front, Schmar glared out of the screen. In a way, Sims thought, the photograph was more telling than real life. Coal black hair and eyes like depthless black pools. The delicate blade of a nose, the thin lips of his smallish mouth gave him an almost ethereal look. But it was the eyes, Sims decided, that made Schmar. Sims had seen those eyes in others, those obsessed with alcohol, drugs, or gambling. But Schmar's obsession wasn't one of those.

"He has to kill," Sims said. "You lock him away where he

couldn't kill anybody and the bastard would kill himself. Just for the pleasure of it."

"Born 11 August 1952," Alberich began. "Košice, Slovakia. Public schools, gymnasium degree. Joined the Czechoslovak Union of Anti-Fascist Fighters in September '70. After basic training, he shows up in the Middle East with a contingent of construction youth."

"Construction?" Riddle asked.

Alberich flicked a button and a younger Schmar appeared. Dressed in a mottled camouflage uniform, he stood in front of a low, patched-together building, a Kalashnikov assault rifle cradled in his arms.

"Construction—building terrorist training camps. Small arms ranges. This's South Yemen, October '71."

Sims raised his eyes.

"The picture?" Alberich asked for Sims. "Got it from the Izzies," he answered. The picture vanished, replaced by a chronology. "Schmar's back in Czechoslovakia in January '72, where he joins the *Lidova milice,* the People's Militia. He must have been on a fast track because four years later, he's attending the KGB school in Novosibirsk, and six months after that—it's October '76 now—the BND reports that he's in East Germany, the KGB field school at Pankow. Teaching tradecraft to Moscow's Third World clients."

Another photograph flashed onto the screen. In the background, the U.S. Capitol; Sims placed it as Pennsylvania Avenue and Fourteenth Street, just outside the Occidental restaurant. Schmar, in a light summer suit, was striding directly into the camera. Beside him, obviously in conversation with Schmar, a handsome blond man about forty or so.

"FBI surveillance shot. It's now June '84 and Schmar's in the Czech Embassy here. Cover: deputy commercial attaché."

Sims reached back into his memory. "And Josef Broz was chief *rezident.*"

Riddle tapped his cane on the floor beside his chair. "Bravo, Mr. Sims. When Broz came here to take over the StB *rezidentura,* he brought one person—his good man Schmar." He waggled the cane at the photo.

"Who's that with him?" Sims asked.

Another picture. It was the same blond man, this time, stiff and upright in a West German *Bundeswehr* uniform. Sims saw from the collar pips that the man was a lieutenant colonel.

"Herbert Spiedel," Riddle announced. "Promising armor officer. A family of Junkers and inveterate Prussians to the core. Young Herbert was the West German army attaché in Washington at the same time Broz and Schmar showed up."

"Anything on Spiedel?"

"The files . . ." Alberich shrugged. "Nothing. As attaché, Spiedel could have been trying to recruit Schmar, or Schmar, Spiedel. But no follow-up in the files."

Spiedel's picture vanished and Schmar came back, this time in an overcoat and carrying a small suitcase. "The last entry on Schmar was dated 9 November '84," Alberich continued. "Surveillance caught him here at Dulles. He flew to Mexico City. Mexico City Station picked him up there. He stayed one night, and the next morning caught a Cubana Illushyin to Havana. From there, nothing," Alberich's voice came out of the dark, "until you ran into him in Prague last year."

The screen flashed. A grainy black-and-white telephoto shot into the front of an Audi. Prague's old town square in the background. Sims's face clearly discernible in the driver's seat of the car. A burly man in a camel-hair overcoat was getting into the backseat. Thick dark hair, tinted glasses in heavy frames above a full, rich-jowled face.

Sitting back in his chair, Riddle, tapped his cane gently against the edge of the conference table and addressed Sims. "Which, young man, brings us to Schmar's relationship to Josef Broz."

Sims identified the photograph on the screen. "January, last year." The picture struck him with a sensation of otherworld unreality. It seemed impossible that he'd been at the wheel of *that* car in *that* photograph. That had been little more than a year ago; it seemed like another lifetime. He had met, for the first and last time, Josef Broz, the last chief of the StB, the *Statni Tajna Bezpecnost,* communist Czechoslovakia's version of the KGB.

"They had shut the StB down two years before that."

Riddle pointed his cane at the photo. "And yet our Mr. Broz still looks quite prosperous. Did you and Houghton ascertain what he was doing?"

Sims shook his head. "No. Houghton made some comment about old spies keeping body and soul together and Broz just laughed at that."

"And nothing, I suppose, about Schmar?"

"No. It was a short meeting with Broz. We concentrated on Valek's defection."

Alberich threw another slide on the screen, another chronology. "Broz and Valek met in early 1966, running an StB front group. They parted company in December '67, when Broz became deputy *resident* for the StB in Madrid. They didn't work together again until April '80. By that time, Broz had been recognized as a comer. He was chief of the StB's North American directorate. Altogether, Valek worked for Broz for four years. Broz then comes to Washington as StB's chief *resident*."

Sims glanced at his notes. "'Eighty-four. Broz and Schmar in Washington." He picked up the trail. "In Prague, Broz told us that when he got back from Washington in 1988, Valek had transferred over to the KGB and was stationed at Center in Moscow—"

"—where he worked until he defected, two days after Christmas 1991," Riddle interjected, "and you brought him in after that lamentable scene in the Rosslyn metro."

"After which I was his case officer, Isaac Felton his shrink, and Mike Gribbins his baby-sitter," Sims finished. "We've come full circle. We're back to now and everybody's dead except Schmar and me."

For a long time, they sat silently, the only sound in the room was the whir of the projector's cooling fan. Sims got up, walked over to the coffee urn, and brought a mug back to the table. He sat for a while, thinking; sorting the pieces and staring at the coffee. Finally he looked at Riddle, then Alberich.

"Valek and Broz are the keys," he announced.

Riddle gave him the cold-fish headmaster look. "They've been dead almost a year."

"Makes no difference. Look, if Schmar had come after

just me it could be revenge. Or he'd been hired by some-body. But there's Felton and Mike Gribbins. And they make it something connected with Valek and Broz."

"That still hasn't put it together, Mr. Sims."

Sims was tired and Riddle pushing him that way made him irritable. He looked for support from Alberich, and finding none, turned back to Riddle. "Damnit, Riddle. This is connected to Valek and Broz. Now, if they're dead, and they damn sure are, then this's something that involved them when they were alive and it's continued on. Let's go back . . ."

"Yes?"

"When Valek and Broz were alive, Schmar was working for Broz. Broz was calling the shots, and whatever Broz and Valek had going, it's still going and Felton, Mike Gribbins, and I somehow, a year later, got in the way."

Riddle considered this, eyes looking into the distance. They refocused on Sims. "And now?"

"I go back to Prague and find out what Broz was up to."

"When?"

"Tomorrow." Sims thought about Rollo Moss who was getting the passport. "Day after at the latest."

Riddle nodded, then consulted a blue index card. "SIGSI cabled this afternoon. They've identified one of the bodies at San Gimignano." Riddle looked at Sims for a moment then at the card again. "One Giuseppe 'Pippo' Calò. The late Mr. Calò was a member of the Porta Nuova clan—"

"Clan?"

"Clan, young man. Mr. Calò was a member of the Sicilian Mafia, a resident of Palermo. SIGSI finds it curious that he turns up so far away from home." Riddle placed the index card facedown on the small table beside him. "They sent their highest regards for the shooting talent that eased him from this mortal coil."

"Why the Mafia?"

Riddle raised an eyebrow. "Why, indeed?"

Sims, Riddle, and Alberich exchanged looks and came up with nothing. Alberich left first, and a few minutes later, Riddle. Sims finished his coffee, which had a sour metallic taste to it.

Out in reception, both blondes were on the telephone. Neither paid attention to him.

Sims checked the outside hallway on the TV monitors. Several doors down, a woman closed and locked a door and made her way to the elevators. Beyond her, a janitor with a pull-along cart of cleaning tools and a vacuum cleaner. Sims watched the woman get on an elevator, waited a few seconds, then stepped out into the corridor. To his right, the elevators, to his left, the janitor, working his way down the corridor in the opposite direction, the noise rising and falling as he pushed a vacuum cleaner back and forth.

The easy route, Sims was thinking, would be to fly to Prague from New York. The safer one would be to drive into Prague. The commies are gone, but old habits die hard, and the Czechs still watched the airports and train stations.

He reached for the elevator button, preoccupied with the advantages of flying to Frankfurt versus Berlin when, inside him, the alarm began screaming.

Later, he would realize he'd been warned by the vacuum cleaner. Instead of the rising and falling sound a vacuum cleaner makes being pushed back and forth, there had been a steady roar. Instinctively, Sims turned, and at the same time, stepped back from the elevator.

As if by magic, a glistening silver furrow peeled open in the metal elevator door just inches from his head.

Sims dove for the floor, rolled left, and clawed for the Colt in his belt.

Down the corridor, some forty feet away, the janitor crouched with a two-handed combat grip on a long automatic pistol. Beside him, still running, the vacuum cleaner.

Bringing his Colt up, Sims saw the long pistol swing toward him and he knew the janitor was ahead of him. Sims fired without aiming. The Colt's flash and roar reverberated down the corridor. Sims saw the answering muzzle flash, tiny and soundless against the ringing in his own ears and the noise of the vacuum cleaner.

The slug splattered against the wall, just above him. Doors slammed open up and down the corridor. A man shouted mindlessly for the police. The janitor shoved the tool cart out into the middle of the hallway, then spun and sprinted away.

Up on one knee, Sims was about to fire again when one of the Trenchard blondes stepped out into the corridor and into his line of fire. Sims scrambled to his feet. Vaulting over the abandoned tool cart, he passed the blonde. He saw she had a small revolver in her hand.

"Get back!" Sims shouted, shoving her roughly back into the office. The janitor had disappeared around the curve in the corridor.

Keeping close to the inner curving wall, Sims ran in pursuit. The curve gave way to the big window at the end and to an empty hallway. Sims stopped in midstride, held his breath and tried to listen; to hear, over his pounding heart, any sound of his assailant. In that fraction of a second, he saw the softly lit exit sign marking the stairwell.

Bursting through the door, he found himself on a landing. Below, the sound of scrambling footsteps on the concrete steps. Sims started down, taking the steps three and four at a time. Soon he was in a controlled fall, covering six or more steps at a leap, maintaining balance with an occasional touch of the steel handrail. In the noise of his own chase, he occasionally heard footsteps below him, but couldn't tell how far away they were or whether he was gaining on them.

At the sixteenth floor landing, he heard a shout of surprise, then the thutting sound of what had to be the janitor's silenced pistol. Coming off a flight of steps, he looked down on the fifteenth floor landing.

"Hurry," Riddle whisper-shouted. The older man leaned against the wall clutching his right forearm, where a dark bloodstain was spreading. In his right hand, a thin sliver of steel, a blade some two feet long.

Sims was beside Riddle. "You okay?"

Riddle let go of his wounded shoulder and pushed Sims away. He pointed the sword cane down the stairs. "I pinked him rather thoroughly. He still has the gun."

Sims picked up the blood trail halfway down the stairs to the fourteenth floor landing. At first, scattered drops, then increasingly larger smears on the raw concrete. Still the sound of steps below. It seemed to Sims they were slower now—more erratic. This was the killer's escape route. The way he would have come if he'd been successful, Sims was thinking. The man wouldn't have taken a chance on an elevator.

Sims had just left the eleventh floor landing when the footsteps below him abruptly ended. For a second, his back against the stairwell, he stopped and listened. Nothing. Cautiously, he rounded the bend in the stairs that would give him a shot at the tenth floor landing. And anyone there a shot back at him.

The landing was empty. And that's where the blood trail ended.

It picked up in the tenth floor corridor, darker stains on a dark blue carpet. A bloody handprint smeared along one wall. Sims felt a gusting decompression. Rounding the corner, he recognized, even at a distance, another handprint, this one on the door at the end of the corridor.

Sims threw the door open, and ran out into the swirling snow. A terrace extended into the darkness beyond the glow of the building, with footprints and blood marking a trail in the snow. Farther out, he glimpsed the briefest flicker of movement, a dark shadow slipping into the blackness of another shadow.

Chasing the shadow, Sims dodged a sawhorse and found himself running through a maze of construction debris. Suddenly, the terrace just . . . ended. No balustrade or guardrail. Inches away, and a sheer ten-story drop below, Wilson Boulevard. He realized he was on the elevated roadway. And with the realization came the headlights, and an instant after that, the winding-up sound of an engine.

The lights bucked as they lurched at him over the unfinished pavement, the eyes of an attacking animal. Sims, glancing from the headlights to the more distant building, knew that he could never in a million years make it off the roadway in time. The building was too far and the headlights too fast. The thought never came to him consciously, but he decided if he were going to die, he damn sure wasn't going to do it running away.

* * *

70

In the van, Ahmed's heart surged at the sight of a man now pinned in the white glare of his headlights. He jammed the accelerator to the floorboard.

"Faster! Faster!" Hassan, in the passenger's seat, shouted encouragement, one hand beating on the dashboard, the other clutching the wound in his side. Hassan didn't care about his wound. The only thing that mattered was the man before them, frozen in the headlights—his target. And the target became everything.

The van bearing down on him, Sims crossed into a realm of timelessness, as if he had stepped into a wax museum display. In football, there had been plays when it had seemed that everyone else on the field had been frozen in place and all he had to do was think about where he wanted to be and instantly he was there. It was that way now: the van had stopped, absolutely motionless, even the snow hung suspended in the night sky. With all the time in the world, he deliberately brought the Colt down in a two-handed grip, aimed it directly into the headlight on his right, then raised his aim the merest fraction of an inch.

In the passenger seat, Hassan screamed even louder, pounding the dashboard. "Faster, kill—" He saw the black man in the headlights make a swift motion and suddenly the black man had a gun and the gun pointed—

Hassan's fist hit the dashboard and a shower of blue-green glass shards erupted into the van. His first stunned thought was that he had somehow caused the windshield to explode. Hassan was still thinking it when he saw Ahmed's head wrench violently and the back of his skull disintegrate in a shower of blood and brain matter.

The van veered violently to the right. Hassan reached for the wheel and wrenched it left. He knew instantly that he'd overcompensated. He felt an immediate sickening twist of vertigo as the boxy vehicle careened into a violent skid.

Time and motion returned for Sims and he watched the van careen wildly, trailing behind it a rooster tail of snow. The right headlight shattered as the van ricocheted off a concrete railing with a shower of sparks and the sound of tearing metal. Then, striking a stack of reinforcing bars, the vehicle vaulted off the roadway as if launching itself toward Washington across the river.

The van fell in slow-motion silence until, partway down, it bounced off a steel support beam. The beam tore open the gas tank and a thin tongue of flame shot down the column of gasoline, licking after the falling van. The vehicle smashed into the street and the flame caught up with it, blossoming into a roiling orange-red fireball.

Sims stood for a moment and watched the flames devour the van. The flaring heat warmed his face and made him think of the sun. From a distance came the sound of sirens. He turned and walked toward the building. Riddle waited for him at the open door.

Still clutching his upper arm, Riddle leaned on his cane, the snow gathering on his hat and shoulders.

Sims motioned to Riddle's arm.

"Only a nick, young man." He pointed with the cane toward the roadway. From an adjacent building, windows reflected the flames below on the street. "I see you've kept your touch."

Sims looked toward the flames, then nodded to Riddle. "Hope the Judge's cleanup crews have kept theirs."

The Judge's cleanup crew that evening consisted of CIA's deputy director and two Agency lawyers. They were backed up by a series of phone calls from a former and well-respected attorney general—an Agency alumnus—and from Virginia's senior senator who was the ranking Republican on the Select Committee on Intelligence. By 11:30 that evening, the Arlington police had finished a preliminary investigation into what would ultimately be declared the county's eighth drunken driving accident of the new year, and the duty surgeon at Bethesda Naval Hospital had removed the bullet from the fleshy portion of Riddle's upper right arm.

Riddle's room was in the tower at Bethesda, one floor beneath the suite kept ready for the President of the United States. At the nurses' station, Sims slipped the magazine from the Colt, jacked the operating slide back to empty the chamber, then handed the weapon over to the security guard. The guard made an entry in a small pocket ledger, then pushed a hidden button and another plainclothes came from out of nowhere to take Sims down to Riddle's room.

Swathed in white, his arm bandaged and in a sling across his chest, Riddle sat propped up in the hospital bed, looking like an unhappy Roman emperor. His sword cane was hooked over the head of the bed next to the call button. Sims's escort left, but Sims imagined the man waiting just outside the door. He ignored the straight-backed metal chair and walked over to stand by Riddle's bedside.

"You okay?"

Riddle, groggy, made a sour face. "Considering . . ."

"They found the real janitor"—Sims paused to let Riddle catch up—"stuffed in a maintenance closet. Shot in the back of the head. The twenty-two slug matched the one they took out of your arm. The van was stolen."

"Identification?"

Sims shook his head. "Not yet. The fire . . . it'll take some time."

Riddle shut his eyes. Just as Sims was beginning to think he'd drifted off to sleep, Riddle opened them again. "It was my fault, you know."

"What do you mean?"

Riddle took a deep breath. "This morning. After we talked. I went for my usual walk, then breakfast at the Army and Navy Club. When I left, I cut across Farragut Square . . . the park . . ." Riddle trailed off, pressing his lips together.

Sims waited for Riddle to continue.

"I was followed." Confession made, his voice picked up in a forced businesslike briskness. "And they undoubtedly followed me to Rosslyn."

"How do you know?"

Riddle got a cross, incredulous look as if asking himself if he'd heard right. *How* would he know? How would *he* know? One might as well ask how one would know that God belonged to the Church of England.

"I *know,* young man, because I *know.* One doesn't spend

73

half a century in the business without knowing that." He pulled a sour face. "I noticed a man behind me before I went into the club. I saw him again an hour and a half later when I came out and walked back to the shop."

"Coincidence." Sims tried to pass it by, but he saw Riddle wasn't having any of it.

"Nonsense. They followed me, calculating that sooner or later, I'd lead them to you. I got sloppy and did just that. Bloody damned awful." Riddle shut his eyes. "Awful," he said again, this time the edge wasn't as hard, and the frown lines were beginning to soften. Sims stood silently until Riddle's breathing became slow and regular and the older man drifted off.

One thing, Sims thought to himself, whoever it was at the *USA Today* building, they hadn't followed him here from Europe. They knew the area. This was local talent. They'd been here all along.

6

At four o'clock, Thursday afternoon, Rollo Moss's blue Chrysler sped along the limited access roadway to Dulles International. Payton was driving and one of the heavyweight bodyguards was riding shotgun. The glass between the front and back seats was up. Rollo sat deep in his corner of the backseat, worriedly searching the left, then the right sides of the road.

"Looking for an ambush?" Sims teased.

Rollo didn't smile. "You need somebody to watch your back," he said, fretful and cross.

"I'll be okay."

"You'd a said the same thing about Rosslyn before yesterday."

Sims shrugged, knowing Rollo was right.

A half mile ahead, floodlights already illuminated Dulles's concrete and glass control tower in the early winter twilight. Farther out, beyond the runways, the landing lights of stacked-up incoming aircraft looked like strings of flares dropped across the Virginia countryside.

That morning, his second in the States, Sims had slept until just before eleven. After breakfast near Eastern Market, he had called Rollo, then the control number the Judge had given him. A man had answered. Young, precise, whitesounding. Vaguely disappointed he hadn't gotten the woman with the smoky voice, Sims had gone through the Kabuki verification dance with his old badge number, and his date of birth, then asked for ten thousand dollars: four in dollars, three in Czech koruna, and three in German marks.

The voice took this in and using a laconic tone, asked Sims to hold. Thirty seconds later, the voice came back with instructions. An hour and a half later, Sims retrieved an envelope from a mailbox rental storefront on M Street, then walked to the Lufthansa office on Connecticut, where he paid cash for a business class seat on flight 419, departing Dulles at 5:40 that afternoon.

It had taken Sims only a few minutes to pack and meet Rollo at Casa Miguel. Rollo had talked with an old friend on the Arlington, Virginia, police force: the van had definitely been stolen, but the bodies as yet unidentified.

Rollo eyed the sweeping glass and concrete terminal building, then turned to Sims.

"I'd still feel better, you had somebody with you."

Sims nodded to tell Rollo he'd heard, then both men stared straight ahead as the car turned up the ramp to departures.

Payton pulled over to the curb where cars were double- and triple-parked, trunks and doors opening, luggage and people crowding the sidewalks.

Sims grabbed his carry-on bag and opened the door. He had one foot out the door when he felt Rollo's hand on his arm.

Rollo's face was crossed with worry. "You watch out, Bradford," he warned. "You keep your eye on the ball. You don't, you end up dead."

Lufthansa 419, a DC-10, landed at Frankfurt's Rhein-Main airport at 7:15 the next morning, a Friday. The airport was already filling with weekend travelers, and it took Sims well over an hour to retrieve his luggage and clear customs. Racing to A concourse, he caught his connecting flight as the gates were closing. Fifty-five minutes later, the FASTEN SEAT BELT sign flashed on, and from his window seat in the small Dornier turboprop, he caught a glimpse through the low clouds of the Elbe River and, alongside it, Dresden.

Dresden's airport north of the city showed that West Germany's wealth hadn't taken root in the east. Behind the flimsy yellow-and-black plastic facade of the Hertz counter, years of indifferent patch jobs made a pasty collage on the plaster wall, and a flat, sweetish odor of cooking gas and soft coal smoke filled the chilly terminal. A thin woman in an ill-fitting green sweater made out a car rental contract by hand with a ballpoint pen, then verified Sims's credit card in a dispirited telephone conversation punctuated by long pauses and sidelong glances at Sims.

Sims tried to figure out whether she didn't want to rent him the car or she didn't want to be finished so soon with the only work that would come her way the rest of her day. He hadn't decided when the woman pushed the keys, a copy of the contract, and an international green insurance card across the counter, and pointed toward the parking lot.

The lot was a barbed-wire enclosure paved with cinders and guarded by an old man with bad teeth who came out from a dilapidated gate shack to examine Sims, then the contract, then Sims again. Finally he pointed to a soot-grimed Mercedes.

The clouds had dropped lower and now snow was mixing with the spitting rain. Driving south, Sims soon entered Dresden itself and crossed the Elbe near the Theaterplatz. Scaffolding covered most of the Hofkirche, the soaring seventeenth century cathedral, and everywhere construction cranes filled the ancient city's skyline. The midmorning traffic was light, and by ten-thirty, he was heading south on Route E-15 toward Prague, 150 kilometers away. After a late breakfast of sausages and roast potatoes in a *gasthaus* in Altenburg, he crossed into the Czech Republic at the border station near Teplice.

An hour later, row after grim row of Stalinist apartments abruptly sprang up in the midst of acres of plowed fields north of Prague. The sterile concrete blocks reminded Sims of the tank traps in the grainy old black-and-white World War II newsreels. The apartments mercifully gave way to a belt of small houses, then shops, and then Sims began recognizing landmarks from the past. A sense of homecoming hit him when he got to the Vltava River. There, the panorama of Prague burst upon him, the old city gauzy and gray with subtle tints of prayer and eternity. Ignoring the traffic behind him, he pulled to the side of the bridge and stopped.

The Vltava shapes Prague. Flowing south to north, the river abruptly swings east, then doubles back and heads north again, making an almost perfect question mark on the map. Most of old Prague lies just below the bulge—on the question mark's stem—with bridges connecting the Old Town on the east, or right bank, with the *Malá Strana,* or Lesser Quarter, on the left bank.

Sims lifted his eyes from the river, and, as he expected, he was drawn to Hradčany. The Hrad, a sweeping cliff on the northern edge of the *Malá Strana,* was crowned with Kafka's castle, and, reaching for the greater glory of God, the spires of Saint Vitus Cathedral, nearly a thousand years in the building. On his first visit to Saint Vitus, Sims, who'd been raised in the African Methodist Episcopal faith, had stood transfixed near the high altar when the midday sun came through the massive rose window, bursting in a kaleidoscope so dazzling and so defiant of human description that he understood why no one could see such a sight and deny the existence of God.

It'd been a year ago, he thought, that he and Houghton had come here to see Broz. And a year ago, Broz had something going that wasn't finished yet even though Broz was dead. The mystery fit Prague. It was a city where no line was truly straight, no corner truly plumb. Even its landmark, the Charles Bridge, bent itself at a weird angle for no apparent reason. Prague—how had Houghton described it?—a wilderness of mirrors?

Sims passed up the Esplanade, his favorite hotel, and chose instead the larger and more impersonal Intercontinental on Curieových. Whatever the business was, it seemed to be good in the Czech Republic; as he made his way through the crowded lobby to reception, Sims picked up bits of conversation in English, Polish, German, Italian, French, and Farsi. The desk clerk, however, was Czech, and he looked sadly at Sims and shook his head when Sims told him he had no reservations. Sims switched to Czech and passed the clerk his credit card with a twenty U.S. discreetly folded under it, and the clerk got a look of recollection, as if he'd just remembered the overlooked room on the twelfth floor.

The large room looked out on the river and Hradčany. Sims found a cold Pilsner Urquell in the minibar, snapped the top off, and stood at the window, sipping the beer from the bottle and gazing across the rust-red roofs of Prague to the castle. Dark against a darker winter·sky, it seemed austere and forbidding, a grim guardian of the city below it. For almost eight years, off and on, Prague had been his home. He'd walked every street and alley and had met sources and potential recruits in nearly every conceivable situation. But no day passed in Prague that he didn't see the castle and feel its presence.

"This village," Sims recited aloud the passage from Kafka, "belongs to the castle, and whoever lives here or passes the night here must have the Count's permission." He finished the beer, showered and changed into a suit, then walked through the mist to Wenceslas Square and a pay phone at the Můstek subway station where he called Ceska.

Half an hour later in the run-down working-class suburb of Smíchov, Sims found a window seat in a coffeehouse where he could watch Ceska's shop across the square. He knew the place well. When he'd first been assigned to Prague in 1978, the square had been dominated by a Soviet tank, perched on a huge granite slab.

Supposedly, the tank had been the first into Prague in 1945, and supposedly, the Czech people had asked that it stay as a reminder of Soviet bravery and sacrifice. Actually, the tank had been nowhere near Prague when the Germans retreated, and actually, the Czechs detested the thing.

During his years at Prague station, Sims had used the graffiti on the tank as a barometer of Czech discontent with the Soviets. The ultimate had come in the summer of 1991.

In broad daylight, a Czech artist had painted the entire tank a bubble-gum pink and then erected a massive penis on its turret. A month later came the coup against Gorbachev and the beginning of the end for Marx, Engels, and Lenin and all that the pink tank represented. Now, Sims saw, there was nothing left of the tank. Only the bare granite base remained, and on that someone had spray-painted *"Adios, Sovětskýcy."*

Satisfied as much as possible that there was no surveillance, Sims paid for his coffee and struck out across the square. Ceska's door was covered by an accordion-folded security grate. He pressed a bell by the door and heard it ring somewhere inside.

He had recruited Jan Ceska in early 1989, just months before the Czech Communist government went belly-up. Prague station had needed a local who could, on short notice, come up with an unregistered rifle, pistol, or shotgun. Ceska, a former master machinist at the Skoda Works, could also turn out quality specialty items such as jimmys, lock picks, and tuckaway knives. And, being in that kind of business, Ceska always knew the latest alliances in the shadow world of Prague's intrigue.

With much noise, Ceska unlocked the door and swung it open. He stood in the doorway, an elfin-looking man: ruddy complexion, high, domed forehead that pushed thinning curls of gray hair back to the top of his head, and protruding blue eyes over a small, almost girlish mouth. He wore a thick woolen shirt and a leather shop apron, and he carried with him the sleek odor of machine oil.

"Dobrý večer, Herr Sims." Ceska extended a stubby, squared off hand. Sims took the hand and stepped into the shop. A narrow central aisle led toward a frosted glass door at the back. Midway down the aisle, a single bulb in an industrial shade threw a cone of light onto the floor. The ceiling and far corners were lost in darkness. On either side, sewing machines—Singers and Elnas, Olivettis, Vikings, and Berninas—modern electrics, old treadle machines. Some ready for use, others disemboweled on workbenches. Ceska stopped under the light and turned to Sims.

"It's been how long?"

"Since August '91," Sims answered in Czech.

Ceska pursed his lips to help him remember. "The coup against Gorbachev. They say you came out well after that one."

"I got shot."

"A wound of honor. The gossip had it that they decorated you."

"Did the gossip have it that they threw me out?"

Ceska pursed his lips and dropped his eyes delicately. "That too. And that there was much killing after." Then he got a sly look. "You are now working for the embassy again?" He asked it as if he didn't quite expect an answer.

Sims ignored him and looked around the shop. "You've been busy?"

"A whole new world of opportunity. Serbs, Croats, Muslims. But no business from your old offices. Your new president—this Clinton—he has talked much about sending Americans to stop the fighting." Ceska's bulging eyes glistened at the prospect.

Sims shrugged. "Politicians say one thing before elections, another thing after." He paused, then: "I need a pistol."

Ceska gave Sims a small nod of acknowledgment, then, motioning for Sims to follow, Ceska turned and walked toward the door at the back of the shop. Through the door, they entered a small wood-paneled office. On an ancient rolltop desk, a gooseneck lamp, like a periscope, raised itself out of a sea of papers. Over the desk, a *Playboy* centerfold, an apparently real blonde, stretched languorously on a leather sofa. At the desk, Ceska reached inside a pigeonhole.

Sims heard a faint buzzing as a section of the wood paneling next to the desk swung inward. Dim lights lit a spiral iron staircase leading down. With another follow-me motion, Ceska descended, footsteps making ringing noises on the metal steps.

Ceska flipped a wall switch. The room was much as Sims remembered it. With walls of exposed redbrick, it extended under the entire length of the shop, a distance of perhaps sixty or seventy feet. The chief feature was a metal I beam in the ceiling that ran down the entire length of the room. On his right under a high-intensity light, three shop stools were pulled up to a workbench as clean and pristine as an operating room table. Above the workbench and on both sides of it, banks of metal cabinets reached to the ceiling.

Ceska pulled a fat key ring from under his leather shop apron. "Revolver? Automatic?"

"Automatic. With a silencer."

"You have been using . . . ?"

"A Colt 2000."

Ceska unlocked a cabinet to the left of the workbench and scanned the banks of labeled drawers. "Yes," he muttered to himself, selecting a drawer. He took out an oiled paper package and opened it on the workbench.

Three quarters of an inch of threaded barrel extended beyond the operating slide, giving the weapon a curious snouted appearance. Sims watched as Ceska cleared the pistol, removing the magazine, pulling back on the operating slide, checking to ensure the chamber was empty, snapping the trigger. Ceska handed the weapon to Sims, grip first.

Sims took the pistol, repeated the clearing ritual, and turned the weapon in his hands to find the balance of it.

"Llama M-82," Ceska said, watching Sims handle the pistol. "Nine millimeter parabellum, fifteen-round magazine."

"Heavy."

"Heavier than the Colt—yes. But very accurate." From another drawer, Ceska took a silencer, a fat steel tube six inches long. Yet another drawer produced a square cardboard box of cartridges that Ceska put on the workbench beside the silencer. Then he walked to an electrical junction box on the wall and threw a switch. With a clanking grinding start of pulleys and cables, a heavy wood frame suspended from the overhead I beam raced toward them from the far end of the basement.

From a shelf beneath the workbench, Ceska took a large folded square of paper. Unfolded, Sims saw it was a silhouette target, the upper torso of a man. Ceska clipped it to the frame and, throwing the switch again, sent the target down the length of the basement. He motioned toward the adjacent wall and two noise-suppressor headsets hanging on a wood rack.

Sims slipped one of the headsets on, thumbed the stubby cartridges into the magazine, then slid the magazine into the pistol grip. Stepping past Ceska, he pulled the operating slide back and let it slam forward, chambering the first round.

In a swift, flowing motion, Sims took up a crouch, the automatic extended toward the target in a two-handed grip. Three shots reverberated as one, the basement walls flaring with the muzzle flash, and the air filling with the peppery smell of burned cordite.

Sims slipped on the safety and lowered the pistol. The lights behind the target shone through three holes, bright against the black of the silhouette. He studied the target for a moment, then walked back to the workbench where he had left the silencer. Screwing the silencer over the extended barrel, he took up the crouch position again and fired another three shots.

Again the muzzle flash, but this time only a quick series of soft, pneumatic sounds, *thut . . . thut . . . thut.* And the lights shone through another cluster of holes in the target.

Ceska worked the switch and the target flew toward them, jerking to a stop a foot or so away. The two clusters of shots had literally punched out the center of the silhouette's head. He continued to stare at the still fluttering target for a moment, then he turned to Sims. The Czech had a glum expression.

"I thought they taught you to aim at the chest. The center of mass."

Sims gazed at the target. "They did," he said.

Ceska waited to see if Sims would say something else, but instead, Sims handed the pistol back to Ceska.

"There is a slight roughness in the pull."

Ceska took the pistol but held it out in front of himself, paying no attention to it. The head shots obviously bothered him. His eyes searched Sims's face. "You are alone and you are looking for someone."

"Yes."

Ceska stiffened. "I cannot be connected to . . ." he trailed off.

Sims nodded toward the pistol in Ceska's outstretched hands. "The pull. Try it."

Ceska looked down at the weapon as if seeing it for the first time. He worked the slide back once and pulled the trigger on the empty chamber. He did it again. "Yes," he said hesitantly, "there is a slight roughness." He walked to the workbench. Sims followed. Under the light, the Czech passed his stubby hands over the pistol several times and as if by magic, the pistol was transformed into a neat array of parts.

Ceska picked up the sear, a flat, beveled bit of metal less than an inch long. He fished in his shirt pocket and came up with a jeweler's loupe. Blowing the dust off the lens, he screwed the small black cylinder into his right eye and took a closer look at the piece of metal.

"I notice they've taken the pink tank away," Sims said.

"The tank?" Ceska rotated his hand, looking at the sear, then at Sims. "The authorities," he said, as if letting Sims in on a family secret, "have it stored away someplace. In case the Russians come back."

"It's like a picture of your mother-in-law. A tank in the attic."

The loupe still sticking out of his eye, Ceska stood for a moment with his mouth open. It took him a second to register on what Sims had said, then he nodded and smiled. It was a small smile, like he didn't want to, but couldn't help himself.

Ceska spun the handle on a small metal working vise and clamped the sear in its jaws. From a drawer in the workbench, he withdrew a small triangular file.

Sims maneuvered toward his next topic. "The old crowd, the *nomenklatura,* I thought they'd go down the drain."

Ceska twisted his face in a cynical grimace and mimed a spitting motion off to the side. "The little fish, perhaps. But little fish are always the first to fall on hard times. That is their role. That is why they are little fish."

"The big fish?"

"The big fish always get along. Some even get bigger. The *nomenklatura* didn't give a shit about Marx. All they cared about were their connections. Take away the Marx and they still have their connections. The secret accounts, the business deals—that's what made them big fish."

Hunched over the vise, Ceska drew the file, once, twice, then three times across the sear, making crisp, rasping sounds.

"What were Broz's connections?"

Ceska froze, the file motionless against the piece of metal in the vise. The bulging blue eyes rolled to lock on Sims. "He's dead," Ceska finally said.

"I know. But before . . ."

Ceska turned his attention to the vise. He ran the file lightly over the sear then blew the filings away, then leaned close to look at his work. Nodding to himself, he unclamped the vise and removed the sear. From a round tin, he took a crocus cloth which he used to polish the filed area. He used the loupe again, turning the sear to catch the light under different angles. Then, still holding the part up, Ceska turned to Sims, the loupe in one eye giving him a squinting, curious look. "The talk is that you were connected with him—that that is why he died."

"Somebody killed him, but later. I think the Russians. It was about a year ago."

"A year ago . . ." Ceska, taken with the phrase, paused, his eyes going off into middle distance. "A year ago we were Czechoslovakia. Now there is Slovakia and we are something called the Czech Republic." He focused and looked worriedly at Sims. "Tomorrow has always been a long time away in Eastern Europe. And next year might as well be eternity. We are in what you call, a free . . ." He gestured helplessly with his hands, reaching for the phrase.

"Free-fall," Sims supplied.

"Free-fall," Ceska muttered to himself. The loupe went back into his pocket, and from a tube he found on the bench, he applied a microscopic dab of graphite grease to the sear. He put the part back in its place among the other parts and turned to Sims. He gave Sims a quizzical, challenging look and stepped back from the bench and extended a hand, palm up, in invitation.

Sims moved to the bench and stood for a second, scanning the parts. As if some inner signal had sounded, his hands darted out and he began reassembling the pistol. His only misstep was the recoil spring, which refused to go over the blued steel guide rod. Sims flipped it over and tried once more. It went on smoothly. Seconds later, he had the pistol together. He pulled back on the operating slide, let it slam forward, and squeezed the trigger. The sharp, metallic click echoed in the basement.

Ceska rewarded him with a small smile. "The recoil spring is slightly tapered on one end. It always causes problems."

"Broz's connections . . . ?" Sims prompted.

Ceska shrugged, obviously reluctant to get into it. "Who knows? He was chief of the StB. He knew everyone."

"When the Communist government fell, the democrats sent him to jail."

"For perhaps a day," Ceska said scornfully. "Then he was out. He stayed out of sight, but he was comfortable enough. Kept the apartment, the Mercedes, the actress—"

"The actress?"

"Gabriela Rys." Ceska got a lecherous grin. "Older, now, but still"—he held both hands out, cupping them inward toward his chest—"a very *out*standing woman."

The pistol lay on the workbench, the overhead lights causing dark glints on its angles and planes. Sims put his hand on it. "How much?"

"Fifteen hundred in your dollars."

"Silencer? Ammunition? Holster?"

"Everything."

Ceska pushed the box of ammunition toward Sims, then stood back and looked Sims up and down, measuring him.

"The holster . . . you want for the belt, or for under the shoulder?"

Sims looked at the heavy pistol. "For under the shoulder."

Ceska nodded his agreement. Opening another cabinet,

he took a shoulder holster, shook out the dangling straps, then handed the rig to Sims. The holster had been used and well-cared for; the leather was firm, yet supple. Sims slipped the automatic into the holster, then pulled it out. It worked smoothly against the leather.

"Well broken in," Ceska said, watching him, "like a good woman."

Sims took off his coat and worked into the rig, right shoulder first, then left, then snapping the holster's stay-down loop over his belt. He counted off fifteen hundred dollars and handed them to Ceska. The Czech folded the bills once and they disappeared under his leather shop apron. Ceska went to the switchbox. The workbench lights went out and there was a grinding of pulleys as the target frame sailed back to the end of the basement.

Upstairs, Ceska stopped once more under the solitary light. "Coffee?" he offered. "Perhaps a *koňak?*"

Sims shook his head. "Been a long day." He walked with Ceska to the front door. There, he paused and put his hand on Ceska's shoulder. Ceska turned his head, keeping his hand on the doorknob.

"One thing more about Broz," Sims said. "What ever happened to his muscle . . . Schmar?"

Ceska's eyes went flat. He said nothing for a moment, then: "The head shots . . , he is the one you are looking for, isn't he?"

"He's looking for *me.* I have to find out why."

"The story is that you nearly cut his hand off."

"He took a knife through his hand a year ago, that's all. It wasn't enough to chase me down for," Sims said dismissively. "He was with Broz until Broz died. What were they up to?"

Ceska got a cornered look. He shook his head. "I don't know. All anyone would say about Broz was that his old friends were helping him."

"The Ks?" Sims asked, using the vernacular for KGB.

Ceska nodded.

"They went out of business," Sims said. "What kept him going after that?"

Ceska shrugged as he opened the door. "I don't know. He

must have had something, though; he never bought cheap wine."

Sims stood for a moment in the open door. Outside, the snow darkened the sky, turning white as it flew through the light of the street lamps. He turned back to Ceska. "The actress . . ."

"Gabriela Rys." Ceska supplied the name, accompanied by his lewd grin.

"Where can I find her?"

Ceska rolled his eyes upward, looking for the answer somewhere in the space above Sims's head. Then the eyes rolled back to Sims. "I don't know."

"Can you find her?"

Ceska looked past Sims, out into the square. "It is cold and late."

"Five hundred?"

"American?"

"American." Sims peeled off the bills and held them out. "Half now . . ."

The money disappeared under the leather apron. "How do I reach you?"

Sims uncapped his pen and scribbled a number on the inside of a matchbook cover. "You will hear a voice speaking in English. When the voice finishes, there will be a tone. Leave a message. Or a phone number."

Ceska studied the matchbook, read off the numbers to himself, then handed the matchbook back to Sims. "The animal game?"

It took Sims a moment to remember, then he nodded.

"How soon?" Ceska asked.

"Yesterday?" Sims said, thinking that was about right— that somehow he was running a day late.

Ceska stayed at the closed door for moments after Sims left, then pulled the bills out, counted them, and stuffed them back in his pants pocket, patting the bulge with a satisfied, proprietary air. He reached around behind his back, untied the heavy leather apron and exchanged it for a thick woolen overcoat hanging on an antler coat rack. It *was* cold and getting late, but the Prague Gabriela Rys moved in was a small town. And the American dollars would pay for a first-class expedition: dinner at Zatiši or the Golden Pear, coffee in the Lesser Quarter, then a wine bar or two over in the New Town, a few discreet inquiries, and perhaps a woman who would come back to the shop with him.

7

It was 7:15 when Sims left the subway at the Národní třída station and made his way to Wenceslas Square. The snow was coming down heavier, and the sidewalks were packed with couples heading for the taverns and dance clubs to start a Friday night in Prague. Just off the square, Sims pushed through the steamed-up glass doors of the main post office. Entering the queue for international calls, he waited for ten minutes until, at the counter, he wrote down the number he wanted, handed over two hundred *koruna* to a clerk, and took a numbered plastic chip.

Five minutes later, a scratchy voice called his number over a loudspeaker and directed him to a booth. At the booth, an old woman took his plastic chip and a few coins for a tip, and ran a dirty rag over the booth's seat.

In the booth, Sims connected the fountain pen scrambler. "Hello."

"Prague—you're on the move."

It was the woman with Lourdes's smoky voice. She sounded playful and Sims got a warming knot in his stomach.

"Yeah . . ." Sims felt the knot in his stomach growing hotter. He tried without success to push the image of Lourdes from his mind. "Yeah, I need an address."

The voice got more serious. "Name?"

"Felix Janik. Czech. BIS. Prague station ought to—"

"You got your pager?"

"Yes."

"Be back to you. Anything else?"

"Else?"

"Anything you need?" The voice was playful again.

Sims sighed to himself. "No," he told the voice, "nothing else."

"Back to you later, then."

Sims found a place at the bar of *U Rudolfa*, a small restaurant in Josefov, the Jewish Quarter of the Old Town. Watching the chef work in the open kitchen, he had a dinner of potato dumplings and grilled beef with horseradish, topped off by an almost-cold Krušovice beer.

At 9:10, the beeper vibrated in his pocket. Fifteen minutes later, he was at a pay phone. The woman with the voice gave him an address across the river, and fifteen minutes after that, he was walking across the Charles Bridge into the Lesser Quarter.

The snow had moved on, leaving the bridge and its statues of Baroque saints under a mantle of white. On his right, Saint Vitus Cathedral, a ghostly green from hidden floodlights, floated above Prague on the dark bulk of Hradčany. The snow lay undisturbed by footsteps, and the thought occurred to Sims that it could as easily have been six hundred years ago, when the bridge was new and the world a far simpler one.

Felix Janik followed Darina up the stairs. As they neared his apartment, he slid his hand up under her coat and skirt and cupped the firm roundness of her bottom. She laughed and made a playful gesture of swatting his hand away. On the landing, Janik, now beside her, pulled her close and caressed the nape of her neck. She turned to face him and they kissed, not for the first time that night, but this time with a deeper and growing urgency.

Janik fumbled with his keys and somehow got the apartment door unlocked. Pushing the door open, he stood aside to let Darina go first. As she brushed by, she reached behind her and found him with a teasing, stroking caress. Janik kicked the door shut behind him, and pulled her to him in the darkness of the apartment. He was struggling out of his overcoat when the lamp in the corner flared.

"Hi, Felix."

Part of Sims couldn't help enjoying it. If there was ever a time when everything just stopped, he thought, this had to be it. Janik and the woman stood there stunned, like wide-eyed statues.

Janik recovered first. "Sims," he said, still not quite believing it. "You . . ." Surprise gone, he was now getting angry. "What are you—"

Sims got up from the overstuffed chair and motioned toward the door. "Can we talk, Felix? Maybe you and I can take a walk and let your friend stay here"—Sims waved at the woman—"and, keep, ah . . . warm."

Janik looked from Sims to Darina and back to Sims. He paused, then, as if seeing no other choice, nodded ruefully, and shouldered back into his overcoat.

"I won't be long." Janik said it to Darina, but looked murderously at Sims.

The two men said nothing, even after they were out in the street. Janik led the way down a narrow cobblestone lane.

Several inches shorter than Sims, Janik had been a gymnast in his university days, and his compact body and his balanced assurance and the way he combed his thick brown hair straight back from his forehead always reminded Sims of a sleek otter. A midlevel professional in the StB, he had nonetheless survived the fall of the party and transitioned smoothly into Czechoslovakia's determinedly democratic intelligence service, the *Bezbecnostni Informancni Sluzba,* or BIS.

Although Janik had been a party member, he hadn't been a *real* party member. Not one of those generations of functionaries who had sucked up to Marx and Lenin and Brezhnev and Gorbachev and that dreary procession of bulky men who always seemed to be lining up for funerals and military reviews with the medals they gave each other pinned across the lapels of their badly cut suits. He'd joined the party because that's what you had to do to be an intelligence officer. And, he had once confessed to Sims, he had wanted to be an intelligence officer, because spies got the best apartments, salaries, and women.

The lane made a dogleg turn and suddenly they were in a small tree-lined square. Rising above the trees at the far corner of the square were the stone support arches of the Charles Bridge.

Janik turned left onto the broad sidewalk that worked its way around the square. As Sims fell into step beside him, the Czech turned to him. "Now, what the hell are you doing?" he asked in flawless American English.

"You haven't heard?"

Janik gave an impatient look. "You know Prague. You can hear anything."

"The CIA killings—"

Janik seemed genuinely shocked. "That was you?"

"Schmar tried to kill me in Italy at the same time those guys went down in the States."

"Schmar? Italy?"

"I was taking a year off. Reading, learning Italian, doing a little writing." Sims shook his head as if to clear it. "Anyway, the two guys—me—all three of us had worked together on Valek's defection. It's connected to Broz, somehow."

Janik's eyes narrowed in skepticism. "But Broz's been dead nearly a year now."

"He and Schmar were in on something. Whatever it was, it's still going on without Broz."

"Broz's dead," Janik repeated, "and Schmar's nowhere around. He's wanted by the federal prosecutors for murder. So why are you here?"

"The StB couldn't have destroyed all its files. And after the fall you kept watch on the old commies, at least the high-ranking ones like Broz. His finances, travel, communications—"

"And so you come to Felix Janik."

Sims heard the tightness in Janik's voice and said nothing, knowing the Czech was building up to something. The men walked together in silence for several paces, then Janik stopped and Sims turned to face him. Janik's face had stiffened.

"Leave this alone, Bradford."

"I didn't start it, and anyway, it's too damn late."

"You *did* start it," Janik countered. "You started it when you came here last year and pressured me into arranging for you to meet Broz."

"Shit, Felix!" Exasperated, Sims had to remind himself to keep his voice down. "Everything we do leads to something else. Your way, we'd sit on our asses all our lives."

Janik stared at his feet, looking unhappy. He ground one shoe into the snow then examined the result. As if finding his answer there, he looked back at Sims. "Okay. Broz's files. I will see . . ." he said, letting it trail off.

"Don't bust your ass, Felix."

Janik got a small incredulous smile as if he couldn't believe what he was hearing. "I can't believe you, Bradford." Janik had slipped into Czech. "You offer me nothing but trouble and then you wonder why *I* don't thank *you?*" He shook his head in wonder.

"You Americans amaze me," Janik continued, now stoked up. "You wander around the world, interfering with everyone. But you only make matters worse. You go to Somalia to rescue starving children and now you are shooting up half the country. And Bosnia! Bush did nothing, and he encouraged the killing; and now this Clinton— he talks a big war but does nothing and *he* encourages the killing. And *you*—you've just come here and already, I'm out here in the snow when I should be in bed, fucking."

Across the square, under the arches of the Charles Bridge, a man staggered out of a pub. The man was singing something off-key, but Sims couldn't make out the words.

For a moment, Janik seemed to be listening to the drunken singer, too, trying to understand him, and then, as if giving up, he came back to Sims, his resentment still working on him.

"You Americans cannot see what is in front of you, Bradford!" Janik swept his arm in one of those theatrical gestures that only Europeans seem able to carry off; a gesture that took in not only the square but everything beyond it, from the Atlantic to the Urals—Janik's civilized world.

"We are falling apart and you *refuse* to see it. You want to believe that nice words and dressing toy soldiers in blue berets of the United Nations can stop what is coming. But you can't stop the killing in your own streets. You can't protect yourselves, how can you protect us?"

Sims studied Janik's face. The Czech's smooth features had hardened and the humanity had drained out as Sims watched. For the first time that day, Sims felt the cold. It was a soaking cold that left him feeling weary and washed out.

The drunken singer, making uncertain progress across the square, suddenly stopped in the middle of a slurred note, leaving an abrupt silence in the air.

Sims pulled his coat tighter around him. "Thanks for the civics lesson, Felix," he said softly, then turned and walked across the square to the bridge.

The pager chirp brought Sims awake with a violent clutch of uncertainty. He bolted upright in bed, right hand holding the automatic he'd bought from Ceska. The dream had been buried so deeply within his sleep that he remembered only that he'd been running through rooms in an old house; that the house had been familiar yet terrifyingly strange. Looking around, he remembered he was in Prague and, from the light filtering through the drawn drapes, he knew it had to be late morning.

He fell back to the pillows, still holding the pistol. It'd been—what?—ten time zones in five days and maybe a total of twelve hours sleep? For long groggy moments, he thought about rolling over, going for some more sleep. Instead, he sat up again, this time swinging his feet onto the floor. His watch and pager were on the bedside table. The watch said eleven-thirty and the pager signal was blinking.

Forty-five minutes later at a pay phone near the hotel, Sims dialed the pager number. The only message on file was Ceska's. The automated date-time stamp put the call just before eleven-fifteen. Sims felt the satisfaction of a puzzle piece slipping into place as he telephoned Ceska and listened to him recite the address. Sims knew the place:

Gabriela Rys lived in a block of apartments in the *Malá Strana* that had been built in the late 1940s to alleviate the postwar housing shortage. Off a side street near the British Embassy, the apartments had been taken over by the Communists who had turned them into luxurious flats for the highest ranking members of the *nomenklatura*.

Overnight, the skies had cleared, and the Old Town Square sparkled under a coat of fresh snow and the clean light of the winter sun. At Bonal, Sims had a stand-up breakfast of coffee, bread, and thick slices of Czech salami. As he ate, he studied a detailed city map with a vague sense of unease.

Deep within his consciousness, something toyed with him, something he should know: a date, a name, a certain fact. He would almost close on it, then it would slip away again. Frustrated, he told himself it was something about Gabriela Rys's address. He looked at the map. But the map told him nothing and so he folded it, finished his coffee, and set out to find a cab.

It came to Sims as he got in the cab. A flash of color and movement caught his eye—a bobbing marionette worked by a street corner puppet master, an old man wrapped in a tattered army greatcoat. A wooden box at his feet held a few dirty bills and a handful of small coins. A full-maned lion danced, prowled, and pounced, its feet just inches above a cleared patch of pavement.

As if from a distance, Sims heard the driver ask for a destination. Sims, totally absorbed by the marionette, ignored him.

The lion reared back on his hind legs, front legs pawing the air.

And then Sims saw the mental replay: *Ceska, standing at the door of his shop, memorizes the telephone number written in the matchbook. Hands the matchbook back to Sims and asks—"The animal game?"*

"Aah, *shit!*" Sims swore loudly as the impact of it hit him. The animal game was the duress code he and Ceska had had between them when Sims was at Prague station. Whoever initiated the contact would always name an animal at the start and end of the message to show that they weren't under someone's gun. Ceska hadn't given an animal and he, Sims, hadn't remembered. "Shit, shit, shit!" Sims cursed again.

The cab driver was a kid with long blond hair and a bright lime green Nike warm-up jacket. On the seat beside him was a tape player jury-rigged with a tangle of wires running up underneath the dashboard. The kid looked warily at Sims.

"Náměstí Sovětských tankistů," Sims ordered, slamming the door. His heart had suddenly ballooned, filling his chest and throat with a cold, choking pulse.

"The pink tank?" the kid asked in his Voice of America English.

Sims motioned in the direction of the Vltava River. "Fast."

The kid still looked questioningly at Sims. "American?"

"American." Sims waved the bank notes.

"American," the kid repeated, and ground the Skoda into gear. "Go like hell," he said in English. As he let the clutch out, he reached over and turned up the tape player and the crash of Bruce Springsteen filled the car.

The kid drove as if Sims had given him a special dispensation to ignore the rest of the human race. Rocketing down the narrow streets of the Old Town, the kid scattered clusters of pedestrians and cut through a labyrinth of bicycles and delivery trucks. At the Smetana Museum, he swung south, skittering onto the wide boulevard along the river. The car picked up a lurching semblance of speed, the engine began a menacing hammering, and Springsteen played on.

Tense and hunched forward over the kid's shoulder, Sims scanned the roadway ahead, urging the kid on. With only one Czech in five owning a car, traffic was light, and the bridges over the Vltava flashed by on the right. Sims heard the engine, now louder, hammering in time with Springsteen.

The last bridge, the Palackého, was coming up fast and Sims thought for a second that they'd miss it. He was about to say something when the kid stood on the brakes and whipped the wheel hard right. The Skoda's front end dipped with a metal-to-metal grinding of brakes and the smell of asbestos and burning rubber, and made a skidding, screeching turn onto the bridge, throwing Sims to the side of the car.

Across the river and into the Smíchov district, the narrow streets closed in again. Rounding the corner on two blocks from the pink tank square, the kid saw it an instant before Sims.

"Shit," the kid cursed, braking violently. Crammed bumper to bumper, trucks and cars formed a solid wall, filling the street ahead and flowing over onto the narrow sidewalks. Pedestrians milled about, looking for some hidden passage through the maze.

The kid threw the Skoda in reverse. The instant he did so, a horn blared from the rear, loud as an oncoming diesel train. A sparkling dark blue BMW had pulled up just behind him and the driver was leaning out his window, face contorted with anger.

"Foking blutty Chermans," the kid muttered, throwing his hands up in disgust, then slapping them down on the steering wheel. Sims peeled off a U.S. twenty, and jumped out, leaving the kid in the rusted Skoda to practice his American-English on the German in the BMW.

Sims twisted his way through narrow openings between fenders. Over the tops of the cars, he got a glimpse of the pink tank square some thirty yards ahead. The sound of angry horns came at him from all sides. In front of him, a truck driver, standing on his running board, cut off his passage with an open door. Sims shoved the man back into the cab, slammed the door, and squeezed by.

At the intersection where the street opened onto the square, two cars had collided. One car had run into the corner of a building. The second car had smashed into its rear, its speed carrying it partially up over the rear of the first car, the two cars looking like metal beasts caught in the act of an obscene mechanical mating.

Emergency vehicles lights flashed across the square and Sims saw crews working to free the cars' occupants. Seemingly oblivious to the warning odor of spilled gasoline, a crowd of curious ringed the wrecks, held back by two uniformed police armed with truncheons.

Sims elbowed his way to the front of the crowd. Ignoring the police, he dashed across the open space toward the cars. Running all out, he vaulted over the wreckage. He landed easily on the cobblestones opposite and sprinted on across the square toward Ceska's. Behind him, the shouts of the police faded into the greater noise of horns and Klaxons.

In Ceska's doorway, Sims paused. The accordion security grate stretched across the door. He pressed the bell, then rattled the security grate. No noise from inside and the grate was locked. He rang again, then, stepping around so he blocked the doorway from casual observation, Sims took out his picks. The grate lock was easy; the dead bolt set in the heavy oak door was tougher. With increasing frustration, he pressed upward with the pick while drawing it out of the lock. On the eighth try, he felt the last pin snap upward.

Opening the door a fraction of an inch, he slipped the pick through the opening and, holding it gingerly between thumb and forefinger, ran it slowly from top to bottom of the door. No trip wires and Ceska hadn't chain-locked the door from the inside. He eased the door open and slipped inside, locking the door behind him, and sliding the Llama automatic from his shoulder holster.

The door shut off all sound and light. Sims stood frozen for what seemed like an eternity, holding his breath and listening, searching in vain for the slightest break in the blackness, willing his skin to pick up the smallest movement in the heavy air around him. Experimentally, he grazed his thumb across his fingertips; he could hear the papery rubbing sound.

Reaching in his pocket, he found the pager and held it out and away from himself. Tightening his finger ever so slightly on the trigger of the automatic, he quickly pressed and released the pager's display button. An instant of dim, grayish light touched the ghostly edges of worktables with their parts and pieces of sewing machines and the aisle leading to Ceska's office.

Sims pocketed the pager and, left hand extended, began a slow advance down the aisle that he saw now only in his memory. The darkness closed more tightly around him as he moved slowly into the depths of the shop, carefully planting each step before taking the next. And after each step, the listening, the scanning, the feeling of the air.

I should be there by now, he told himself, trying to remember how far away the door had seemed in the light of the pager. He stretched his hand farther, forward into nothingness. He fought the nervous impulse to use the pager again. He leaned into the next step and his fingertips brushed wood. Finding the thin crack between door and frame, he traced the crack downward to the knob.

The door opened soundlessly, and Sims felt the slightest caress of air on his face and the sweet-sharp scent of gun oil and nitro cleaner. Partially shutting the door behind him, he chanced the pager. In the instant of dim light, Sims saw that the office was empty. And then it registered that the entryway to the basement—Ceska's hidden panel—was open.

Sims slipped his automatic back into his shoulder holster and moved until his outstretched hand touched the corner of the rolltop desk. Now, he told himself, he was directly in front of the open panel. He pictured what lay before him: the spiral staircase with its metal steps, the long narrow basement below with its workbench and cabinets. And the light switches . . . the switches . . . where were they? Sims recalled Ceska at the junction box. Where had the Czech been standing? At the wall just off where the steps came down—somewhere. But two feet? Or six feet? Sims gave up on the junction box.

Leaning against the desk, he took off one shoe, then the other, knotted their laces together, and hung them around his neck. Then, taking the automatic out of its holster, Sims stepped through the entryway and began his descent into the basement.

He stopped after the first step. His stockinged feet made no sound and the darkness around him was unbroken. Even so, he felt exposed, vulnerable. Every nerve had tightened to a tensile brittleness. He continued down the staircase and as he descended, it seemed that he was immersing himself ever deeper in a danger that was nowhere yet all around him, and he remembered the waiting in the darkness for Schmar at San Gimignano.

Just as it seemed that the staircase would go on forever, Sims's foot touched the rough concrete floor. Standing motionless, he was certain now, more than ever before, that he was not alone in the darkness. He shifted the pistol to his left hand, and with his right, found the wall.

Sims began a crablike progress along it, keeping his back flattened against the wall, sweeping the pistol, covering the darkness to his front with slow, waist-high arcs.

His fingertips touched a round hardness. He remembered that the electrical conduits dropped down from the ceiling, then ran horizontally for several feet before ending in the junction box.

Tracing the conduit, Sims moved with growing confidence along the wall. His fingertips touched the hard edge of the junction box, and at the same time, he felt his right foot brush a small, hard object.

A skittering, metallic chiming sound across the rough concrete floor seemed to draw a neon arrow of sound toward him.

Sims's fingertips grazed the light switches, passing them by, then, desperate, he groped in the darkness for them again, an eternity in which Sims tensed himself, waiting for whoever it was in the darkness to swing toward the sound and fire. With a strength that almost sheared the levers from the junction box, Sims threw the switches.

Blindingly, the lights flashed on. A clanking-jerking sound. The grinding of the electric drive motor. Overhead, cables and pulleys rattled. By Sims's feet, a handful of bright empty brass cartridge cases. And from the end of the basement, the target frame sped toward Sims, carrying with it what was left of Jan Ceska.

8

Janik stared in morbid fascination at Ceska. The gunsmith had been crucified on the target frame. His wrists had been wired to the upper cross member; another length of wire held his head upright against the vertical stanchion.

There were no wounds to the chest, abdomen, or head. Ceska's arms and legs, however, looked like they'd been fed through a meat grinder. Back against the basement wall, back where the target frame had been while they'd been shooting Ceska, pools of blood collected on the rough concrete floor and made the air smell like tarnished copper.

Sims imagined them—two or three, judging from the number of shells—standing here, shooting at Ceska. Probably taking turns. Maybe even making bets. Who could do the most damage without killing him. Ceska's eyes were open, the blue now faded and flat. He had seen until the end what they were doing to him.

"The animal game?" Janik whispered, still looking at Ceska.

Sims and Janik spoke in embarrassed, almost apologetic tones, as if they were talking about Ceska behind his back and he might hear them.

It had to do with recentness, Sims thought. The recentness of Ceska being alive. Sims kicked one of the brass cartridge cases. It skittered across the floor making a cheerful tinkling sound.

Sims looked at Ceska and as always, the permutations of violent death had about them a certain mystic awesomeness. It's not like having cancer or AIDS—something you *know* will kill you. When the sun had come up this morning, Ceska'd been healthy and alive, and he'd no idea that he'd be dead in a couple of hours.

You run into violent death by the slimmest of margins, Sims thought, remembering how his father had walked out of the house to go on shift and had never come back. A little slower answering an alarm and the looter never gets a chance to blow you away. Wake up a few minutes earlier or later and you miss the asshole who runs the red light. An extra cup of coffee and somebody else dies in the elevator accident. If he hadn't come to see Ceska. If Ceska hadn't mentioned Gabriela Rys. If Ceska had asked one less person where Gabriela lived. If he, Sims, had thought about the animal game sooner.

"Duress code—name an animal at the start and end of the message."

"And he didn't?"

Sims shook his head. "And I didn't catch it."

Janik looked from Ceska to Sims, then back to Ceska again. "It wouldn't have done any good. They probably did this right after he called. After that, they had no use for him. They had to kill him."

"Yeah . . . maybe." Sims kicked another cartridge case.

"They used him to tell you where the Rys woman is."

Sims nodded. "Dangling the bait. And now we know where they're waiting, don't we, Felix?" He watched Janik for a moment, and just before the Czech could answer, Sims guessed, "And the files on Broz . . . you didn't find anything, did you?"

Janik, still looking at Ceska, shook his head, obviously not wanting to get drawn into it and just as obviously knowing he already was, "The files on Broz have been vacuumed. There's nothing left—zero. The man never existed. The head of the StB has just disappeared."

"That leaves the Rys woman."

Janik nodded glumly.

Sims saw Janik's predicament. Gabriela Rys was incon-

103

venient, a leftover from the bad old Communist days. Janik didn't want to hear what she might say. No one, even the President of the Czech Republic, wanted to hear. National amnesia would be a blessing. Better that all the memories of four decades of minor treacheries and major betrayals disappear quietly—like Broz. But Janik and his superiors had weighed the possible consequences of not knowing and found them even worse than knowing.

"You're going along with this, aren't you?" Sims asked.

Janik sighed. "If we don't, you'll do something without us." He looked at his watch. "I've got to make a call."

An hour after Janik had called, Ondrej Pajor drove a gray post office step-van by the high garden walls of the Waldstein Palace. Pajor, a tall, cadaverous man, a chain-smoker with a perpetual cough, looked like he'd spent a chronically dissatisfied lifetime in the frayed green coveralls with the yellow post office logo on the breast pocket.

In what passed for real life, however, Ondrej Pajor was BIS's Peeping Tom. Like Janik, Pajor had served in the old StB. Pajor's cameras and microphones had captured an endless parade of businessmen, soldiers, diplomats, and whores—drunk and sober, day and night, universally and foolishly performing all sorts of tricks in rooms they shouldn't have been in.

Just past the British Embassy, he swung right onto a narrow lane and began raining down a steady stream of Slovak curses on the stupid bastards who'd parked their cars like jackstraws, half-on and half-off the curb. He had to ease the van to a crawl to squeeze by. The curses continued as he bent forward over the steering wheel, craning to find the street numbers of the shops and buildings.

"There it is." From the passenger seat, Nemec pointed excitedly.

Pajor didn't like Nemec. Pajor didn't like kids, and that's what Nemec was. Nemec was young enough to be excited about the spying business and if you were young enough to be excited, you were young enough to fuck things up and get yourself killed. Pajor didn't get excited and that's why he was still alive. Pajor cursed the BIS bureaucrats; he would have been safer working alone, but the high lords of the rear echelon said he had to have security and so he'd drawn Nemec. Supposedly to watch his back. God, what an insult.

"There it is," Nemec repeated.

"I *see* it, goddamnit."

Nemec looked up and down the sidewalk.

"Two guys in the silver Audi."

Pajor saw them in the sideview mirror. Nemec was right, which pissed him off more. Two in the Audi watching the front and—Pajor recalled the building plan—probably another two in the back.

The building was a long, dun-colored box with a high-pitched slate roof. The architects had tried to blend it in with the ornate seventeenth century buildings around it by tacking clusters of grotesque *faux* marble columns and arches along the ground floor exterior. Pajor counted three entrances; the apartments inside opened onto vertical stairways rather than long horizontal hallways. The Rys woman was top floor, right stairwell. He grunted in grudging satisfaction; at least registry had given him the plans for the right building.

Pajor slowed almost to a stop, eyeing a narrow opening between a Mercedes and a Nissan. Krauts and Japs, he thought with envy, they *knew* how to lose wars— Czechoslovakia never learned how to lose wars worth a shit.

Looking down the street, he saw no other opportunities, so he pulled the van up onto the sidewalk, wedging it between the two cars. Setting the parking brake, he glanced in the mirror. In the dim interior of the Audi, he saw the whites of faces turn his way. Whoever the watchers were, they'd spotted him. Well, fuck them, he cursed silently. Fat lot of good it's going to do. He got up and, crouched, made his way into the back of the van between bins, cabinets, and coils of wire and insulated cable.

From a storage bay, he pulled a square cardboard cable dispenser box, tucking it under one arm along with a roll of rubber matting. The box was lighter than it looked; instead of copper wire, it contained fiber-optic cable, its individual glass strands finer than a human hair. With the other hand, he found his lineman's tool kit, a leather pouch on a wide web belt. Slinging the kit over his shoulder, he motioned with his elbow at a large metal box. "Bring that," he ordered Nemec, and he opened the van's back doors and stepped out into the street.

With Nemec trailing and complaining about the weight of the toolbox, Pajor entered the left entrance to the apartment building. In the sparse lobby, an old woman sat behind the concierge desk, smoking a cigarette and watching a small television. She looked up from her television program, saw their coveralls and the tools, and waved them past. The elevator, a wrought iron cage, creaked and lifted them to the fourth floor. There, Pajor led the way to a locked door at the rear of the elevator shaft.

As he worked on the lock, Pajor sensed Nemec making a motion behind him. He swiveled his head around. Nemec, the toolbox in one hand, had pulled a stubby Steyr submachine gun from under his coveralls and was waving it in the general direction of the elevator.

Pajor hissed at the younger man. "What're you *doing?*"

Goggle-eyed, Nemec worked his mouth several times, looking like a fish out of water. "Uh, guarding—"

"Guarding?" Pajor curled his lips. He rolled his eyes theatrically upward, begging heaven for deliverance, then snapped them back to Nemec. His voice was a hoarse whisper. "Put that thing away before you shoot your dick off."

The lock gave way, and Pajor switched on a miner's flashlight held on his head by an elastic band. Before them was a flight of dusty stairs to the common attic that ran the length of the building. Seconds later, they were over Gabriela Rys's apartment. Pajor unrolled the rubber mat to serve as a sound-dampener, then he carefully set down the metal box, the cable, and his leather tool kit.

A good news-bad news job, Pajor reflected as he unrolled a tape measure, noting the distance from a major support truss. The good news was that this would be a one-way chore: all he had to do was to set up the surveillance; he didn't have to hide it from later inspection. The bad news was that the subjects would be in the room: That meant you couldn't have an electric drill bit bringing plaster down on some bastard's head. He'd done that once and had gotten a bullet up his ass when the target had started shooting up through the ceiling.

He made another measurement, intersecting the first, and marked the point on the raw wood flooring with a penciled X. Fourteen inches below, give or take a half inch, was the plaster crown molding in Gabriela Rys's living room.

The plan was to drill down through the lath and plaster ceiling, into the molding, and from the molding, cut a hole that looked into the living room. That was the plan. The trick of the plan was that he had to do this without anyone in the room catching on, and the hole had to be clean and round and the size of a pinhead.

In complete silence, Pajor unlatched the metal box, its top opening like a clamshell. Pajor had had the box built by a master machinist in Stockholm. It was the fifth of such boxes, each taking into account lessons learned from its predecessor. Inside, it looked like a grown-up's erector set, with varied lengths of lightweight structural titanium rods and bars fastened by elastic holders to the padded sides of the box. In the center of the box was a dull black-matte finished cylinder perhaps six inches in diameter and beside it, cushioned in foam, a small box with sockets and a panel with knobs, dials, and tiny indicator lights.

Pajor studied the contents for a moment, then selected three bars, each about eighteen inches long. The ends of the bars held ball and socket locking joints. Swiftly, Pajor snapped the three bars together, interlocking them to make a triangle. Less than a minute later, with the triangle as a base, he added three more bars to form a sturdy pyramid.

The black cylinder—an ultraquiet heavy-duty drill drive—he locked into place inside the pyramid. Dropping a plumb bob from the drill's chuck, he watched as the point of the weight quivered a fraction of an inch over the penciled X on the floor. He nudged the apparatus, making a final adjustment. The bob point moved almost imperceptibly to the exact center of the *X*. Pajor squinted at the penciled mark for another second, then removed the plumb bob from the drill chuck and replaced it with the bit. The bit, tipped with industrial diamond, was exceptionally heavy, being custom made to Pajor's exacting specifications from a rod of depleted uranium.

In the reflected light of his miner's lamp, he caught a glimpse of Nemec, eyes wide, totally absorbed. Pajor felt a smug glow of self-satisfaction. Perhaps Nemec wasn't so bad after all—the kid *did* recognize a master at work.

Pajor eased the control box from its foam nest, connected its cables to the drive motor, and pressed the power-on button. Two rows of indicator lights along the top of the panel glowed red, then, one by one turned yellow, then green. He pressed another button and watched as the drill bit spun silently up to speed.

The drill's alignment was so precise and the titanium frame so steady that it was impossible to tell by sight that the drill was moving. Glancing again at the panel, he slowly turned a knurled steel knob. The drill bit lowered toward the wooden flooring. The hole seemed to appear by magic. At just over forty thousand revolutions per minute, the massive momentum of the uranium and the bite of the diamond caused the wood to vaporize soundlessly at the face of the drill bit.

A block away, another van, this one bearing the crest of the ministry of public works, stopped on a side street. Two workmen got out, set up orange traffic cones and began erecting a canvas shelter around a manhole cover.

Inside the van, Sims watched as a tech powered up an oscilloscope and a bank of monitors. One by one the monitors came to life, each showing a circular test pattern.

Janik, with headset and microphone, made a call on a two-way radio while studying a glass fronted map. Gabriela Rys's building was at the center of the map and around it, the neighborhood for several blocks in each direction. Janik listened, then, with a felt-tip marker, drew four fluorescent orange goose eggs on the glass. He pushed the mike away from his lips and looked up to Sims.

"Special section has teams here, here, here, and here." Janik tapped the goose eggs with the marker. "When we say go, they'll take out the people at the front and rear of the building. Then we go up."

Rehearsals . . . Sims thought . . . details . . . practice. In the exercises at the Farm you always had time. Time to find out where the bad guys would be sitting. What they'd be wearing. How they'd be armed. Time to get a helicopter to the roof so you didn't have to go up flights of stairs.

But there wasn't time. Janik's people had spotted two at the front of the building and two at the back. There were at least two with Gabriela Rys. That made six. But then what? Maybe a shooter or two in the stairwell? Maybe someone across the street, a man with a rifle on a rooftop? Wait and you could find out. But if you waited, they could figure you weren't coming and leave the Rys woman in the same shape they'd left Ceska.

Totally absorbed, Pajor studied the small screen on the control box panel. A bright green undulating sine wave traced a snakelike path across a darker green background, the peaks of the wave showing the progress of the drill. Fourteen inches beneath him, a microphone in the drill bit broadcasted a steady stream of extremely low-frequency pulses.

The pulses traveled through the plaster remaining in front of the drill face, then bounced back to a receiver. The computer in Pajor's control box calculated how much plaster was left. As the plaster disintegrated, the peaks of the sine wave flattened. Theoretically, at the precise moment that the last molecule of plaster disappeared, the sine wave would be a flat line on the monitor, and the computer would order the drill to retreat—theoretically.

As Pajor watched the screen, he remembered how it'd felt, the time that the bullets had come up through the flooring. Unconsciously, he cupped his left hand around his testicles as he knelt closer to the screen.

Sims stared at the monitors and their test patterns. "It'll be soon," he heard Janik say. Janik didn't sound all that confident. The monitors filled Sim's field of view and he willed them to life and nodded to let Janik know he'd heard.

The sine wave flattened and Pajor saw the bit backing out of the hole. As soon as it cleared the floor, he moved the drill away from the hole. From another padded compartment in the metal box, he removed a coil of thin flex cable. Carefully straightening the cable, he connected one free end to a terminal on the control panel.

The other end Pajor held at eye level and carefully slid back a plastic protective sleeve covering the last several inches of the cable. A tiny glasslike bead glistened in the light of his miner's lamp. He examined the tiny quartz lens for several moments, taking care not to let his breath pollute the polished surface.

Aiming the lens at his hand, he watched the control panel display. Ten thousand glass fibers bundled in the cable carried the image, and the hand showed up a ghostly white on the small screen. Satisfied, he slid the protective sleeve forward again, covering the lens.

Leaning forward, Pajor slowly fed the lens and its cable into the hole. The cable was marked off in one-inch increments, and when he counted thirteen, he pushed the cable even more gently until finally, he felt it meet resistance. If everything had worked right, the lens was at the pinhole in the plaster molding. He slid the protective sleeve back to expose the lens and pressed the button to activate the view screen.

Nothing.

The screen remained dead black. Pajor felt his throat thicken in disbelief. He turned brightness and gain full up. Nothing. The lifeless screen mocked him. He felt Nemec stir behind him and was suddenly filled with rage at Nemec, at the screen, at the drill, at himself. He closed his eyes and forced himself to breathe deeply and think about the plaster molding just over a foot away.

Slowly he withdrew the cable. He aimed the lens at his hand. As before, the hand came up on the screen. He looked accusingly at the drill and mentally cursed all the slick technology that seemed to work perfectly whenever you didn't need it, and didn't when you did.

He thought for a moment that seemed much longer. Pajor weighed what he'd have to do next against the memory of the bullets that had torn through him the last time he'd done it.

Sims glared impatiently at the monitors. "Where the hell *is* that guy?"

Janik looked at the digital clock, then at the monitors. "He'll be on soon." What little confidence he'd had before was now gone.

Pajor lay belly-flat on the attic floor, right hand extended and over the hole to Gabriela Rys's apartment. No more high-tech solutions. Between his thumb and first two fingers, he held a beryllium rod the thickness of a knitting needle.

Easing the rod into the hole, he felt the slightest resistance. Slowly, he twisted the rod, twirling it between his fingertips. A foot away, the sharpened face of the rod cut into the last particles of plaster molding.

Pajor closed his eyes in concentration, willing himself not to think about the bullets, but to feel the minute change in vibrations that would tell him the point of the rod had made its way completely through the plaster. His chest had become a cavernous vault, echoing and reverberating with each beat of his heart. He felt a tracing down the small of his back, then another and another and realized that in spite of the cold, sweat was running down his spine.

The third monitor lost its test pattern, its screen blackened, then lit again as, a block away, Pajor flicked on the UHF transmitter.

"Thank God!" Janik took a seat beside Sims at the console.

Gabriela Rys's living room, distorted by the fish-eye lens, came up on the screen. Fitting on a headset and microphone, Sims dialed the woman's number. Behind him, tape recorder reels began to roll. As he listened to the clickings in the telephone exchange, he watched the monitor.

The fish-eye lens looked down the length of long room, giving a view like looking through the wrong end of a telescope. A window took up much of one wall. Beneath the window, the glossy top of what looked like a credenza bounced a dark blossom of glare into the lens. Along the opposite wall, a small antique sofa with end tables faced two armchairs. At one end of the room, two more chairs gathered around a fireplace. In one corner, an old-fashioned stereo set, one of those bulky monsters the Czechs had turned out before Sony conquered the Warsaw Pact. The telephone sat on a lace doily on one of the end tables by the sofa.

The telephone rang. The sound of it echoed from the speakers in the van and, at the same time, in Sims's headset.

Before the second ring, a stocky man in a tweed sports coat entered the room and sat on the sofa at the end away from the telephone. Sims watched as the man reached down on the floor and picked up an earphone. As he did so, another man, very slender and in a dark suit, led Gabriela Rys into the room.

"Hello, Schmar," Sims whispered to himself.

With one hand, Rys clutched a robe tight at the front, the other she held against the right side of her face.

Schmar pushed her roughly onto the sofa by the telephone. The man in the plaid sports coat put the earphone to his ear and nodded. Schmar gestured to the telephone then picked up another earphone, keeping his other hand around the woman's upper arm. Rys hesitated for a moment, then picked up the phone.

She answered in an unsteady contralto, and the voice gave reality to the image on the screen and Sims, watching the monitor, felt a flush of anger at the two men with her.

"I am a friend of Josef Broz—" Sims began.

"Yes."

It was a sharp interruption and Sims saw Schmar twist her arm and shake his head in warning. Relax, Sims found himself telling her, you've got to convince them that you're convincing me.

112

"My name is Sims. Josef and I met a year ago. This's my first time in Prague since he . . . since he died. I need to talk with you."

A pause. Sims saw Schmar nod.

"Yes." the woman replied.

Sims knew what they wanted and so he made it easy on her. "I have your address. Would it be convenient—"

"Yes!" This reply was swifter, and this time her fear was nakedly apparent. Sims saw Janik roll his eyes in alarm at the monitor.

"I will be there in an hour," Sims told her. He saw Schmar shake his head, put his hand over the mouthpiece of the telephone and start to coach her. Schmar didn't want to wait. Sims added, "I can't possibly make it before then."

Schmar hesitated, then handed the phone back to Rys, and nodded.

"Yes, an hour," she said in her disintegrating voice, "that is good."

Before Schmar put down his earphone, Sims added, "I will call, Frau Rys, just before I come up."

"Yes," Gabriela Rys said, and hung up.

Sims watched as the two men took the woman back into the other room. He stared for a moment at the empty living room, then got up from the console. Janik, already in a kevlar vest, tossed Sims a similar vest, and swung open the gun cabinet. Sims shouldered his way into the vest while surveying the weapons lined up in their racks. Finally, he selected a stubby double-barrel riot gun and a handful of shot shells.

"Not much for precision work," Janik said, taking a folding stock Kalashnikov.

Sims broke open the breech, peered down the barrels, then snapped the gun shut with a whipping wrist motion. "I don't think we're gonna need a helluva lot of precision."

Glancing out the back window of the van, Janik nodded an all clear to Sims, then opened the door. Outside, the utility shelter flaps had been lashed to eyebolts on either side of the van, hiding the back of the van from the street traffic. A blustery cold wind snapped the canvas sides of the shelter.

Janik nodded and two workers who had been warming their hands by a portable gasoline heater stripped off their coveralls. Underneath they wore the dark brown and green camouflage battle dress of the Czech army *spetznaz*. From their web harnesses hung radios, knives, flashlights, and grenades.

One man, a senior sergeant, carried a folding stock Kalashnikov, the twin of Janik's, the other, a corporal, had slung a Danish Madsen submachine gun over his shoulder. He carried a door-ram, which looked like a three-foot segment of telephone pole with two handholds on each side. The man with the Kalashnikov knelt to one knee, and with an easy motion, lifted and pushed aside a heavy cast steel manhole cover, revealing a conduit-filled utility tunnel.

Janik nodded and the man disappeared down the opening. Janik followed, then Sims, and the man with the Madsen bringing up the rear. The dark tunnel smelled of a sour mix of ozone and damp concrete, and was only high enough to permit the men through at a crouch. Overhead, there was the occasional rumble of traffic. The lead *spetznaz's* flashlight beam bounced through the darkness, and Sims caught glimpses of the eyes of rats, glowing orange-yellow, then disappearing as they fled the light.

Sims's legs were cramping from running at a crouch when the *spetznaz* in front of him slowed, then straightened up as the tunnel expanded. Steel rungs set in the concrete wall made a ladder toward the gray sky above, guarded by a metal grate. The four men crowded the well beneath the grate. Janik glanced at his watch and turned to the sergeant.

"They are ready?"

The *spetznaz* sergeant muttered into his radio, then listened as the teams that would snatch Schmar's watchers reported in.

Sims broke the riot gun open, thumbed in two of the large shot shells, then locked it shut again. He was aware that the sergeant and corporal were watching him. It was measuring time and they had an unknown. Janik they knew. Or at least knew Janik well enough to take him into account. The black American? How would he hold up when everything turned to shit in the space of half a second? Run? Shit his pants?

Kill his comrades in a trigger-happy panic? Sims saw the questions in their eyes and knew the questions because they were questions he'd asked himself in other times like this.

The sergeant cocked his head, listening to the radioed responses. He nodded to Janik. "They're ready."

Janik looked inquiringly at Sims as if to ask, we *do* know what we're here for, don't we? Sims nodded back. The first problem was to roll up Schmar's watchers before they could get out a warning. The second was to get Rys loose without getting her or themselves killed.

Sims banished everything from his mind that didn't have to do with the assault on Gabriela Rys's building. The only things that counted were the men immediately around him and the mental image of Gabriela Rys's apartment and the stairwell leading to it. The world beyond no longer mattered . . . Prague and the Castle . . . Washington . . . Riddle or Rollo Moss . . . past or future . . . none of it existed. Everywhere was here. All time was now.

Janik turned to the sergeant with the radio. Janik pointed to the grate above them. "Go," he whispered to the sergeant. The sergeant nodded, and over his radio, gave the word to the snatch teams. Sims remembered checking his watch. It was 3:48 P.M. Sims, Janik, and the *spetznaz* corporal stood as if frozen, searching the sergeant's face for the slightest splinter of expression as he monitored the radio.

At 3:51, the sergeant's eyes narrowed and he gave a small victory smile. "They have the ones at the back," he told Sims and Janik.

Sims felt the tension around him imperceptibly lessen. The first play had gone well.

He caught Janik's eye. The Czech began a smile that everything would be okay, but the smile froze when a burst of submachine gun fire came from up on the street. There was another burst, then another and another, and the whining sound of bullets ricocheting off the paving stones.

"Ahh, shit!" Sims cursed. The sergeant was already on the radio, but all four men knew that the snatch team at the front of the building had somehow fucked up and that feet above them, bullets were screaming over the street. And in the apartment building, Sims thought, Schmar and the woman . . .

"Go, goddamnit, go!" Sims pointed to the grate, not realizing he was shouting in English. He started toward the ladder, the motion snapping the paralysis of surprise.

The sergeant got to the ladder first, Sims behind him. Scrambling up the rungs, Sims had the sergeant's boots in his face and he had to hold his head to one side to avoid being kicked. The automatic weapons fire came steady, loud, and angry—a sound like heavy canvas being ripped.

The sergeant stopped. Sims looked up. The man braced his shoulders against the grate and heaved upward. He heard the grate clang on the pavement outside. In a quick motion, the sergeant hoisted himself up and out and disappeared, and suddenly Sims realized there was nothing between himself and the gunfire but a square of gray sky.

At the top of the ladder, Sims tensed, then dove up and outward, pushing off from the top rung and throwing himself onto the cobblestones. He rolled once, keeping a tight grip on the riot gun, scrambled to his feet and into a clumsy sprint. The conduit had opened in the middle of the street, and he had to cover thirty or so yards to the apartment house. The noise of gunfire was ferocious and seemed to be concentrated down the street to his left.

The *spetznaz* sergeant had already made it to the shelter of Gabriela Rys's apartment entrance. The sergeant motioned to Sims to come on and at the same time began firing short bursts from his Kalashnikov. Running broken field, Sims dodged between the bumpers of two cars pulled up on the sidewalk and covered the last several yards in a dive, tumbling into the doorway behind the sergeant.

The shooting continued.

A nearby car suddenly flared and began burning.

Out in the street, Janik scrambled across the snow-slicked cobblestones followed by the *spetznaz* corporal lugging the heavy door-ram.

In midstride, the corporal stumbled.

For a moment, Sims thought the man would regain his footing, then the corporal staggered, dropped the door ram, and fell sprawling into the street. Janik, running full speed, had not seen what happened behind him.

The corporal tried to crawl, and Sims saw that one of the man's legs was trailing at a crazy angle. From down the street, the firing intensified and Sims saw bullets chipping the pavement. Whoever was firing was methodically walking the strike of their bullets toward the downed corporal.

Sims heard a shouting and realized it was his own as he willed the corporal to outrace the bullets. His fists clenched as he realized the corporal wasn't going to make it.

Bolting from the doorway, Sims ran at an angle to keep as many parked cars as possible between himself and the gunner down the street.

Janik, still unaware of what had happened in the street behind him, ran toward Sims and the doorway. The Czech got a look of incomprehension and started to stop.

"Keep going!" Sims shouted, passing Janik and slapping his back. By now, Sims was between two parked cars. Ten yards of open pavement separated him from the corporal.

Bullets overhead made a distinctive crackling sound like a snapping whip. Down the street, a booming explosion that a part of Sims reflexively identified as a stun grenade.

Sims paused for a second, crouched in the shelter of the car, held there by a last thread of caution. Pulling himself forward on one elbow, the wounded man inched across the pavement. His face a mix of pain, fear, and supplication, the corporal's searching eyes found Sims.

Sims's caution vanished when the corporal looked straight into Sims's eyes and held out his free hand for help. Another burst of gunfire sprayed the pavement, just inches from the man, a chip of flying stone tearing his cheek open. Sims dashed into the street.

The ten yards to the corporal stretched into forever and Sims felt as if he were trapped in one of those nightmares where he was slogging through quicksand, his legs fighting him with every step. Ignoring the corporal's face, Sims concentrated on reaching the man's hand.

In the open, Sims felt naked and exposed. A steel band was squeezing the breath from his chest and the wounded corporal seemed miles away. The split seconds lasted an eternity, but he finally reached the man.

Sims slipped his hand by the man's outstretched hand to lock onto the wrist. Then, reaching under, he found the other wrist, and, ducking and twisting, got the man up onto his back in a low fireman's carry.

Sims's rush had surprised the gunner down the street. The next burst of fire was high and behind. At a lumbering run, Sims aimed for the partial shelter between two parked cars. The next burst, closer, shattered the windshield of the car to Sims's left. At the same time, the car on his right lurched as its tires exploded with hollow pneumatic gusts.

Getting a firmer grip on his burden, Sims dashed across the narrow space between the cars and the apartment building entry. More bullets, this time rippling across the facade of the apartment building, blasting a ragged line of chips about eight feet off the ground.

Lungs burning from the exertion and cold air, Sims stumbled into the doorway and lowered the corporal, propping the man so he sat with his back against a wall. The sergeant ripped open the corporal's blood-soaked trouser leg, and from a pouch on his web harness, came up with a large battle dressing that he expertly tied around the wound. The corporal, cursing through gritted teeth at the pain, looked up at Sims with silent thanks.

"Let's go!" Sims motioned up and into the building. The sergeant looked to Janik and got a confirming nod.

Inside, a small concierge desk—empty. On the corner of the desk, an ashtray in which a cigarette, still burning, sent a tendril of blue-gray smoke into the air. Off to the left, a staircase that wound upward around an open European-style elevator shaft enclosed only by a flimsy ornamental wrought iron grating.

The sergeant took the stairs two at a time, Janik and Sims, shoulder to shoulder, just behind him. They were soon one floor below Gabriela Rys's apartment. From outside came the muted sounds of gunfire, and it seemed to Sims that the bursts were shorter and more sporadic.

It all came at once: the stocky man in the sports coat on the landing above them, a submachine gun in his hands, gunfire, a splattering rippling noise. The sergeant, collapsing as massive exit wounds tore through his back; Janik, staggering crazily and going down, crumpling on the stairs. More gunfire.

All in one motion, Sims swung the riot gun toward the man in the sport coat and squeezed the trigger. The stubby weapon roared as the grape-size shot left the riot gun's left barrel in a tight pattern no more than an inch and a half in diameter. By the time it hit the man at the top of the stairs, the shot-swarm had spread to eight inches. Striking him just below his belt line, the lead pellets literally tore the man in half as their momentum slammed him backward into the wall.

"Stop, Sims!"

The shout came from around the bend in the stairs. Sims heard a woman's voice in a half-moan, half-cry, and Schmar appeared, pushing Gabriela Rys before him. With one hand, he twisted her arm up behind her. With the other, he held a pistol to her head.

Rys, still dressed in her robe, moved in strained steps as she tried to rise on tiptoe to ease the pain in her arm.

"The gun, Sims . . . drop the gun!"

Sims stooped as if to lower the weapon. Then, cocking his wrist, he swung the muzzle up and fired. The ceiling above Schmar exploded in a hail of plaster and lath. Sims sprang up the steps toward Schmar and Rys, who were now locked in a violent embrace as she tried to twist out of his grip.

Sims was at least ten feet away when Schmar, with a powerful backhand, threw Rys against the wall. Ignoring the woman, Schmar took a two-handed grip on the pistol and aimed at Sims coming up the stairs.

Schmar fired twice—two professionally quick shots in succession. Both tore into the wall inches from Sims's face. Sims saw that the miss hadn't shaken Schmar. Calm, almost casual, the man had a reptilian smile of anticipated pleasure as he swung the pistol a fraction in compensation.

Again, the nightmarish quicksand feeling dragged at Sims. He had to get to Schmar, but no matter how hard he tried, he'd never make it.

A stutter of gunfire.

At first Sims thought it was the shooting outside. Then, slowly at first, then ever faster, Schmar's smile fractured like a broken window, changing to surprise . . . more firing . . .

Schmar jerked upright like a toy soldier at attention . . . mouth and eyes wide open . . .

Another burst.

Schmar's arm flinging outward in an uncontrolled spasm . . . Schmar's pistol sailed into the void of the stairwell and on its way down, crashed against the elevator shaft cage.

More firing . . . Schmar stumbled crazily forward . . . a stop-motion fall headfirst down the stairs toward Sims.

Only when Schmar's body lay crumpled and still on the stairs did Sims realize that the shooting had come from the stairs above. That Schmar was dead. That he, Sims, was alive. And that Gabriela Rys lay in a crumpled heap on the landing.

Sims rushed to her side and knelt on the bloodstained floor. She stared wordlessly at him, a bloodstain darkened the front of her robe. Opening the robe, he saw the wound, a jagged hole under her right breast, and clamped his hand over it to stop the bleeding.

Up the stairs, on the next landing above, a young man in coveralls stood holding a Steyr submachine gun, looking in stunned disbelief at what he had done.

An older man, also in coveralls, brushed by and rushed to Sims's side. When he saw the woman's wound, the older man shouted angrily at the younger man, the one with the Steyr submachine gun.

"Nemec, you stupid bastard!"

Outside, Klaxons replaced the sounds of shooting.

"Doctor!" Sims ordered to the younger man with the Steyr, jerking his free hand toward the street. Then he touched his fingertips to Gabriela Rys's throat. The pulse was weak and reedy. He saw that her eyes were following him. He tried to look reassuring. Tell her help was coming. That she would be all right.

The eyes, steady on him, showed no emotion and seemed to be watching him from a distance. "Cold," she said simply.

A jacket appeared in front of Sims. He looked up. It was

the older man, the sound tech, Sims guessed. He kept his hand clamped over Rys's wound while the man wrapped his jacket around her. Out of focus, Sims saw Janik dragging himself into a sitting position on the stairs, his back against the balustrade, his left hand clutching his right shoulder.

Sims bent closer to her. "Broz—"

Rys smiled. "Josef? He's here?"

"No," Sims said slowly. "Josef's not here." He forced himself to speak even more slowly. "Where did Josef get his money?"

"Money?"

"For you. For his cars . . . where did he get the money?"

Rys smiled again, shock and loss of blood brightening faded memories of other times. "Josef . . ."

"Please!" Sims whispered with urgency, "Give me something to get into this. A place. A name . . ."

Rys murmured something so quietly that Sims barely heard it.

"Karstens?"

"Karstens—"

"Who is Karstens?"

"German," she whispered, and then died.

9

The deputy commercial attaché of the Syrian Arab Republic's Prague Embassy was, in fact, the head of the Syrian Intelligence and Security Service section. Within half an hour after the battle in Gabriela Rys's apartment building, the attaché transmitted a complete report of the action to Damascus.

Two hours later, in Latakia, Lebanon, Sergei Okolovich stood at the penthouse windows of the pyramidlike Meridien Hotel and stared morosely out to the Mediterranean. The bobbing lights of ships waiting for berth in the harbor mocked the former KGB chairman. They were free to come and go while he had to watch every shadow, weigh every footstep behind him on a lonely street. Syria was damned better than freezing your ass off in an Arctic prison camp. And the French had done a pretty good job in building Latakia when the city had been the seat of France's Syrian mandate. At least there were some decent restaurants left. But, Okolovich thought dully, every day seemed to bring him closer to getting dumped in the shit.

Behind Okolovich, Kamäl Zohdi sat in a deep leather armchair, sipping cardamon-laced coffee from a small handleless porcelain cup. Zohdi had arrived ten minutes ago from Damascus, landing on the roof helipad in an unmarked helicopter. He had brought with him the news of Schmar's death.

Zohdi's glistening ebony eyes studied Okolovich over the rim of the coffee cup. The Russian seemed to be collapsing from within. When Zohdi had first met Okolovich ten years before, the man had been a giant, a power in the political jungle of the Kremlin. But now, without the grand offices on Dzerzhinsky Square, without the armies of spies at his command, without the power of an unlimited budget, Okolovich was a shrinking man. Get through the next days, Zohdi told himself, and Okolovich could disappear, and good riddance. But for now, Okolovich still had his uses.

As if reading Zohdi's mind, Okolovich turned away from the window and faced the Arab.

"I'm disappointed in Schmar." Zohdi aimed the barb at Okolovich. "I thought he was more . . . more *professional.*"

Okolovich's depression caused him to lash out. "I didn't notice your holy warriors covering themselves with glory."

"Enough!" Zohdi said, with a cautionary lift of his hand.

Okolovich's cheeks flushed. There'd been a time when a man could die for talking like that to him, Okolovich thought. Now this crazed Arab mystic could treat him like a hired servant. Now this Arab was looking at him as a butcher might study a steer, not just seeing the steer, but also seeing how it would be cut up. Okolovich found Zohdi's stare unnerving, the slightly bulging black eyes raking him over like dark death rays.

"What is it?" he asked Zohdi.

Zohdi's thin red lips pulled upward in a small superior smile. "I was just thinking, Sergei Federovich Okolovich."

Zohdi's superior manner touched off another spasm of anger in Okolovich.

"Yes," Zohdi continued, "you are a useful reminder."

"Reminder? Of what?"

"Of the Soviet Union's rise and fall, Sergei Federovich. Tell me"—Zohdi's excitement climbed as he anticipated another twist of the knife in the helpless Russian—"do you know *why* you are no longer master of the KGB? Why you're not a member of the privileged *nomenklatura* with legions of servants, dachas in the Crimea, fast cars and airplanes to whisk you anywhere at a moment's notice?"

Okolovich ran the tip of his tongue between his lips and it

seemed to Zohdi that the Russian's eyes got a wounded look.

"Do you know why"—Zohdi demanded, boring in for the kill—"why you are reduced to grubbing about so that you can live on the run in second-class hotels in third-rate countries?"

Okolovich winced under the attack. "We . . . economically . . ."

"Economics!" Zohdi sneered. "Don't talk to me of economics! I have a doctorate from those fools in London." He slashed the air with his hand. "No, Sergei Federovich, economics had nothing to do with the Soviet Union's death. What killed you was that you lost your faith."

"Faith?" Okolovich asked. Though he knew it was dangerous, he let a contemptuous note creep into his voice.

"Faith!" Zohdi said, his fervor growing. "You see, at the bottom of it, communism, although it was godless, required faith. Lenin had it. So did Stalin. Even, I think, Khrushchev. They *believed!* They believed with the zealot's passion that communism would overcome the Americans and the materialist world that Washington wanted to build."

"And we lost the faith," said Okolovich, a slight mocking tone in his voice. "When did we do that?"

"You lost it when you tried to compete with the Americans instead of destroying them. They lured you onto their playing field. After Khrushchev, every Soviet leader gave way, selling off your faith bit by bit. Brezhnev, Andropov, Gorbachev—they tried to keep communism and at the same time, tried buying off the masses with *things*—apartments, color television, fancy foods. But you lost it all because you could never become what America is."

"And that is?"

"The Great Satan."

Okolovich couldn't suppress a scoffing laugh. "You sound like those crazed mullahs in Tehran." He cringed at his impulsiveness, his fast tongue. The one thing you didn't call a crazy man was crazy.

But Zohdi got even calmer. "I know what it *sounds* like, Sergei Federovich. But Satan is an apt metaphor. You see,

America is the great tempter. We Arabs cannot keep what is our core, our inner being"—Zohdi jammed his stiffened fingers into his own chest—"and become like the Americans. Either we accept everything America offers or we reject it totally. There is no middle way!—no compromise! Islam is great because it has the unique ability to satisfy the human soul. America denies the soul. The struggle has already begun."

Zohdi craned his head toward Okolovich. "Listen," he commanded softly, with great intensity, "do you think that what is happening now in Bosnia is merely tribal warfare?

"No!" Zohdi answered his own question. "Bosnia is the opening battle of the West against Islam. It begins with the Serbs and their ethnic cleansing. The Americans play a sham game, protesting to that fool's circus—the United Nations—but secretly, America's allies see this as an opportunity to rid the continent of Europe of an Islamic outpost that has frightened them for centuries. And the Americans are going to let that happen." Zohdi paused for a deep breath, then shook his head. "No, Sergei Federovich, America *is* the Great Satan. It is the source of all evil and thus the enemy of Islam."

Zohdi paused for a moment, letting the silence emphasize his concluding point. "And America being the enemy of Islam, America must be destroyed." He bit off the letters: "Q . . . E . . . D."

Zohdi pinned Okolovich with a warning look. "I have worked too hard," Zohdi said, his eyes flashing with an inner fire. "We can't let this man Sims keep after us. I am too close."

At 2:15 the following afternoon, Eastern Standard Time, a sleek Gulfstream IV jet with white and blue U.S. Air Force markings entered the Air Defense Identification Zone thirty-seven miles over the Atlantic off the coast of Virginia. In the approaching distance, Sims saw the dark horizon smudges of land, and less than five minutes later, through breaks in the thick cloud cover, he glimpsed the barrier islands north of Hatteras and then the sprawling shipyards at Norfolk.

125

Nine hours before, he'd been in a Mercedes at a well-guarded military ramp at Prague-Ruzyně airport, watching the Gulfstream taxi in. The Gulfstream's copilot, a shoulder holster over his grayish blue flight suit, had met Sims at the bottom of the plane's boarding ladder. The pilot had pulled a photograph from a sleeve pocket, checked it against Sims's face, then motioned him aboard. The crossing had been made in silence: Sims had seen the crew only when they passed through the cabin for head-calls and once when he'd been given a box lunch of rolls, coffee, hard-boiled eggs, and cold sausage.

A massive cold front had the coast in its grip. As the plane dropped through the clouds, Sims saw that the air was thick with snow. The Gulfstream landed smoothly, and Sims, peering out the window, recognized the small control tower—they were at the Farm. The jet rolled to a stop less than twenty yards away from a black government-issue sedan. The back door of the sedan was open and beside it, like a great Buddha, stood Riddle, watching, alone in the blowing snow.

"We are staying in ISO," Riddle announced, settling comfortably in his corner of the backseat and working himself deeply into his Burberry coat. "Mr. Alberich will meet us there."

"Why this?"

"This?"

"The Judge's plane," Sims replied, "the Farm, you, Alberich—*this.*"

"Because, young man, I don't think killing Schmar ended it. We must explore some leads, do some thinking. I thought a few days away from the distractions of Washington"—he waved at the wooded scenery—"would help us wrestle this to the ground."

"Alberich?"

"He has been here since yesterday, fiddling with his computers."

Riddle reached into an inner pocket and came up with a yellow message flimsy. "Prague station update on your Mr.

Janik's condition." He handed the paper to Sims. "Abominable language," Riddle sniffed. "In the old days, we would have never transmitted such vile language."

Sims unfolded the message. Harrington, Chief of Station, Prague, had visited Janik in the Czech military hospital near Karlín. Harrington reported that Janik was serious but stable, and that Janik very specifically wanted Sims to know, as Harrington put in quotes, "You owe me, Sims. I could be fucking Darina instead of in this *pissoir* of a hospital with these damned tubes running in and out of me."

"He's all right," Sims said, folding the message. Then, looking at Riddle: "What's next?"

Riddle pursed his lips for a moment. His cheeks were rosy red from the cold, and his hazel eyes seemed to dance in secret excitement. "Here, we shall confer with Mr. Alberich and his marvelous machines. In Washington, the Judge is doing battle with the fellows at the fudge works."

The Farm is tens of thousands of acres of weapons ranges, barracks, airfields, and training sites along the York River, next to Williamsburg, Virginia. Federal registers list it as Camp Peary. And Camp Peary supposedly belongs to the Pentagon where official records describe it as an experimental training facility. But the Farm has belonged to the Agency for almost fifty years, and its architecture accidentally reflects the academic and military antecedents of the Agency: its later buildings, done in a redbrick New England-style stand next to original World War II barracks and mess halls.

Security at the Farm is like a set of nested Chinese puzzle boxes; figure out how to open one and you're faced with another, very different challenge in the next box. First there is the perimeter, constantly scoured by motorized and helicopter patrols, over a hundred miles of chain link and razor wire fencing, each foot monitored by remote devices that can see through the darkest night and can sense motion or body heat.

Within the perimeter, there are islands of even tighter

security, protected by yet more fencing, watchtowers, foot patrols, sentry dogs, and special identification tags for those authorized within. As might be expected, these islands comprise the Farm's airfields, long-range communications complexes, satellite down-link stations, and the massive storage bunkers for weapons and ammunition.

The most sensitive and carefully guarded area is a close-set cluster of rustic buildings on fifty double-fenced acres along the river. This is Isolation, or, in Agency-speak, ISO. ISO is a jumping-off place where individuals and teams make a final stop before special missions. ISO is a self-contained world with its own living quarters, medical support, chapel, classrooms, and gymnasium, and even a small-arms range.

In ISO, the most sensitive secrets are divulged, the most delicate operations planned. In ISO, espionage skills are given final sharpening, the latest spy gizmos unveiled. When the brief-backs are completed, ISO's guests leave in closed vans or trucks, usually bound for the Farm's airfield, sometimes in parachutes and full combat gear, sometimes in J. Press suits and carrying only expensive attaché cases. All this is done in confidence that nothing will leak in time to endanger the mission, since agents and support staff who go into ISO remain there until the mission is either launched or scrubbed.

ISO's operations center is a replica of the one at Langley, down to the state-of-the-art Cray computers, the billions of gigabytes of electronic records, and the all-important shielded networks that link those computers and records with other U.S. and foreign intelligence agencies. And like at Langley, Matthias Alberich's computers in ISO were housed in a labyrinthine bunker, complete with its own independent electrical power, and an air supply that met the most exacting standards for cleanliness, humidity, and temperature.

In an underground office of the computer complex, Sims, Riddle, and Alberich sat in easy chairs, facing a screen that took up much of one wall. On-screen, the Judge appeared in his office at Langley. On his desk, a small monitor showed

Sims, Riddle, and Alberich gathered around a conference table at the Farm.

He looks like hell, Sims thought, *shot at and missed, shit on and hit.* The Judge, drained of energy, hunched forward over his desk, leaning on his elbows for support. It alarmed Sims to see how beaten the Judge seemed, his face drawn and etched with deep sad furrows making him seem old and fragile.

"Hello, Bradford. I'm glad you made it back from Prague."

Sims wondered how he looked to the Judge. "I guess the White House's pissed off."

"Pissed off?" The Judge winced, then gave Sims a tired smile. "That's an understatement, Bradford. I haven't had such an ass chewing since I was an ensign. Ralston Dean started off with a tirade about what he called 'the shootout at the Prague corral' and ended accusing me of letting the Agency get out of control—"

"Shit, Judge," Sims protested, his temper flaring. "Like I invited Schmar to San Gimignano! Why's Dean pointing the finger at *us?*"

The Judge straightened up from his slouch over his desk and sat back in his chair. "It's Dean's makeup," he explained, talking slowly as he put together his thoughts. "As I said earlier, Dean's got an agenda. He's frightened that we're going to upset his apple cart. He wants a smooth-sailing first hundred days for the new administration—"

"And so he wants to keep a lid on us."

The Judge cocked his head. "I wouldn't put it that way, exactly."

"Exactly?" Sims asked. "What do you mean by that—*exactly?"*

The Judge got a cross look. "I often think, Bradford, you'd make a helluva trial lawyer." The Judge sank back into his thinking, then: "We will continue to pursue the intelligence aspects of this . . ." The Judge's pause seemed like it was meant to be interrupted, so Sims did.

"But?"

"Well," the Judge said, putting it delicately, "someone

else was already in Dean's office when I got there. Lars Nesbith."

"The FBI director?"

"Yes."

Sims felt the slippery, pissed-off feeling he got when he suspected he was being had. "FBI? They haven't done shit investigating Gribbins's and Felton's murders. Why's Lars Nesbith in on this?" he asked, even though he thought he pretty well knew why.

"Dean's position," the Judge said evenly, "is that the FBI should investigate the breaking of U.S. laws." The Judge paused. "Results," he continued in a neutral voice, "will be reviewed and coordinated by a committee comprised of Ralston Dean, Lars Nesbith, and me."

Sims felt the surprise working deeper into his consciousness. Its implications unfolded, softly at first, then with gathering intensity. Riddle must have sensed it, because he nudged Sims with his knee and gave him a warning look out of the corner of his eye.

"Do you have any questions of me?" the Judge asked.

For a moment, no one spoke, then Sims shook his head. The Judge looked out of the screen for a second longer as if he wanted to say something but thought better of it. Sims saw the Judge's hand reach for a control panel set in the desktop, then the Judge's image flashed, then faded to a bright point of light on the screen and then, that too, went away.

In the silence that followed, Alberich worked the controls that shut the video system down and Riddle watched as Sims traced invisible lines with his index finger across the polished tabletop.

"The Bureau . . ." Sims muttered. The two words, along with Sims's undertone of anger and disbelief conveyed a sense of the rivalry between CIA and FBI. Begun in World War II when J. Edgar Hoover tried to cripple Wild Bill Donovan's Office of Strategic Services, the OSS had given way to CIA, but Hoover's enmity had remained. Sims had bloody firsthand experience with that hostility when he'd exposed the King assassination conspiracy the year before.

Alberich finished shutting down the video system and

turned to Sims and Riddle. "Hell, Dean's got Nesbith under his thumb," Alberich said. "Nesbith's scared shitless. He wants to stay on and he's afraid Clinton might appoint somebody new. Dean will say shit and Nesbith'll ask how high."

Alberich had it right, Sims thought. George Bush had appointed Nesbith to the FBI top job and Bill Clinton, as an incoming president had every right to replace him. TV news clips had left Sims with the impression that the silver-haired Nesbith was an utterly *nice* man: earnest, innocent face, clear Scandinavian complexion, expressionless pale blue eyes, and the perpetual professionally understanding smile of a bartender or a parish priest.

"The Judge's playing defense," Sims said, still thinking about the added wild card of the Bureau coming in, "and he's going to have to until we get our shit together."

The session with the Judge had ended just after six. Alberich stayed behind in the computer complex to establish communications with the Germans and begin the preliminary search for Karstens. Sims and Riddle left the operations center and made their way to the parking lot where the motor pool had left a white Jeep station wagon. The wind had dropped, and the snow was now falling straight down in a thick lace curtain.

Sims drove the Jeep down the winding road to a junction at the foot of the hill. Ahead, through the trees, he saw the York River, a black vein cutting through the whiteness of the snow.

"We go left here. Just over a mile." Riddle pointed down the narrow road, lined on both sides with thick stands of pines, their dark green branches already heavy with snow. "We're staying at the Judge's lodge."

Sims, eyes on the road ahead, grunted a nonreply. The windshield wipers beat at the snow with a somber metronome precision.

Riddle's hazel eyes measured Sims's face for a long time, then, quietly breaking the silence, he asked, "You're still bothered, aren't you?"

"Yeah." Sims hunched his shoulders. "I got the feeling a

lot of people'd be happier if I'd gotten my ass blown away in Italy."

Riddle gazed through the windshield into a distance beyond the road and the snow. "You shouldn't be surprised, Mr. Sims. New presidents and the people around them don't want to buy into a picture of the world that would keep them from getting on with what they believe they were voted in to do."

"We killed the dragon, but somehow it's gotten harder rather than easier. At least before, we knew who our enemies were."

"Yes,"—Riddle paused as if to fix his sights on a thought that was evading him—"over the years, we and the Soviets achieved a kind of peace because we each held a gun at the other's head. It was dangerous, but it was easy thinking. Now that we've won, it doesn't seem fair that the thinking would get harder."

Riddle motioned to the road ahead. "That next branch to our right."

Sims made the turn. The snow was thicker on the branch road and he downshifted and threw the Jeep into four-wheel drive. "But what happens, Riddle, if you run up against a bunch of bastards who don't want to play it like the Soviets? Who don't give a shit about your missiles and bombers?"

"First, we must recognize, Mr. Sims, that we *have* run up against this bunch of bastards."

"You think anybody wants to hear that?"

"After every victory, there is a natural urge to put down the sword. That urge is particularly strong now."

"No more enemies."

"Not that anyone can see—"

"Or *wants* to see."

"You shouldn't be surprised, Mr. Sims. After killing the dragon, the knight is supposed to return home to live happily ever after."

"And I'm a reminder that happily-ever-after isn't here yet."

"Exactly." Riddle motioned off to the left front of the road. "And here we are."

"Here" was a row of rustic cabins on a low bluff overlooking the river. A paved path linked the cabins with a single-story lodge built of large cypress logs.

Riddle motioned to the lodge. "I believe the bar is open."

Alberich returned from the computer center just before dinner. The menu was a Farm specialty: a spicy seafood gumbo, grilled filet of grouper, baked potato, and key lime pie. Conversation around the table was general, as if there had been an unspoken agreement to talk about everything but the one thing that had brought them to the Farm. For much of the meal, Riddle and Alberich probed Sims for details of his year in Italy. Riddle spun a fascinating account of meeting Hemingway during the liberation of Rome in World War II, and Alberich told a raunchy story about the computer tech who had recently quit the Agency to explore the commercial potential of virtual reality sex.

It suddenly struck Sims as remarkable that in the telling of his story, Alberich gestured so normally with the mechanical arm that it no longer seemed like a prosthesis.

"That is one hell of an arm," Sims said admiringly.

Alberich smoothly brought a forkful of pie from his plate, ate it, then, as an encore, twirled the fork like a baton between his metal fingertips. He grinned. "And watch this, bro'." Alberich reached across the table and snagged a crown bottle cap from a bottle of mineral water. He closed his hand then opened it. The bottle cap had been bent in half.

"Awesome," Sims applauded, laughing. Riddle got a prim look as if disapproving of the table manners.

Alberich spun the bottle cap on the table. "That's the easiest trick tonight," he said, at last getting to the subject. He looked from Sims to Riddle, as if still not anxious to get into it. He fiddled with his chair, jockeying minutely forward, then back. "There are," he said finally, "eighty million Germans. And those are just the ones in Germany. It doesn't count ethnic Germans in Switzerland and Austria. Hell, there're several million Volga Germans who've lived in Russia for centuries."

"How many Karstens?" asked Sims.

Alberich picked up the bent bottle cap and spun it again.

"Thirty-two thousand, four-hundred and seventy-nine—more or less."

"More or less," Sims echoed, reaching out and picking the bottle cap off the table in midspin.

"Well, shit." Obviously tired and frustrated, Alberich tossed a pencil onto the desk and stared accusingly at his computer screen. Sims sat back in his chair and gnawed absentmindedly at a cuticle. His computer screen, too, said nothing. He was deadly tired. His back and shoulders were knotted and tense and his eyes felt as if someone had poured granulated glass into them. The air in the underground room was flat and had the acid smell of ozone.

He and Alberich had attacked the thirty-two thousand Karstens after dinner. They had intended to put in a few hours and had ended up working all night. Sims looked up at the digital clock. Somewhere outside the windowless room, morning had come to the Farm. He dully wondered if it had stopped snowing.

Alberich had derived the basic list from German tax rolls under the assumption that any Karstens sending money to Josef Broz was a Karstens who was paying taxes. The night had gone in an endless series of log-ins, passwords, verifications, files searches. They had set up an electronic pipeline across the Atlantic to Europe, to an alphabet soup of espionage agencies. The Brits, the French, the Russians. And of course, the Germans.

They'd focused on German intelligence, where they'd crawled through the massive files of the *Bundesnachrichtendienst* (BND) as well as its counterintelligence organization, the BfV. Nothing. They had gone to the German Foreign Ministry for a review of visa and passport issuances. Thousands of Karstens had traveled throughout the world. Holidays in Majorca, Norway, and Pago-Pago. Business trips to Sheffield, Vladivostok, and Sydney. Any of the Karstens could have met Broz or Schmar or an unidentified partner in any of those places or in their own living rooms anywhere from the Swiss border to the North Sea.

"So much for the files," Sims said.

"So much for the files we can get to," Alberich amended.

"There's probably ten zillion goddamn pieces of paper stuffed in folders and cabinets all over the world that'll never get put into computers. And we don't know that our friends are letting us read all their mail."

"I was hoping we'd get lucky." Sims logged off his computer, then stood and stretched.

"Where now?"

"Where?" Sims asked as if the thought had just occurred to him. "I'm going over to supply and get some running gear."

"Run? In this snow?"

"I need to clear out some fog."

Alberich shook his head. "You're a goddamn masochist. Even if I had two legs, I'd still be going to bed."

The storm had blown out to sea during the night, but another front followed it in from the north, and the morning sun turned the underbelly of the clouds a silvery salmon. Forty minutes later, Sims started out at a slow trot, making his way north along the York River, each footfall crunching crisply in the dry snow. To his left, the dense forest of black-green pines interspersed with water oaks and sycamores. To the right, towering knob-kneed cypresses dotted the river's tidal flats.

The first mile was the toughest, as Sims had expected it'd be. Calf and thigh muscles protested and his lungs hurt from the cold air. But gradually he adjusted to the effort and settled into a long-strided pace. After another mile he was running easily, and the steady exertion swept his mind free of the morass of fragmented ideas and thoughts that had built up during the night into layer after suffocating layer. Just as he got the feeling he could run forever, the running started getting more difficult. He slowed as the path began to wind its way up a steep hill.

He began a driving effort to keep his pace up the hill. As the trail's pitch increased, its course began twisting and turning. Soon Sims felt a flush of sudden warmth beneath his nylon jacket and sweat suit. Pushing harder, the perspiration soon streamed down his face, back, and legs. The crest was no more than forty yards away, and he heard only the rasping sound as his breathing became almost a cry of agony as he strained to pull precious oxygen into the bottom of his lungs.

Twenty yards from the top, he forced his protesting legs and lungs even harder. Nothing in the world existed but the top of the hill, and it became everything that was opposition and everything that was achievement, and when he crested the hill, he felt the protesting pain vanish.

For several minutes he walked in small circles on the top of the hill, hands clenching his waist above his hips, head thrown upward to the graying sky, trying to suck in more air and listening to the hammering in his chest, and feeling the blood throttling through the veins in his neck and feeling so alive that he felt like shouting in triumph. And that's when it came to him, the one question he and Alberich hadn't asked the computers.

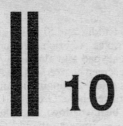

10

Still perspiring from his run, Sims knocked twice, then opened Alberich's bedroom door.

"Matthias! Remember—"

Alberich rolled over and groggily registered on Sims. "What the hell, Bradford—"

Sims held up a hand, cutting Alberich off. "Remember the FBI surveillance photo of Schmar in Washington? A German was with him. A *Bundeswehr* officer."

Alberich reached for the overhead bar and pulled himself upright in bed. "Spiedel?"

"Herbert Spiedel," Sims supplied.

Alberich, his eyes heavy with sleep, glared at Sims. "And I suppose you want to go through with Spiedel what we went through with Karstens?" He looked at the bedside clock. "Goddamnit, Bradford, I haven't gotten an hour's sleep. Can't you wait—"

"Look, Matthias, Karstens was just a name. Spiedel is . . . was . . . a person. A specific person." He paused, then dismissed Alberich with a casual wave. "You get your sacktime. Riddle and I will go on down and fire up the computers." He was at the door when he heard the sounds of Alberich swinging himself into his wheelchair.

"Riddle and you? Fire up . . . ?" Alberich's voice cracked

in disbelief and alarm. "Just a goddamn minute, Bradford, at least let me brush my teeth."

Half an hour later, Alberich, Riddle, and Sims sat side by side at adjoining computer consoles. Alberich, with headset and lip microphone, worked a keypad and a mouse. Above the consoles, a large projection screen charted his electronic dialog with a communications satellite hanging in an orbit twenty-three thousand miles above Thule, Greenland. That link established, the satellite beamed down to a field of antennas on the roof of the U.S. Embassy in Bad Godesberg, a suburb just south of Bonn proper.

The Agency's Bonn station took up the embassy's entire fourth floor. Within the station's bunkerlike comm room, a teleprinter chattered noisily and when it finally stood down, the duty officer tore off the yellow flimsy bearing Alberich's message and noted the "eyes-only" address and the immediate precedence. Calling for his relief, he hand-carried the message to the chief of station at a dead run.

Six hours later, Sims was working out on the Nautilus machines in the gym when Alberich called. Ten minutes later, he and Riddle sat facing Alberich and the projection screen in the operations center.

Alberich had the expression on his face that Sims had long ago identified as the bomb-thrower's buildup, so he sat back in the high-backed swivel chair and waited.

"We got Bonn station's take from Spiedel's military records and tax records." Alberich read off his screen. "Herbert Kraft Spiedel, born November 12, 1941, in Kehl." Alberich made an entry and on another computer screen a map of Germany appeared. A small red light blinked in southern Germany, just across the border from Strasbourg, France. "Gymnasium first degree, 1956. Baccalaureate, University of Tübingen, 1960. Twenty years service in the *Bundeswehr*—armor—1963 to '83. Current occupation: businessman. Married to Ursula Frank, 1965. Two sons, Eric and Friederich, born 1966 and 1970."

"The nature of Herr Spiedel's business?" Riddle asked.

Alberich grinned. "Our friend Herbert Kraft Spiedel is a busy, busy business executive. A regular Type-A workaholic. When he left the German army, he founded a private export-import company. Founder, president, and chief executive officer of his own private trading company."

Alberich's grin grew wider. "Get this," he announced smugly. "Spiedel called his company *Karstens*-Export, Bremerhaven."

An image of the port city flashed in Sims's memory: docks, freighters, the smells of the waterfront.

"What're you doing now?"

Alberich keyed the computer and a form in German filled the projection screen. "Corporate tax declaration," Sims translated.

"See that number?" Alberich asked. The cursor darted to a block in the middle of the form. "Identifier number of Karstens-Export's bank. The Germans require it so they can check to make sure corporate submissions are on the up-and-up." He danced the cursor around excitedly. "There's the end of the thread," he said to Sims and Riddle. "Now, if you computer illiterates will get out of my way . . ."

Sims and Riddle stayed out of Alberich's way. Reading, napping, reading some more. Dinner, then coffee. Sims looked at his watch. It was after eight. Nothing from Alberich.

"Play for the Farm's February chess championship?" suggested Riddle. Sims played badly, but they kept at it, Riddle winning game after game, the losing only adding to Sims's impatience. Sims, wired from expectations and too much coffee, was about to call Alberich, but Alberich called first. It was just after one in the morning, Wednesday, February 3.

Alberich had his chair pulled up to a small conference table. Before him on the table, a bulky accordion-folded computer printout. Alberich's face was lined, his eyes dark smudges.

"You look like somebody pulled you through a knothole, Matthias," Sims said.

Alberich yawned. "I *feel* like somebody pulled me through a knothole." He tapped the printout. "But we got the goodies on Karstens-Export." Paper clips, like shiny pitons, worked their way up the face of the thick stack of paper.

Riddle eased into his chair and directed a headmaster's fish eye at Alberich. "Now, young man, before we get into the results of your cybernetic virtuosity, would you be so kind as to explain—layman's terms, please—how you went about this?"

Alberich shot Sims a sideways glance as if to mark yet another proof that certain things with Riddle never changed. "The first assumption, Riddle, is that Karstens-Export made regular payouts to Broz."

"Rather conservative, Mr. Alberich, given the dying testimony of the Rys woman. And the second?" he asked placidly.

"That it'd be too hard to hand over a certified check or a bag of bucks to Broz, so we assume that Karstens-Export made the payouts through some form of banking transaction."

"And the nature of such a transaction?"

"Probably an international electronic transfer."

"And such a transfer can be traced by—?"

"Tapping into the network."

Riddle thought about this for a moment, staring at the stack of printouts. "Indulge me," he looked up and said in his plummy Charles Laughton voice, which made him sound like an officious English judge, "I still live in a world of checks, paper bank notes, letters of credit. I even have a certain empathy for those who bury a bit of bullion in the back garden. Give Mr. Sims and me a layman's description of your 'network.'"

Alberich settled back into his chair and for several moments, twirled the yellow pencil between the burnished fingers of his metal hand. It struck Sims as one of those perfectly natural unconscious gestures, the kind of physical doodling most people do, and he wondered if there was now any dividing line between the man in the chair and the metal arm he had made for himself.

Alberich started his tutorial. "You have a bank account, Riddle. Probably several; a personal account, maybe one for Tabard Books too?"

Riddle nodded.

"Are those accounts made up of separate boxes into which the bank tellers put in and take out dollar bills?"

"Of course not."

"That's right. Those accounts are *numbers*. And those numbers represent the dollars the bank would let you have if you asked for them?"

"Yes."

"Now, Riddle, you see the evidence of those accounts in a monthly statement. You open an envelope, pull out a piece of paper, and there's your accounts."

Riddle nodded.

"Now," Alberich continued, "it used to be that tellers settled up accounts every day: entering deposits and withdrawals on a ledger, a big sheet of paper. But now, Riddle, paper's no longer the base record of your accounts. Your account numbers are in a computer. Your money's nothing but an image on a cathode ray tube. Electrons, not dollars or gold bars tell how much you're worth."

Riddle pursed his lips primly. "I never measured personal worth in money, Mr. Alberich."

Alberich and Sims both gave Riddle a come-on-now look. Riddle caught it and waved a hand in surrender and smiled at his own pomposity. "I know what you mean . . . go on."

"Okay, Riddle, now that your accounts and everyone else's are numbers in computers, imagine that all these computers are connected—that they can instantly communicate with each other. Then let's add some more connections. Connect the banks with all the world's stock exchanges, bond markets, commodity exchanges, with credit card giants like Visa, American Express, Barclay's.

"This network handles every transaction on a minute-to-minute basis, from a Japanese cartel buying a Hollywood movie studio to Joe Schmuckatelli in Yonkers paying for a tank of high-test with a credit card."

Alberich, enjoying himself, shifted into high gear. "Some gee-whiz numbers: every day, the fiber-optic circuits beneath Wall Street transfer two *trillion* dollars. The same in Frankfurt, Geneva, London, Hong Kong. You can move a billion dollars from New York to Buenos Aires faster than you can ship a truckload of oranges across the California-Arizona line."

"And so Karstens-Export was in this network?"

"The first step was to find Karstens-Export's bank. Got that from a standard open source reference directory— Deutschesbank, Frankfurt, was the bank of record from the start of Karstens-Export's existence. Deutschesbank belongs to SWIFT—"

"Acronyms," Riddle grumbled.

"—which stands for Society for Worldwide Interbank Financial Telecommunications. SWIFT's headquarters is in Basel, Switzerland. Thousands of banks transfer money around the world over the SWIFT network."

Sims saw where it was going. "So you broke into SWIFT."

Alberich put on a look of mock horror. *"Broke into?* Mr. Sims!* We pay our dues! We're members in good standing."

"The Agency?"

"Well, not the Agency, exactly. But a Bahamian commercial bank, E. and K. Hill, Unlimited."

"Agency proprietary?"

Alberich nodded.

"But," Sims persisted, "membership would only get you into the net. The transactions would be encrypted—"

Alberich cut him off with a shrug and a larcenous grin. "Well, *that* did require a little help from our friends in Maryland."

Sims nodded. The Maryland friends lived at Fort Meade behind double chain link fences and spent their lives picking transmissions out of the air or off the sea bottom, and cracking encryption systems—reading other people's mail.

Few people knew, however, that Alberich's Maryland friends also designed algorithms and computer encryption chips for banks, international corporations, AT&T and all the Baby Bells. The algorithms and chips together made up something called the Digital Encryption Standard. DES let companies communicate around the world without fear of interception. DES could be broken, but only with one of the most powerful Cray supercomputers and about two hundred years of uninterrupted effort. SWIFT used the DES system. What SWIFT didn't know was that the friends in Maryland had built a secret window into DES, one that they could open at will, or when Alberich had a special request.

"Braggadocio aside, Mr. Alberich," Riddle said reprovingly, "what do the Karstens-Export accounts tell us?"

Alberich's metal hand found the first clip and delicately unfolded the printout to a page with two parallel columns.

"We did a run, matching Karstens-Export's transactions"—he tapped the first column with a pencil—"with Josef Broz's activities." The pencil skated over to the second column.

"Leaving the army, Spiedel incorporated Karstens-Export with substantial capital assets in West Germany in August 1983."

"The source of Spiedel's capital?" Riddle asked.

Alberich shrugged. "These"—he ran his hand over the printouts—"start with the founding of Karstens-Export, nothing before that. We don't know where Spiedel got the money."

"We just know what he did with it," Sims said.

Alberich picked up the pencil and went back to the printout with the two parallel columns. "As I was saying, this first column with the dates and numbers represents Karstens-Export payouts that probably went to Broz."

"Probably?"

"Probably," Alberich answered Sims. "Obviously, there's no direct transfer from Karstens-Export to an account we know *now* belonged to Broz. We might find that later. All we have now are consistencies—"

"The second column," Sims guessed.

"That's it." The pencil rapped the first column. "Now, here, August '83—the first month Karstens-Export was in business, it began payments into the Habsburgerbank, Vienna, into a numbered account. Spiedel—or Broz—knew what they were doing when they picked an Austrian bank. The Austrians are nuts about confidentiality, even more than the Swiss."

"So we know the account, but we don't know who owns it?"

Alberich nodded. "And so we have our own little network. From Bremerhaven to Frankfurt to Basel and finally, to a numbered account in Vienna." The pencil dropped to the bottom of the first column. "This went on for almost nine years. The last payment was in February '92."

"The month Broz was killed," Sims said.

"What," Riddle asked, "were the amounts?"

Alberich found another paper clip and turned to the page. "Varies, but the payments were never less than five hundred thousand and not usually more than eight hundred thousand—"

"A *month?*" Sims asked incredulously.

"Hell," Alberich replied, "I said 'not *usually* more.' There were several payments in the millions. One in February '88 was for one point five million, another in December '89 was for three point six."

"But," said Sims, "we don't know that Karstens-Export was pumping money into Broz's account."

"You're right," Alberich admitted. "Not yet, anyway. But look here." He opened the printout to another clip. The pencil jabbed at a column of dates. "Broz goes to the States in May 1984." The pencil moved to an adjoining entry. "The Karstens-Export payouts stop going to the numbered account in Vienna."

"And?"

"And they start flowing into a bank in the Caymans."

"Broz's account?"

Alberich frowned in frustration. "I don't know . . . yet." He moved the pencil down the column. "Four years later, Broz returns to Czechoslovakia—"

"January '88," Sims recalled.

"The payments stop going to the Caymans that same month and swing back to—"

"Vienna," Riddle finished. "Impressive. Very impressive, Mr. Alberich. But still coincidental."

Sims reached out to the printout and riffed the pages through his thumb and forefinger. "Wouldn't stand up in court," he admitted, "but then, we aren't in court."

Alberich nodded wearily at the printout. "Well, that's all there is for now. There's a helluva lot of digging left to do. I've got traces working on funds coming into Karstens-Export, but working back on those will take some time."

Riddle yawned politely behind a hand.

"Me too," Alberich said, and began shutting down the console. As he was doing so, a blue light flashed accompanied by a chirping sound. Alberich pressed a button and answered, using his lip microphone. He looked up to Sims. "You have a call—your control." Alberich rolled his eyes. "Sex-x-x-x-y voice."

Sims felt a sudden small shortness of breath and didn't want to answer in front of Riddle and Alberich. "Go on," he told them. "I'll be along in a little while," he said, reaching for the phone.

"You're a man who gets around."

Again an image of Lourdes haunted Sims and he felt a stream of warmth in his guts. Then his curiosity did a jump-shift and he found himself wondering what the woman on the phone looked like. "I don't know that I'm getting anywhere."

"You had a call from a man named Rollo. He said he had to meet you. He left a number. He sounded like somebody good to have on your side."

"You always want Rollo holding your rope."

She gave him an 800 number.

"Bradford," Rollo Moss's voice grated like a rusty hinge, "you near here?"

"I can get there."

"You might do that."

"Something breaking?"

"No. Not exactly. But there's somebody you ought to talk to."

"Can't they—?"

"They don't want to use the phone."

Sims weighed Rollo's message. The tone was steady and substantial, like it was wrapped around a sure thing. He glanced at his watch. It was three-thirty.

"Where? When?"

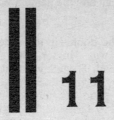

11

Wednesday afternoon, twelve hours later, Sims scanned the Virginia countryside from the copilot's seat of a small, bubble-nosed helicopter. Flying north from the Farm, they had run into a new cold front whose low, scudding clouds promised yet more snow. The small helicopter's bucking and pitching got steadily worse and it was with relief that Sims spotted the pad, a concrete square tucked away in a back field of a mansion in the horse country outside Middleburg, Virginia, some fifty miles west of Washington. A pickup truck, blotched white by splattered road salt, waited on an adjoining road.

In a springy squatting motion, the helicopter settled on the pad, its windmilling blades churning the fine snow into a sparkling vortex of white flecked with flashes of diamond. The pilot cut pitch and throttle and gave a thumbs-up, and Sims opened the door and stepped out of the helicopter and made his way to the waiting truck. As he got nearer, he saw the driver reach across and unlatch the passenger side door and push it open.

The driver, an older white man in a red nylon parka and plaid wool cap with earflaps motioned him into the cab. Deep furrows ran down the face from eye corners to the points of his mouth, giving him a sad hound look. The glacier blue eyes, however, were clear and focused.

The man looked oddly familiar. "I've seen you before," Sims said, trying to place the man and the name. "With the Judge."

"I'm Hunter."

Sims got in and slammed the door. He took the older man's extended hand. This was Hunter, the Judge's driver—Hunter, an Agency legend. The talk was that Hunter had parachuted alone into North Vietnam. After an initial entry report, nothing. A month after he'd been declared dead, he'd trekked out to Thailand, having racked up three very important kills to his credit. But complications from dengue and a gut wound took him out of fieldwork and entitled him to a disability pension. Hunter had turned down retirement to stay on with every director since Helms.

Hunter and Sims watched the helicopter take off. Hunter then turned to Sims. "You got a place to stay?"

"Yeah."

Easing the truck into gear, Hunter looked over at Sims. "The Judge was going to have somebody pick you up. I volunteered."

Hunter crouched forward over the steering wheel and Sims saw the webbing of a shoulder holster.

"I know who you are," Hunter said, as the truck jolted over the frozen ruts in the road. "When they medevacked you from Prague Station, I took the Judge to Bethesda Naval Hospital, him and Mr. Riddle. To see you after they operated on you. Saw you again at that funeral at Arlington."

"That was a while ago."

"You got the Intelligence Star and the Exceptional Service gong, didn't you?"

Sims laughed. "Thought that was supposed to be secret."

Hunter laughed with him. "You gonna keep secrets in a building with fifteen thousand spies?"

Up ahead, the private road intersected with Route 50.

"Now," Hunter asked, "where you going?"

An hour later, Hunter swung the pickup off the George Washington Parkway onto the ramp to National Airport.

Less than a minute later, he pulled to a stop in front of the 1930s style main terminal.

"You sure you don't need some backup?" Hunter said it hopefully.

Opening the door on his side, Sims reached across to offer his hand to Hunter. "Maybe next time."

"Soon." Hunter ordered with mock severity, then grinned. "You call, I haul."

Over half a century of remodeling and expansion have changed the face of National Airport, but National's heart remains the original waiting room. The room was designed in a pretelevision age, when families drove to the airport on Sunday afternoons to watch the airplanes land and take off. Rows of seats face a giant floor-to-ceiling window. Outside, the main runway, the Potomac, and in the distance, the white dome of the Capitol.

Sims couldn't find Rollo, but he spotted Payton, Rollo's driver, standing by the newsstand, off to the right of the seating area. Payton had seen him too. Sims watched as the thin man casually lifted a hand, apparently to scratch his nose, but Sims knew he was muttering into a microphone clipped to the cuff of his shirt. Sims stood in place, playing the role he was supposed to play.

The voice came, as he thought it would, from behind him. "Afternoon, Bradford." A hand cupped Sims's left shoulder.

Rollo Moss, black homburg and cashmere overcoat, stood beside him, as if materialized from nowhere. His right hand on Sims's shoulder, his left hand gripped a carry-on bag. A few steps behind Rollo stood one of Rollo's heavyset bodyguards, big, bulky, and dangerous in a tan trench coat and a fierce look.

"Hi, Rollo." Sims looked down to the carry-on bag. "Goin' somewhere?"

"Stage prop, Bradford. You right on time."

"For what?"

The hand on his shoulder exerted a gentle pressure forward. "Let's walk and talk, my man, and I'll tell you what."

They left the waiting room, taking the main corridor south toward the TWA gates. The corridor was thick with travelers rushing past souvenir shops, bookstores, and airline service desks. The bodyguard moved in front of them and set a slow pace down the corridor. Glancing over his shoulder, Sims saw that Payton had fallen in behind ten yards away. Rollo edged closer.

"We meetin' Roy Cantrell." Rollo said it CAN-trull.

"And he's—?"

"Roy-Boy's chief of Arlington police CID."

"Criminal Investigation Division?" Sims guessed.

"Criminal *Intelligence.*"

"Who's he think I am?"

"I told him you were Agency."

Sims cocked his head very slightly, but Rollo caught it.

"My judgment call, Bradford. I've known Roy a lotta years. We do each other favors, time to time."

"And?"

"I call him ever so often. Talk about a lotta things—you know?" Rollo rolled a hand, palm-up, palm-down. "Anyway, I happen to ask him about those fellas that got fried up in Rosslyn, and he . . . well, shit, Bradford, it's his story." Rollo pointed down the corridor. "We'll let him tell it."

Rounding a bend in the corridor, Sims saw the bodyguard walk into a coffee shop. Sims and Rollo followed. The place was a standard airport layout, cafeteria line for pastries, fruit juices, cellophane wrapped sandwiches, dispensers for soft drinks and coffee. Past the clerk at the register, several rows of stand-up tables.

"We get some coffee, Bradford. You bein' a government employee and all, you think they'll let me buy?"

The bodyguard went through the line ahead of them, paying for a cup of coffee and taking a place at an empty table toward the back. He positioned himself so that he partially blocked the very last table. There, a thin white man sipped a Diet Coke from the can while turning the pages of the *National Enquirer.* He wore a camel hair sport coat with pale blue shirt and a striped burgundy tie. By his elbow, a dark brown topcoat draped across the table, discouraging company.

Rollo, coffee in one hand, carry-on bag in the other, walked past his bodyguard to the table with the white man. He set his coffee down opposite the man, who moved the topcoat to one side, then continued to thumb through his tabloid. Sims followed on Rollo's right. The white man lowered the paper and, looking past Sims and Rollo, scanned the coffee shop.

Sims watched the flat gray eyes work their way around the room in quick, sweeping arcs. Sims estimated the man was in his late forties, early fifties. He had the look of someone who'd never gotten rid of yesterday's scuff marks. A badly done skin graft covered his right cheek, shiny and tight-looking under the fluorescent lights. The hands were square and strong. Masonic ring, no wedding band. Workmanlike stainless steel watch with metal band.

"That's your man at the next table, isn't it?"

Sims heard the words, but the man's lips hadn't seemed to have moved.

"Mnh-hunh," Rollo murmured, concentrating on his coffee. Then, to Sims, "This's Roy Cantrell."

Cantrell made another sweep of the coffee shop before looking at Sims. When he did look at him, it was a long appraisal, with flat gray eyes that resembled camera lenses. Sims knew that Cantrell would go to his grave remembering what Bradford Sims looked like. Cantrell gave the slightest of nods.

"We ID'd one a the assholes who burned up over in Rosslyn." It was a gravel and Marlboro voice.

Sims, coffee cup at his lips, locked eyes with Cantrell and nodded slightly.

"At least we got a name and some a his belongings," Cantrell continued. "Illegal alien named Naji Mohammed Hassan."

"That his real name?"

Cantrell shrugged. "Shit, what's real these days? That's the name he rented his apartment under. Same name's on the immigration stuff."

"Immigration stuff?"

Cantrell fished in a pocket of the camel hair sport coat and came up with a cheap wirebound notebook that he cupped in one hand. "Yeah. Mr. Hassan entered the United States on"—he wet a thumb and peeled back several pages in the notebook—"on 20 December '91."

"You said he was illegal."

"Yeah." Cantrell straightened up as if to stretch a stiff back, then leaned forward again. Sims noticed that the man made another sweep of the coffee shop. "Hassan arrives at Kennedy, New York, on an Air France flight from Paris. Syrian passport, but no U.S. visa. Claims political asylum. Gives a mosque in Jersey City as sponsoring organization. Immigration and Naturalization Service takes his name, prints and photos him, tells him to stay in touch for hearings, and turns him loose."

"Just like that? They let him in?"

Cantrell looked at Sims like he would a backward child. "You Agency guys know how to get into every country in the world except your own. Immigration and Naturalization has a flood of these fuckers every day. The judges won't let them send them back, and INS can only warehouse a couple hundred. So they have to turn them loose."

"How'd you ID this one? The fire . . ."

Cantrell's eyes went off for a moment in thought, then focused back on Sims. "There's a guy—call him Willie." Cantrell paused again, like a man on ice, testing his next step before he put his full weight on it. "He's a small-time gunrunner. Willie somehow doesn't have a record. He buys a few guns a week at a place down near Richmond. Not enough to draw attention. Pays a couple hundred bucks for a pistol, say, then resells it in D.C. no questions asked for five-six hundred." Cantrell moved his can of Diet Coke around on the tabletop. "Anyway, two a Willie's sales ended up in the wreckage of that van."

"This Willie," Sims guessed, "he's a source of yours." He knew from Cantrell's eyes that he'd guessed right.

"Yeah." If anything, Cantrell got more cautious. "Technically, I oughta throw Willie in the slammer. But with Willie workin' on the outside, I got a little window on the gun business—and Willie's customers. I put Willie in, I got nothin'. He'll be back on the street in a couple a months and even while he's away, the badasses will get their guns from somebody else."

Out of the corner of his eye, Sims saw Rollo nodding in agreement.

"Willie's a cautious guy," Cantrell continued. "He keeps a list of serial numbers and the guys he sells them to. This guy gave him a phony name, and that would a been the end of it, except the guy comes back to Willie for more ammo and another pistol. Wanted one a them Ruger .22 target pistols. Not the equipment of choice for stickin' up liquor stores or shootin' Koreans."

Sims flashed back to the *USA Today* building and the man with the long-barreled .22.

"This gets Willie curious," Cantrell went on. "He figures this guy might be into something that could turn a few extra bucks on top of the gun deal. So he follows the guy. Guy does a couple of turns around the block, but Willie stays on his tail. Guy lives in one a them tenements down off South Glebe."

Sims knew the area, a place of seedy rent-by-the week garden apartments in Alexandria where you had to pay in advance for newspaper delivery. "The bodies in the van were burned?"

"Crispy critters," Cantrell said casually, taking a sip of his Diet Coke.

"How do you know the guy Willie tailed was one of the guys in the van?"

Cantrell gave Sims another slight roll of the eyes. "DNA. There was enough stuff in the apartment, hair in a comb, skid marks on dirty underwear—that kinda shit—to come up with a DNA match on one a the bodies."

"The other guy?"

Cantrell shook his head. "Nothin' on him yet. Just Hassan."

"Anything else in Hassan's apartment?"

"Immigration papers. New Jersey taxi license. Couple hundred bucks in twenties hidden in a Ziploc in the toilet flush tank. Couple a changes a clothes. Kmart stuff. You gotta remember, he was in the place only a month before he got fried in Rosslyn." Cantrell paused, as if making a decision, then reached into his pocket, and brought his hand out and extended it toward Sims, fist closed. "Besides the pistols, two a these made it through the fire in the van." He opened his hand. "Hassan was wearing one, so was the John Doe in the van with him."

Sims picked a gray metal medallion out of Cantrell's hand. About the size of a silver dollar, it carried a relief of a scimitar, the point of the curved sword buried in the ground, and in the sky above, a large crescent moon.

"Can I have this?"

Cantrell studied Sims for a long moment. "S'posed to get a receipt, but," he said, shrugging, "you could sign anything with any name. Let's just say it's a loan." He nodded to Rollo. "He's my collateral." A troubled look came across Cantrell's face. "I was a grunt in Viet Nam; Combat Infantryman's Badge, Silver Star with oak leaf cluster. And I been in police work for almost thirty goddamn years— I've seen a lotta killin'." Eyes off into the distance, he shook his head, wrestling with a thought. "Killin' in war, killin' in robberies, killin' for jealousy, killin' for hate." The eyes came back to now and Sims. "I understand that kind a killin'. But now I'm beginning to see killin' just for killin', and it's scaring the shit outta me."

Cantrell took a deep breath as if to shake off the mood. "Anyway, here's this." He reached under the topcoat beside him on the table, brought out a large manila envelope, and nudged it across the table to Sims. Sims covered it with his own coat.

"What's this?"

"Copy of our Hassan file. Interviews, autopsy and lab reports, inventory of personal effects, prints—"

"Prints? I thought he was burned to—"

"He was. These were from the apartment. All over the place. Matched those immigration took when he showed up in New York." Cantrell stuck his hand out to look at his watch. "Gotta go." He gathered up his topcoat. As he passed Sims, he paused. "When Rollo asked me about how we were doin' on IDing the van guys, I thought it was funny."

"Funny?" Sims asked. "How?"

"Well," Cantrell drawled, watching Sims for a reaction, "I thought you government guys talked to each other."

"What do you mean?" Sims asked, sensing a hidden hook.

Cantrell shrugged, a cynical smile playing at the corners of his mouth. "We told the FBI about IDing Hassan three days ago." He gave Sims a last measuring look with his flat gray eyes, shrugged into his coat, and walked away.

Sims watched Cantrell walk out into the corridor and into the crowd.

"Well, well," said Rollo, "what do you make of that?"

Sims said nothing, but watched until Cantrell disappeared. All that was left was the medallion and the envelope with the Hassan file.

"Bait-and-switch, Rollo. You get one answer, but you get another hundred questions." He picked up his coat and drained the last of his coffee.

Again in the airport's waiting room, Sims saw through the huge windows that the snow was coming down outside like it meant business. He found a phone booth and called control. This time it was another woman with an older voice. Sims told her what he wanted.

"Meet?—tonight?" the woman asked.

"He's in Washington?"

A pause filled with electronic noises, then: "Yes."

"Then I want to meet tonight," Sims said brusquely. "Call me with time and place."

Rollo was standing just outside the booth.

"I'm staying overnight," Sims said.

"Place over in Southeast's open."

"I got a meeting tonight."

Rollo looked at his watch. It was just after four.

"In town?"

"Probably. Yeah, most likely."

"Let's go home. Dee'll fix us supper, then I'll take you."

"No need. I—"

Rollo held up his hand. "You gonna dig your grave with that hard head a yours, Bradford."

Sims recognized Rollo's no-give tone and gave in with an answering shrug.

Outside, Payton had the car waiting at the curb.

Sims got in and shut the door as a dusting of snow swirled in. As the car pulled into the traffic, Rollo touched the button and the window between front and back seat silently rolled up. "Now—you want to tell me where you been?"

Sims started out with meeting Ceska in Prague, and ended with the killing of Schmar and Gabriela Rys. Rollo listened, face stony, never taking his eyes off Sims. They were crossing the 14th Street bridge, and through the gaps in the buildings crowding the Southwest Freeway, Sims got an occasional glimpse of the Capitol dome, already lighted from within, and pristine white against the dark purple clouds. Sims finished as the car dropped down the 6th Street ramp.

"An' today Roy-Boy gives us this Arab, Hassan," Rollo said, as if taking inventory. "An' didn't you say they ID'd one a those guys who tried to do you in Italy?"

"Yeah," Sims said tiredly. "Sicilian Mafia." Outside the car, the scenery had changed. Off the freeway, no more shots of the capitol or office buildings. Now they were in the projects of Washington's southeast. Rollo, his large head at a slight angle, stared off in thought, then looked at Sims.

"You thought a the drug angle?"

"You mean the Mafia and—"

"Yeah," Rollo rumbled unhappily. "Lotta street talk says heroin's makin' a comeback. Italian connection and the Arabs. That kinda talk." He looked anxiously at Sims. "You ever cross the drug boys somewhere in your past?"

Sims shrugged in frustration. "No. At least, not that I know of."

"Well, whatever, looks like you picked up a new batch of bad company from somewhere."

They rode for a while and it was Sims who broke the silence. "Bad?" He shook his head. "Not bad. The Russians—the commies—*they* were bad. But you knew how bad. They played on the same field as we did. It was sorta like football. You knew they'd cheat. And they'd knee you in the balls. But you knew all that. It was part of the game. *These* guys"—he threw his hands up in a helpless gesture—"who the hell knows?"

"A different kinda bad?"

Sims shook his head, trying to work it out, what was bothering him. "No," he said finally, "more than just bad."

"More?"

"Yeah," Sims answered, thinking he was getting it more clearly, now, "I think they're evil."

"Evil?" Rollo rolled the word around experimentally. "You mean like the preachers talk about?"

"Yeah," Sims said.

On the way to Rollo's, the snow began falling faster. The traffic was already thinning out as the last of Washington's office workers left early to avoid the inevitable snarls that came with the slightest snowfall.

Sims turned on the backseat radio to get the news, but instead, got a rap station. Before he could change stations, the killing beat of the words stitched out a staccato line of hate.

> *Rat-a-tat and a tat like that*
> *Never hesitate to put a nigga on his*
> *back . . .*

Angrily, Sims punched the select button until he found NPR. For the third consecutive day, Serb gunners had pounded the outskirts of Sarajevo, Corey Flintoff reported. Two school children had been killed and a number of adults wounded when shells fell on a funeral procession for an earlier victim. Meanwhile, in the United Nations Security Council, the debate continued—

Sims snapped off the radio. "Shit," he cursed.

"Whole world's on a killing binge," Rollo muttered. "If they not singin' about it, they out doin' it."

In Washington's northern neighborhood of Shepherd Park, Payton pulled the Chrysler into a drive, stopping before a massive iron grill gate. Through the gate, Sims saw a large two-story brick house with slate roof and dark blue shutters. Set back from the street on a large wooded lot, the house was surrounded by an imposing eight-foot wrought iron fence.

"New, Rollo," Sims commented. "Looks like Fort Knox."

Payton pressed a button on the dash and the driveway gate swung open.

"Unh-huh," Rollo grunted unhappily. "Shit's gettin' bad, even with the mayor livin' just down the street. Used to be thieves worked on a profit motive. Weigh gains against risk. Now"—Rollo ran his fingers thoughtfully across his chin— "now they just want to grab somethin' that'll get them their fix. They go in anywhere. Steal anything." He eyed the gate as they drove through and nodded as if it had passed his inspection. "Be bad advertisin' for me to get robbed."

Dee, Rollo's wife, a plump, matronly woman, smothered Sims at the front door and led him through the house to the kitchen, leaving Rollo to follow in her wake. Sims had stayed away too long. He was too *thin*. Still *single?* she frowned. No shortage of charming young women. *Moral* young women, Dee added pointedly.

The three ate supper at the kitchen table. Pork chops smothered in sausage gravy, rice, and vinegar-laced collards. After, Sims and Rollo moved to the den. Sims sprawled on the worn leather couch while Rollo tilted back in his BarcaLounger and the two of them endured the first half of an uninspiring Bullets-Sixers game. Shortly after seven, Sims's pager went off.

Standing while making his call from the phone in the hall, he saw through the small windows set in the front door that the snow was still falling, thick and white in the glare of the security lights. Warm and with a full belly, the last thing he wanted tonight was to go out again.

A voice answered and gave Sims a time and place. He hung up and walked back to the den. Rollo, head thrown back and eyes closed, was snoring gently. Sims bent and shook him gently by the shoulder.

"Come on, Rollo. We better get movin'."

* * *

Thirty minutes later, Payton turned west onto Constitution Avenue just below Capitol Hill. The snow and streetlights turned Washington into a confectioner's masterpiece. The town was empty and only a few tire tracks broke the white expanse of the avenue, and the scattered cars that had been left parked along the curbs huddled like snow covered beasts in hibernation.

Farther down Constitution—near the Ellipse, Sims guessed—the sparkling yellow lights of a snow plow. At Fourth Street, Payton turned left, then hooked an immediate right into a driveway. The driveway led to an underground garage where a uniformed guard stood waiting just inside the large open doorway, smoking a cigarette and watching the snow fall.

Payton pulled the Chrysler into an open space. Rollo and Payton got out with Sims. As the three walked toward the guard, the man flipped his cigarette onto the slush covered floor and wordlessly beckoned them to follow.

Two flights of stairs brought them into the rotunda of the National Gallery of Art. Massive dark green marble columns encircled the fountain with its statue of the god Mercury, and Sims remembered standing here with Houghton two years ago, just after Valek had defected. Somewhere along his trail, Valek had kicked a pebble off a cliff and now there was an avalanche. Connections—the goddamn connections—Valek had led to Broz and Schmar and that had somehow led to the killing in San Gimignano and that . . . that to here and—

"This way." The guard stood some twenty feet away, motioning impatiently, and Sims realized that he'd stopped at the fountain. Rollo and Payton following, he caught up with the guard, their footsteps making hard hollow sounds off the dark marble floor.

Down the long arched corridor, Sims recognized a figure standing just inside an open doorway that led off to a warren of galleries.

"Who's that?" whispered Rollo.

"Judge's driver."

The guard nodded to Hunter, then left.

Sims introduced Rollo and Payton to Hunter.

Introductions done, Hunter looked at Sims, jerked a thumb over his shoulder toward an open doorway. "He's waiting."

Alone, Sims walked into the gallery. Inside, a ceiling spot focused a tight beam on Auguste Renoir's *Pont Neuf, Paris*. The light left the walls of the gallery in darkness and the painting seemed to be suspended in midair, a window looking out on the Paris of 1872, sunlight and blue sky and puffed white clouds, the wide stone bridge over the Seine filled with carriages and men with walking canes and women with parasols, children, and small dogs.

The Judge was seated on a sofa slightly off to the side of the painting.

"Dramatic," Sims said.

"Very." The Judge stood and gestured to the Renoir. "The Germans had it. Not Hitler," the Judge added. "He hated the Impressionists but Goering was a collector. We almost lost it when the Russians took Berlin."

"No. Dramatic . . . meeting here."

The Judge turned, rimless glasses bouncing a sliver of light. He gave Sims a slightly quizzical look. "The gallery director and I are classmates," he said, as if that explained everything. "And at this hour there are few more secure places in Washington." The Judge took his place on the sofa and patted the space beside him.

Sims sat down, and for a moment, both men stared at the Renoir.

"I met with the head of the Arlington PD intel section this afternoon."

"Yes?"

"And he gave me a file. A file on a dead man named Naji Mohammed Hassan. One of the guys who tried to kill Riddle and me last week in Rosslyn."

The Judge looked at Sims, then back to the painting. "And what else does the file tell us?"

"That Hassan, if that's his name, was one of your basic militant Muslims. He was wearing a medallion with a sword and crescent on it. The other guy in the van was wearing one too."

"How did the Arlington police identify this man?"

"Traced his weapon. DNA match of the corpse matched stuff found in his apartment." Sims paused. "Funny thing about the ID."

"Funny ha-ha? Or funny strange?"

"Funny strange."

The Judge tilted his head slightly.

"Arlington PD thought we should already know about the ID."

"Know? How?"

"They passed the information to the FBI three, four days ago."

The Judge winced slightly, then sighed. "So much for cooperation."

Sims was silent for a while. Then: "Why'd the Bureau hold out?"

"Why?" the Judge shrugged cynically. "In this town more than any other, knowledge is power. There're always more reasons to hold out than to share."

"I feel like I'm running blindfolded in a damn minefield."

"Complaining?"

Sims shook his head. "No. Just telling." He gripped one hand around the fist of the other.

"I'm just as blind as you are."

"You going to hit the Bureau on that crap?"

The Judge stared past Sims to the Renoir. "I don't come here often enough," he said, as if confessing to someone other than Sims. "But when I do, this painting always draws me. I imagine living in the Paris of that time, and it's peaceful and everything is as you see it."

The Judge fell silent, looked wistfully at the Renoir for a second more as if telling Paris good-bye, then turned to Sims. "Confront the Bureau?" The Judge paused, then nodded, agreeing with a private thought. "It might be more useful to lie low with it. For now, anyway." He focused on Sims. "And where're you putting your foot down next in *your* minefield?"

"Germany," Sims said, "if I can arrange some transportation."

* * *

By nine the next evening, Sims looked ten years older, his sideburns touched with silver, new wrinkles sprayed outward from around his eyes, and he walked with a slight arthritic limp. Now a CPA at Arthur Andersen & Co., Sims in his new identity worked on K Street, and lived in a moderately expensive high-rise apartment building on N Street, Southwest. He belonged to the Downtown Y, the University Club, and the University of Pennsylvania alumni association. His passport, five years old, bore visas and entry stamps testifying to regular business trips to France, Great Britain, both sides of the formerly divided Germany, and occasional excursions to Italy and Greece.

Cover staff had provided a well-worn but expensive leather briefcase that carried thumbed-through copies of correspondence between Andersen's D.C. office and its Berlin branch, and a thick, multitabbed draft plan for an American client with hopes of breaking into commercial shipping. Everything, the paper specialist said, had two levels of backup behind it.

At ten o'clock, Hunter, this time driving a Red Top cab, dropped Sims off at Dulles departure where the Arthur Andersen travel section had booked business-class reservations on the eleven-thirty KLM flight to Amsterdam's Schiphol Airport.

12

At dawn on Friday, February 5, in Lebanon's Bekáa Valley, a lone shepherd stirred in his blankets, the ground cold and hard beneath him. He sought vainly for the slightest warmth. His small fire had died to smoking embers and the north wind sliced through his thin blankets. The female goats, their udders swollen, bleated and cried to be milked.

The shepherd got slowly to his feet, hobbling slightly from a familiar arthritic stiffness in his right hip. Wrapped in his blankets, he took a few steps away from the fire and, back to the wind, urinated. Finished, he walked to the goatskin bladder suspended from a rough tripod. Turning the hand-carved willow spigot, he caught a few drops of precious water which he used to wash his hands and forearms. A few more drops for his face, and finally, for his feet.

As the sun broke free of the mountains, he faced south-east toward Mecca. With open hands, palms forward at head height, he began *al-fajr,* the dawn prayer. In his second repetition, he included a plea for his goats. It was a small herd and he its only keeper. The shepherd's home village was Boudaï, six miles to the west, but forage there had become scarce. Which was why he had come here, to graze as close as he dared to the forbidden zone.

The zone was directly ahead, about a mile away, marked by a cluster of low buildings. The shepherd had suppressed his curiosity about the forbidden zone. There were many such up and down the valley, and life was difficult enough without running afoul of the authorities. Still, when the goats had to eat or die, one had to take certain risks.

Toward the end of *al-fajr*, the shepherd, now kneeling, heard a faint clattering sound. Looking up, he saw a helicopter lift off from the forbidden zone, a dot in the morning sky. Then the ground trembled, and he heard a rumbling sound, muffled and indistinct, like a giant coughing within the earth. As he watched, a windblown cloud of dirty yellow smoke swept toward him from the distant buildings, reaching for him like a clutching hand.

By nine, the sun had taken the edge off the cold, and the shepherd had forgotten the cloud as he herded his flock toward a *wadi* where he knew there'd be water. The man, who prided himself on his vigilance, heard a cry and knew instantly it was a nanny in distress. Peering over the gathered backs of the goats, he searched toward the right fringe of the small flock.

At first, nothing.

Then he heard the cry again and at the same time, saw a kid stagger. The young goat, a male, white with black and brown spots, was one of the last born in late fall. The kid's mother circled protectively around it, anxious, tossing her head and bleating mournfully. As he started toward the nanny, the shepherd saw a rippling seizure overtake the kid, the animal shaking as if it were in the grasp of an invisible giant hand. The hand flung the young goat to the ground, where it thrashed, its legs kicking in violent spasms. The young goat whinnied, a high, keening shriek of pain. The shepherd ran to the stricken animal.

The kid fell quiet, and for a moment, the shepherd thought of a twisted leg, or perhaps a snake bite. Then the small animal gave a deep, hiccupping cough and vomited a rush of thick, blackish blood. The dark blood splattered the ground, staining the golden stubble of the bunch grass. Another cough and the blood became a torrent, erupting from the mouth and nose, then the ears and anus. The kid's mother's cries became disconsolate as she knew, before the shepherd did, that her offspring's life had flown.

Careful to avoid the blood, the man knelt and touched the young goat's throat. Beneath the fur, the skin, even in death, was feverish hot. He had been a shepherd all his life. Over half a century. In all that time, he had seen nothing like this. He fought down a rising gorge of fear, forcing himself to think. He could not carry the carcass back to Boudaï, but there was the blood. He could take some of that. Perhaps the authorities . . . in their laboratories . . .

He was reaching for a clump of the bloodstained grass when he heard another cry of distress. Then another. And another. He stood and saw his flock bucking and heaving, tearing at themselves as if possessed. Frozen in disbelief, he watched as one goat, then another, collapsed. And the cries of pain and suffering filled his ears with torment. And the blood of the flock joined to become a dark pool.

The last goat standing looked at the shepherd. As if finding the death around it unremarkable, the goat began nibbling at the grass stubble.

The shepherd stared in desperation at the survivor. The living goat was reality; the dead a nightmare. Stepping over the carcasses of his flock, the man made for the goat. He would clutch the animal to him and feel its life and this horrible dream would go away.

Suddenly, one of the goat's front legs crumpled, then the other, and the animal dropped to the ground. And as it did, the shepherd felt a tiny stirring within himself. At first nothing more than a spark somewhere beneath his stomach, then the warmth flashed through his body. As if a valve had turned, perspiration suddenly poured from him and he felt as if his blood were on fire. And deep within, from the same place the spark had come, the first knifing pains.

13

Sim's KLM Flight 652 touched down at Amsterdam-Schiphol in the early afternoon of Friday, February 5. An hour later, he was headed east in a rented Volvo. Crossing into Germany, he picked up E-8, the east-west autobahn that would carry him to Berlin. Bypassing Hannover, he stopped for a light dinner in the Ritter St. Georg in Braunschweig, and by nine-thirty, he was on the autobahn again. At eleven, he passed through Potsdam and entered Berlin.

At the end of World War II, American, British, French, and Soviet forces staked out their occupation zones in Berlin and Vienna. When the Iron Curtain fell across the continent, the four powers, now no longer allies, retained control of the two cities.

In no time, Berlin and Vienna became the Sodom and Gomorrah of espionage as CIA, MI-6, and SDECE squared off against the KGB. The Agency burrowed tunnels to tap top-secret Soviet cable communications to Moscow. The KGB's "wet teams" crossed into the American, British, and French sectors to assassinate or kidnap troublesome defectors. Finally, in 1955, the show closed in Vienna with the signing of the Austrian peace treaty—center ring was now Berlin.

Berlin held a special fascination for Sims. Berlin base had

been almost independent of the mammoth Bonn station with its layers upon paralyzing layers of worriers and retrospective analysts. First as deputy, then as chief of base, Sims had had the freedom to develop a network of sources that had performed minor miracles when terrorism came to Europe in the spring of 1986. As he drove into the city through the Grunewald forest, he experienced a pang of nostalgia for the times when you could tell yourself that you knew the rules of the game.

It was almost eleven when Sims stopped at a curbside pay phone in Charlottenburg and dialed a number given him by cover staff during the briefings in McLean the day before. A woman answered. As scripted, Sims, in German, identified himself as Erich Mueller, and asked for Herrdoktor Vogel. Herrdoktor Vogel, the woman replied, was not in. Perhaps a message? Sims said no and hung up.

Sims mentally traced what he'd set in motion. He'd given Berlin base duty officer two confirmation signals: first by calling from the Charlottenburg exchange, then by identifying himself as Erich Mueller. As he walked back to the car, he imagined the duty officer alerting the security detail at the safe house, then calling the chief of base to let him know that the expected company had arrived.

Cran Zachary, the base duty officer, met him at the safe house address, a seven-story Bauhaus-era apartment building overlooking the Spree River, just north of the Tiergarten. Zachary was a small, compact man with a gravel voice and a thick black mustache who reminded Sims of G. Gordon Liddy, the Watergate burglar.

The apartment, on the top floor of the building, offered a commanding view of nighttime Berlin. To the east, the living room's large picture windows framed a panoramic view of the Brandenburg Gate. In one direction off the living room, two comfortable bedrooms with baths faced each other across a narrow hallway that led to a small library. In the other direction, a dining room and kitchen. From the refrigerator, Zachary produced a covered plate of Emmentaler cheese and a chilled bottle of '81 Pfalz which he put on the kitchen table.

"For a nightcap," he explained. He opened an attaché case and withdrew a shoulder holster which he placed beside the wine and cheese. "And a Llama nine for you." Zachary went through the ritual clearing of the weapon before handing it to Sims.

Just before midnight, Friday, Matthias Alberich lay in bed, staring through the dark toward the ceiling, a feeling of unknowing panic clutching in his chest. He'd taken a Halcion, but still sleep wouldn't come. As soon as he'd doze off, everything would accelerate. As if he'd stepped on a speeding conveyor belt. Jumbles. Bits and pieces. Parts of dreams, parts of reality flashed by at the speed of light. He would reach out but couldn't make contact. He couldn't grasp *this* and connect it to *that*. Everything sped away, just beyond his grasp.

"Shit! Shit! Shit!" He gave up, swung himself out of bed and into his chair and in fifteen minutes, he was back in the operations center, staring at the floor-to-ceiling board with its colored patchwork of notes. The board seemed curiously flat and lifeless.

On the desk before him, a thick stack of files in tan manila folders. Because he couldn't think of anything else to do, he reached for the first folder and began reading, searching for the smallest undigested particle.

An hour later, he pulled out Naji Hassan's file. Again he went through the Arlington police paperwork: the initial report of the first officer on the scene at the *USA Today* building, the narrative entries of the follow-up investigation, loaded with jargon and passive-voice descriptions of the detectives, the weapon-trace, DNA analysis, fingerprint card, and finally, the medical examiner's report, consisting of the ME's summary, a four-page document, and a thick stack of tabbed attachments.

Alberich worked his way through the ME summary. Large chunks of the document were now familiar to him. He found himself starting to skip through the dry description of the pathologist's examination and forced himself to slow down. Along the summary's left margin were tabbed attachments, the details of the lab work. Details the ME had brought together in his summary. Alberich had read the ME summary, but not the tabs. For long moments, Alberich stared sleepily at the multicolored tabs, then plunged in.

In spite of his fatigue and the obtuse technical language, Alberich found the lab reports interesting. Mitochondrial DNA analysis . . . gas chromatography . . . ballistics evaluation . . . X-ray . . .

The dental report was two pages. There was a full-mouth diagram showing upper and lower jaws with their molars, incisors, and bicuspids. On this, someone had mapped out Hassan's teeth, marking those teeth missing or filled. There was a copy of a memo, an obviously standard notation that a postmortem impression had been made and was on file with the Arlington County ME, and identified by an alphanumeric code designator.

Alberich started to go on to the next inclosure when a brief entry on the full-mouth diagram caught his eye. He looked closer at the handwritten note beside the upper left molars. For an instant, he couldn't tell why the note had attracted him, and he turned the page to the next report.

Suddenly, a jittery tremor of excitement shot down his spine. He turned back to the full-mouth diagram and stared at it for a moment, then pulled up a classified telephone directory on his computer screen. He highlighted the number he wanted and over the loudspeaker came the sound of a telephone ringing.

"Hello?" A voice thick with sleep and slightly irritable answered on the third ring.

"This's Alberich," he identified himself. He didn't wait for a response. "Get down to the Arlington medical examiner. Corpse by the name of Hassan. He's got a stainless steel tooth."

"Stainless steel—"

"*Tooth!* I want to know all about it: who, what, when, where, how."

A dead space as the party on the other end put things together. "You want it now, I suppose," the voice finally came, carrying with it a pout.

"You guess good," Alberich said.

* * *
169

A light rain fell on Berlin the next morning. It was Saturday, and Sims easily found a cab to Kirchstrasse, in southwest Berlin, where Zachary met him in the lobby of the American consulate. The pair passed through the Marine security on the first floor, taking the elevator to the second floor where another Marine greeted them.

The consulate's second floor had housed Berlin base since Riddle had set it up in 1947. Berlin base was small: the single corridor formed a perfect square: you got out of the elevator and turned right or left at the Marine security window. Either direction and you walked down a windowless cream-colored corridor with unmarked doors, and you came back to the elevators and the Marine guard. The glare of the fluorescents overhead washed out all traces of skin color and the air had a sealed-in staleness to it that Sims associated with submarines.

"Home sweet home," Sims muttered to himself, partly in irony, partly in genuine nostalgia for the years he'd spent here.

Zachary opened a door, led Sims past two busy secretaries, and into Sam Durney's office. Sims felt a momentary shift back in time: the office was the same as he'd left it seven years ago: same ornate carved walnut desk in the center of the room, same burgundy carpet, and the same heavy blue velvet drapes hiding a window that no longer existed because Riddle had had it bricked in forty-five years before, when Berlin base had come into being.

Durney, a stocky red-faced Irish-American on the long side of forty, bent over the desk, laboring with a pencil over a pad of paper, obviously deep into a draft. Judging from the wadded up balls of paper strewn around him on the floor, Durney was having a tough time of it. He looked up with surprise, then stood and shook hands as Zachary did the introductions.

"Let's sit over here." Durney motioned to a camel-back sofa and a low coffee table surrounded by three upholstered armchairs. Sims sat on the sofa and turned down Zachary's offer of coffee, as did Durney. Zachary paused for a moment, then disappeared.

Durney settled himself into a chair opposite the sofa and

studied Sims with unconcealed curiosity. "Welcome home," he said to Sims. "The Judge said you get a blank check." Durney paused for emphasis. "What do you need?"

"I need," said Sims, "to know about Herbert Spiedel and a trading company he set up called Karstens-Export in Bremerhaven."

"With the Wall down and peace everywhere, we're a smaller place than when you were here. My deputy, four case officers."

"TOPS?" Sims asked—technical operations specialist.

Durney motioned with his head toward the door. "Zachary. Good on audio and visual. We would have lost him years ago to headquarters but he has this thing about Berlin. We're pretty thin here, compared to before. Bonn station could've given you more support."

Sims shook his head. "I know Berlin better than Bonn."

"We've set up an accommodation address and phone under the Arthur Andersen cover, but headquarters didn't say anything about your story."

"I'm a senior director for Andersen's international operations. We have a client—unnamed, of course—who is considering acquisitions in the merchant shipping business—"

"—and the possibility of Bremerhaven as a port of call," finished Durney. "What's next?"

"Tomorrow," Sims said, "I'd like to start scoping out the Bremerhaven real estate market."

At CIA headquarters forty-five minutes later, Alberich passed through the security gates, picked up a sandwich and container of soup at South Cafeteria, and took everything with him to the basement. The concrete block walls echoed the sound of his chair's drive motors as he wheeled down a dim underground corridor. Just past the gym and indoor running track, he came to another bank of elevators. Unlike the first elevators, Alberich had to slip his ID card into a slot by the closed doors. He did so and the doors slid soundlessly open. Once inside, the doors whooshed shut with a sealing hermetic sensation, and the elevator automatically began a stomach fluttering drop through the granite ridge that runs along the west bank of the Potomac.

The elevator slowed, then stopped. It opened onto an eggshell white corridor that seemed to go on forever. Bright indirect lighting and walls unbroken by doors heightened the sense of dimensionlessness. Curving gently to the right, the corridor's ceiling and floors blended smoothly into walls without joint seams, the whole thing giving the impression of a spatial infinity.

This was Alberich's world. He had designed everything: the independent power source, the exquisite air filtration system, even the corridor which traced a perfect segment of a Keplerian ellipse—all to support the massive room at the end of the corridor where Alberich had put together the Agency's nerve center. The computers that filled the cavernous room bore no brand names. Alberich had built them all, with the benefit of a near limitless budget and the personal backing of the Judge and his predecessors. It was a world in which intellect meant everything; wheelchairs and withered limbs nothing.

A hidden bank of sensors detected Alberich's approach, identified him against a coded set of algorithms, and sent a signal that opened the massive vault door. As Alberich entered, a gust of ozone-laden air greeted him. To his right, rows of computer processors, arrayed in parallel, capable of sifting through man's accumulated knowledge in fragments of seconds. Rows of lights, blinking and steady. Demanding lights and passive lights. Mostly greens, some yellows, and a sprinkling of reds. He steered up the ramp to the mezzanine.

This was Alberich's bridge, and from it, he commanded the voyages of his earthbound spaceship. From here, he surveyed the entire floor: the computers and above them a huge wraparound projection screen, three stories tall, a marvel of display technology, a screen fed by computers that could carry you out through the solar system in three dimensions, then switch in a dizzying nanosecond and transport you to the inner core of an atom. And like the captain returning to his ship, he felt a sense of completeness and well-being.

He set the soup and sandwich on the desk of his command console. Nearby on his left, a drawing board the twin of that in the smaller operations room at the Farm. He inserted a floppy disk into a computer drive slot in the console and worked a command into the keypad. As if written by an invisible hand, the drawing board filled with a copy of the multicolored notes he'd first put together at the Farm. He started at the top, and again, for at least the hundredth time, began to work his way down.

The chirping sound came as Alberich was studying the medallion the Arlington police had found on Hassan. Keying the video phone, Alberich noted it was ten past nine. A man wearing a white lab coat came on the small screen on Alberich's console. In the background, Alberich recognized a small electric arc furnace. Alberich pressed the keypad button that allowed his image to be transmitted to his caller's screen.

"The tooth was definitely Russian," the man reported. "KGB work. It was done five, six years ago."

"Okay, Russian. And the date? The five or six years?"

"Easy"—another shrug—"carbon dating."

"So Hassan would've had to have been in the USSR to get that done?"

Another nod.

"No other possibilities?"

"No place else to get that kind of dental work," the man in the screen said emphatically, then signed off.

For several minutes, Alberich stared at the blank screen, sifting, sorting, matching. He glanced at a digital clock that told him that it was just after five in the morning in Moscow. Alberich keyed the secure circuit for a transatlantic call. If Isaacson wasn't awake by now, he ought to be.

Carl Isaacson had been awake. By eight o'clock, the Moscow station chief had received copies of Hassan's fingerprint card, dental records, and DNA profile. And by nine, he'd set up a meeting for that afternoon with Yegor Kulikov, deputy chairman of the Russian Intelligence Service.

14

At nine, Berlin time, Sims caught Deutsche BA's first commuter flight of the morning out of Tempelhof. Fifty-five minutes later at Bremerhaven, a slender, precise man in his fifties with thinning gray hair and yellow nicotine-stained fingers stood at the terminal gate holding a neatly hand-lettered placard with the name ARTHUR AN-DERSEN.

Sims introduced himself.

The man came to near-military attention and bowed slighlty. He was, he said in good but slightly archaic English, Herr Bernhard Quandt, senior agent for Kober and Zimmermann, one of Bremerhaven's larger commercial real estate firms. Quandt ceremoniously opened an antique silver case and handed a conservatively engraved card to Sims.

In return, Sims turned an Arthur Andersen Washington business card over and scribbled the Berlin accommodation address and phone numbers Durney had set up.

The exchange of business cards completed, Quandt waited for questions from Sims. Satisfied there were none, he nodded vigorously and marched off through the terminal to a well-preserved Opel Rekord. At the car, Quandt asked a pro forma question about breakfast, and when Sims shook his head, he seemed relieved.

"We will now"—he smoothly eased the old Opel into gear—"conduct our inspection."

Bremerhaven is a put-together city without cathedrals or significant history. Built in 1827 where the Wesser River joins the North Sea, Bremerhaven is a city of a single strictly utilitarian purpose. It was and is a deep sea port, a fact testified to by a perpetual odor of fish and diesel fuel.

A lifelong resident, Bernhard Quandt knew the waterfront, from Fischereihafen in the south where half of Germany's fishing fleet is based, to the Containerkreuz in the north where the sea-land container ships put in to feed the German economy.

During the course of the day, Sims fed Herr Quandt bits and pieces of requirements that by the process of elimination led them in the afternoon to the Columbuskaje terminal area. Finally, Quandt turned the Opel onto the numbered street where, Sims knew, the Karstens-Export warehouse stood.

Along the right side of the street stretched a long expanse of asphalt parking lot. Massive trucks waiting to load and unload filled the lot. On the left, identical dirty gray warehouses followed one another like bulking elephants on the march. Each warehouse bore a number painted in fading white at each corner end. Some warehouses were in the open, others had fencing.

Sims showed no interest as they passed warehouse fifty-seven which carried a metal sign with Karstens-Export in bold black lettering against a tan background.

Sims, however, muttered a silent curse to himself. Karstens-Export's neighbors had no fencing; Karstens-Export, however, had an eight-foot chain link fence topped with barbed wire arms jutting outward. They were at warehouse fifty-nine when Sims said casually, "Herr Quandt, I think something like this might do."

Quandt made a brief call on the car phone to a central registry, then pointed down the street. "There is a vacancy," he announced. "A watchman will let us in."

Fifteen minutes later, Sims and Quandt walked through

the vacant warehouse, the watchman trailing a discreet distance behind. It was a melancholy building, having endured half a century of Bremerhaven's industrial fallout which had darkened the redbrick walls to a soot-grimed gray. Dim yellow lamps high in the black rafters added little to what feeble winter sun managed its way through the dirty panes set in the skylights. The place was an inventory of smells: the dusty dryness of grain chaff mixed with the dampness of aging concrete, all underlaid with spilt oil and grease.

Sims produced a camera from his attaché case and took photographs, then paced the length of the building. Just over three hundred feet long, Sims noted, standing at the far end, and, he estimated, perhaps one fifty wide. A large cubicle, perhaps thirty feet on each side and ten feet high filled one corner of his end of the building, providing space for offices. Overhead, just below the rafters, a motorized hoist on an orange primer painted I beam ran the long axis of the building, from the cargo door at one end to the similar door at the other. Sims walked back to rejoin Quandt.

"Utilities?" he asked the German.

"Standard fifty cycle, two-twenty volt electricity," Quandt read from a large black notebook, "two water mains, each twenty centimeters in diameter, heating by fuel oil."

"Alarm systems?" Sims asked, trying to keep his voice flat.

Quandt leafed through the book. *"Nichts."* He shook his head. "I imagine that is up to each tenant."

"Our client will require an alarm," Sims said. "Can you provide us a list of contractors who have done work in these warehouses?"

Quandt nodded and made a notation in his notebook.

"And are blueprints available?"

Quandt consulted the notebook, and nodded. *"Ja,* however, there is a deposit required."

"You have our address," Sims said.

"I shall mail—"

"Courier would be better," Sims cut in, adding, "We, of course, will cover that expense."

"Your client must be in a hurry," Quandt ventured.

"Yes," said Sims, looking around the warehouse. "Probably more than we even know."

At five that afternoon, Carl Isaacson took the Moscow Metro to the Sportivnaya station just east of Lenin Stadium. Stepping off the escalator, he took a moment to orient himself in the afternoon darkness, then struck out toward the bright streetlights along the Bol'shoy Pirogovskaya, a block away.

Ten minutes later, he stood before the Church of the Transfiguration. The church with its stylized belfry was a masterpiece of Moscow Baroque, a study in rich redbrick set off by ornate white granite window surrounds. A high crenelated brick wall extended right and left from the church proper. To the west, the wall ran to the banks of the Moscow River. In the opposite direction, it went as far as Pirogovskaya, then bent around and out of sight. The long brick walls were broken at intervals by watch towers and the whole thing reminded Isaacson of the forts in one of those old *Beau Geste* movies.

A massive iron chain stretched across the entrance to an arched cobblestone passageway through the church. A rusted sign hanging from the chain said CLOSED.

Isaacson stepped over the chain and continued down the passageway. The passageway opened onto a huge courtyard that was not really a courtyard but in itself a small city. Isaacson's eye was captured, as it always was, by the Cathedral of the Virgin of Smolensk with its bulbous onion domes. Beyond it was the Church of the Intercession and beyond that, the cemetery where Gogol was buried.

Narrow paths had been swept through the snow, cutting dark lanes across the white of the courtyard. Isaacson made for a long brick building, the Lopukhin Palace, where Peter the Great had stashed wife number one after he'd gotten tired of her.

As Isaacson approached a kiosk guarding the entrance of

the palace, the kiosk door cracked open. An old man's face appeared in the opening, and Isaacson took in the hearty smell of *schchi*—cabbage soup—and tobacco.

"I am here to meet Ivan Baklinov," he said, using the name Kulikov had given him.

The old man stared suspiciously at Isaacson for a moment, then closed the door. Bumping, stirring sounds came from inside the kiosk, then the old man came out, wrapped in a bulky blue quilted nylon overcoat, a yellow and green knit balaclava over his head, the earflaps tied securely under his chin. In his ungloved hand, he carried a large ring of keys. He unlocked the huge oaken door and entered without a backward look to see if Isaacson was following.

Inside, the old man led him up a spiral staircase to the second floor, down a corridor paved with alternating black-and-white tile squares, coming to a stop before a doorway of two high double doors. From inside, Isaacson heard fragments of music, but the sounds were too faint to identify.

The old man spoke his first and last words. "He is here." He eyed Isaacson to make certain the American understood, then turned and shuffled off.

Isaacson twisted the ornamental bronze handle and swung the doors open. The music took form, the rich throaty tones of a cello, warm and vibrant like a glass of Bordeaux.

The room itself was a study in light. Devoid of furniture, the room nonetheless seemed filled with light and the music. Two crystal chandeliers blazed against pale yellow walls and waxed parquet floor. Splintered reflections came from the latticework of small panes set into three French doors dividing the far wall. To Isaacson's right, a fire in a large fireplace framed by Delft-blue tiles, and in front of it, Yegor Kulikov, seated on a fragile Louis XIV chair, a cello clasped between his knees, playing and looking into the depths of the fire. A single chair sat empty beside Kulikov.

"Mozart?" Isaacson took the empty chair. It was a good guess, he told himself. An honest one. Not the kind you just throw out hoping you hit it by sheer luck.

Kulikov, firelight glistening in his dark eyes and glowing on his bald head, nodded, still playing, still absorbed in the cello and the music. He finished the bar, and sat motionlessly for a moment, bow in hand, watching the fire with his head cocked as if listening to the music fade within himself.

"The String Quintet in G minor. Vienna, 1787," Kulikov finally answered, his eyes now taking in Isaacson. He waved the bow around the room. "I come here for lessons and practice," he explained. "A quiet place . . . a place to refurbish the soul." Cradling the cello in the crook of his arm, he loosened the bow and set it in its case to the side of his chair.

Then, grasping the cello by its throat, Kulikov held the instrument out and away from himself and smiled reflectively. "The cello is wonderful—like sex." His eyes fastened mischievously on Isaacson. "The position is ludicrous, but the effects are magical." He put the cello in its case, then sat back in his chair, crossing one leg over the other, all business. "And now?"

"We need your help."

Kulikov gave Isaacson a sly horse-trader's look. "Help that requires you come to a convent in Moscow on a Sunday evening?" His lips pursed in a smile of anticipation.

"Headquarters wants it quickly."

The Russian laughed cynically. "All headquarters want everything quickly. That is why they are headquarters."

Isaacson didn't laugh with Kulikov. "And quietly," he added, a somber note in his voice.

Kulikov sobered. He dropped his chin and regarded Isaacson through hooded eyes. "You and I, Carl, we cannot make blind promises."

"I'm not asking for promises, Yegor. I'm just telling you how Langley wants it."

"What?"

"A man named Naji Hassan tried to kill one of our people."

"The shooting in Langley?"

Isaacson shook his head. "This one didn't get in the papers."

"Go on."

"Hassan ended up dead. He has dental work our people say was done here—here when—"

179

"I understand. You want to know what we know."

Isaacson nodded and pulled a thick legal-size manila envelope from an inside overcoat pocket. Holding it with his right hand, he tapped it for a moment in the palm of his left hand, then gave it over to Kulikov.

"The details. Dental records. Fingerprint card. DNA profile."

Kulikov held the envelope gingerly out in front of himself, bobbing it up and down slightly as if to judge the weight of it. "This man . . . the name probably wasn't Hassan in our . . . in the old files."

"I understand."

"We can't do a computer search. We'd have to search manually all the fingerprint and dental records. It could take some time."

Isaacson remembered the conversation that morning with Alberich and he let the worry show on his face and hoped Kulikov caught it. "Make it front burner, Yegor. I don't think we have a lot of time."

15

High marks for Teutonic efficiency." Zachary came back from the apartment door carrying a large cardboard mailing tube. Sims sat at the dining room table, going over his photographs of the warehouse he'd taken the day before.

Sims opened the tube. First out was a letter from Quandt. "One alarm contractor covers the docks," Sims said, passing the letter to Zachary.

Next, Sims pulled out a tight roll of blueprints which he laid on the table and anchored down with a pair of bronze candlesticks. Off to one side of the table Zachary had set up, a large white drawing board stood on an easel with a plastic cup full of various colored felt-tip pens.

"We've got a blank check"—Sims motioned to the blueprints—"we better start filling in the amounts."

The discussion that followed was a case study in espionage tradecraft. Sims and Zachary had been taught that surreptitious entry is, in its simplest form, an attack on a building. The defender, the building's occupant, combats the attack with three weapons: denial, detection, and deterrence.

At the Farm, experienced practitioners teach that denial depends on physical measures such as high fences, thick doors, guards, locks, safes—all intended to stop the amateur and delay the professional. Detection covers alarm systems and other warning devices, and deterrence is a psychological factor incorporating both denial and detection: both, if formidable, may erode the attacker's confidence and make him or her prone to mistakes.

The discussion rose and fell. Both men would try to talk at once, only to be followed by long periods of silence. Finally, two hours later, a silence fell that seemed to be final, and Sims got up, and walked to the picture window, and stretched.

Across the rooftops, he gazed at the Brandenburg Gate, its twin pillars glowing from hidden floodlights. A steady rain was falling and it seemed that the gate was the only thing that kept the heavy clouds from falling to earth. No city in the world, he thought, could look as gray as Berlin.

Sims walked back to the table where Zachary was measuring distances on the blueprint. Sims put his sheaf of notes and sketches in order, picked out a felt-tip marker, and jotted TIME? and SECURITY? on the white drawing board.

Sims underscored TIME with the marker, the red line like a cut opening up in the white board. "We don't have much."

"How much?" Zachary asked.

Sims shrugged. "You want a wild-assed guess? We got to be in and out of that warehouse in forty-eight hours."

He watched Zachary weigh that. The bald man didn't like it. The more time you had, the better the odds. A week, two weeks—you could find at least a half dozen weak points. You could take any number of unobtrusive set-up actions that would make the actual entry a piece of cake. Forty-eight hours was a higher risk: wham-bam thank you ma'am.

"Okay," Zachary said, frowning under his thick black mustache. "Forty-eight hours."

Next on the board was SECURITY. It had two indented subheadings: ACTIVE and PASSIVE.

"Under active we need to know who's in the warehouse, where they are, when they're there."

"This isn't like a residential or business area," Zachary said, talking out loud to himself, looking at the sketch of the warehouse area layout. "No way to rent a room across the street. And we damn sure can't park a van outside the warehouse. . . ." He trailed off and was quiet for long moments, studying the sketch. "Okay." He nodded, hesitantly at first, then with more confidence. "We can do something."

Under PASSIVE, Sims jotted "alarm system."

"We know the possibilities of the alarm system." Zachary put in. "The company that Quandt gave us is a major German security firm. We got specs on all their products. But that just gives us individual components and general setups. Doesn't give us the configuration inside that particular warehouse." Zachary pointed to the blueprints lying on the table. "They might combine noise pickups with heat detectors, maybe even motion sensors. Or they might have nothing but intrusion tape on the windows and mag switches on the doors. I sort of think they'll go for something in between. Moderate."

"Why?"

"Hasn't been a high-crime area," Zachary answered. "Isn't human nature to drop a lot on alarm systems unless they're needed. You always see a lotta shit being sold after break-ins. Closing barn doors—that kind of thing."

There was a long silence that came from both men having said everything that could be said. Sims broke it. "You get me in—and out?"

Zachary rubbed the back of his neck as he studied the blueprints, the drawing board, and then Sims. "Forty-eight hours," he muttered. He thought for a while longer. Finally he nodded. "Yeah."

"You don't like it." Sims said, reading Zachary's body language.

Zachary rubbed his neck some more. "Shit, Sims, I don't like *any* of it."

Three hours later, two trucks pulled out of the walled compound that housed the motor pool of the American army's Berlin Brigade. The first was a heavy commercial transport truck, a canvas tarpaulin lashed securely over its cargo bed. The second was a large yellow repair van with the hunting horn logo of Telekom, the German government telephone service. Despite Berlin's rush-hour traffic, the vehicles stayed in sight of each other, both making their way west on Heerstrasse through Charlottenburg and Spandau, and finally out onto the autobahn to Hamburg.

By eight that evening, the trucks were fifty kilometers east of Hamburg. At the autobahn rest stop near Gudow, where the former East German government had maintained a border crossing station, the trucks pulled off the road. Zachary, at the wheel of the Telekom van, parked facing the woods. Behind him, Sims slowed the cargo truck to a stop. It took them less than five minutes to exchange the van's Berlin license plates for those of Bremerhaven.

Bremerhaven's commercial waterfront's expansion created two harbors. With relentless Teutonic logic, the city fathers came up with the inevitable names of *Neuer Hafen* or Newer Harbor, which is just north of the original port, and *Alter Hafen,* or Older Harbor.

Dockyards rely on perpetual maintenance and repair, and in the predawn darkness the following morning, dockworkers clocking in early paid no attention to the flares and reflectorized warning signs at the entry of *Neuer Hafen,* nor to the two men in parkas, hard hats, and climbers working at the top of a utility pole, leaning backward, braced against their wide safety belts.

"Shit, Sims," Zachary cursed softly, ducking his head to see into the junction box. "If you're going to hold the fucking light, then *hold* the fucking light."

Sims said nothing, but, pushing against his belt, angled himself closer to Zachary and aimed the light deeper into the j-box.

In the circle of light, Zachary carefully weeded through a tangle of thin multicolored strands from a cable as thick as a man's wrist. Finally, he had four wires between thumb and forefinger. He reached into a pouch and came up with a dull black device the size of a book of matches. Working smoothly, he laid the selected wire strands in a groove in the box, then taped the groove closed. He rearranged the wires so the thickness of the cable hid the induction tap, then punched in a series of numbers on the keypad of what appeared to be a folding cellular phone. He studied the pattern of lights that flickered in the phone's window, then grunted with satisfaction.

"We're in," he whispered to Sims as he started closing up the j-box. "Now you're gonna buy breakfast."

Several miles north of the docks, Sims and Zachary pulled the Telekom van into a commercial garage that had been rented by a phone call from the American Embassy's logistics section with a week's advance rent paid to an eager and uninquisitive broker. No heat, the tin roof leaked, and the place smelled of urine, grease, and rat droppings, but it had electricity—for an extra thousand marks—and it was large enough for the Telekom van and the cargo truck.

By seven, the tailgate of the cargo truck had been let down and the tarp thrown back, revealing a large boxlike shelter built into the truck bed. A thick black power cable snaked its way from an electric main across the dirty concrete floor and up a metal ladder leading to the shelter entry door. Inside the shelter, halogen lamps cast a warm sun-yellow light down from the ceiling and the heat generated by bays of electronics along one wall took the edge off the chill.

Sims and Zachary sat at a small fold-down worktable drinking coffee from a thermos and watching a control panel ablaze with green, yellow, and red lights. A digital clock above the panel ticked off the seconds. It was just after eight, and each fifteen seconds, lights on the control panel would ripple and a loudspeaker carried the sound of a telephone ringing.

The waiting seemed to stretch into forever, and by nine o'clock, the intermittent ringing sound cut through Sims like a dentist's drill. The small shelter was closing in, the air thickening with the strain of sustaining two humans and the electronics. Sims thought he was imagining his own discomfort until he saw a bead of perspiration run down the side of Zachary's face. He was about to step out of the van—even the ammoniacal odor of the garage would have been an improvement—when the ringing sound was interrupted by a rapid-fire series of clicks and a woman's high-pitched voice. The woman was annoyed.

* * *

"Hello! Hello!" Frau Geissler spoke into the telephone, at the same time impatiently tapping the instrument's cradle. The telephone had been ringing strangely when she'd opened the small office at her usual hour of nine. Karsten-Export's only full-time employee, Frau Geissler, sixty-seven, a widow and a government pensioner, was office manager and bookkeeper.

Frau Geissler jiggled the phone cradle. There *were* certain standards. The office telephone *must* work. It was not an office without a telephone. The jiggling worked. The static disappeared and the dial tone came on. Finding the Telekom repair number at the front of the phone book, she dialed.

"There she is." With a predatory smile, Zachary flicked a switch on the control panel and spoke into his lip mike. *"Ausbesserndienst,"* he announced in clipped German.

An hour later, Zachary pulled the Telekom van in to a stop at the Karstens-Export warehouse gate. Sims got out and walked to a call box by the gate. The world seemed freshly minted. The wind off the North Sea had scattered the heavy cloud layers, revealing patches of pale blue sky, and the winter sun, low and bright on the horizon, turned the wet pavement into a sheet of silver. The air was damp and clean with the salt, and overhead, the circling gulls seemed to be calling out in revelry at the freedom of flight.

Sims paused for a moment, watching the gulls, then opened the call box at the gate. He spoke briefly to a male voice, and before he got back into the van, a watchman in a dark blue uniform made his way from the warehouse to open the gate.

The watchman waved them through the gate, motioning to a small parking area marked off by yellow stripes. One of the slots was filled by an old Volkswagen beetle, another by a small commercial BMW van. By the time Sims and Zachary had pulled two large tool kits from the back of the van, the watchman had closed the gate and joined them.

Sims recognized the shoulder patch on the uniform as the logo of a commercial security outfit. The same logo was on the BMW van. The man's scuffed black leather equipment belt held a large three-cell flashlight, a watchman's clock key, and a 9mm Browning automatic with an extra ammunition clip. The uniform was sharply pressed and the heavy boots well shined. The watchman disappeared into the warehouse through a small personnel door set in beside the large sliding freight doors.

Sims and Zachary followed. As Zachary had shown him back in the garage, Sims tripped the small lever hidden in the handle of his toolbox and was answered with a short confirming vibration.

The freight door was open at the opposite end of the warehouse, the large rectangle of gray morning light framing a long aisle lined with towering stacks of wooden crates. Down near the door, a worker on an electric forklift loaded a massive steel shipping container, the whining of the straining forklift accompanied by the crashes of heavy loads lifting, shifting, dropping. Backing out of the container, the lift operator spun the stubby vehicle around and scooted up the aisle to slip steel forks under his next load, a piano-size wooden crate. A flatbed truck had been backed into the building, and Sims noted that it had already been loaded with two containers. From here to the docks, Sims thought, and from there to . . . where?

Sims visualized the interior as a huge *I*. The wide central aisle with smaller corridors at either end of the warehouse making up the top and bottom crossbars of the *I*. Sims oriented himself on the mental diagram, imagining a "you are here" sign with an arrow pointing to the bottom of the *I*.

The watchman led Sims and Zachary straight ahead, down the short corridor to the office. The door opened into the center of the office. To the left, a large, freestanding vault. Both its doors were open. Against the right wall, by the window, Frau Geissler sat at a large dark oak rolltop desk. She looked up and dismissed the watchman. She was a woman who had once been very pretty and, Sims thought, was still good looking. Her thick iron-gray hair was cut several inches above the shoulders, framing a delicate face dominated by high cheekbones and blue eyes. She wore a burgundy cardigan against the chill in the small office.

An accounts ledger lay open on the desk before her. She took in Zachary, then Sims, then closed the ledger. Sims saw more of the ledgers neatly stacked in the vault.

"The telephone." She got up and moved away from her chair, at the same time, pointing to the instrument on the side of her desk. The phone obviously connected with other lines. Sims noted a row of clear plastic push buttons below the keypad. One of the buttons glowed, the others were dark.

Sims set his tool kit on the floor and knelt to open it. Zachary moved to the desk, picked up the telephone and listened. Frau Geissler, now standing by the window, watched Zachary for a moment, then, seemingly losing interest, turned to the window and gazed out to the sky and the gulls.

"Static," Zachary announced. "There are other telephones connected to this line?"

"Yes." The woman nodded, not taking her eyes off the gulls.

Zachary began taking the phone apart, using a screwdriver from the leather tool pouch on his belt. Frau Geissler glanced over at him, then back to the window.

Having opened his tool kit, Sims found a circuit tester. He stood, the instrument in hand. As he did so, he shifted slightly so that he faced squarely into the open vault. He squeezed his right arm against his side, tripping the automatic shutter on the belly camera held by the harness beneath his coveralls. The camera was totally silent; only a slight, tingling vibration told Sims the camera was working. Sims released the arm pressure, moved a fraction of an inch left, then right, each time squeezing again. Zachary was still disassembling the telephone. Frau Geissler was still staring out the window, her mind apparently a thousand miles away.

Sims passed the circuit tester to Zachary who poked around in the telephone innards, then began reassembling the instrument.

"This is working properly," he told Frau Geissler, pointing with his screwdriver to the telephone. "We must trace the circuit."

"Do whatever," she said, sighing in helpless resignation, obviously impatient to have this all over and to get back to her routine.

"Do you know where the terminal box is?" Zachary asked.

Frau Geissler looked as if Zachary had asked her about the back of the moon. "No," she said, exasperated, "I do not know where such a thing is."

Zachary handed the circuit tester to Sims, who closed up the toolbox. "We'll have to look," Zachary told Frau Geissler.

"*Ob*viously," she said. She pressed a button by her desk. Sims had just picked up the toolbox when the watchman knocked, then opened the office door.

"These men"—Frau Geissler waved a hand at Sims and Zachary—"must find a . . . a thing related to the telephone," she told the watchman. "They must look through the warehouse."

The man nodded and jerked his head toward the main part of the warehouse. As he shut the office door, Sims saw that Frau Geissler was already back at the desk, deep into the ledger book.

Zachary led the search for the terminal box. He and Sims, the watchman trailing, walked out to the start of the central aisle. Zachary motioned to the left. "You take that side," he told Sims, and started off to the right aisle.

"No!"

Zachary stopped and turned to the watchman. "No? No what?"

The watchman jerked his chin up at Zachary. "Together."

"Together?"

The man made a show of putting his hands on his hips, the fingers of his right hand tapping the grip of his pistol. "You must work together. I watch."

Zachary shrugged. "Come on." He motioned to Sims.

Standing in the wide aisle, Zachary aimed his flashlight down the narrow gaps between the stacked crates. Sims noticed that the crates had been stored according to size; here the smaller crates, down the aisle toward the open freight door, the larger ones. The gaps were barely wide enough to permit a man to crab his way between them. Zachary started down one gap.

"Where're you going?"

Zachary turned to the watchman. "To look for the terminal box. You don't expect," he said, laying on the sarcasm, "they'd put one right out here in the middle of the floor for us to stumble over. They put them on the walls. It could be behind any of these containers." Zachary waved down the long aisle.

The man considered this for some seconds, then: "Very well. You go. I will watch you."

Zachary sneered. "Very good, watchman, you watch." And Zachary worked his way down the first narrow passageway while the watchman stood in the aisle and played his flashlight on Zachary. Sims put his toolbox down and sat on it, watching, a bored look on his face.

Zachary wriggled down to where the containers met the interior wall, played the flashlight right, then left, then made his way back out to the aisle.

Sims glanced at his watch. It had taken just over a minute and a half. Not long, but it seemed longer, and he noticed that the watchman was restlessly shifting his feet.

Zachary slowed down on the next gap and the next. When he came back out after the fourth inspection, the watchman sighed heavily.

"What?" Zachary asked.

"I said I don't have all day."

Zachary shrugged. "Well, we have a job."

"Can't you go faster?"

"I'm going as fast as I can." Zachary said, beating the dirt off his coveralls with the back of his hand. "You want to try it?"

The watchman eyed Zachary with distaste. "No. But can't you—"

"I could," Zachary interrupted, "if you'd let him"—he pointed to Sims—"help me."

"Two of you go down one of those . . ." The man flashed his light down the gap Zachary had just come out of.

"No," Zachary said patiently. "He checks one, I check another."

"But," the man said dully, "I've got to watch you both."

"Stand farther back," Sims said, trying to sound helpful. "Then you can see down both sides." He saw the watchman take this in. The man studied the gaps between the containers, then the long aisle and Sims saw him waver. "We'll be done twice as fast," Sims added.

"Go ahead." The man made it an order, as if trying to climb back on top of the situation.

Zachary found the terminal box five minutes later. Prying it open, he fiddled around for several minutes, then closed the box and came out into the aisle where Sims stood with the watchman. "Trouble's not in here," Zachary announced. "It's got to be outside."

Frau Geissler got up for a cup of tea. Passing the window, she saw the Telekom van. It was outside the gate, parked in the street. The unpleasant little man and his black helper were high on a pole, apparently checking connections with the main cable. She picked up the telephone, heard a burst of answering static, then irritatedly hung up. On the way back from the kettle, she paused again at the window to watch and sip her tea.

As she stood there, the telephone rang.

"Hello?"

"This is Telekom repair," the voice came. It had to be the unpleasant little man with the mustache and bald head. "We are outside on the—"

"Yes," Frau Geissler said shortly. "I can see you."

"We have found the problem. Your telephone is—"

"It sounds satisfactory. There are charges? The bill—"

"There is no charge," the voice came back, and then there was a click and the line went dead, and then the dial tone came on, clear and steady.

Frau Geissler finished her tea, standing at the window, watching the men close up their work on the cable, covering it with a large black protective cylinder. She stood there for a moment longer then got back to the books. The books, she thought, there will always be the books.

16

An hour and a half after Sims and Zachary left the docks, Zachary flicked a switch and a large TV monitor in the cargo truck shelter bloomed to life.

"Great picture," Sims muttered, looking over Zachary's shoulder.

The field of view, angling down from a height, took in the entire front of the warehouse and much of its roof and the chain link fence. Unwittingly, Frau Geissler had watched Sims and Zachary set the camera up. They had done it in plain sight as they worked on the utility pole outside the warehouse. The camera was hidden inside the round rubber splice boot they had attached to the telephone cable. At dark, Zachary could switch to an infrared or low-light level television mode.

Sims saw that the BMW security van and the Volkswagen beetle that he assumed belonged to Frau Geissler were still in their parking slots. Zachary, satisfied, got up and crossed the shelter to a small workbench. Sims slid into Zachary's seat and moved a joystick controller forward. The resulting camera close-up gave him the numbers on the VW license plate.

Zachary had moved to the other workbench where he'd taped to the wall an enlargement of a photo Sims had taken of the front of the safe. Micrometer in hand, he measured dimensions of the combination dial, jotted them down, then measured the internal dimensions of a metal hemisphere about the size of a large half-grapefruit.

Sims, meanwhile, unlatched the toolbox he'd carried through the warehouse. Removing the tools, he scraped away a soldered joint and lifted out the false bottom of the box. From a recorder, Sims thumbed a latch, removed a large tape cassette and held it up to the light. The take-up reel was almost full.

"I damn near used it all," he told Zachary.

Zachary put the metal hemisphere down. "Let's see what you captured." He slipped the cassette into a player hooked to a computer and hit rewind. While the tape picked up speed, he flicked on the computer monitor and power supply.

The tape player finished rewinding and Zachary hit forward. The reels moved slowly, and the tape began feeding billions of electrons into the computer. A sawtoothed horizontal line flickered across the monitor. Zachary pressed a key and a tongue of paper rolled out of a printer with a copy of the screen. Zachary brought up other screens, repeating the procedure.

Ten minutes later, Sims sat at the workbench, now covered with computer printouts, as Zachary explained.

"These are printouts of all the electronic frequencies your toolbox picked up inside the warehouse." Zachary scanned the printouts, his lips pursed in thought. "I have to work out the details—"

"The outlines," Sims prompted.

Zachary looked at the printouts again as if making sure he wasn't missing something big. On a blank writing pad, he sketched a rectangle.

"This's the warehouse." He erased portions of the rectangle, leaving three openings. "The two freight doors and one personnel door," he said, making tick marks in the openings.

Just inside the rectangle, Zachary drew another rectangle, this one a continuous unbroken line. "This"—he traced the inner rectangle—"is what we see here." He motioned to the other printouts.

Sims bent closer to the diagram. "And that's—"

"A motion alarm system." Zachary touched the pencil to the four interior corners of the warehouse. "They have ultrasound transmitters here, here, here, and here. The transmitters send beams along the interior of the warehouse and—"

The beams, Sims noted, overlapped. There was no opening to exploit. "Anything that breaks into that field . . ." Sims finished, trailing off, eyes widening at the implications. Spiedel hadn't skimped on the alarm system.

"There's more," Zachary said. He drew three *X*s on the sketch: one by each of the two freight doors, another by the smaller personnel door. "Time-clock punch stations," he explained. "The watchman has to activate them every hour with a special key. If he doesn't do that, a signal goes to the main security office and they send a reaction patrol." He added another *X*, this one inside Frau Geissler's office.

Sims pulled his chair up closer to the workbench and reached for Zachary's sketch of the warehouse, its alarm systems and the watchman's patrol path.

Two hours later, just past four on the afternoon of Tuesday, February 9, the entry plan had been roughed out. After entry, Sims would go for the crates first, then, just after the watchman had done his check-in, go for Frau Geissler's office and the safe. Time of entry: just after the watchman's one A.M. rounds, Thursday morning, February 11. Agency shrinks, in one of their many arcane studies of human behavior, had found that the level of alertness took a dive in the hours shortly after midnight. Then, subjects were most weary, and morning still seemed impossibly far away.

He and Zachary would have a day and a half of surveillance to work out the routine of the warehouse. More time would be better, Sims thought, but forever still wouldn't be enough.

The following morning, two thousand miles southeast of Bremerhaven, a lone airplane circled lazily above the Sea of Galilee. With its slab-sided body, fixed tricycle landing gear, and pusher propeller at the end of a boom-tail, the plane could have been taken for a hobby builder's model. But the graceful, tapered wings spanned fifty-nine feet, and the two-stage turbocharged engine swung a ten-foot propeller.

The pilotless plane had taken off four hours before. From an underground bunker ten miles southwest of Nazareth, Israeli controllers had flown the plane in a racetrack flight pattern, each ten-mile lap gaining altitude. Now the plane was in its final lap, approaching sixty-five thousand feet. Carrying over four hundred pounds of high resolution cameras, the plane could fly at this altitude for several days, but today's mission would have it back at its home field before dark.

At 11:18 A.M. Jerusalem time, the cameras passed a final check and two minutes later, the plane's on-board computer took over. A navigation fix from a Global Positioning Satellite gave the computer the spy aircraft's position within an accuracy of three feet. From the GPS data, the computer calculated a course north-northeast, into Lebanon's Bekáa Valley, and over the city of Baalbek, ninety-five miles away. At Baalbek, the plane would take another GPS reading, swing northwest to circle the village of Boudaï, then return to Israel, all the while its cameras recording every detail of the terrain below.

17

At 12:15 on Thursday morning, February 11, Sims wheeled the ponderous cargo truck through the gates of the Columbuskaje container terminal. The truck now bore Swedish license plates along with a black on yellow tag with the initials T.I.R.—*transports internationaux routier*—which identified it as a licensed trans-European carrier. A light rain had fallen and large puddles reflected the blue-white light of the terminal's mercury-vapor lamps. Sims continued down a wide road off which jutted numbered streets. The streets were laid out with warehouses along one side, parking lots and loading dock along the other. At the third corner, Sims turned left. Just past the Karstens-Export warehouse, he slowed to a walking pace, and pulled in behind another T.I.R. truck with Spanish license plates.

Sims switched the engine off. For a moment, he and Zachary sat quietly. The truck, cooling, made creaking and popping sounds.

"How do you feel?" Zachary asked, his voice hushed and solemn.

Sims leaned forward, resting his elbows on the steering wheel. He was dressed in black: snugly fitting black trousers, black wool jacket over a thick black turtleneck sweater. On his feet, soft rubber soled canvas boots. "Scared."

"Yeah," Zachary said, apologetically, "stupid fucking question."

"Let's go," Sims said, opening his door.

Outside, the two men slipped beneath the cargo bed of the truck. Zachary worked a latch, opening a trapdoor, and pulled himself up into the shelter. Inside, the shelter was dimly lit by the glow of red night vision lamps.

Zachary slid into his chair at the main console and started the fuel cells that powered the shelter's electronics. As the lights on the console blinked green, Sims opened a locker and began shouldering into what looked like a parachute harness without the backpack: sturdy black nylon web leg and shoulder straps snapped together in a matte black metal quick release plate in the center of his chest. Sims worked to adjust the harness for fit, shrugging, bending, tugging at straps and buckles, shrugging and bending, then tugging some more.

Finally Sims stood still. "Okay," he said to Zachary, while raising his right arm.

There was the ripping sound of Velcro as Zachary peeled open a small nylon pouch on Sims's harness, slipped in a black metal box slightly larger than a cigarette pack, then pressed the flap closed.

Sims lowered his arm, swinging it experimentally several times to make certain the box wouldn't get in the way. Satisfied, he reached into the locker and came out with a knit ski cap and pulled it over his head. Zachary, moving around behind Sims, reached under the back of the cap and came out with a coiled length of wire with a shiny silver connector. He stretched the wire out and snapped the connector into the black box.

Sims felt for the small buttonlike receivers inside the cap, found them, and worked them into contact with the mastoid bones just behind his ears. Though not as comfortable as earphones, they wouldn't interfere with his hearing. At the console, Zachary did a countdown into a microphone. Sims heard the countdown and responded by squeezing the black box under his right arm. A series of Morse dits and dahs came over the loudspeaker spelling out QSL— "acknowledge receipt."

"Now the no-see-um suit," Zachary said, handing Sims a pair of coveralls patterned with blotches of black and shades of gray. Stepping into the coveralls and zipping them up, Sims bent, and worked at tie tapes on one leg, then the other, wrapping them securely around his thighs and calves and knotting them so no material flapped loose to snag or pull. Then the shoulder holster and last, a pair of black gloves.

Finished, Sims straightened up to see Zachary watching him intently. It was the look of expectancy that he'd seen in football, when in the huddles men had looked at him and when, no matter how much noise was coming from the crowd, it always seemed frozen and quiet for a split second that was an eternity.

"Break a leg," Zachary said, shattering the quiet. His face was solemn and deeply shadowed by the red night vision lighting that turned the shelter into a two-dimensional study in scarlet and black.

Zachary knelt, hooked a finger through the pull ring, and opened the trapdoor.

Sims eased through the opening in the floor. Then, standing on the street below, he turned and looked back up into the shelter as Zachary lowered a rucksack made of the same black and gray as the coveralls. Sims gave a small wave and was gone.

For several minutes, Sims crouched beneath the truck, scanning the warehouses across the street and letting his eyes get used to the dark. He heard the faraway sound of a crane, laboring somewhere down by the docks. Otherwise, the night was still. The roadway between him and the warehouses was dark, and the only light came from the glow of Bremerhaven reflecting off the low clouds to the east.

Out from under the truck, Sims swung the rucksack onto his back, jerking the chest and belly straps tight. That done, he stood quietly, listening and watching for any sign of life on the dark landscape before him. The crane was still working away, but otherwise, nothing. He squatted slightly several times, bouncing on the balls of his feet to loosen his calf muscles, then crossed the road in a smooth, flowing motion that was to ordinary running as silk was to sandpaper. Keeping his body low on flexed knees, he glided across the ground, maintaining his weight and balance on the grounded leg while moving the other leg into position to bear the weight. In seconds, he had soundlessly disappeared into the deep shadows surrounding the warehouse closest to the Karstens-Export fence.

As planned, he moved toward a loading dock that jutted out from the warehouse. Diving under the dock, he rolled twice and came to rest belly down. For seconds, he lay frozen on the damp cobblestones, straining to detect any sign that he'd been seen. Finally, he sat up and shifted the rucksack off his back and opened the rubberized fasteners. He had packed the rucksack in sequence: what he needed first would be on top, last, on the bottom. And, he'd prayed, everything else he'd need would be somewhere in between.

He took out the rope ladder. Twenty feet long, with sturdy plastic stirrups each thirty inches, one end of the rope ended in a three-pronged grappling hook of titanium alloy covered with a thick padding of molded rubber.

Duck-walking under the low beams, he carefully straightened out the rope ladder on the cobblestones, then, as carefully, coiled it in two-foot loops. Again, Sims crouched motionlessly, searching along the fence some twenty yards away, mentally rehearsing every move, feeling his heartbeat swelling into his throat.

With the coiled rope ladder in his right hand, Sims flowed into the same soundless motion that had carried him across the road. Coming to the fence, he dropped to the ground, breaking his fall with a forward pushing action of his forearms and hands. And there was no sound except the crane down on the docks and a rising of the wind.

Rising to a crouch, Sims stepped back a pace or two from the base of the fence while transferring the rope ladder coils to his left hand. Eyeing the top of the fence, he took the grappling hook in his right hand, and let out several feet of slack. He began with slow, pendulumlike motion swings of the hook, getting the feel of it, calculating its trajectory. The swings grew larger. Sims released the hook as it approached the top of its arc. The hook soared up and out, and the rope ladder whispered urgently as it played out across the palm of Sims's glove. Over the top of the fence, the hook jerked to a stop as the line snapped taut. Then, dropping, the hook fell on the other side of the fence. Sims gently tugged and a barb of the hook secured itself in the chain link fencing. He pulled again, this time putting his weight behind it. The hook held.

He paused a moment to scan the area—his stage, his stadium, his world: the cargo truck across the road to his right, behind him, the loading dock where he'd had a few minutes' shelter, and through the fence before him, the Karstens-Export warehouse.

Sims climbed easily, keeping his body close to the rope ladder. In seconds, he rolled over the top of the fence and dropped down on the far side, landing soundlessly on the balls of his feet. He stood, then tugged at the rope ladder that snaked up and over the barbed wire overhang to fall in a tangled heap on his side of the fence. Coiling the rope ladder, he looped it over his left shoulder and started for the warehouse.

A dozen or so empty shipping containers, like so many eight-foot high dominoes, lay scattered about the open space between the fence and the warehouse. Slipping between the containers, Sims paused frequently, straining to detect any sign that another person might be in the yard. Nothing.

He hesitated at the last container, then sprinted across the ten yards of open space to the warehouse. Back against the warehouse wall, Sims looked down the long length of the building. Eighty yards of brick, uninterrupted by doors or windows. Two stories above him, the roof.

Sims stepped back several yards and scanned the distance to the roof. The architectural drawings were one thing; this was another. Standing out here in the night, the building seemed more impregnable and menacing than when he'd studied it in the safety of the van.

Eyes still on the roof, he shrugged the rope ladder off his shoulder, catching it in his left hand. Taking a few more steps back, Sims fed the grappling hook and several feet of slack to his right hand. Now facing the wall again, and focusing intently on the roof, he swung the grappling hook, first back and forth, then in complete windmilling circles, the hook making a low whirring sound in the night air.

On the fourth revolution, Sims released the hook just as it began its upward climb. The hook sailed skyward, hung for a moment in midair, and began a graceful fall, disappearing out of sight over the edge of the roof.

He held his breath, listening for the sound of the hook, but heard nothing. Even so, he flattened himself against the warehouse wall, waiting for sirens, lights, or the creak of a door. He counted to thirty, then thirty again. Nothing. He pulled gently. Several feet of the rope ladder slid noiselessly off the edge of the roof before he felt a firm resistance.

Moments later, Sims stood on the flat roof, looking down on the dim outlines of the yard with its empty containers, the fence, and across the road, the cargo truck. He pulled up the rope ladder, coiling it again over his left shoulder. That done, he squeezed the Morse transmitter under his right arm, signaling that he'd made the roof. Zachary's acknowledgment, a terse "okay," was immediate. The voice, traveling through the bones behind his ears sounded as if it wasn't coming from a radio at all, but from someplace in the middle of Sims's head.

Gravel covered the roof. Sims planted each foot carefully, coming down on the back edge of the heel, rolling across the sole, and off the toes, compacting the small stones in a downward motion, avoiding the scraping sound of stones moving sideways against themselves.

Four skylights punctuated the flat expanse of roof, two and two—a pair on each side of the building's long axis. Sims passed the first one by. The second skylight was closer to the office and farther away from the watchman's corner.

Resembling a miniature greenhouse, the skylight was composed of a grid of metal frames holding panes, each pane approximately one foot square. Kneeling, Sims swung the rope ladder from his shoulder, then wriggled out of the rucksack, placing both beside the skylight. Then he pulled off a glove and ran his fingertips along the soot-gritted panes and frame until he found the joint of the section of the skylight that could be lifted for ventilation. He traced the joint: three panes by three panes—a reassuring match of the architect's plans.

A side pocket in the rucksack surrendered a springy coil of insulated wire, one end connected to a slightly concave metal disk the size of a quarter, the other to an electrical connector. Partially unzipping his coveralls, Sims plugged one end of the wire to the radio beneath his right arm. Stretching out the wire, he placed the metal disk flat on a pane of the skylight, then reached back into his coveralls and flicked a switch on the radio, turning the device into an electronic stethoscope. The sound of footsteps came through his earphones. He glanced at his watch. The luminous dial on his watch said one o'clock; the watchman making his rounds, punching in at the time-clock stations.

Sims listened, mentally tracing the watchman through the warehouse. It was 1:08 A.M. when he heard the footsteps fade, then stop. He waited no more than a few seconds before attacking the skylight.

In a rotating, pressing motion, Sims flattened a six-inch gum rubber suction cup to the pane of glass nearest the skylight's interior latch. Then, holding the suction cup's ring handle in his left hand, he bent forward and worked a pencil-size ultrasonic probe along the pane edge, loosening the glazier's putty sealing the pane into the metal frame.

Another listen through the stethoscope: dead silence, then, so faintly as to be almost lost, the strains of music. A little night music, Sims thought—the watchman was listening to a radio.

With a small blade of his pocketknife, he lifted the square of glaziers' putty out intact and set it aside. Then, slowly, taking care not to scrape its edges, Sims lifted out the glass pane.

Air from the warehouse rose through the opening, bringing with it a vaguely sour odor. Sims leaned headfirst down through the opening. Far off toward the watchman's corner, he saw the dim glow of a light. Angling so he could look back against the interior of the skylight, Sims took a penlight from a sleeve pocket. A needlelike beam shot a tiny spot of red light against the skylight frame. He worked the beam around the entire frame; no intrusion tape, no magnetic sensors, no wiring. Shifting the penlight so he held it in his teeth, he reached into his sleeve pocket again, this time coming out with a small aerosol dispenser. He carefully directed two puffs of watchmaker's oil over the panel's hinges, then stowed the aerosol and penlight.

The panel opened soundlessly, and Sims propped it open with a strut that'd been welded to the skylight frame for that purpose. The rucksack again on his back, he gathered the rope ladder, and, securing one of the hooks over the skylight ledge, lowered the ladder into the darkness. He tested the hook to be certain it would hold and wouldn't scrape along the skylight's steel frame, then stood and sent the Morse signal that told Zachary he was going in. His watch said 1:12.

He's running late, Zachary fretted to himself. He sat at the workbench staring at the architect's drawings as if he could see Sims in them. *Two minutes late,* Zachary thought, looking unhappily at the drawings.

Belly down, legs extending into the open skylight, Sims inched backward until he hung from the frame of the skylight. His feet searched for, and finally found the first stirrup in the rope ladder. He tested his weight against the ladder and its hook. The ladder swayed, but the hook held fast. Moving down the ladder, he reached up and slowly pulled the skylight shut. It wouldn't close all the way because of the grappling hook, but some was better than nothing.

Now Sims hung among the wood rafters. Fifteen feet directly below, the tops of stacked crates. Off to his right, the central aisle connecting the building's freight doors. Toward the end of the building, and out of view behind the walls of crates, the glow of the lamp in the watchman's corner reflected dimly off the walls and rafters.

The sound came from behind him as he reached for the next stirrup. A scratching, fleeting noise on the rafters, just behind him at neck level.

He twisted on the rope ladder. A huge rat, not six inches away from his face . . . glowing orange eyes . . . Sims choked down a wave of revulsion.

For a moment, Sims and the rat stared at each other. Then, deciding that whatever it was on the rope was too dangerous to attack, the rat scurried away, its claws whispering along the wooden rafters. Now Sims saw other dark shapes swarming in the rafters making the beams seem to undulate with a sinister life of their own.

Hanging for a second on the ladder, Sims breathed deeply, then started down again. Another stirrup, then two, then three.

He was reaching for the next stirrup when he heard another sound, this time footsteps ringing off concrete. Feeling a cold stab of alarm, he glanced at his watch. It was 1:15. A flashlight beam bobbled and bounced down the central aisle, coming from the direction of the watchman's corner. *What the hell was this? This wasn't in the plan!*

The footsteps closer, now, Sims estimated the man was fifteen or twenty feet away, while he, Sims, was a foot, maybe two feet from the tops of the crates. Flattened out on top of a large crate, he'd be less visible.

Could he get to the crate below? He might have time . . . *but then, he might not.* Move fast and you can make it, he told himself.

Another voice warned: You don't know what kind of crap might be on top of those crates. Metal banding straps. Nails. Wood dunnage scraps. Try something now and you make noise.

Caution won. Sims froze on the rope as the footsteps grew louder, averting his eyes to avoid losing his night vision in the chance glare of the flashlight. The beam played along the concrete floor. The watchman wasn't searching, but using his flashlight to light his way.

The man would pass less than four feet away. Sims willed himself to blend with the darkness. Concentrating on legs, then arms, Sims forced his muscles to relax so no nervous tremor would betray him. He slowed his breathing, but couldn't quiet the blood roaring through his head and it seemed impossible to him that the man, now just below, could not hear the sound of it. Below him, Sims heard the creak of the man's leather belt with its holster and smelled a mix of garlic, sweaty wool, and cigarette smoke.

Sims hung suspended between the freedom of the skylight now so far away and what waited for him in the darkness below. He waited for the footsteps to stop. For the blinding flash of the light on him. For the watchman's shout of surprise and alarm. His pores tingled and danced crazily across the surface of his skin. And centuries crept agonizingly by between the sounds of each footfall.

And the footsteps passed on and the bobbing progress of the flashlight disappeared around the corner some forty feet away.

Relief swept Sims, along with a flash of irritation at being surprised. Then Sims heard the sound of a door opening. A sliver of light behind the far row of crates. The unmistakable sound of a man urinating. A toilet flushing. Nature's call, Sims reminded himself, could screw up the best of plans.

By the time the watchman made his way back from the toilet, Sims was off the rope ladder and flattened on top of a tall crate. It was 1:20 when Sims lowered himself to the floor. He would have until 1:55 to work the crates, five minutes to get under cover for the watchman's 2:00 A.M. round, then an hour to be in and out of the office.

He chose as his first target a desk-size crate, one of a dozen or so stacked together, separated by heavy wood forklift pallets. Kneeling at the crate's corner, he wriggled out of his rucksack, swinging it off his back and onto the concrete floor in front of him. Two minutes of work with the silent high-speed drill and he had a hole three-tenths of an inch in diameter cut into a splintered portion of the crate.

Wrapping a turn of masking tape around his fingers, sticky-side out, he patted around the hole to pick up any stray shavings. Putting the drill aside, he reached into the rucksack for a small plastic case. Opening the case, he lifted a pistol handgrip from its foam slot. A four-foot flex probe hung coiled from the grip, and behind the pistol grip, a funnel-shaped eyepiece.

Two separate fiber-optic bundles ran through the flex

probe. The image bundle of seven thousand fibers was surrounded by an illuminating bundle of fibers that carried light from the pistol-grip handle to the tip of the probe. At the tip, the image bundle would pick up everything in the field of view and bring it back to the eyepiece.

Sims took ten minutes with the first crate, working the probe between the cartons inside, making notes of the markings, then, withdrawing the probe, filling in the hole with wood dough from a small tube and rubbing dirt from the floor over the filler.

One for one, Sims thought, looking at the crate thoughtfully. Herr Spiedel's sticking to the business he knows best. Then, before he moved on to the next crate, he radioed Zachary.

"Five point five six millimeter small arms ammunition," Zachary whispered to himself as he decoded Sims's Morse message. "Lots a need for that in the farming business."

At 1:45, Sims entered his last crate. It had been one discovery after another: belt-fed Spanish Ameli light machine guns nestled next to Russian AGS-17 grenade launchers; Italian Beretta pistols stacked with American Stinger SAMs. And Herbert Spiedel had been loyal to his own firm: one of the crates had been filled with Heckler and Koch MP5 submachine guns.

The last crate was an apparent cropper—a pinkish orange substance blocked the probe. Sims tried twice more with the same result. The fourth time, he squeezed a trigger set into the handpiece, and at the face of the probe, a tiny scoop flicked out, twisted thirty degrees, then withdrew back into the probe. Whatever it was, Sims thought, he had a small sample.

"Watchman started rounds." Zachary marked Sims's message at two o'clock sharp.

The minutes and seconds ground by. A light flashed on Zachary's communications console, accompanied by an insistent chirping.

Zachary started with alarm. It was from Berlin base. "Yes?" he said into the mike. He listened intently to the message, nodding once, asked for a repeat, then broke the connection. He turned and glared at the clock as if it were his enemy. It was 2:11. Sims should be going into the office, now. Four minutes later, Sims's message said that's what he was about to do.

Edging through the narrow spaces between the crates, Sims came out into the short corridor just feet from Frau Geissler's office. Reaching under his coveralls, he pressed a detent button on his radio, and in his headphones heard a steady high tone as the converters picked up the ultrasonic beam of the warehouse motion detector and brought it down to the range of human hearing. He stepped nearer the office and its protecting beam and the tone rose in pitch, becoming a buzz like an angry hornet.

The transmitter, Zachary had said, was on the left wall of the warehouse as you face the office door, the receiver on the right wall. Break the beam, the receiver senses the interruption in the transmission—and all kinds of bad shit happens.

Gently lowering the rucksack to the floor, Sims opened the top flap into the main compartment and took out two parabolic reflectors about the size of large soup plates. Next, he unfolded the legs of a tripod, locking each leg in place with a twist of a knurled set screw. The reflectors fit one over the other on studs projecting from the tripod's upright. Another adjustment of the tripod, and now the reflectors stood chest high.

Sims flicked a switch behind the top reflector and watched as its transmitter warmed up. Tiny indicator lights, each the size of a grain of sand, glowed red, then green. Facing the reflectors toward the warehouse receiver, Sims moved the tripod into the alarm system beam. Zachary's rig would detect the exact frequency of the original ultrasound beam and adjust its own transmitter to mirror it. All this, Sims knew, was done in millionths of a second. The receiver would detect no interruption in the beam.

The tripod's two reflectors were now fully intercepting

the original beam and transmitting a phony one of their own. Another series of indicator crystals turned green; the warehouse receiver had bought the counterfeit signal.

With the original ultrasonic beam no longer protecting the office door, Sims opened his lock pick kit and went to work the door's dead bolt. The lock gave way on the third rake. Sims pushed the door open, stepped in, then reached out, brought the tripod in with him, then shut the door. The time now was 2:28.

The office smelled of lavender, and in the dim light that came through the window, Sims noticed a vase of cut flowers on Frau Geissler's desk. Slipping the rucksack off his back, he lowered it to the floor and withdrew a large, blanket-size blackout curtain that he secured around the window. A similar but smaller curtain fit snugly over the door.

He then knelt in front of the safe. On hands and knees, he worked around all four sides of the container, playing the red beam of his penlight along the base, looking for any signs of an alarm that the sensors in Zachary's toolbox might have missed.

Back at the front of the safe again, he sat back on his knees and stared for a moment at the combination dial and handle. He grasped the handle and turned. He didn't expect it'd open. But he'd sure as hell feel foolish, he told himself, if he went through all he was going to go through only to find Frau Geissler had forgotten to lock it in the first place.

First came a small metal ruler with which Sims carefully measured the location of the combination dial in the safe door, jotting the dimensions on a small plastic tablet hung by a chain around his neck.

Back into the rucksack. This time he came out with the grapefruit-size hemisphere in which Zachary had cut out the interior to the measurements he'd taken off Sims's photo of the combination dial. A protective plastic tape masked the circumference rim. Sims peeled the tape off, revealing a sticky adhesive. Penlight in one hand, Sims slowly eased the hemisphere over the combination dial, alert for any resistance that would warn him of an imperfect fit.

Sims detected a slight pressure as the hemisphere encountered the combination dial. He jiggled the hemisphere slightly and felt it slip easily over the dial. Even without the adhesive rim, the hemisphere would have clung tightly to the dial. Prying off a protective plastic cap on the back of the hemisphere, Sims uncoiled two thick insulated cables.

From the rucksack, he lifted a metal box. Not much larger than a telephone book, the box was surprisingly heavy. Sims worked around the perimeter of the box, releasing spring-loaded legs from each of the four corners. He set the box on the floor in front of the safe, directly under the dangling leads of the hemisphere. The legs gave the box a standoff distance of two inches from the floor—sufficient for insulation. Sims connected the leads to the box.

After checking to make sure the leads were tightly connected, Sims went into the rucksack for a second hemisphere. This one was the same size as the one covering the combination dial except that its interior hadn't been hollowed out. Moving around to the rear of the safe, Sims consulted the plastic tablet and measured off the same dimensions on the back of the safe. Checking his measurements again, he peeled the tape off the second hemisphere and stuck it to the safe's back. The second hemisphere was now directly opposite its twin covering the combination dial on the front.

Like the first hemisphere, this one had two insulated leads. But unlike the hemisphere on the front, Sims wired the leads to a small radio transmitter. After checking the connections, he extended a telescoping antenna and placed the transmitter on top of the safe. He stood back from the safe and sent his second coded message to Zachary.

Zachary looked at the clock as Sims's message came through the loudspeaker. It was 2:33. Zachary had been fine-tuning the receiver and recorders, running through sequences on the computer console. He was tempted to tell Sims to hurry, but forced himself to settle back and wait. And so he sat back and concentrated on the digital clock and tried to will the numbers to quit changing.

* * *

At 2:34, Sims sent a warning to Zachary. Sims got an immediate go-ahead, then pressed the firing button on the large metal box connected to the hemisphere on the front of the safe. He felt an intense flare of heat from the box.

The process would take place in thousandths of a second, Zachary had said, and it would be entirely silent. Inside the titanium composite box, the sodium-lithium hydroxide thermal batteries melted, producing a massive jolt of twenty thousand volts of electricity. The gigantic surge lasted only thirty-five millionths of a second, but this was long enough to fire up the tiny neutron generator in the grapefruit-size hemisphere.

In the next millionths of a second, the generator created a miniature volcanic eruption of neutrons. The hemispheric shielding around the generator focused this storm of subatomic particles forward in a stream against the face of the combination dial . . . through the dial . . . through the safe . . . and out the back, to be captured by the second hemisphere.

On top of the safe, the transmitter picked up the digital information from the hemisphere and instantly beamed it to the cargo truck.

"Hot shit, he got it!" Zachary slapped a hand explosively on the flat surface of the console before him. Frozen on the display screen above Zachary was a clear X ray of the safe and the settings for the combination tumblers.

"Right three to twenty-three," he transmitted to Sims, "left two to forty-eight, right to seven, left to zero." He waited a second and repeated the message.

A short silence, then in Morse, Sims repeated the combination back to Zachary for confirmation. Zachary confirmed, then checked the time. It was 2:36.

The safe's heavy doors swung noiselessly open. Four clothbound ledgers occupied the top shelf. On the shelf below, Sims recognized Frau Geissler's in-box, filled with what Sims supposed were current transactions and correspondence. An old-fashioned strongbox took up the bottom of the safe.

Sims photographed the safe's contents with a small Polaroid camera, then sent another progress transmission to Zachary while waiting for the picture to develop. Examining the Polaroid picture carefully, he grunted in satisfaction, then tacked the photo to the inside of the safe door with a small piece of masking tape.

From the rucksack, Sims carefully removed a container the size of an attaché case and set it on the floor near the open safe door. He unlatched the case and opened it. The half nearest him resembled a rectangular tray.

Reaching into the safe, Sims pulled out the first ledger and opened it faceup on the tray. From the other half of the case, he opened a compartment and withdrew what appeared to resemble a large electric razor, except for a narrow glass window where the cutting head would be. He flipped two switches, watching a small liquid crystal display screen, then ran the instrument over the ledger, taking two sweeps to cover the page. The page appeared in the display screen, then vanished. A green light flickered to tell Sims that the page had been recorded in the machine's memory. At 2:39, Sims sent another coded message to Zachary, signaling that the copying had begun.

Forty-four, forty-five pages—2:48 A.M. Just one more page, Sims told himself, knowing he was pushing it. He had sampled three of the ledgers and was now working on the fourth.

"You about closed up?"

Zachary's disembodied voice in the headset came as a surprise. Sims closed the ledger and put it back in the safe. As he did so, Frau Geissler's in-box caught his eye. He glanced at his watch—2:49. He looked longingly at the in-box. As he did so, he remembered the cookie-jar story from boyhood and heard his mother's voice, warning about the penalties of greed. But the in-box was *there,* just inches away.

Sims's caution shattered. He plunged his hand into the safe, and grabbing the thick sheaf of papers, he ran the scanner over one, then another, and another. As he did so, he noticed his hands were trembling in excitement. He started to scan another document, then, with the fierce determination of a reformed alcoholic, he stopped his hand in midreach and began closing up.

Papers back into the in-box. In-box back into the safe. Peeling the Polaroid photo off the interior of the safe door, he held it up and compared it against the contents as he'd stowed them. Something was wrong. He checked the Polaroid again. Everything was back in place, yet—

The ledgers! a voice in him shouted. He flashed his light into the safe. The ledgers were numbered on their spines, and he had put them back on the shelf in reverse order!

Hurriedly, he restacked the ledgers. Another comparison, then he stuffed the Polaroid photograph into the rucksack, closed the safe door, and locked it, spinning the combination dial several times and bringing it to a stop with the zero on the index marker where he'd found it.

By 2:53, Sims had repacked the rucksack and had searched the office for any small clue that he had been there. At 2:54, he left the office after working the ultrasonic transmitter into the beam of the motion detector. Removing his gloves and stuffing them in a coverall pocket, he knelt behind his transmitter and locked the office door's dead bolt with his lock pick.

He was slipping the tension tool from the lock when he heard a distant scraping sound on concrete, a faint cough, and footsteps. Lock picks zipped securely in a pocket, his hands flew over the folding tripod of the ultrasonic transmitter. The watchman was in the central aisle, walking this way . . . no time to get back to the rope ladder.

Tightening the rucksack on his back, Sims quietly slipped a few feet farther down the short corridor, away from the central aisle. To his left, an eight-foot wall formed by a bank of shipping containers; to his right, the invisible ultrasonic beam, now restored and dangerous.

He thought about hiding in the shadows where the shipping containers butted up against the warehouse wall. He shook his head. He'd be trapping himself—the watchman would face that way when he unlocked and opened the office door. The narrow corridor was dark, but not that dark.

The footsteps were louder and now Sims saw the bobbing reflection of the flashlight beam. Turning to face the container on his left, Sims crouched, then sprang, arms extended, hands reaching for the top of the container.

His hands closed on the sharp edge of the container and he felt a massive pulling pain in his back and shoulder sockets. For an instant, he hung there, shutting the pain out, concentrating on what he had to do, then, arms burning with the effort, Sims pulled himself slowly up, each inch an agony, until he was just over chest level with the container top, then bent forward and twisted around, swinging his legs up and over the edge. As he did so, he felt his left leg hit something. He froze in place, but it was too late to stop whatever it was that he'd hit. A drumming sound echoed through the warehouse as a hard object banged against the side of the container and crashed onto the concrete floor.

The footsteps stopped. *"Was ist das?"* The watchman's rasping voice carried an undertone of fear. The flashlight now streaked up and down the central aisle.

Sims cautiously turned his head and peered over the edge of the container down into the small corridor still hidden from the watchman. On the floor below, not far from where he'd stood, shards of glass. It must have been a bottle, he thought, perhaps a beer bottle, left over from some workman's lunch. Whatever—now it was a sign pointing to him.

He shifted slightly to get away from the edge of the container, knowing it'd do little good. The rope ladder hung somewhere in the darkness, not more than thirty or forty feet away. It might as well have been on the moon.

Immobile, Sims listened to the watchman approach. The man moved slowly, his footsteps quieter, cautious.

Another noise, undefinable, but closer, more furtive. Searching the darkness, Sims saw a shifting of shadows on the next container over. At the same time, he placed the sound. It was the sound of claws.

You do it because there's nothing else you can do, Sims

thought, forcing the gorge back down his throat. In a quiet, swift motion, he opened his pocketknife and sliced into the web of skin between the thumb and forefinger of his left hand, and as he felt the pain, he felt also the warmth of his blood.

Ten feet away, the Norway rat paused and sniffed the air. Over a foot long, the rat was in perpetual competition with the other warehouse rats for food. The rat was a pair of inch-long teeth driven by a blast-furnace metabolism. It had found little so far tonight—it'd had to fight with three other rats over a small crust of moldy bread. The bread had only whetted the rat's ravenous appetite. Now its hunger was a twisting, churning demand within its guts, and the salty rust smell of Sims's blood drove it into a paroxysm of greed.

Sims lay motionless, cheek against the metal of the container, his wounded hand stretched out before him. The watchman's footsteps sounded nearer—no more than thirty or forty feet away, Sims estimated. He strained, but there was no sound of the rat. There were only the watchman's footsteps. Then Sims felt a soft thud on the top of the container.

Before he heard the rat, he smelled it, a nauseating stench of musk and urine. Then the hollow sound of the claws . . . a brush of air against his hand . . . a warm dampness as the rat's nose, tactile and soft like a fleshy probe, nuzzled the blood spoor, making its way to the wound.

Sims clenched his teeth and forced himself to wait.

The rat lost all caution as its lust to feed became a raging frenzy. Its total consciousness focused on the blood and the wounded flesh and it urinated in excitement as it sank its long teeth into Sims's hand.

Though Sims expected it, he almost cried out with the piercing shock of the pain. He brought his right hand around, catching the rat in a viselike grip around the neck and front legs, tearing its teeth from his left hand, then pinning the struggling animal against his body, fighting the impulse to crush it and kill it. Sims heard the watchman's footsteps, just scant feet away and saw the flashlight beam as the watchman searched the spaces between the containers.

Sims listened to the footsteps, forcing himself to wait until they were closer, just a little closer. The rat's struggles grew more frantic. Sims, surprised at the animal's lithe strength, held it against his chest. Then he heard the sound of glass grinding underfoot. He cocked his arm back, the rat wriggling wildly in his hand.

The watchman swung his flashlight to the floor and the spray of broken glass. He turned the flashlight upward, toward Sims. The beam caught a flash of sudden motion. He twisted away as the rat glanced off his shoulder.

Stunned when it hit the floor, the rat sprawled motionless. The watchman's surprise and fright turned to hatred and disgust. He aimed a kick at the rat.

The kick missed as the rat came to its senses. The animal darted toward the watchman, then changed course and disappeared into the dark. Winded, the watchman stared at the broken bottle and the place where the rat had landed. Filthy beast! He kicked at the glass shards. Watchman was job enough. It wasn't up to him to kill rats or clean up the messes they made.

Clutching his wounded hand, Sims lay on his belly, listening to the watchman unlock and enter the office, then, less than a minute later, come out, lock up and go on his way for the three o'clock check-in.

At 3:23, Sims crossed the roadway, ducked beneath the cargo truck and rapped on the shelter's trapdoor. Five minutes later, he sipped a cup of scalding coffee and watched as Zachary worked on his wounded left hand with peroxide and Merthiolate.

"That shit stings."

Zachary frowned in concentration as he swabbed on more Merthiolate. He sat back and screwed the cap tight on the Merthiolate bottle. "And you've got a rabies series to start."

"Tomorrow—"

"This *is* tomorrow, and you got a busy day ahead."

Sims looked at Zachary, then shook his head. "Okay. I give."

Zachary put the Merthiolate away and snapped the medical kit shut. "Base called while you were rat-wrestling. After you get your shots, you got a meeting with the Judge and a guy named Riddle."

18

Sims stood at the picture window in the wood paneled room, looking out at the lake. The water, a cobalt blue, glinted cleanly in the winter sunlight, and on the opposite shore, birches spread into the forest, cutting white veins through the darker stands of ash and oak. It could have been a hundred lakes around the world if it hadn't been for Berlin's low skyline in the distance.

He and Zachary had gotten the cargo truck and Telekom van back to Berlin just after dawn. While the doctor at Berlin base had stitched Sims's hand and given him the first rabies shots, a team from base had opened the lodge to air it out and run an electronic sweep. It was almost eleven, and Riddle and the Judge's plane had landed ten minutes ago at the nearby airport at Gatow.

He went out to wait on the veranda. It was a glorious false spring day, an unseasonably warm day that winter-weary Berliners would worship from a thousand outdoor cafes that would spring up like mushrooms throughout the city. A short flight of steps below, a white gravel drive emerged from the thick curtain of evergreens, looped in front of the lodge, then disappeared back into the woods again.

Sims heard the cars before he saw them, their tires making roaring crunching sounds over the gravel. The cars, three embassy BMW sedans, glistening black and perfectly synchronized, exploded from the woods like a train hurtling out of a tunnel. Before the convoy came to a complete stop, a pair of Sam Durney's security officers leaped from the lead BMW and took up stations on either side of the middle car.

The Judge and Riddle got out and stood blinking in the bright sunlight. By that time, Sims was at carside. Riddle gave Sims's bandaged left hand a long look.

"Rat," was all Sims gave in the way of explanation, enjoying Riddle and the Judge's looks of mystification. "There's a story to it—but why're *you* here?"

"We're here," the Judge answered, "to meet Dimitri Petrovich Aristov."

"Shit," Sims said, awed.

"And Yegor Kulikov," Riddle added.

"Big company," Sims said as they entered the lodge. "Boris Yeltsin's chief of staff and the Russian service's number two. But"—Sims looked from Riddle to the Judge—"why're they coming here?"

The Judge shook his head. "I don't know. Obviously, it has to be something to do with . . ."—the Judge gestured to Sims—"with *you*. Alberich probably got them spun up."

Sims and Riddle took chairs in front of the picture window. The Judge started pacing as he summarized Alberich's visit to the Arlington coroner and the stainless steel tooth that connected Naji Hassan to a KGB dentist.

"Alberich cabled Isaacson at Moscow station, asked him to check it out with the Russians."

"And that's it?" asked Sims.

The Judge nodded. "Yesterday, just after lunch, Washington time, Aristov called me from the Kremlin direct, no explanation. Just said it was a matter of highest concern and we had to meet." The Judge shrugged. "And here we are."

"And they're due here—?"

The Judge shot out an arm and glanced at his watch. "We said noon." He tugged at his shirt cuff, took a chair facing Sims and Riddle, and crossed one leg over the other. "We have time. Now, how about the rat story?"

Sims skipped the details of the entry, for he had a premonition that though the Judge knew such things were done, the fastidious part of the Judge that was an officer of the court didn't want to hear about breaking and entering. Instead, Sims detailed what he'd found in the crates, describing the weapons and their countries of origin.

"Add it up," Sims concluded, "Josef Broz set up Herbert Spiedel as a front to sell weapons on the terrorist market."

"And the Mafia?" asked the Judge.

"Drugs," Sims answered. "Heroin's on the upswing again. Almost half the shit on the street today comes out of the Middle East. The terrorists give heroin to Spiedel and Broz for guns, Spiedel and Broz sell the drugs to the boys in Sicily for cash. While Broz was alive and while he was head of the Czech intelligence service, he probably used STB connections to help the Mafia move the stuff around the world."

The Judge got up and walked to the window and looked out at the lake for long moments. He turned from the window. "Tidy package," he said to Sims and Riddle. "It explains everything except why they killed Gribbins and Felton and the attempt on you."

"We were in the way," Sims replied.

"How?" the Judge asked.

Sims shrugged. "Maybe we'll ask the Russians."

Ten minutes later, Sims again stood on the lodge's veranda, this time with Riddle and the Judge, this time watching Dimitri Aristov's car door being opened by one of Durney's security officers.

The American bodyguard was big. Aristov was bigger. The shoulders, chest, and head carried the great bulk of his body, and as he got out of the car and straightened up, his posture and size reminded Sims of a bear standing on its hind legs.

Dimitri Petrovich Aristov, Sims knew, had been no Communist party hack. Enlisted man, then officer, Aristov had risen through the ranks of the Red Army on merit. In Afghanistan as a general, he had commanded a tank division. Twice wounded, Aristov came out of the debacle with a reputation as a soldier's soldier.

Aristov hadn't sought Yeltsin; Yeltsin had sought him. Russia's first president needed a troubleshooter. "Tough bastard," George Bush had supposedly remarked about Aristov to Yeltsin. "Tough times," Yeltsin had supposedly replied. If the story wasn't true, it was at least accurate. If reform in Russia was to succeed, the insiders said, it would need Dimitri Aristov or someone just like him.

The Judge and Aristov, who'd met before, shook hands, Aristov growling a good morning greeting in English to the Judge and clapping his free hand on the American's shoulder. The Judge introduced Riddle and Sims as Yegor Kulikov climbed out of the car to stand a pace behind Aristov.

Aristov shook hands with Riddle then stepped over to Sims and gave him an up-and-down parade-ground inspection. Aristov nodded curtly, as if Sims had passed muster.

Dimitri Aristov poured thick cream into his coffee until it took on a light tan color. He sipped, rolled the coffee around his mouth in appreciation, and set the mug on the table before him. "Let me explain why we are here. Your man in Moscow . . ." Aristov paused, a look of irritation at forgetfulness on his face, and spun an index finger in an impatient winding-up motion.

"Isaacson," the Judge supplied.

"Yes." Aristov nodded. "Your man Isaacson asked Kulikov here, for an identity." As if scripted, Aristov nodded to the RIS officer.

Yegor Kulikov picked up smoothly. "This was four days ago—Sunday. Carl Isaacson gave me the fingerprints, dental records, and DNA profile of a man with the name of Naji Hassan. I turned these over to the head of our registry on a priority basis. Yesterday, we found matches on the fingerprints and teeth. The man's name then was not Hassan but Hassan is as good as any for now. At any rate, Hassan was in Moscow in 1984, a student at Patrice Lumumba University."

Sims squinted at Kulikov. "Student?"

Kulikov shrugged again. "Phony names, phony occupations. What matters is that he was under KGB control.

What started the alarm bells was Hassan leads us to someone we are looking for."

It was Aristov's turn again. "You know, of course, Sergei Okolovich?" he asked.

"Sergei Federovich Okolovich," Riddle recited, "formerly Chief, First Directorate, KGB, then Chief of the entire KGB. He was in power when the Soviet Union fell in December 1991. There was some speculation at the time that he would be the head of the new Russian intelligence service." Riddle fixed Aristov with a hard stare. "Speculation also had it that you and he had a falling-out."

A smile hovered at the corners of Aristov's mouth. "You have good speculators, Mr. Riddle. I had Okolovich jailed. We found he'd been running his own little international currency exchange. Building dollar accounts for himself in Switzerland and Austria. He escaped seven months ago—" Aristov's nostrils flared contemptuously. "Escaped?" he asked himself. "No. That implies daring and courage. Sergei Okolovich stayed in character. He bribed his way out.

"But let me start at the beginning," Aristov continued. "After the fall of the Shah of Iran in 1979, the Politburo saw its chance to push you Americans out of the Middle East, particularly out of Egypt and Saudi Arabia. They gave that job to the KGB." He paused and nodded to Kulikov.

Kulikov picked up. "Inside the KGB, the task was passed to Sergei Okolovich. Okolovich decided that the pickings would be most lucrative among the Islamic fundamentalists, given their hostility to the West in general and America in particular. But Okolovich had to find an Arab leader.

"In 1981, Josef Broz, of the Czech service, came to Okolovich. Broz had found the Arab Okolovich had been looking for. Miloslav Valek, who worked for Broz, had recruited a promising Palestinian named Zohdi."

"Kamāl Zohdi?"

Kulikov's eyebrows shot up. "You know him?"

"He's got a reputation," Sims said. "Let me guess. Hassan was one of Zohdi's guys."

Kulikov nodded. Aristov gave Sims a somber, appraising look, the kind of look a poker player uses to size up a stranger across the table who's started raising the ante.

Sims asked, "And now that Hassan has shown up . . . ?"

"It means that Zohdi is not far behind."

"But you don't care about Zohdi, do you?" Sims guessed. Aristov gave Sims a look that told him he'd guessed right.

"It's Okolovich I want," said Aristov.

"So?" asked Sims. "What's that got to do with us?"

Aristov's blue-ice eyes worked their way over Sims, as if he were still filling in the details missed by an earlier measurement. When the Russian spoke, it was with a rough intimacy, as if he and Sims were old soldiers in a bar, reliving a long-ago campaign. "You know my history." Aristov said it matter-of-factly.

Sims nodded.

"Do you know that I have cancer?" Aristov asked it softly, but without self-pity. His eyes locked with Sims as if they were the only people in the room.

"It's supposed to be in remission," Sims said.

"Yes," Aristov acknowledged wistfully. Then he reached out and grasped Sims's forearm. "Russia had a cancer." The voice got harsh. "Sergei Okolovich and his kind ravaged the Russian people for over seventy years. They are out of power, but they are not gone. Russia is in remission, but it is not cured.

"*Comrade* Okolovich"—Aristov hung "comrade" with contempt—"wishes to come back to Russia. He and his friends want to bring back the good old days. Meanwhile, they are building their networks abroad with help from Zohdi, waiting for their chance to return."

Aristov shook Sims's arm for emphasis. "Things are going to be very bad in Russia. They will be better. But first very bad. A delicate balancing act. There are a lot of people in the streets who listen to the poison Okolovich and his kind are spreading. As long as he is out there, he is dangerous."

"But why us?" Sims repeated.

"Boris Yeltsin is president," Aristov explained, "but he is not czar. He doesn't control the parliament. The old Communists—the antireform elements—would never stand for an open attack on Okolovich." Aristov drew himself up, throwing his head back, and added almost formally, "Understand—we are not asking that you do the . . . the job. Just for cooperation."

"Cooperation?"

"Cooperation." Aristov repeated. He cut a glance to Kulikov.

Kulikov served up the deal: "We will help you find Zohdi; you will help us find Okolovich."

The Judge's eyes met Sims's in a silent conference. The Judge sat expressionless for a long moment, finally nodded to the Russians. "That's reasonable." He turned back to Sims. "Bradford?"

"We need access to your files," Sims said to Kulikov. "Zohdi's, also Valek's, Broz's, and the Czech service."

"You understand I can't just turn them over."

"No one's asking you to. A liaison arrangement. Someone to work with you. Someone who knows the case." Sims offered.

"There is a name? This person?"

"Alberich." Sims thought he saw a flicker of recognition pass across Kulikov's face.

"Matthias Alberich?"

"Yes."

Kulikov seemed to relax. "When?" he asked.

Aristov and Kulikov had barely left before the scrambler telephones in the lodge's small communications room began ringing. One call, from Langley for the Judge, the other for Sims.

Sims picked up the receiver. It was Zachary. He listened for several minutes, thanked Zachary, then hung up and walked back into the lodge's living room.

Riddle stood looking out the picture window. On the lake, a small white ferry was pulling away from the docks at Kladow. Sims came to stand beside Riddle and both watched the boat in silence.

"That was Berlin base," Sims finally said. "The orange crap—the sample I got out of one of the crates? It was Semtex."

"Ah, yes," said Riddle, still looking out the window, "and we know where that comes from, don't we?"

223

Sims stretched and kneaded the back of his neck with both hands. Semtex, he thought. American C-4, British PE-2, German Cyclonite—all plastic explosives had a distinctive odor. All except Semtex. That was completely odorless, one reason the dogs at Frankfurt airport hadn't found the bomb aboard Pan Am 103 before it exploded over Lockerbie, Scotland. The Rolls Royce of plastic explosives, Semtex was made only in Czechoslovakia.

"Josef Broz's contribution to the partnership," Sims said, remembering his meeting with Broz a year ago in Prague: the out of work Communist spy-master, still sleek and well-dressed. The tailored Italian suit, the camel hair topcoat, the French designer eyeglasses, the mistress in a plush apartment. Paid for with Semtex laid away during the good times. Had Schmar inherited Broz's cache of explosives? And had he passed the inheritance of death on to someone else?

"Broz's dead," Sims said wonderingly, "and he still keeps killing." His attention slipped back to the boat. "It's going over to Wannsee."

The two men stood quietly and Riddle's hazel eyes registered on another time. "Wannsee," Riddle echoed, his voice coming from a long way off.

The boat was now passing a small island, the Schwanenwerder. The conference at Wannsee, Sims thought. January 1942. A secret meeting of Hitler's top Nazis. Where Reinhard Heydrich and Adolf Eichmann put together the conveyor belts of the Holocaust. Where six million people began the journey to the gas chambers of Auschwitz and Bergen-Belsen.

Wannsee had been a case study when Sims had gone through training at the Farm. He'd learned how Riddle and his partner, Bazdarkian, had gotten a copy of the conference minutes. How Riddle had spent a long night at the Morse key transmitting his report to London. How . . . nothing.

"They didn't listen, did they, Riddle?"

"No." Riddle sighed. "It was too monstrous for them to believe."

* * *

Five minutes later, the Judge, Sims, and Riddle left the lodge for the Judge's plane. In the car, the Judge turned to Sims, trying to focus on a lost picture. "Zohdi . . . Zohdi."

"Achille Lauro," Sims prompted.

The eyes flicked back to Sims. "Ah, yes. *That* one. There are so many of them that you lose count. Maybe we ought to have the bubble gum people do cards on terrorists." The Judge frowned, trying to remember. "Yes . . . 1984. The tour ship hijacking . . ."

"It was 1985," Sims corrected. "Kamāl Zohdi's Popular Liberation Front. There was a passenger. Leon Klinghoffer. He had everything going against him—American—Jew—confined to a wheelchair."

"Pushed him overboard, didn't they?"

Sims nodded. "In front of his wife."

"Zohdi was there?"

Sims shook his head. "But he set it up. I was chief of base here"—Sims pointed a thumb back in the general direction of Berlin—"and one of our assets came up with Zohdi's name. Then NSA intercepted an Egyptian radio message about Zohdi who had a plane waiting in Cairo for the hijackers. Zohdi collected his friends, and took off for Tunis. Navy F-14s off the carrier *Saratoga* intercepted the plane, forced it to land in Sicily."

Sims frowned, remembering his disappointment. "We had those bastards like *that!*" He held up an open hand, then clenched it shut.

"The Italians tried them."

"Three of the hijackers got fifteen to thirty years. But they were just the hired help. Zohdi'd planned it, and we were pushing Rome to put him on trial, too, but Qaddafi started raising hell. The Italians didn't want to screw up their deals in Libya, so they turned Zohdi loose. We tried to pick him up again, but he got away." Sims winced as he made a connection between then and now. "Oh, *shit!*"

Riddle's eyebrows arched, and the Judge tilted his head inquisitively toward Sims.

"It just hit me. We traced Zohdi through Yugoslavia and Hungary, but we lost him—"

"In Czechoslovakia?" the Judge guessed.

"Where his buddy Josef Broz helped in the disappearing act." Sims frowned. "A month later, Zohdi showed his gratitude to the Italian government. Remember the machine-gunning of the El Al ticket counters at Leonardo da Vinci airport? Zohdi again. His brave liberation fighters killed twenty civilians, six of them little kids." The numbers came to Sims the way baseball addicts recalled batting averages of a half century before. "Wounded over a hundred."

Riddle looked through the windshield. They were at the Gatow terminal. "He seems to be back in the game."

Sims shook his head. "He never left it. We just lost him."

"It's a big world," the Judge said, sounding slightly defensive. "We can't keep track of everybody. Those things happen."

Sims nodded, suddenly feeling tired and vulnerable. "Yeah, they happen, Judge. But why're we always stuck paying the bill?"

Sam Durney waited for them planeside and handed over a heavy leather and canvas pouch containing copies of the warehouse documents. On board, Sims and Riddle took seats facing the Judge across a worktable. After takeoff, and with a cold green bottle of Beck's at his elbow, Riddle unfastened the pouch and began reading through the documents.

Five minutes later, Riddle gave a soft "oh" of surprise. He studied two documents again as if to make certain he hadn't been mistaken, then handed the first to the Judge.

"This is a copy of the manifest of a recent shipment from Bremerhaven," Riddle explained. "It is to a final destination in Latakia, Lebanon."

The Judge scanned the document and passed it to Sims.

"Enough for a small army," Sims said, eyeing the second print, the one in Riddle's hand.

Riddle handed it to the Judge. "And this one is to the same destination. Note the odd entry toward the bottom of the page."

Sims watched as the Judge's eyes flicked down the page. The eyes stopped and the Judge's mouth tightened. The

Judge closed his eyes then opened them again. He had a disappointed expression as if he'd hoped the paper would have disappeared.

He passed the two pages to Sims. "We better track that down. Then let's get our friend Ralston out from the White House." He thought for a moment, then added, "And Lindahl, the science adviser." Another pause. "And be sure to invite Nesbith too. Don't want the FBI feeling rejected."

19

The Judge's plane landed at Andrews Air Force Base at 5:53 P.M. where Hunter was waiting.

"If Mr. Hunter could drop me by the bookshop . . ." Riddle suggested.

Sims started to protest, but Riddle held up a hand. "Time for me to disappear back into the woodwork. There's nothing I can do to help you tonight, and my presence at a meeting would raise questions from the White House worthies." He wagged a cautionary finger at Sims. "You will, of course, stop by after . . . ?"

Back at the Agency, the Judge's special assistant showed Sims to a small office in the Judge's seventh floor suite. Dropping his bag in a corner, Sims reached for the phone and called Alice Brenner, the Agency's senior biologist.

Brenner, a tall attractive woman in her forties, showed up ten minutes later. Sims motioned to a chair beside his desk. He caught her glancing at her watch and her frown. "You had plans," he guessed.

Brenner shrugged. "Oh, just the usual Thursday night— president's box at the Kennedy Center, dinner at Bice with Tom Cruise, but for you, Sims . . ." she let it trail off. She cocked her head at him. "Where've you been? I thought you were in Spain somewhere."

"Italy." Sims pushed a copy of the Bremerhaven transaction register across the desk to her.

Brenner took the chair, picked up the register, and scanned the first page. "Guns," she said with distaste. She combed her fingers through a thick shock of chestnut hair, pushing it away from her blue-gray eyes and the high Hepburn cheekbones. She turned a page. "More guns." She looked at Sims, puzzled. "Guns aren't my *shtick.*"

Sims pointed a pencil at the documents. "Next page. Toward the bottom."

Brenner went back to the register, tracing the entries with her index finger. Midway down the page, she stopped, then bent closer as if to make certain of what she'd read. Her face tightened in concentration, then, holding her finger on an entry to save her place, she looked up to Sims. "Vacuum pump? Autoclave?"

"Don't fit with the guns, do they?" Sims paused, then went on. "We didn't get all the pages of the register," he explained. "On what we got, there's only one entry like that. Can you track the pump and that autoclave back to the suppliers? See if there were other buys? Get dates, quantities?"

Brenner gazed past Sims, weighing the effort. Finally she swung her eyes to Sims and nodded. "I know the major supply houses in the U.S. and Europe. You've got a serial number on this"—she tapped the register with her finger— "I ought to be able to scare up something by next week."

"By tomorrow."

"Tomorrow?"

"Tomorrow *morning."*

"Morning?" Brenner gave Sims an incredulous look. "Sims, my contacts will be home. My God, it's midnight in Europe."

"Call them at home. Wake them up."

"We're going to burn a lot of chits on this."

Sims nodded. "Burn them. And by the way, you'll be briefing tomorrow morning."

"Brief who? What?"

Sims looked at his watch. "I got to see Louis Vee." He motioned to the register. "Get started on the traces, I'll fill you in after I see Louis."

He stopped at the door. Brenner was already making

notes in the margins of the register. "Sorry about dinner with Tom Cruise. I'll buy tonight."

Brenner looked up skeptically. "At Bice?"

"South Cafeteria."

"No *cavatelli Genovese?*"

"Tuna salad."

"You don't offer a woman much choice."

"Rye or whole wheat?"

Louis Velasquez had run the Counterterrorism Center from its inception. That had been 1986, when William Casey, the Judge's predecessor, set up CTC to coordinate America's war against terrorism. Tucked away behind a double set of steel vault doors on the sixth floor, CTC was manned around the clock. Velasquez recruited his talent from across government. He tapped the usual intelligence agencies, but CTC was also staffed with men and women from Treasury, DEA, and Agriculture as well. And Louis had even managed to get a small contingent on loan from Congress's Office of Technology Assessment.

Velasquez was universally known as "Louis Vee," to separate him from another Louis (Louis Carboni, a.k.a. "Louis Cee.") who also worked in CTC. Louis Vee, a mountain of a man, chewed on an unlit cigar, laced his fingers behind his head and tilted back in his armchair to listen to Sims. Velasquez made listening into a contact sport. When Louis Vee listened to you, you walked away afterward feeling like you'd been worked over by a world-class sumo wrestler. His dark liquid eyes impaled Sims, registering every facial expression, every hand gesture, every dip or twist of the shoulders. All the while, Louis Vee produced a stream of grunts. Grunts of astonishment, of doubt. Grunts of dismay, of sympathy.

Five minutes later, Louis Vee brought his hands from behind his head, took the cigar from his mouth, and tilted his chair forward in a controlled crash to rest his forearms on his desk.

"You want this fucker Zohdi," he summarized. Sims hadn't finished nodding before Louis Vee got to work, and the search for Kamāl Zohdi branched out, rippling like a tremor through the nervous system of the international espionage establishment.

Louis Vee made his first scrambler call to London, to Grayson, MI-6's unofficial favor banker. More calls followed: to DGSE's DeGuerin in Paris, to Aref of Egypt's *Mukhabarat el-Aam,* and finally, to Aman headquarters in Jerusalem. After each call, Louis Vee filled in the Agency chiefs of station in the countries involved, giving them a concise "ears only" account of his conversations. No paper trail, of course, remained of the conversations.

Meanwhile, Louis Vee's chief of biographical research ordered a priority search of DESIST, CTC's computer system that tracked all known terrorists, their backgrounds, and organizational affiliations. She then began her local calls on the scrambler, spinning her web among her longstanding contacts in the U.S. intelligence community: NSA, DIA, State INR, Army INSCOM, Office of Naval Intelligence, and, of course, the FBI. Forty minutes later, her terminal beeped, announcing that DESIST had compiled an initial update of Kamāl Zohdi's file. She tapped a key on her console and the printer in her office whirred to life.

Morning brought a slate gray sky to Washington with a snow line of flurries marching in from the northwest. It was a few minutes before ten as Sims put the first slide on the tray and switched on the projector. The machine squatted on one end of the conference table, throwing its images down the length of the table to a screen at the far end. In between, eight cushioned armchairs to the side.

"Look at it this way: it's not an inquisition." Alice Brenner said from the semidarkness of the room as she watched Sims focus the picture. Fuzzy at first, the picture sharpened, then fuzzed over again as Sims twisted the lens too far. A bearded man, dark and angry, looked out of the screen.

"Oh?" Sims answered, with heavy irony. "A little friendly show-and-tell?"

"We've got a story."

"This's a town full of stories," Sims said, still fiddling with the projector and watching the man on the screen.

"But—"

"That's got it." Sims said softly, finally satisfied with the focus. He snapped the machine off and scanned the long, windowless room, taking in the details. This was the director's conference room on the seventh floor of the old building, a decorative hangover from the sixties infatuation with Danish modern. Pale teak paneling, soft indirect lighting, and dark blue plush carpeting. Beige drapes around the room that could be opened for map boards, status charts, and other paraphernalia of crisis management. Between each set of drapes, crests of America's intelligence agencies. Tompkins was setting out legal pads and sharpened yellow pencils, lining them up neatly in front of each chair.

Sims fought the desire to throw himself into one of the padded high-backed chairs. Close your eyes, he warned himself, and you'll be out for the rest of the day.

Just after nine last night, Louis Vee had called from the Counterterrorism Center—DESIST had begun spewing out the initial files on Zohdi. Sims had worked through the night putting together Zohdi's story. Some of it was new; some of it he'd known but forgotten: born 1950, Wahdat refugee camp, Jordan. Family part of the four hundred thousand Palestinians who fled Israel in advance of the Arab-Israeli War of 1948. Father killed by Israeli security patrol two months before Zohdi's birth.

Wahdat refugee camp, Sims thought—the spawning ground for the killings at the '72 Munich Olympics, bombings of schools, hospitals, and airports, hijackings of half a dozen international airliners—a regular graduate school for a generation of terrorists.

Zohdi had an uncle who worked for Gulf Oil in Kuwait. The uncle took Zohdi in, and several years later, Zohdi showed up as a student at the London School of Economics. Arrested in the bombing of an Israeli consulate, but released due to lack of evidence. A return to Kuwait . . . meteoric career in oil speculation . . . multimillionaire before the age of thirty.

The early eighties: Zohdi now united with a childhood friend from Wahdat, Abu Nidal. Zohdi as chief of finance directorate, funding terrorist operations from Iraq, Czechoslovakia, Syria.

Then Zohdi on his own, shuttling between Damascus and Khartoum, bankrolling his own army of Egyptians, Palestinians, and Saudis, building an Islamic Legion to fight the Russians in Afghanistan. Hijacking of the *Achille Lauro,* bombing American GIs in Berlin discos. An increasing appetite for terror and blood.

The files were deceptive. The computer information seemed impressively authoritative—this was truth complete and unarguable. But when you got into it, one piece of information only raised another ten questions. He had chased follow-ups to follow-ups and the most basic questions remained unanswered—like where is Zohdi now?

Twice during the night he'd taken a coffee break, taking the stairs down to the fifth floor where Brenner had been tracing bills of lading and shipping documents, tracking transactions across four continents. By eight, they'd roughed out the briefing and turned the mass of notes and sketches over to the Agency's senior graphics technician who had taken just over an hour to put together the deck of slides that Sims now stacked beside the darkened projector.

Sims picked out the slim deck of pale blue index cards on which Riddle had outlined the other important biography for this morning—Ralston Dean.

Ralston Eggers Dean, forty-six, born in Ithaca, New York. As an undergraduate at Oberlin College in the sixties, Dean had been attracted to the Arab world by the fiery revolutionary rhetoric of Frantz Fanon.

Dean went on to a Ph.D. at Columbia. Blessed with a high-brilliant IQ and a stubborn perseverance, Dean mastered Arabic, a difficult language. Under the tutelage of Edward Said, he immersed himself in the Arab world, a culture even more complex than its language. Appropriately, Dean had written his thesis in Arabic: *'Emdat ha-*

'Aravim b'Sikhsukh Yisrael-'Arav ("The Arab's Position in the Israel-Arab Conflict").

Dean rose to the top of his profession: president of the Middle East Studies Association, consultant to the Ford, Rockefeller, and MacArthur foundations, a regular participant in Aspen Institute seminars and Ditchley House weekends, consultant to ABC-News and Peter Jennings during the Gulf War.

Dean's books and articles described the Arab world as mystical, spiritually elitist, and aesthetically pure. The West, on the other hand, was infected with antiintellectualism and crass materialism. In the margins of the blue index card, Sims saw Riddle's ironic note in neat cursive that Dean always drove a new Mercedes convertible and was known as a collector of rare wines. All paid for, Sims suspected, with the royalties from fucking over the West.

Riddle's commentary noted that Dean consistently protected his beloved Arabs from Western criticism, a task to which he brought a formidable arsenal of intellectual and rhetorical weapons. Dean could appeal to multicultural sensitivity, and on other occasions, Riddle noted, Dean simply overwhelmed critics with his encyclopedic knowledge of the Middle East. And, if all else failed, he deployed the seasoned academic's well-honed skills in the construction of euphemism. Thus what seemed to be obvious and blatant violations of human rights—stonings in the marketplace, death sentences pronounced for wayward writers—Dean dismissed with a shrug of superiority. "One can expect," Dean once wrote, "that when certain activist Islamic movements come to power, human rights issues will be a source of tension."

Sims glanced at his watch. Ten o'clock—bring on Mr. Dean. Show time.

20

Thank you for coming on such short notice."

From his customary seat at the middle of the table, the Judge did the opening honors. Three men sat across from the Judge. Ralston Dean directly across, and to Dean's left, Lars Nesbith, the FBI director, a professional smile on his face. On Dean's right, a large man in rimless glasses, a shaggy tweed suit, and burr haircut whom Dean had introduced as Lewis Lindahl—*Doctor* Lewis Lindahl. Sims and Alice Brenner sat to the Judge's left, Sims closest to the projector. A few feet from the conference table, a mahogany podium stood to the side of the projection screen. A large Agency crest, the round blue shield with a white eagle head in profile decorated the front of the podium like a protective shield.

"When we met last week, we agreed that the Bureau"— the Judge gave Lars Nesbith a small nod—"would look for domestic leads and that the Agency would work foreign intelligence to see if these events were somehow connected. I believe we've found evidence of that connection." The Judge motioned to Sims.

Sims rose and flicked on the projector. Two views of a bearded man: full face and right profile.

"It looks like a booking photo," Lars Nesbith murmured.

"The missing link: Kamāl Zohdi," Sims said, and nodded

to the FBI director. "And it *is* a booking photo. Rome, October 1985."

"Kamāl Zohdi's resume." Sims put on the second slide, a sparse chart with dates and events—the essential Kamāl Zohdi. He stood silently for a moment, watching the eyes around the conference table scan the slide.

Sims then took them through Zohdi's biography: the child of the Jordanian refugee camps turned promising student turned accomplished terrorist. Zohdi's descent into the darkening well of fundamental Islamic militancy, every move gaining increasing influence: as Abu Nidal's financial wizard, as the ruthless planner of the bloody purges of Muslim moderates in Egypt and Algeria, as the organizational genius behind the Islamic Legion's campaigns in Afghanistan.

Ralston Dean listened, eyes never leaving Sims, face emotionless, right hand twirling a pencil Tompkins had laid out. Point on the legal pad, half turn, then eraser on the legal pad, then point again.

Lars Nesbith kept his hands folded on the table, occasionally jotting a series of notes. Lindahl, the White House science adviser, sat deep in his chair chin down on his chest, arms folded across the top of his paunch, eyes fixed on the tabletop.

"Behind all this"—Sims gestured toward the screen—"is a series of relationships that took shape in the early eighties. We don't know the details, except that the relationship involved Zohdi, the Soviet and Czech intelligence services, and the Mafia."

Sims put a new slide on the projector.

"This gives you an idea of the quantity and types of arms that were being shipped from Bremerhaven to Latakia, Lebanon."

Sims paused. All quiet around the table. Dean was still fiddling with the pencil, Nesbith the FBI director was still wearing his opaque smile, and Lindahl had gotten a mystified look as if he'd taken the wrong turn somewhere on a country road.

Using his pencil as a drumstick, Dean beat an impatient

staccato on the table top. "Okay. We have a terrorist. We have a bunch of old commies in the gunrunning business." Dean tossed his pencil onto the legal pad in front of him. "It's not a pretty picture, but it's nothing new." He motioned to Lindahl sitting beside him. "And certainly nothing we needed Dr. Lindahl for."

The Judge held up a restraining hand. "Excuse me, Ralston." He twisted slightly in his chair. "Dr. Brenner?" He turned back to Dean. "Dr. Brenner is our chief biologist, Ralston." The Judge shifted his eyes to bring in Lindahl. "Ph.D., Caltech. Member, National Academy of Sciences and fellow, Royal Academy of Sciences, London."

Brenner and Sims exchanged places at the projector. Two slides in one hand, Brenner rested her other hand on the projector and looked down the table to Ralston Dean.

"What is new, Mr. Dean," Brenner said in a voice with the softly implied menace of a razor shearing silk, "is that Kamāl Zohdi is accumulating the equipment he can use to put together a biological weapon."

Sims watched the three visitors. Washington briefings were an art form. And part of the art—a major part—was the opening line. You had less than fifteen seconds of undivided attention once you stood up. Too many briefers squandered that attention with pointless jokes or maundering scene-setting monologues and let their audiences slip away into daydreams or outright napping. He and Brenner had gone over her opening line repeatedly, honing it to the bare essentials, weeding out the multiple qualifiers that Washington favored that turned concrete to mush. No gauzy conjectures of Zohdi's intentions, just capabilities, only what Zohdi *could* do, nothing about whether he *might* do it.

Sims was satisfied. Dean's expression had not changed, but his face had visibly paled. Nesbith had brought a hand up to the side of his face, and Lindahl, the science adviser, had an open-mouth, open-eyes look.

Next pitch, Sims sent a mental message to Brenner, keep them off balance.

As if she'd heard Sims, Brenner flicked on the projector.

"This next slide," the soft implacable razor voice-over came, "is also from the register of the Bremerhaven warehouse."

A register page flashed on the screen, a bright green band highlighting one entry.

"This transaction—September '91—didn't fit the Bremerhaven warehouse pattern," Brenner said. "On September 4, Bremerhaven shipped a laboratory-quality vacuum pump and an autoclave. We see here"—Brenner worked the laser pointer and a bright red arrow nicked an entry on the screen—"the brand names and serial numbers. This consignment was shipped to the same destination—Latakia— as the previous and subsequent consignments of weapons."

"You've got more than that," Ralston Dean guessed in his cynical voice, as if he were watching a carny pitchman ineptly setting up a shell game.

Brenner looked at him impassively, then nodded. "Kardis and Mayer Incorporated, a specialty machine shop in Oak Park, Illinois, manufactured the vacuum pump. On 23 July 1991, they sold the pump to Eustis Precision-Tech of Evansville, Indiana. Eustis is a supplier for laboratories. Eustis Precision reports that less than a month later, on 19 August, they shipped the pump to Karstens-Export in Bremerhaven. Eustis also reports shipping five biohazard cabinets to Karstens-Export along with the vacuum pump. The cabinets had been built by Saf-Aire of Oakland, California."

"Excuse me," Lars Nesbith cut in, a puzzled look on his face. "Biohazard?"

"Cabinets that allow you to work with biological agents without fear of contamination," Brenner explained. "Simple ones look like large glass boxes with rubber-glove ports. The models Eustis shipped were state of the art. You hook the vacuum pump to them and the pump maintains a negative pressure—a slight vacuum in the box so that if there is a leak, air from outside comes in—"

"But the bugs don't get out."

"The bugs don't get out," Brenner repeated to Nesbith. "The exhaust from the hoods is usually run through an incinerator which kills any organisms that make it through the filtration system." She waited for a follow-up from Nesbith, and when that didn't come, she continued. "The second item, the autoclave, was built by a Danish firm, Gamma Chemical in Copenhagen. Gamma also reports the sale to Karstens-Export of a lyophilizer—"

"A what?"

Lindahl put his hand on Ralston Dean's forearm. "A lyophilizer," the scientist repeated slowly. Sims caught the undercurrents of a European accent. "It is a machine that does freeze-drying."

Dean took that in, then turned back to Alice Brenner. "Anything else from the Bremerhaven warehouse?"

"No."

Dean looked at her for a moment, as if still sizing her up, then held out his hands, palms up. "And so from *this*"— Dean sounded as if he'd expected better—"you tell me that we have a terrorist out to bring a plague down on the world."

Sims eyed Brenner. The woman stood motionless.

"I am *not* telling you that at all, Mr. Dean," Brenner said slowly, emphasizing each word. "I *said* that Kamāl Zohdi is accumulating the equipment he *can* use to put together a biological weapon." She paused for a moment. "That he *can* use," she repeated, with the slightest hint of a school teacher's scolding tone, "with the emphasis on 'can.'"

Nesbith raised a hand. "I should think the technology would be out of his reach."

Brenner shook her head. "Most doomsday scenarios involve terrorists and nuclear weapons. People haven't paid much attention to the biologicals.

"It is useful to compare and contrast nuclear and biological weapons. Both can be mass killers. We know about the hundreds of thousands killed at Hiroshima and Nagasaki. We know about the death toll from Chernobyl.

"We know less about biological weapons. While biological warfare has never been conducted on a large scale, the *inadvertent* spread of infectious diseases during wartime has caused far more casualties throughout history than actual combat. Few realize that bioagents were stockpiled during World War Two and continue to be developed as the poor man's atomic bomb by a growing number of countries.

"Weight for weight, dollar for dollar, biological weapons have a potential for mass destruction that can exceed nuclear weapons. Nuclear and biological weapon production offers very different challenges. The slides compare those challenges."

The first slide flashed on the screen.

"The first comparison is raw material. Biological weapons require pathogenic microorganisms. Nuclear weapons require enriched uranium or weapons-grade plutonium. As we see here," Brenner said, gesturing to the slide, "biological 'starter kits' are widely available. Pathogenic microorganisms are indigenous to many countries and can be cultured from infected wild animals, living domestic animals, infected remains, or even spoiled food.

"On the other hand, to obtain enriched uranium or weapons-grade plutonium for nuclear weapons, one must have access to expensive and exotic equipment such as molecular vapor lasers, precision high-speed gas centrifuges, massive pumps and compressors. And all enrichment technologies require enormous amounts of electricity."

The next slide contrasted scientific and technical personnel. "Again, biological weapons pose the lesser challenge," Brenner noted. "While nuclear weapons require a variety of rare skills such as precision machining of high explosives, electronics integration, and metallurgy, bioweapons can be developed by a few well-trained single-expertise scientists. And to produce bioweapons after the experimental stage is finished requires very little skill at all.

"Equipment," Brenner announced the following slide. "Nuclear weapons production requires highly specialized tooling and equipment that are difficult to buy or to build. To the extent that we have prevented the spread of nuclear weapons, it is because we have been able to control the sale and distribution of such exotic items as numerically controlled multiaxis milling machines, vacuum induction furnaces, and high pulse rate lasers.

"For bioweapons, all that's needed is the same laboratory

equipment needed to produce vaccines, antibiotics, or even yeast. And this is the fundamental problem in countering proliferation of biological weapons—the fact that much of the necessary know-how and technology is dual-use, with legitimate applications in fermentation and biotechnology industries."

Brenner put on another slide. "And the cost of building biological weapons is quite attractive compared to going nuclear. Because of the easily available equipment, small-scale facilities, and relatively common knowledge of the science involved, you could build a considerable biological arsenal for less than ten million dollars. The nukes?—a moderately sized nuclear weapon production facility could easily cost in the billions. And you would have to have a physical plant that could easily be picked up by our surveillance satellites.

"Last slide," Brenner announced. "A comparison of weight between nuclear and biological weapons." She addressed Ralston Dean and his side of the table. She waited until Dean raised his eyebrows, then: "A first-time builder of a nuclear weapon, even if he were successful, would have a device weighing at least several thousand pounds. It would take a very sophisticated operation to put together what the thriller writers describe as a 'suitcase bomb.'

"In World War Two, Japan's Unit 731, a top-secret biowarfare outfit, produced botulinal toxin in pound batches using a fermenter ten feet high and five feet wide. Botulinal toxin is the most poisonous substance known. The fatal dose is about seventy nanograms."

"*Nano*grams?" Dean frowned.

"About two billionths of an ounce. Perfectly distributed, several thimblefuls of botulinal could kill every man, woman, and child in America . . . three times over."

Brenner continued. "America also went into the botulinal toxin business in World War Two. We completed a plant in Vigo, Indiana, in 1945 but never went into production. Had it done so, the plant could have turned out over two hundred fifty thousand toxin bombs a month." Brenner paused to make a point. "The plant cost eight million dollars."

"Chump change for Kamāl Zohdi," murmured Sims.

"You said something about Zohdi being able to put together a"—the Judge glanced at his notes—"a serviceable facility if he were willing to take risks." He looked up to Brenner. "What kind of risks?"

"What we call 'containment.' We grade bio facilities on the degree to which they isolate the human operators from the infectious agents. The highest grade is BL Four. In a BL Four facility, for example, each operator would wear a self-contained 'spacesuit,' and would enter the work area through a series of air locks, and leave through disinfectant showers and ultraviolet rooms.

"But if someone were willing to risk the lives of the workers, they wouldn't have to go to the BL Four level. The Japanese Unit 731 in World War Two produced vast amounts of very dangerous agents with workers protected only by rubber suits, masks, gloves, and vaccinations. After the Gulf War, the UN inspection teams in Iraq found that Saddam Hussein's people were handling all kinds of violently infectious stuff at what would barely qualify as a BL Two level—they weren't wearing masks or protective clothing.

"So," Brenner concluded, "if you had someone who didn't care about risk—"

"—or workers who thought that if they died, it would be a one-way ticket to Paradise," the Judge interjected.

"—you could do some very nasty work in a bare-bones facility."

Sims glanced around the table while Brenner stood waiting for more questions. No more, Sims guessed. Dean, arms folded across his chest, gazed over the Judge's head toward some point on the far wall. Next to Dean, Lindahl sat back in his chair, doodling on his writing pad, shaking his head in small motions. Nesbith was a study in neutrality, hands folded primly and resting on the table before him. After a second, Brenner shut off the projector and took her seat at the table.

Dean brought his eyes down to the Judge, turned to look down the table toward the now-dark projection screen, and then back to the Judge.

"A lot from one entry on a pilfered document, Judge."

*"Poss*ibility, Ralston, not *prob*ability."

"But not the *only* possibility." Lindahl dropped his pencil on his pad, which was now full of looping swirls. He leaned forward, resting on his elbows, burr-cut head thrust forward at Brenner, looking, Sims thought, like a gross snapping turtle reaching out of its shell.

"In fact," Lindahl continued, "both Lebanon and Syria have legitimate industries that would account for the shipments you find so suspicious. As you point out, Dr. Brenner, anyone who knows how to make beer has access to equipment like that." Lindahl jerked a thumb toward the screen. "Besides brewing, such equipment is found in basic pharmaceutical manufacturing and food processing as well: food colorings, flavorings, yeast, vitamins"—Lindahl spread his hands expansively—"why it has any *number* of uses."

Sims, already exasperated by Lindahl's arrogance, cut in. "I don't think Zohdi's setting up a Budweiser franchise, Doctor. Or going into the aspirin business." Too late, he felt the Judge give him a knee under the table. "This bastard's a goddamn *terrorist!* He's slaughtered school buses full of kids, thrown grenades into theaters. Why the hell should we think—"

Ralston Dean smiled wolfishly at the Judge. "Ah, yes. Now Mr. . . . . Sims brings us to the hard part—intentions." He turned to Sims. "Perhaps we can explore why Zohdi—or any terrorist for that matter—would use some kind of . . . bug bomb. Admittedly, Zohdi is a bloodthirsty creature. But he's a political creature as well. He is cunning and he is . . . *rational."* Dean made it a final pronouncement, putting heavy emphasis on *rational.* "Why would he build a weapon that would kill several thousand people—"

"More than that," Brenner muttered.

Dean gave her a courtly condescending smile. "Kill several *hundred* thousand people, then, Dr. Brenner." Dean looked from Brenner to Sims and then to the Judge. "Zohdi has a weapon that will kill several hundred thousand people. Where"—Dean threw his hands up—*"where* would he use it? It'd have no extortion value. No one'd believe he had something so terrible. So he'd have to pop it off. So then he kills all those people. If he did it to us, we'd flatten him. We'd destroy any nation that gave him refuge."

Dean paused to lean back in his chair. He shook his head. "No," he said emphatically, "it is ab*surd*. I refuse to believe it."

The Judge tried patience. "Ralston," he said, soothingly, "again, what we're trying to say is that this is a possibility. We've gone through this kind of thing before—an increase of terrorist alert. During the Gulf War, we put the clamps down. Closed down foreign immigration, shut down everything except diplomatic travel into the States. We could—"

"No!" Dean stormed, slamming a fist on the table. "I don't give a shit how secret this meeting is, we go to some heightened alert and the story'd be out in no time. And you know damn well what that'd do. Once it got public, Congress'd raise all sorts of hell, demanding we *do* something. The Jewish lobby'd be pointing fingers at Syria. Then Damascus would walk out of the talks, and that son-of-a-bitch Rabin"—Dean scowled as he mentioned the Israeli prime minister—"would say he'd told us so, and the peace process would go into reverse."

Dean sat for a moment in his chair glaring belligerently across the table at Sims, the Judge, and Alice Brenner.

Suddenly, it came to Sims, how tired he was—everything seemed one universe removed from him. Incredibly, less than thirty-six hours ago, he'd been jimmying the warehouse skylight, and just yesterday in Berlin, he and the Judge had been waiting for Dimitri Aristov to show up. The fatigue invaded him, aided by the throbbing pain in his hand. It took a wrenching physical effort for him to bring himself back to the conference room. He looked around, startled to see everyone was standing. Show time was over. Sims got to his feet, his legs feeling like lead beneath him.

Seconds later, Sims, the Judge, and Alice Brenner stood alone in the conference room. Sims looked at the door through which Dean, Nesbith, and Lindahl had just left.

"Over the piano was printed a notice," the Judge quoted, also looking at the door, "'Please do not shoot the pianist. He is doing his best.'"

"Yeah," said Sims, "we just aren't playing Dean's tune."

Leaving the conference room, Sims's eye was caught by the Judge's special assistant. Telephone to her ear, she waved to him from her glassed in office, then held the phone out and pointed to it.

"He just called," she said to Sims as he came into her office. "You weren't in; it rolled over to my phone. Says he has to talk to you." Eyebrows raised, she offered the phone to Sims. "Name's Cantrell?"

21

You got squatters rights here?" Sims asked.

It was as if Roy Cantrell had never left the stand-up table in the coffee shop at National Airport. A new Diet Coke, but as far as Sims could tell, the same camel hair coat, pale blue shirt, and striped burgundy tie. Cantrell took a sip of the Diet Coke, his flat gray eyes scanning the coffee shop behind Sims over the rim of the raised can. He put the can down and moved his topcoat to the side to give Sims a place to put his coffee.

"Good meeting place," Cantrell answered in his rasping voice, "and they keep the Coke cold." Then, thin lips barely moving and the flat gray eyes still searching the coffee shop, "You been out a town."

Sims nodded without asking how Cantrell knew. Sims had known people like Cantrell; they could get to know anything. Unless they offered to tell you how, there wasn't any sense asking.

"I didn't know you guys were interested."

Cantrell gave him a long glance. "Heard there was going to be a meeting—you, the Judge, Dean, and Nesbith . . ." Cantrell let it trail off to see if Sims would fill in the blanks, but Sims just nodded and waited.

Cantrell gave up with a shrug, and continued. "My friends in the Bureau say Lars is keepin' his head down. Don't want to piss off the White House. Might show up for work one morning and find his parking slot's taken by some state trooper from Little Rock."

Sims said nothing, but made as if it took all his attention to remove the lid from the Styrofoam cup and stir in an envelope of sugar.

"A course," he heard Cantrell continue, "in this business, your sources, they keep workin', no matter what people like Nesbith and the Judge say—sources, they just keep workin'." He gave Sims a conspiratorial look. *"You* know how it is. When the boys on the top floor drag their feet, you can't always stay in step with them. They might want you to stonewall. But you can't slow down. Can't just not listen when you get a call."

Sims tried his coffee. It was scalding hot, and in spite of the sugar, bitter as hell. He put the coffee down and looked wearily at Cantrell.

"I'm tired as hell, Roy."

Cantrell casually glanced around to check for listeners, then hunched forward, resting his elbows down on the table and bringing his face closer to Sims. "This guy Hassan, the guy who tried to kill you in Rosslyn—"

"Yeah?"

"He belonged to a mosque in New Jersey—al-Salam, Jersey City."

"Okay, Jersey City," said Sims, wondering where it was going.

"Well,"—Cantrell's eyes made another circuit of the coffee shop—"the Jersey City PD has a source in the mosque."

"Source?"

"This guy was a walk-in. The Jersey City PD kept getting indications the mosque was . . . well, *militant.* They were wondering how to get a line on the mosque and this guy shows up on their doorstep. Code name's Neptune.

"Neptune checks in yesterday afternoon with his handler. A new guy has shown up in the mosque"—Cantrell pulled a small wire-bound notebook from an inner pocket and found the page he wanted—"a Palestinian named Yousef. Ramzi Ahmed Yousef." Cantrell folded the notebook shut but kept it under his hand on the table. "Now, that mosque's like Grand Central Station, anyhow, with all kinds a people coming and going. What makes this guy Yousef unusual, is that he's what they call an Afghani. That's a guy who—"

"Fought in Afghanistan," Sims supplied the explanation.

Cantrell nodded. His voice dropped lower. "Neptune said Yousef wears a medal. On a chain around his neck." Cantrell opened the notebook, withdrew a folded slip of paper, and passed it over to Sims. "Here's Neptune's sketch. Look familiar?"

Sims unfolded the paper. It wasn't to scale and the proportions were screwed up, but there was no mistaking the circle surrounding a curved sword, point buried in the ground. And above the sword, a crescent moon. Hassan had been wearing such a medallion, and so had the other guy who'd been in the van with him when the two of them had burned to death in Rosslyn.

"What's Neptune's access?"

"Don't know. Like I say, he's new."

"What's his background? Where'd he come from?"

Cantrell got a put-on look. "Damn, they teach you a lot a questions out there at Langley, don't they?" He shook his head wonderingly. "All I got from Jersey City is that Neptune walked in. They said they inherited him."

"Can we get a photo of Yousef? Maybe a print or two? Names of associates? Address?"

Cantrell sighed. "I already went back to the Jersey PD for that kinda stuff."

"And?"

"They haven't got back."

"You can't push?"

Cantrell got a face like he tasted something bad. "I'll do my best. It's not like we can work through the Bureau. Like I said, Lars is keeping his ass down. One thing Lars is good at is reading where trouble is."

"And his trouble comes from the White House." Sims picked up his coat. "You'll get what you can on Yousef?"

Cantrell drained his Coke, then nodded. "You?"

What the hell was he going to do? Sims couldn't think. How long had it been since he'd had any real sleep? Forty, fifty hours? Suddenly, the most important things in the world were food and sleep. Miragelike, a vision of a thick steak shimmered before him. Crisp and sizzling on a metal platter, surrounded by thick-cut fries. A cold beer. Crisp sheets on a firm bed.

"Me?" Sims said. "I'm goin' to see a man about a steak and fries."

As if from a great distance overhead, he felt a physical tugging, persistent, irresistible. Struggling, he rose through layers of consciousness, feeling as though he were being dragged from a secret cave within the central core of himself. As he rose, his awareness slowly expanded to take possession of the inert mass of his body. Somewhere toward the surface, he realized it was the ratcheting clatter of the phone that had caught him. He swung his feet to the floor and sat on the edge of the bed. Nerve endings, now awake, told him of the pain in his hand, of a need to urinate, of a dryness in his mouth. He felt under the pillow and came up with the Llama automatic.

He looked around, placing his surroundings: he was in Rollo Moss's apartment in southeast Washington. After leaving Cantrell, Sims had called Riddle and the two of them had met at Sam and Harry's. In little more than two hours, Sims had filled Riddle in, had the steak, a shower, and made it to bed. The bedside digital clock said eight. Six, maybe seven hours sleep, he thought. Then he saw the bright light filtering between the gaps in the drawn curtains. More like twenty hours, he corrected himself, getting out of bed, the last of the sleep-warmth still huddling in his chest and groin.

He answered the phone.

"Hi," came the throaty voice. "You been getting around."

In his sleep hangover, Sims imagined Lourdes's breath on his neck and took a deep breath himself.

"Line secure?"

"Wait a minute." Still thick-witted with sleep, he fumbled through his suitcase, finally found the fountain pen scrambler, and hooked it to the phone.

"On," he told her.

"Here we go," she said, and was gone, replaced by an echo-chamber effect that told him it was a satellite hookup.

"Hello?"

After a slight delay, "This is Will Uhlmann. From WE. Remember?"

The voice and image clicked into place. Small, dark-haired man. Neat. Precise. Good writer, desk with lots of pictures. Wife. Kids' soccer. Sailboat on the Bay. He had had an office two doors down from Sims in Western Europe division. That'd been seven years ago, before Sims's last posting to Prague.

"Sure. Where you now?"

"Calling from Tel Aviv, I'm chief of station here."

Sims carried the phone over to a chair and sat down, the instrument in his lap.

"I didn't know you were back . . ." Uhlmann's voice trailed off, leaving an aftertone of friendly curiosity.

"You know how it is," Sims said, thinking he was going to have to ask Uhlmann why the call, but knowing it had to do with Louis Velasquez and CTC.

"Uh . . . yeah," as Uhlmann caught onto it himself. "Anyway, we got the buzz from CTC, and the Izzies have come up with something on Zohdi. I called Louis Vee and he said you made the request."

"Yes," Sims said, now fully awake.

"Anyway, they got something—the Izzies do."

There was something else, Sims thought, a reason Uhlmann simply didn't call into CTC. "What do they have, Will?"

The pause was longer than the satellite bounce time.

Uhlmann finally came on. "I don't know. Aman's uncomfortable sending it out."

"You mean letting us have it." Exasperated, Sims felt his stomach knotting. "But if Aman told us they had something, why the hell won't they share it? Why say anything if they aren't going to say what?"

Another long pause.

"Bradford," the voice was lower, "they'll talk, but they say it has to be face-to-face—here."

22

"The Izzies aren't happy about this."

Uhlmann hunched forward over the wheel, keeping his eyes on the furious early morning traffic. The road to Jerusalem resembled a racetrack, with automobiles, motorcycles, trucks, and even army troop carriers, all blaring horns, all hurtling at maximum speed, as if each driver had to be first into the Holy City. They had left the coastal plain, and now the raw limestone outcroppings were covered by evergreens planted to reforest the broken hills of Sh'aar Hagai.

Uhlmann's call had come Saturday morning. Saturday afternoon, Sims was back at Andrews Air Force Base. Just after dawn, Sunday morning, the Judge's Gulfstream had touched down at Sde Dov military airfield near Tel Aviv. There, Will Uhlmann had been waiting to hustle him into the embassy Buick he'd parked discreetly off to the side of the main terminal.

"I think we're walking into a family squabble."

"About what?" asked Sims.

The chief of station shrugged dramatically. "Not sure. The Izzies pretty much keep their infighting to themselves. But rumors, body-language, a few hints here and there . . ."

Uhlmann glanced over to make certain Sims had caught the caveat, then plunged in. "Reuvan Eitan's the head of

Aman, good professional record. He's a climber, though, and Aman's too small a playground for him.

"Eitan's problem is this lieutenant colonel, Mordecai Ben-Ezra. Former para, lost an eye in the Yom Kippur war. One of those hairshirt kinds of guys—wakes up every morning convinced that the fate of Israel's on his shoulders—all that. Word is, Ben-Ezra's got Eitan over a barrel. Whatever it is that Ben-Ezra's got, Eitan doesn't like it because it means having to do something about it, but Eitan can't stifle Ben-Ezra, just in case everything goes to shit, Eitan's career'd be finished."

Sims mentally surveyed the landscape of Israeli intelligence. While the Mossad was Israel's better known intelligence agency, it is Aman that is the shield of the Jewish state. Mossad runs HUMINT, or human intelligence, but Aman holds the key to SIGINT, or signals intelligence. And it is on Aman, not Mossad, that rests the heavy responsibility for preparing the most sensitive document of the Israeli government, the annual Risk of War Estimate. In early 1993, no nation posed a greater threat to Israel than Syria; and each day, every day, it was Aman that stood watch for the point of the Syrian spear.

"And so Eitan gets us involved and, like you say, if it goes to shit, his ass's covered."

Uhlmann leaned on his horn and swung the Buick out to pass a loaded farm truck belching a thick blue cloud of exhaust. Then he looked at Sims. "Something like that."

"Nine days ago, on the fifth of February, we intercepted radio traffic of the Syrian air force attacking the village of Boudaï. On the basis of this information, we flew a photo reconnaissance mission into the Bekáa Valley."

Sims watched as Mordecai Ben-Ezra began his briefing. Uhlmann's description fit. Everything about the rail-thin lieutenant colonel said intensity: the eye patch, the hawklike face, the tight-ass voice. Other than the lieutenant colonel's pips on the epaulets of his faded khaki shirt, Ben-Ezra wore no medals except his silver parachutist wings.

When you had those wings and a patch where your right eye had been, Sims reflected, you didn't need pretty medals across your chest. From the corner of his eye, Sims scanned the decorations on Eitan's neatly tailored gabardine tunic—three rows of "be there" ribbons. The kind you got for hanging around, ceremonial medals that you got for staff work. Not the kind you got for facing fear in the night. Ben-Ezra, Sims decided, was a man with his mind on his business.

The windowless room resembled a medical theater, with six terraced rows of chairs with wide armrests for taking notes. Sims sat in the first row, with Uhlmann on his left and on his right, Reuven Eitan, head of Aman, Israel's military intelligence.

Eitan had been correct but cool when they'd met. Sims got the impression that the pudgy general would rather be anywhere else. When Ben-Ezra had entered the briefing room, Sims had noticed that Eitan went from cool to downright freezing doing the introductions. For a clumsy moment, the four of them had stood facing each other uncomfortably until Ben-Ezra muttered something about getting started and took his place at the podium.

Ben-Ezra worked a button on the podium, and a projection screen unreeled from the ceiling. Another button, the lights dimmed.

"Photos, please," Ben-Ezra requested a hidden projectionist.

The first black-and-white photo filled the screen. From sixty-five thousand feet, Aman's pilotless spy plane's camera had captured hundreds of square miles of the Bekáa Valley.

"The Lebanon Mountains," Ben-Ezra said, using a wooden pointer to trace a ridge of mountains framing the left of the photo—"and the Orontes River"—the arrow traced a thread running north to south—"and Boudaï"—the pointer flew to the center of the photograph.

Sims saw only a large smudge, dark against the valley floor, with darker random lines running through it.

"Next, an enlargement," Ben-Ezra announced.

The enlargement kept the same orientation as the original photograph. The dark random lines, Sims saw, were the outlines of buildings. Or where the buildings had been.

"Boudaï was a typical Bekáa village," Ben-Ezra said. "Mostly one story flat-roofed houses and shops. This had been the village square . . . and here the mosque . . . here and here the schools . . . you can still see the soccer field . . ."

"There's nothing left," Sims said.

"We counted thirty-two firing runs on the village," Ben-Ezra said in a flat voice, the impersonal tone adding chill depth to the desolation on the screen. "Fourteen with fragmentation bombs, eighteen napalm. We have tapes of the pilot's radio transmissions as they machine-gunned children trying to escape into the fields. They machine-gunned them, then they napalmed them."

Sims thought he detected a tremor in the Israeli colonel's voice. "How many people?" Sims asked.

"Our records show just over six hundred."

Unable to take his eyes away from the scorched devastation, Sims found the shape of an ox-drawn cart tilted on its side with one of its huge wheels facing skyward. He couldn't find the remains of the ox or any trace of the people who had been in the cart. The sterile photograph was all the more gruesome because he knew what it was hiding. He found his eyes filling and a corrosive wave of anger harsh in his throat.

"We didn't understand this," Ben-Ezra said. Sims noticed that he cut a hard glance at Eitan, who shifted minutely in the next chair. "But your request for information on Zohdi raised the question if he, in some way, was connected to Boudaï."

"Connected?" asked Sims.

Ben-Ezra nodded. A flicker of light and the previous photo seemed to have been shifted in its frame. Sims saw the Lebanon Mountains and the Orontes River again, and the scorched area that had been Boudaï, but now, Boudaï was moved farther west.

Ben-Ezra tapped the screen with his pointer, circling two straight dark lines against the valley floor.

"Yaate," he announced, tapping the screen again. "It is well known that the Syrian government allots territories in the Bekáa to various terrorist groups—among other things, it keeps the peace in Syria. Yaate was allotted to Zohdi. It is an airfield, built long ago when the French controlled Lebanon. It had been abandoned for some years. This photograph was taken in March 1990."

Another photograph, an enlargement.

"You see here the runways and parking ramps and the foundations for hangars. The hangars themselves were dismantled years ago."

Sims stared intently at the screen: the two runways crossed, looking almost like partially opened scissors, cutting their way east. By the scissors' pivot, the parking ramp and hangars.

"Then, in October 1991, a source reported that the local authorities had declared Yaate a forbidden zone. That same month, we detected construction activity. Along with that, we picked up transmissions suggesting that a tactical radio net had been established to control security in the area. These are signature events—they've happened before when Damascus has parceled out land for terrorist camps in the Bekáa."

Ben-Ezra paused and scanned his small audience, a silent invitation to questions. There were none.

"And now . . ." Another flicker of the screen. "This is a photograph taken on December 17, 1991."

South of the runways, behind where the hangars had been, Sims saw a cluster of buildings. Light tracings showed new roads. Small rectangles that Sims took to be trucks were parked throughout the area, and on the ramp near to the runways, he saw what looked like a helicopter.

"French," Ben-Ezra said, as if reading Sims's mind. "An Aérospatiale Gazelle. Sold in great numbers to Kuwait. That particular one is Kamāl Zohdi's personal play toy."

"What are the buildings?" Sims asked, beginning to like the stiff-necked colonel.

The pointer rapped the screen. Set back from the runways, two long narrow buildings paralleled each other, leaving what Sims estimated to be a gap of thirty feet between them. "These are barracks—see the smaller buildings behind each? Latrines. And here"—a square building at one end of the barracks and equidistant from them—"a mess hall." The pointer flew to an area surrounded by earthen berms. "Generators."

"The building by the runways?" Sims pointed to an L-shaped building, set off from the other buildings. It was as if someone had taken the two barracks buildings and butted them together.

Ben-Ezra shook his head while gazing at the photograph for some seconds. As if he might figure out the answer with just another look. He shook his head again. "We don't know." The pointer worked its way around the building. "There is a fence around it with but one entry." He pointed out a small building. "This's the guard shack at the entry, it is—was—manned around the clock. And watchtowers here, here, and here." He rapped the pointer on the screen.

"What's that in the L of the building?" Sims eyed a square box of a structure, estimating its size to be about that of two of the trucks that were scattered around the photograph.

"This?" Ben-Ezra slid the pointer over the screen with a rasping sound, finding the building. He looked at it for a moment, then shook his head. "Another thing we don't know." He hung the pointer on a hook on the side of the podium and folded his arms across his chest. "As I said"—he jerked his head to the screen—"this was Yaate on 17 December 1991.

"We put it on our watch list, but over the year, it dropped in priority. Nothing going on. Little communications traffic besides the guard network. No human source reports from the area of anything, even in the marketplace gossip in Baalbek.

"Then came the destruction of Boudaï on February 5, then your request for information about Zohdi, and now this photo of Yaate." Ben-Ezra reached across to the podium and another photograph flashed onto the screen.

The runway first caught Sims's eye; then he noticed the difference. "The L-shaped building . . ." The barracks and mess hall still stood, but the building by the runway was rubble. The trucks were gone. No helicopter waited on the parking ramp.

"When was this?"

"Wednesday. The same overflight that took the Boudaï photographs. Yaate was in the vicinity; standard procedure calls for us to get as much as possible from each mission."

"Signals traffic?" Sims asked.

"Nothing. Last transmissions the morning of 5 February. Five hours before the destruction of Boudaï."

"Human sources?"

"Nothing. Absolutely nothing."

Sims glanced left out of the corner of his eye at Eitan, the Aman chief. The general's round face had tightened into a pout of . . . disapproval? . . . no, Sims decided, unhappiness. Sims twisted in his seat to face Eitan. "And what's the interpretation of this, General?"

Eitan's reaction was subtle, as Sims suspected it'd be. Subtle but telling—a microscopic flinching as the surprise flickered across the face, a reflexive dropping of the jaw, a tongue run quickly across the lips. Sims had to hand it to Eitan, though. In less than a second, the general turned to Sims, fully composed, with a small smile of calm assurance and professional competence.

"Those of us in this line of work have been here before," Eitan said smoothly, as if dealing with a sympathetic but not too bright member of the Knesset who saw to Aman's yearly appropriations. "Outsiders always picture us coming up with the absolutes . . . the certainties. The secret plans for an Arab atomic bomb, the date and hour of the next coup in some back of beyond country that has yet to discover the flush toilet."

Having reached his peak, Eitan paused theatrically, then rushed down the slope on the other side. "They never know how tenuous most of it is. How little we have to go on. The haggling . . . the negotiating. The sorting out of that which is wheat, and that which is chaff."

Sims stole a glance at Ben-Ezra. The thin lieutenant colonel stood frozen by the podium, watching the general with a cobralike fixed stare.

"One version of Colonel Ben-Ezra's *'events,'*" Eitan continued, managing a set of verbal quotation marks around *events,* "is that Zohdi's men at Yaate had families in Boudaï, that the destruction of the village and the camp at Yaate was the result of infighting among the Arabs. That Zohdi somehow crossed the wrong faction in Damascus. Brutal . . . inhumane . . . but not without ample precedent." Eitan folded his hands on the wide arm of his chair and gave Sims an "I'm finished" look.

Sims had to hand it to Eitan—he was sure that the *one* version was *Eitan's* version. But the general hadn't chiseled his name on it. At the same time, he'd pissed all over Ben-Ezra with that "events" shit. Sims's dislike of the smug Eitan climbed another notch.

"You said 'one version,' General. Those of us in this line of work know there're usually more."

Eitan realized Sims had thrown his "those of us in this line of work" back at him, and a small smile pulled at his mouth, but his dark eyes were guarded and watchful.

"Our hawk." Eitan waved a foppish hand in Ben-Ezra's direction. "Colonel Ben-Ezra, give our guests another variant."

With a bleak, stony look, Ben-Ezra straightened his shoulders and picked the wood pointer off its hook on the side of the podium. Instead of using it to point to the screen, he held it point-down along the side of his leg, as he might have held a sword.

"The version General Eitan gave is persuasive . . ." Ben-Ezra put a coat of grease on "persuasive," paused a beat, then delivered the rest of it, ". . . on the surface."

Sims forced himself to suppress a smile. Ben-Ezra might be a tight-ass, but he wasn't a suck-up.

Ben-Ezra continued. "Careful analysis, however, raises certain questions." He smacked the pointer squarely in the middle of where the L-shaped building had been. "The rubble pattern here"—Ben-Ezra traced the destruction—"is relatively even. It is all blown outward." He snapped the pointer away from the screen and slapped it against the side of his leg. "Had the Syrians bombed Yaate the way they bombed Boudaï, we would have seen a more random distribution of rubble. This pattern"—another crisp slap on the screen—"is more indicative of an explosion from within, not from bombs dropped from above. Moreover, had the building been bombed, there would have been craters. This explosion was too neat. Too precise."

Ben-Ezra scanned the eyes locked on him. "Questions?" He paused for a moment, then, "Next, we monitored radio transmissions from Yaate until early Friday morning. The transmissions were scrambled and we are still working on breaking them. But the traffic intensity was normal. At oh-six hundred hours, just after sunrise, the net shut down."

"How long had the net been in operation?" Sims asked Ben-Ezra.

"Continuously. Since October '91."

"Well, then," Sims argued, "wouldn't that buttress General Eitan's version?"

Eitan's composure slipped a fraction. "That . . . ah . . . that wasn't *my* . . . I mean, it was . . . *a* version."

"Of course, General, just a version," Sims said, not sounding very sincere. He turned back to Ben-Ezra, whose eyes held a lurking amusement. "Wouldn't that buttress . . . the original version?"

"Not exactly. You see, the transmissions from Yaate didn't just end"—Ben-Ezra made a downward slashing motion with the pointer—"each station in the net signed off. Very disciplined, very professional. They ended their own transmissions, they weren't ended for them."

Another pause for questions. There were none. Ben-Ezra, having laid his foundation, went on to build upon it. He slapped the pointer against the side of his leg.

"Third point: We had no difficulty monitoring the air activity in the destruction of Boudaï. We detected no air activity hours earlier over Yaate."

Again, no questions. Another slap of the pointer.

"Fourth, no other buildings in the Yaate complex were destroyed. The barracks, the mess hall—these remain intact.

"And the last point: The Syrians still classify Yaate as a 'forbidden zone'; they still run occasional patrols around the area for security."

Ben-Ezra brought the pointer across his body and grasped the free end with his left hand, and stood, legs slightly apart, alert, yet relaxed.

"And this means?" Sims prompted.

Coolly, Ben-Ezra tilted his head back slightly, jutting his jaw out. "I don't deal in guesses, Mr. Sims."

"I didn't *ask* for guesses, Colonel Ben-Ezra," Sims replied evenly.

A tense silence stretched across the room. Eitan, arms folded across his chest, eyes on the floor in front of him, smirked in satisfaction. Uhlmann, an uneasy spectator, shifted in his seat, his shoes rasping on the floor. Then Ben-Ezra swung the pointer down and tapped its point against his leg.

"What it indicates is a deliberate evacuation of Yaate. Something about Yaate was serious enough to cause Syrians to destroy Boudaï and kill six hundred people. It indicates, too, that Zohdi's purpose at Yaate is over. He either failed or succeeded at whatever it was that he was doing there."

Sims shifted in his seat. "Let us go back to the beginning." He waved at the screen and the photograph. "How did you identify this as Zohdi's in the first place?"

Ben-Ezra rewarded Sims with a tight smile. "Zohdi didn't live at Yaate. The security radio net would invariably warn its guards and watchtowers when Zohdi's helicopter was on its way in." Ben-Ezra gave another small smile. "Our man Zohdi is a great one for ironic metaphor. His radio call sign was Abaddon."

Head tilted to one side, Ben-Ezra looked at Sims. "You know the Bible, Mr. Sims? Do you know Abaddon?"

Sims nodded. "Revelations—the angel of Hell."

The room fell into a silence that was finally broken by Eitan. "As you Americans say, Mr. Sims, we've put *our* cards on the table." He looked expectantly at Sims.

"Three days ago," Sims began, "we uncovered a connection between Kamāl Zohdi and a German export firm. The firm had been shipping weapons to Zohdi for some time."

"Ah, yes," murmured Eitan, "the good Germans."

"But we found an unusual transaction." Sims described Alice Brenner's detective work as Eitan and Ben-Ezra listened intently. It seemed to Sims that as he spoke, Eitan's inner vitality drained away, that the man was becoming a lifeless statue. Ben-Ezra, on the other hand, was racing along with Sims, as if taking the pieces Sims was offering up and fitting them against gaps in his own mental puzzle. When Sims finished, it was Ben-Ezra who spoke first.

"Again—the date of the transaction?" he asked Sims to repeat it.

"September. September 4, '91."

"A month before the construction began at Yaate."

Eitan said nothing but sat staring off into the distance, his face looking old and drawn. He finally came to life, wearily rubbing a hand across his forehead. "As you might expect, Mr. Sims, the possibility you raise of weapons of mass destruction has a certain . . . ah . . . resonance here."

"Here?"

"Israel."

Sims thought for a second. "Yes." He nodded. "I guess so." Sims rose from his chair and faced Eitan. "It looks like if we want to know about Yaate, General, we got to go there."

23

Sims had forgotten how cold it could get in the desert. A few minutes before, the blast doors of the hangar had been rolled open and now the Negev Desert's night wind knifed through the arched concrete structure, bringing with it a fine pumice grit that stung the exposed skin.

Some thirty feet away in the semidarkness of the vast hangar, the small MH-6 helicopters resembled fragile eggs onto which a child had glued rotor blades and pencil-thin tail booms. Ground crews were busy closing the last of the helicopters' service panels. The men and the helicopters looked oddly two-dimensional in the flat red glow of the blackout lights, and the panels snapping shut made tacking metallic sounds.

Sims saw that Ben-Ezra was finishing a conversation with one of the pilots. In a moment, the Israeli colonel would look around, find him, motion, and they would be under way. Sims shifted the Galil assault rifle to his left hand and with his right tugged at the shoulder straps of his rucksack, working the heavy load higher on his back.

By the helicopters, Ben-Ezra made a come-on gesture.

"Time," Sims whispered to himself.

Ben-Ezra waited by the lead helicopter. With him, Jibril and Yariv, senior noncoms in the *Sayeret Matcal*, loosely meaning reconnaissance regiment—Aman's counterpart to the American Green Berets. The three men stood leaning slightly forward to offset the heavy rucksacks. Sims was dressed as they were, rough leather combat boots, camouflaged battle dress uniforms splotched with irregulars and and earth tone blots, soft floppy bush hats.

Wordlessly, the four men boarded. Although the doors had been taken off the passenger compartment, loading took work because of the small space and the bulky rucksacks. Ben-Ezra climbed in first, then Sims, strapping themselves side by side into the two forward-facing nylon mesh seats.

Jibril and Yariv took up positions facing them. Jibril, opposite Sims, stuffed his floppy bush hat into a leg pocket of his battle dress trousers and, reaching into an overhead compartment, came down with earphones and lip mike that he slipped over his head.

Sims, following the man's hands, saw what looked like a trombone case latched into an overhead rack. He nudged Ben-Ezra. "Stinger?" he asked.

Ben-Ezra nodded. Jibril, hearing Sims's question, pulled a grin made sinister by a gold canine tooth. "We go down," he said, still messing with the lip mike, "the first airplanes we see might not be our own."

Jibril muttered something into his lip mike and the helicopter came to life. The Allison turbine jutted into the tiny passenger compartment, its thin aluminum casing just inches from Sims's left ear. As the pilot increased rpm's, the turbine's high-pitched whine became a physical sensation and the vibrations seemed to blur the air inside the cramped compartment. Just as the sound reached the intensity of a dentist's drill, the helicopter lifted several feet off the hangar floor, dropped its nose, and, tilted forward, flew out of the darkened hangar into the overcast sky.

Fifteen minutes later, the helicopter had reached its initial cruising altitude. The chase helicopter had taken up station a thousand feet behind and slightly higher. Sitting in the open doorway, held in only by his seat belt, Sims looked down on the landscape five thousand feet below. He saw only the dimmest outlines of a rough and craggy terrain. The cliffs soon gave way to a flat even blackness of what could be water, and the slipstream rushing past the helicopter carried an odor of rotten eggs.

"The Dead Sea," Ben-Ezra leaned over to shout in Sims's ear. He pointed down into the dark. "We are passing over Masada somewhere down there."

Masada, the mountain stronghold where a thousand Jews had held out against the might of the Roman empire long after Jerusalem had fallen. And where the Jewish men had killed their families, then committed suicide rather than surrender.

Sims glanced at Jibril directly across from him. The man was asleep, as was Yariv. Sims turned to Ben-Ezra who was rocking back and forth in small mournful motions, staring into the well of darkness below.

A man with a mission, Sims thought. Ben-Ezra had obviously been planning a crossborder operation before Sims had brought it up. Within minutes after Eitan had given final approval at Aman headquarters, Ben-Ezra had had a helicopter waiting to take Sims and himself to the secret Aman camp near Dimona in the Negev Desert. That evening and the following day had been a blur of preparation.

There had been the pairing up with Jibril and Yariv. The two professionals had made no attempt to hide their critical inspection of him and Ben-Ezra, nor did they hide the looks of skepticism on their faces.

Jibril had taken Sims through processing, with Yariv accompanying Ben-Ezra. First, supply, then the armory. Boots, socks, rucksack, woolen underwear, thick ribbed sweater, freeze-dried rations, camouflaged battle dress uniform. Then the silencer equipped Galil rifle with grenade launcher, claymore mine, first aid kit, night vision goggles, three hundred rounds of rifle ammunition, four canteens, five two-pound blocks of plastic explosive, and finally, a single side-band radio.

After the firing range where Sims and Ben-Ezra had zeroed their weapons, the four began a nonstop assessment of Yaate and the surrounding Bekáa Valley. Aman's intelligence specialists had tried to fill in the blanks: the Syrian patrols, their strength, weapons, routine, frequency. Regular troops? Or local militia? Vehicles—jeeps? trucks? armored cars? Syrian communications—frequencies? net structure? discipline? Photo analysts had dissected the Yaate airfield and its surrounding terrain—size of the demolished building? length of runway? power capacity of generator? where is the high ground? the gullies and wadis? Even the meteorologist had his day—BMNT? (beginning, morning nautical twilight?) cloud cover? precipitation? temperature and visibility? wind speed and direction? EENT? (end, evening nautical twilight?).

Sims leaned slightly out into the slipstream and looked down. They were now headed north over the Dead Sea. They would follow the Jordan to the Sea of Galilee, the same flight path routinely flown by Israeli border surveillance aircraft. Then they would drop down to the deck to throw off Syrian and Jordanian radars, and begin their run up the Bekáa.

Settling back against his seat, he saw that Ben-Ezra had been watching him. Feeling awkward as their eyes met, Sims put on an overly large grin and gave a thumbs-up gesture. Unsmiling, the Israeli nodded acknowledgment, then shifted his gaze to the terrain below his side of the helicopter.

Sims studied Ben-Ezra: the profile of a hawk, the high cheekbones, the hard mouth and its thin lips. And the black patch. During the intensity of the past thirty hours in the desert camp, Sims had seen Ben-Ezra show only the slightest sign of what might be weariness when the man had slipped his fingertips under the patch to massage the empty eye socket.

You don't get to know men like this in thirty hours, Sims thought, maybe not in a lifetime. They're proud of not bullshitting anybody. But they bullshit you and themselves. For all the what-you-see-is-what-you-get, there's always something secret inside them they'll never tell you and they'll never tell themselves.

Jibril and Yariv were different. Hard as Ben-Ezra, probably tougher, certainly younger. Jibril, dark, compact, lively, a Druze whose family had lived for centuries in the land that straddled what was now the Golan Heights and the lower Bekáa Valley.

Yariv was a quiet Pole whose grandparents had settled in Palestine before World War II and the holocaust. Blond with quick blue eyes. Big hands that cradled a Belgian Minimi machine gun as if it were a child's toy.

Jibril and Yariv had joined the Israeli army after high school, met in the paratroopers, and, lured by the excitement, signed on with Aman. They had run crossborder operations into every neighboring Arab country and had stopped counting missions after the two hundred mark. Sims watched them nod, chins down on their chests, heads bobbing slightly with the vibration of the helicopter. They weren't faking—they were asleep.

Half an hour later, Sims sensed a subtle change in the helicopter's vital signs. It was nothing he could pin down: a slight drop in the pitch of the turbine, a vague feeling of slowing, the rotor blades overhead seemingly taking a shallower cut out of the air. Then, unmistakably, he felt the helicopter descend. Down below was the Sea of Galilee, dark under the overcast sky, its outline only hinted at by sprinklings of lights from Tiberias and the small towns and settlements along the shore. To his right—the east—the Golan Heights and Syria.

According to plan, the two helicopters would fly the last ninety miles into Yaate on the deck to evade the Syrian surveillance radars covering the southern entrance to the Bekáa. Sims felt his ears popping under the increased pressure and he saw that Jibril and Yariv were wide awake.

Like two tethered dragonflies, the tiny helicopters zipped down canyons, over rises, under power lines—in near pitch-dark, twenty to thirty feet off the ground, at a hundred and thirty miles an hour.

Inside the lead helicopter, Sims was being thrown violently about in spite of his seat belt. Every hard angle, edge, and corner dug into him as he slammed against his rucksack, seat back, and Ben-Ezra. Outside the open doorway, the scenery flashed by like one of those manic scenes shot hurtling down a bobsled run. The eye would catch a mosque, a cliff, a stand of cedars, but they would be gone long before the brain registered.

Sims imagined the view from up front where the pilot was flying with night vision goggles. It helped—and it didn't help—that Sims knew what that meant. Night vision goggles let you see, but just barely. They cut your peripheral vision down to keyhole size and depth perception to zero.

The ride got even rougher as the pilot threaded the small craft through the rising terrain of the Hula Valley north of Galilee. Here, Sims remembered, the elevation was no more than several hundred feet; minutes ahead of them lay the Lebanon Mountains, the western wall of the Bekáa Valley. The valley floor averaged around three thousand feet above sea level, the mountains another three thousand or so above that.

"Metulla," Ben-Ezra nudged Sims and leaned over to shout in his ear. The lights of the Israeli border town flashed by a mile or two away out the port side of the helicopter. Minutes later, they bypassed Marjayoûn, the first major town in Lebanon. Sims felt the helicopter bank sharply to the right. He checked his watch: 11:40 P.M. They were on time and in the Bekáa.

For twenty-five minutes, the two helicopters hedge-hopped up the valley, keeping close to the Lebanon Mountains, jinking and twisting to skim over hills, cultivated fields, tiny farming villages.

Several minutes more, and the fields of the lower Bekáa gave way to the arid flatlands, and Sims felt the helicopter slowing, almost imperceptibly at first, then more so. In the distance, their last checkpoint before Yaate—the lights of Baalbek.

A buzzer sounded in the passenger compartment, harsh and rasping over the engine noise. Over each doorway, a red signal light came on. Sims looked up to see the copilot extending a hand back into the passenger compartment. Two fingers made a V—two minutes to touchdown.

Outside, the rotors changed pitch, making slapping sounds against the cold night air. Checking again to make

267

certain the safety was on, Sims swung the muzzle of his
assault rifle out into the slipstream and worked the charging
handle, chambering a round into the breech. Jibril watched
with a small smile, then followed suit.

The buzzer sounded again. One minute. Jibril was the
first to unsnap his seat belt. The helicopter was slower, now,
flaring into its approach. They were directly over Yaate;
Sims picked out the dim shape of the runways several
hundred yards off to his left and beyond the runways, the
less distinct outlines of what had to be the footings for the
hangars.

The helicopter was almost at a standstill, six to seven feet
above the ground. The red light over the door changed to
green and the buzzer gave a last, angry command.

Gone!—one instant Jibril was there, the next, gone.

Sims jerked his head left. Ben-Ezra and Yariv's seats were
empty. The helicopter pitch increased.

Sims jumped. Hitting the ground as the helicopter began
picking up speed, he swiveled on the balls of his feet,
twisting slightly to roll onto the side of his right leg, then
onto his back, taking the shock up with his rucksack. He
scrambled to his feet, shaking the rucksack higher up on his
back and changing his grip on the Galil so that his thumb
was over the safety, ready to flick it off. The helicopter was a
faint noise disappearing into the night.

Ben-Ezra got to him first. "Are you all right?" After
getting Sims's assurance, Ben-Ezra needled him. "I thought
you decided to go back."

Sims felt his face flush. "I'm okay," he told Ben-Ezra. He
dug his floppy hat out of a trouser pocket, jammed it on his
head, then pounded Ben-Ezra on the back of his rucksack.
"And I wouldn't go back without *you,* my man."

Ben-Ezra motioned toward a low hill beyond the runways
and set off toward it. The rest followed in a strung-out single
file, Yariv next, then Sims, with Jibril bringing up the rear.
The ground was dry and hard and Sims could smell the
pinching odor of the alkali dust kicked up by their boots.
The wind, coming from his right, drove icy slivers into his
face and he was thankful for the sweater, gloves, and thick
woolen underwear.

They moved quickly across the runway. As they did so, Sims came to realize how exposed they were. The terrain offered little cover; the small hill they were making for was no more than a gentle rise peppered with basalt and limestone boulders. No trees, no vegetation except a winter-burned grass stubble. He knew it from the maps and photographs, but the barren artificial flatness of the runway brought it home: they were as vulnerable as ants on a tabletop.

Within minutes, they had made it to the top of the hill where Yariv shrugged off his rucksack beside a large lime-stone boulder and began setting up his radio. Sims, Ben-Ezra, and Jibril spread out and surveyed the land around them through night vision binoculars. Sims saw that the hill was a low oval, its long axis parallel to the main runway and pointing directly to the hangar footings and foundations. He swung his binoculars several degrees to the right of the hangar footings and found the chain link fence that had secured the L-shaped building. The rubble, about two hundred yards away, was a linear jumble of what appeared to be broken concrete panels, as if a giant, tired of his game, had carelessly tossed a deck of cards onto the ground. Still farther to Sims's right, the two barracks buildings and their mess hall.

He walked a few paces to Ben-Ezra, who was lowering his binoculars. "Nothing here."

"Or here either," replied Ben-Ezra.

"Nothing." Jibril joined them, shaking his head.

Yariv, sitting cross-legged on the ground in front of his radio looked up and gave Ben-Ezra an okay sign, making an O of thumb and forefinger: he had made contact with base operations and filed his initial entry report.

Sims checked his watch: 12:30 A.M., Jerusalem time. So far, the plan was working. Sun and moon and helicopter vulnerability had shaped the plan's outlines. The helicopters wanted to be in and out of the Bekáa during darkness. There would be a quarter moon at 2:43 A.M. But getting into Yaate at night meant you had to wait until daylight to go through the Yaate wreckage. And if you came out too early in the day, you'd risk discovery. You wanted minimum time between coming out of hiding and pickup. Sunset would come at 5:30 P.M. So the plan was to hole up for most of the day until just after 3:30 P.M. That'd give you two hours of daylight: maximum time to work through Yaate, minimum time for the Syrians to tumble to you. Then, with darkness falling, the helicopters would come pick you up. That was the plan.

Sims and Ben-Ezra followed Jibril and Yariv as they walked their inspection of the hilltop, looking down on the terrain below it, the two sergeants talking among themselves in the infantry soldier's professional jargon, gestures and incomplete sentences about observation, cover and concealment, fields of fire. Positioning Yariv's machine gun was the most important thing. They had no way of knowing the direction from which any enemy might come, so the discussion centered on the most likely approach and the next most likely approach. Cover one and find an alternate to cover the other.

Having settled the issue on the approaches, Jibril and Yariv pointed to where Sims and Ben-Ezra would take up positions. It came down to this: the four men occupied a roughly circular position on the crest of the hill, each making best use of the boulders for cover. Yariv set up his machine gun on its folding tripod so that it covered the southern slope of the hill which was the most gradual. Jibril assigned each of them clock times: he, facing north, was twelve o'clock, Sims east, was three, with Yariv at six, and Ben-Ezra, facing west, nine o'clock.

As if on silent command, Jibril and Yariv then moved to the next task, that of camouflaging their positions. Sims watched as Jibril dug into his rucksack for a rough-weave net that unfolded to ten feet on a side. Next, a length of dirty-colored nylon line and a half dozen metal pegs almost a foot in length. In seconds, the two men had strung and staked the netting over their positions, then turned to help Ben-Ezra and Sims.

Sims's position looked directly down on the airfield some two hundred yards away. Scanning from left to right through the night vision binoculars, he saw the greenish glow outlines of the runways and ramp, the L-shaped building—or what remained of it—then the barracks and mess hall. Five miles to the southeast, Baalbek. Six miles due west, what had been Boudaï. His netting stretched out from a flat-faced boulder on his left, making a lean-to with enough headroom so that he could sit up. He crawled in, dragging his rucksack with him. For the next several minutes, he unpacked, rucksack in a crevice back by his feet, spare magazines for the Galil to his right front, and beside them, two fragmentation grenades.

Although Ben-Ezra was by far the senior, he'd wisely left the security decisions to Jibril and Yariv. The two NCOs had divided the remaining four hours of darkness into two watches; Jibril having the first, Yariv the second. Sims hadn't liked it, the implication that the night watch was too important to be left to amateurs like himself. But thinking it through, he saw that he was very much the straphanger, and that Jibril and Yariv had made this line of work their profession.

Close behind, he heard the sound of boots grating on gravel. He turned. Jibril knelt, holding a length of nylon line into which he'd tied a loop.

"Here." He handed the loop to Sims. "To put around your wrist. Our alarm," he explained, motioning down the hill from Sims's position. "I see something, hear something—I will pull. Bring you orange juice in bed." Jibril flashed a gold-glinted smile and went off into the night, paying out his nylon line, making his way to Yariv and Ben-Ezra.

Sims felt a sharp tugging. Before fully awake, he realized it had come from the nylon loop around his wrist. He had been dozing on his belly, cheek on the forestock of his assault rifle. Rolling into firing position, he pushed his rifle into his shoulder and scanned the land below over its sights. His heart was still pounding as he listened to the quiet and realized it had been Jibril's wake-up call: everyone awake at first light.

The sun was still behind the Anti-Lebanon Mountains,

fifteen miles away, and the sky and the land were the same shade of dingy gray. Some four or five miles away, Sims estimated, a thin column of smoke from an open fire rose straight up, then, as if running into a glass barrier, it bent abruptly as it hit a low-lying inversion layer and heeled over to the west. Breakfast, he thought, for a shepherd or a Syrian army unit. He hoped it was a shepherd. His watch said 5:58 A.M. Remembering Ben-Ezra's briefing, the MiGs out of Khalkhalah would be airborne for their morning patrol, and would be overhead in half an hour or so, looking down at Yaate and the four of them on the hilltop.

Without the night binoculars, the airfield seemed shrunken and farther away. Even in the dim light, the disrepair was evident, wide cracks in the parking ramps, and in places, dunes of windblown limestone grit covered large portions of the runways. The fencing around the ruins of the L-shaped building was torn in several places and he could now see more clearly the square structure that still stood in the interior corner of the L. As far as he could see, with the exception of the column of smoke, there was no sign of life.

He laid his assault rifle down, then reached into his rucksack, coming up with a foil-wrapped fruit bar. Sitting up with his back against the boulder, Sims nibbled at the fruit bar and unscrewed the top from a canteen. Still chilled from the night before, the water tasted clean and slightly alkaline, as if it had come from a spring. Taking another sip, he sloshed the water around in his mouth, then spat it out. Within seconds, the parched soil had absorbed the water without a trace.

For a moment, Sims stared at the patch of soil where the water had been, thinking idly about the water's rapid disappearance. He glanced at his watch: 6:15. He had been awake now all of seventeen minutes. How many minutes until 3:30, when they would go down to the airstrip? Thinking of time, he realized today was February 15. For a second, he knew it was a significant date, but couldn't place it.

Then it came to him: today was his father's birthday. Resting back against the boulder, Sims let his memory work on dim and faded images, shifting images, mostly of his father's face: stern, demanding, laughing, sad. A father who was proud in his police blue with creaking leather and polished brass and gleaming shoes. And he wondered, not for the first time, where he would have been without those images of his father. Dead or in jail, he thought, that's where I would have been. And he thought about that as his eyes grew heavy and he drowsily settled into spying and soldiering's oldest job—waiting.

Half an hour later, the sun, climbing higher, had burned away the thin mist, leaving a deep blue dome over the creamy limestone of the flat valley floor. In the glare of daylight, the hilltop appeared barren and lifeless, the only movement being the slow shifting of shadows among the boulders.

At seven, Sims heard a faint roar from the sky, and through the camouflage netting, he saw two white contrails overhead—the Syrian MiGs from Khalkhalah. The next hours Sims spent beneath his camouflage net, studying the airfield through his binoculars, napping, and when tired of both, sitting up to read a tattered paperback he'd picked up in the Negev camp, Conroy's *The Lords of Discipline*.

At three-fifteen, he methodically repacked his rucksack. At three-twenty, he checked his rifle and dusted the grit off it with a small cleaning cloth. He was finishing when Ben-Ezra, in a crouch, rounded a boulder and came to squat just outside the overhang of Sims's camouflage net.

"It is almost time." On his hands and knees, he crawled under the net to get a look at the airfield.

Sims motioned with his binoculars. "You look at the crowds in a city, you know all kinds of things are happening. "This"—Sims waved at the airfield—"totally lifeless. They left last week, but it's the same as if they'd left a thousand years ago. Hard to believe anything ever happened there."

Ben-Ezra studied the airfield for a long time, then shifted a questioning gaze to Sims. "How did you come to be here?"

273

"Here? On this hill?"

"Doing the kind of things that put you on this hill."

Sims remembered the morning and the images of his father. "You make choices about your life. I made mine because I wanted to be one of the good folks."

"Good folks?" Ben-Ezra asked, clearly puzzled.

"My dad and mom always told me the world was made up of good folks and bad folks."

"A basic definition."

"Yeah. Dad and Mom were basic people. For them, good folks were people who worshipped God, loved their family, obeyed the law, and defended their country." Sims turned to Ben-Ezra. "And you? Why're you here?"

"I had a choice after . . ." He touched the eye patch. "Into civilian life or into intelligence. There was no market for one-eyed paratroopers."

"How'd you lose it?" As soon as he asked the question, Sims wished he hadn't. The Israeli officer got a bleak walled-off look that told Sims he'd gone too far. Suddenly, to Sims's surprise, Ben-Ezra's face softened and he looked past Sims thoughtfully.

"I was a lieutenant in the '73 War—the Yom Kippur War. A platoon leader of parachute infantry. Fine men . . ." Ben-Ezra's eye focused on a time and on the faces of the men he'd known twenty years before. "The Arabs caught Israel by surprise. My platoon was thrown into a breach in the lines. We had to hold a pass in the Golan against Syrian armor . . . lightly armed parachute infantry against armor. . . ." The Israeli's voice faded in the remembered horror of long ago shelling and dying.

When Ben-Ezra picked up again, he'd gone back into his professional armor. "Syria and Egypt's surprise attack had come close to destroying Israel. Our agents and listening stations had for months been collecting massive files on Arab military preparations.

"The information had been there but not the courage to recognize it for what it was, the warning of war. The generals, the pompous bastards like Eitan, didn't want to listen because to do so would have meant abandoning *ha-Konseptzia.*"

"The concept?" Sims guess-translated.

Ben-Ezra nodded. "The Concept," he repeated bitterly. "After we smashed the Arabs in the six-day war of 1967, the Concept had spread like rot up and down the Israeli chain of command: The Arabs would never again launch an all-out war since they now knew they could not win.

"No one had questioned this until the Arab armies surprised us on Yom Kippur." Ben-Ezra touched his eye patch. "When I chose to stay in the army and go into intelligence, I swore to my dead comrades that I would make certain that, whatever else, I would question, and I would be heard."

Sims looked down on the airfield. "Well, you've been heard. We're here." He turned to Ben-Ezra. "You'd like the eye back?"

Ben-Ezra gave Sims an incredulous look, then the look faded as he thought more about it. Then, with an expression of surprised self-discovery, he shook his head. "No, maybe not." He thought about it some more, then, "With one eye I see differently. Even if I had both again, I don't know that I could look at things the way I used to."

"I don't think it has to do with the eye . . . the seeing differently."

"No?" A note of challenge crept into Ben-Ezra's voice.

"No," Sims said, starting to realize something for the first time, himself. "It's what we've done. We live through what we've lived through and we'll always look at things differently."

"You sound as if you tried to walk away from it—from this." Ben-Ezra waved at the airfield and the gesture took in more than just Yaate and the Bekáa.

Sims didn't know that he really wanted to answer, but couldn't think of a way out. "I did," he admitted. "I thought I could. But it came back for me. And then I realized that I couldn't let the bad folks score."

Sims felt his face flushing the way it did when he thought he'd talked too much, and he looked at his watch. "Three-thirty." He looked up at Ben-Ezra and motioned with his head to the airfield. "Want to see what's down there?"

* * *

Sticking to the plan they'd developed in the Negev, they would work in a large circle, hitting the L-shaped building first, then the barracks and mess hall. When they had finished, they would make it back to the hilltop for the helicopter at five-thirty.

Cramped from the long hours of waiting, Sims welcomed the weight of the rucksack on his back, the tug in his legs as his muscles came into play. With a ten-yard interval between them, the four men made their way down the hill in an extended single file, Jibril walking point, Yariv bringing up the rear.

The afternoon sun warmed Sims's back. As they got closer, the proportions of the L-shaped building took shape, a massive jumble of broken concrete panels that in some places jammed up against each other, forming dark cavelike openings.

At a hand signal from Ben-Ezra, the men stopped and dropped their rucksacks to the ground. Within minutes, they had donned gloves and lightweight plasticized coveralls and had fitted air filtration protective masks over their faces. Clumsily, they shouldered their rucksacks, picked up their weapons, and made their way to the edge of the rubble. Although he had walked less than a hundred yards, Sims already felt the heat building up inside the coveralls and he knew it would be a long two hours.

"Whatever's in there, gonna be a bitch getting to it," Sims said, eyeing a thick panel, its reinforcing rods splayed out like so many steel fingers.

Slowly, the four men clambered to the top of the rubble. Once there, Ben-Ezra took a compact 35-mm camera from a pouch on his web harness.

While Ben-Ezra methodically snapped photographs of the rubble, Sims studied the nearby structure he had first seen in the aerial photography. Crouched about twenty feet away, it was a squat windowless cube of redbrick. A low, round metal chimney jutted out of the center of its flat roof and a row of utility poles carried a pair of thick power lines to a junction box beside its only entry, a set of sturdy looking steel double doors. The utility poles led past the L-shaped building back toward the earthen berm that surrounded the generator shed. One of the poles was down, barely visible under a large fragment of concrete panel.

"Maybe we check that first," Sims suggested, pointing to the brick building.

Ben-Ezra looked at the building over his lowered camera, then glanced back at the tangle of broken concrete they were standing on and nodded.

Minutes later, Sims, Ben-Ezra, and Jibril watched as Yariv knelt by the doors, checking for trip wires or pressure switches.

Getting up, Yariv stood back and experimentally pressed down on the door handle with the muzzle of his machine gun. No give. "Locked," he said to no one. He pushed harder. Nothing. He looked thoughtfully at the door, as if sizing up an opponent. "Very well," he said to the door, swinging off his rucksack, "if you want to be difficult . . ."

Like kneading dough, Yariv shaped three charges, ribbons of plastic explosive about six inches long, no thicker than a man's thumb. The first two ribbons he pressed over the heavy steel hinges of the rightmost door. The last he molded around the door handle and lock plate.

From a foam-cushioned box the size of a deck of cards, Yariv took three electrical blasting caps, slender aluminum tubes an inch and a half long, each with a two-wire pigtail. With a pocketknife, he stripped the insulation off the first two inches of each wire. Splicing the caps together in a series circuit, he then molded one cap into each charge, then connected the remaining two free ends to a coil of insulated wire.

Sims, Jibril, and Ben-Ezra followed Yariv as he played out the slender two-conductor wire, leading them to a sheltered position fifty feet away, behind an upended concrete panel in the rubble of the L-shaped building.

Huddled against the panel, Sims watched as Yariv connected the free ends of the wires to a palm-size blasting machine, a small black matte box with a twist handle. Sims's eyes met Yariv's as the Israeli sergeant cradled the blasting machine against his chest. Sims had seen that kind of smile before; it was the kind of smile some quarterbacks got as they dropped back in the pocket on a play they knew in their sleep.

Yariv winked, then twisted the handle with a vigorous cranking motion.

It's not how big a bang you make, Sims remembered his demolitions lesson at the Farm, it's how little juice you use.

A sharp, whip-cracking sound split the air and was gone. No heavy crumping explosion, no clouds of dust, no flying debris. Yariv still had the lazy grin on his face as they stood up.

The doors were seemingly untouched. Just as Sims was about to turn to Yariv, the door on the right quivered, then, in slow motion, fell forward, slamming the ground in a belly-flopper of ringing steel and flying dust.

Ben-Ezra was the first to move. It was a cautious advance, assault rifle brought up at a low port across his chest. But there was nothing but the sound of the wind, slight and whispering.

Jibril and Yariv took up positions covering the outside of the building. Ben-Ezra paused, then ducked in with a rush, Sims following close behind.

"Oh God!" Ben-Ezra half prayed, half cursed.

Sims took a breath. Even through the mask, the odor was overpowering. It was a primal smell the knowledge of which every human carried in their genes. "Something dead," he said, knowing it didn't need saying.

The two men stood on a rough concrete floor in a room not more than twenty feet wide. Facing them, ten feet away, a brick wall with a large gray metal control panel with duplicate sets of dials and control handles. On either side of the panel two large metal doors resembling the hatches on submarines with large locking wheels set in the middle.

Sims stepped past Ben-Ezra and spun the wheel of the door on the right. The wheel turned with a machined smoothness, withdrawing the dog latches at top, bottom, and on the sides. He tugged, and the door opened and the odor hit him full force, a nauseous wave he could almost touch. The odor seemed to writhe and coil like a thing alive, a sweet oily putrescence reaching all the way into the bottom of his lungs and stomach. The revolting smell of death mixed with the smell of soapy ash. He gasped, thankful for a nearly empty stomach.

"Furnace." Ben-Ezra's voice seemed to come from a long way away.

"No," Sims said, staring at the feet, "a crematorium."

The feet—human feet—two pair side by side, toes up, purplish black, with the skin over them swollen almost to bursting, like the skin over a ripe grape. Sims saw the dim outlines of the bodies, laid out on a heavy wire mesh stretcher suspended inside the crematorium on iron racks.

He gripped the rough steel handles of the stretcher and pulled. The weight of the two bodies and the stretcher fought him. Ben-Ezra pushed in beside him and between the two of them, they inched the stretcher out.

Sims motioned with his chin toward a stretch of floor where a shaft of sunlight angled through the open doorway. "Over there."

Slowly lowering the stretcher to the floor, the two men stood back and looked at the bodies.

Ben-Ezra was the first to speak. "The color . . ." The corpses' skin was the same purplish black as that of the feet.

Sims turned around and looked at the panel between the doors. The two control handles had been turned far right, their indicator pointers resting against raised metal stops.

"Where're you going?" Ben-Ezra asked.

"Look at something."

Sims stepped outside the door, blinking in the bright afternoon sun, and followed the power lines away from the building. He came back in and stared at the two bodies for a moment, putting it together.

"They were cremating these when they blew the building," he said, talking toward the corpses. "Debris from the building took out one of the utility poles. No electricity . . ." trailing off, he looked around to Ben-Ezra.

Ben-Ezra nodded. "And so they didn't finish the job." Keeping his eyes on the bodies, he walked around to the other end of the stretcher, taking his camera out of his pouch.

"They were shot in the back of the head."

Both bodies were missing their faces from just above the eyes. Sims imagined that if you turned them over, you'd find nearly identical entry wounds, a little-finger size hole in the lower base of the skull. Small going in, mess coming out.

Ben-Ezra began taking pictures as Sims knelt by the nearer body and turned the hand of the corpse palm up into the light. The flesh was firm and Sims tried not to think of a well-done slab of beef.

For several seconds, Ben-Ezra circled the stretcher, getting shots from all angles. Then he lowered the camera and looked at Sims. "What are you doing?"

"Prints."

Sims had unscrewed his ballpoint pen cartridge and was bending the slender brass tube back and forth. It broke and carefully smearing the sticky black ink over the corpse's fingertips, Sims opened his pocket notebook and began rolling prints onto a clean page. Repeating the process with the second corpse, he stood up and slipped the notebook into an interior jacket pocket and zipped it securely shut. He looked around to find Ben-Ezra spinning the locking wheel of the other crematorium door.

"What . . . ?" Ben-Ezra stood blocking the open door, looking into the furnace with astonishment.

Sims came up to look over the Israeli's shoulder.

"Rats," Ben-Ezra said. The metal stretcher was a duplicate of the one on the floor, except this one was full of furry singed bodies. The smell, if anything, was even more overpowering than that of the human corpses. Ben-Ezra took two pictures then started to slam the door in distaste.

"Wait!"

"Wait?"

Sims pushed past and looked into the stretcher. Pulling the long hunting knife from its boot scabbard, he turned a rat on the top layer over.

"There must be hundreds," he heard Ben-Ezra say.

Sims turned a second rat over. Unlike those on the upper layer, these were unscorched.

"White," Sims said to himself. "White rats."

"We have to be going." Ben-Ezra was putting his camera away, snapping down the canvas pouch on his web harness.

"A minute." Sims searched through his rucksack and came up with a water bladder. Unrolling it, he handed it to Ben-Ezra. "Hold that."

Uncovering yet another layer of rats with his knife, Sims picked one out that looked relatively unburned and, balancing it on the knife blade, lowered it into the bladder that Ben-Ezra was holding open. Taking the bladder, he double- and triple-folded the neck, secured it with a rubber band, and thrust it deep in his rucksack. Looking up at Ben-Ezra, he grinned. "Never can tell when you'll need an extra meal."

Ben-Ezra grimaced and jerked a finger toward the door. "We're running out of time."

Sims shouldered the rucksack and picked up his assault rifle. The air outside the crematorium was effervescent, like a long swallow of crisp champagne, the blue sky seemed to go on forever, but even in the relief of being outside again, he thought of the two men lying inside there, together on the metal stretcher and wondered who they were and why they had been in the furnace with the rats.

"Yariv's found something." Jibril pointed away from the crematorium, down the line of rubble that had been the L-shaped building. Thirty, forty feet away, Yariv squatted, peering under a concrete panel tilted at a forty-five degree angle.

By the time Sims, Ben-Ezra, and Jibril got there, Yariv had crawled under the panel. All that was visible was a pair of boots. Ben-Ezra knelt by the boots.

"What is it?" he called in to Yariv.

Nothing for a moment as the boots shifted and twisted. "Machine of some sort," came the muffled reply. The boots began backing out. Yariv emerged, belly down, then rolled to his side and sat up, his eyes blue against the white of limestone grit and concrete dust on his face. "Looks like an air compressor." He jerked a thumb into the stacked debris.

"Mind?" Sims gestured to the opening.

"My guest," Yariv said, standing up gesturing to the narrow opening.

The air was prickly dry with the smell of concrete, and after the brightness of the sun, Sims had to use his flashlight.

It wasn't an air compressor; it was a vacuum pump. The concrete debris had crushed the control box where the power cables came in, but the electric motor was intact, its drive connected by a heavy rubber belt to the flywheel of a finned two-stage pump. Sims rubbed the dust away from the data plate riveted to the crumpled control box, and, in the cramped space, held the flashlight in his teeth while he jotted down the manufacturer—Kardis-Mayer—and a long alphanumeric serial number. What *was* a vacuum pump doing here?

Sims back-crawled out of the rubble cave, and as he was beating the dust off his uniform, Ben-Ezra pointed to his watch. "Four forty-five." He motioned south toward the buildings a hundred yards away. "We do the mess halls and barracks, then get back to the hill."

Ten minutes later, the four stood outside the mess hall. The mess hall and the two barracks buildings made a U, the three buildings facing onto a rocky courtyard. The tin roofs extended out to cover a rough concrete walkway bordering the courtyard. Each barracks room opened directly onto the walkway. Halfway down the courtyard, a volleyball net sagged between the buildings. Sims counted ten rooms on either side of the courtyard. Not enough for the security detail; they'd probably slept in tents.

The mess hall had yielded nothing. It had been cleaned out except for two broken tables, several flimsy folding chairs, a dried-out pomegranate and a moldy cheese in an institutional refrigerator, and a ragged dart board hanging on the wall. One dart was in the bull's-eye; another, having missed the board entirely, stuck in the wall.

Ben-Ezra motioned down the right walkway. "You and Jibril take those rooms," he said to Sims. "Yariv and I will take these."

The room clearing went quickly, Jibril checking the doorway for signs of a trip wire or pull device, then, as both stood to the side, Sims pressed the door handle with the muzzle of his assault rifle and flipped the door open.

The rooms were simple ten-foot cubes: one window, smooth concrete floor, ceiling fan, and in one corner, an open closet with a single clothes rod. The rooms had been stripped of furniture. All that remained of human habitation was a scattering of cigarette butts, a tattered wall calendar advertising a textile shop in Damascus, a single well-worn Nike athletic shoe, the sports section of a Beirut newspaper.

Glancing across the courtyard, Sims saw Ben-Ezra and Yariv coming out of the next to last room on their side of the courtyard. The Israeli colonel shook his head and made an empty-handed gesture as he and Yariv prepared to enter the last room.

The last room was like the first nine. Sims and Jibril poked among the litter on the floor: a copy of *Paris Match*, a thin roll of waxy toilet paper, a bent safety pin, a stained purple tank-top T-shirt with Pakistan label. As Sims turned to leave, a square of paper in the corner of the open closet caught his eye. It was the size—about three inches on a side—and the crinkle-cut edges that whispered photograph. He picked it up and stared at it.

Jibril, partway through the door, looked back. "What is it?"

"Two girls," Sims answered, still looking at the photograph.

"Pinup?" Jibril grinned, looking wolfish and at the same time unbalanced because of the gold tooth.

"No." Sims flashed the picture at Jibril, then glanced at it again as he stuck it between the pages of his notebook. Two little girls, six, seven—maybe eight years old. Holding hands on a riverbank, looking up into the camera, squinting into the sun. Dressed in their finest. Two little blond girls. In the distant background, a large city on the river's far bank.

"Sims!"

Sims and Jibril were out into the courtyard before the shout died down.

Ben-Ezra, flattened against the wall of the opposite barracks, pointed south, away from the mess hall, toward the crest of a rise some two or three miles away. Yariv, beside Ben-Ezra, had extended the whip antenna of his radio, and was talking into the handset, his attention fixed in the direction of Ben-Ezra's point.

At first Sims saw nothing, then a bright flash—the glint of

the setting sun off glass. He searched the rise—nothing. Then he made them out as they came over the crest: four dark shapes moving toward them across the butter yellow limestone of the valley floor.

"Back!" Ben-Ezra pumped an arm toward the hill.

For a moment, Sims hesitated. They'd be seen as they crossed the open land between the airfield buildings and the hill. But if they stayed here, the Syrians would find them anyway and they'd have to fight here, where they'd have no cover, and—he glanced at his watch—it was 5:10: the helicopters were already on their way.

It was a race. The Syrian patrol spotted them, as Sims had thought they would, as he and the Israelis sprinted across the open ground between the airfield and the hill.

The first ragged bursts of fire sounded like the distant popping of firecrackers. Out of range, Sims thought. Even so, he felt his breath suddenly push against a constriction of fear in his chest and his bladder signaled a need to urinate. The gently sloping hill had become a mountain and the rucksack weighed a thousand pounds and he was moving as if he were underwater, constricted by the coveralls, breathing made even more labored by the protective mask.

The shooting intensified and now Sims heard an occasional round crack through the air. He imagined the Syrians behind him, now out of their trucks, working their way through the buildings, getting their range.

Directly above him on the hill crest, he saw the boulder— *his* boulder—where he'd spent an eternity earlier in the day. It called out sanctuary and no place in the world was more appealing, more desirable.

More shots. Bullets ricocheting, chipping limestone splinters . . . overhead crackling sounds thicker, closer. A quick glance right, then left: everybody still up, Jibril, Ben-Ezra, Yariv, all leaning into the hill, legs driving, arms extended as if reaching for a hidden handhold to pull themselves to the top.

Suddenly Sims found himself belly-flat behind a boulder, Jibril, Ben-Ezra, and Yariv strung out to his right. He couldn't remember getting there. It was as if he'd been magically transported the last ten yards. The shooting had stopped. There was only the sound of his own breathing. Somewhere on the way up, he'd pulled the protective mask down to hang around his neck. He left it there and listened to Yariv, in the background, calling in on the radio.

Sims brought his rifle up to search for a target. On the far side of the airfield, beyond the buildings, four dark green Russian trucks, stopped where their drivers had abandoned them. One of the trucks' cab doors hung open, and from another truck, Sims could see a dark plume of diesel exhaust from an engine left running. Trucks, no people. He imagined the Syrians, spread out among the buildings, their lieutenant or captain, choking down his fear and excitement, trying to think about what to do next. Sims scanned the buildings over the sights of his rifle, then realized his weapon was still on safety. He flushed, flicked the selector to fire, then twisted to get a spare magazine from the ammunition pouch on his web belt.

There was a scrabbling sound as Ben-Ezra crawled up to lie beside him. He said nothing, but looked for a long time down on the airfield. Sims felt better, noticing how heavily the Israeli was breathing.

"How many?"

"Can't tell," Sims answered, continuing to search among the buildings and rubble. "Figure four, five, each truck." He saw Ben-Ezra scanning the airfield, thinking. "How far out are the helicopters?"

Ben-Ezra stared at the airfield another moment then glanced at his watch. "On time. Seven minutes out."

"They know?"

The Israeli frowned. "Yariv's told them. They're still coming."

In the Aman operations center outside Jerusalem, Major General Reuven Eitan and Will Uhlmann sat in the command balcony facing three massive electronic situation screens covering the opposite wall, some fifty feet away.

On the floor below, two rows of desks; the first row, senior controllers, air force, army, and naval forces officers in contact with the operational arms of their individual services. In the second row, Aman's communicators maintained constant contact with listening posts across Israel, with the cloister-quiet groups of photointerpreters and, of course, with Ben-Ezra and Sims now in Yaate.

Will Uhlmann worriedly gnawed on a fingernail. Eitan hunched forward, and held up a restraining hand as he listened to the words coming to him over his headset. With his other hand, he pressed the headset into his ear as if that would make the words come clearer, or so that maybe he wouldn't hear what he was hearing.

Straightening, Eitan slipped the headset down around his neck and turned to Uhlmann. He motioned with his head to the situation screens. As he did so, two red X's blinked into existence below Damascus, some fifty miles east of Yaate.

"Two MiG-23s"—he waved his free hand to the X's on the screen—"are on their way to Yaate. They—"

Eitan jerked his attention away from Uhlmann as someone came on the phone. Issuing a terse command, Eitan slammed the instrument down, then turned back to Uhlmann. "I have just scrambled F-15s from Ramat David," he explained.

The two men watched the screen. After an eternity that lasted no more than thirty seconds, four blue Xs appeared, streaking north from the Israeli Air Force base near Haifa. Simultaneously, a bright yellow square flashed on the screen, bobbing and weaving just north of Yaate.

"What is that?" asked Uhlmann.

"The four blue Xs are our F-15s."

"And the yellow square?"

"The square?" Eitan smiled mirthlessly at the station chief. "That is where the computer says that our F-15s and the Syrian MiGs will come together. As you Americans put it," he rasped, "that is where the shit hits the fan."

24

The shout, high-pitched and strident, came floating up from the airfield. It was the first sound from the Syrians and it caught Sims by surprise. He was still wondering if it meant anything when a stream of green tracers suddenly materialized, silently drifting toward him, followed by the sound of automatic weapons fire. High at first, the tracers dropped as the Syrians adjusted their fire, and bullets now struck sparks off the boulders around him and whined angrily as they ricocheted into the air.

To his right, Yariv's machine gun opened up with a hammering roar. It had been less than a second between the tracers and Yariv's first shots. In that time, three Syrians dashed from the rubble toward Sims and the hilltop. The three, distinguishable in silhouette only, ran well, keeping a good spread between them, dodging among boulders.

Sims saw them head for a small rise at the foot of the hill. Once there, the rise would provide them protection from fire from the hilltop. He swung his rifle up, but he knew he wouldn't be fast enough. Yariv's red tracers were already tracking the three men. Two more bursts, then Yariv stopped firing. All three had made it to the rise and safety. The covering fire from the airfield dwindled to a ragged scattering of shots, then stopped.

They were putting together a classic assault, Sims guessed. Next, the three guys behind the rise would provide covering fire and another element from the airfield would dash forward. The elements would leapfrog each other, one firing, the other advancing, up the hill until they were in a position for one last rush to the top.

The Syrian lieutenant or sergeant down there was no great shakes for imagination, but conservative and effective. If the Syrian leader had been a football coach, Sims thought, he would've been an up-the-middle, four-yards-and-a-cloud-of-dust guy.

Sims scanned the terrain below. Down the hill to his left, a large cluster of boulders looked like it would offer good protection for three or four men. The boulders, he estimated, were about two hundred yards down the hill. To get there from their airfield positions, the next group of Syrians would have to cover about one hundred yards in the open—about fifteen seconds exposure, max.

Reaching to his right, he grasped Ben-Ezra's arm. The Israeli colonel turned, and Sims's index finger traced a path from the airfield to the boulders. Ben-Ezra looked, then, understanding, crawled over to Yariv, a few yards to his right. Yariv and Ben-Ezra held a brief whispered conversation, then Yariv nodded, and traversed his machine gun to cover the hundred-yard gap between the airfield rubble and the cluster of boulders. Sims looked around to his left and slightly to his rear. Jibril, cradling a 40mm grenade launcher, gave him a thumbs-up, flashing the gold tooth—he had seen Sims's mimed conversation with Ben-Ezra.

Sims gave Jibril an answering smile, then rolled onto his side and pulled his rifle in. The Galil, firing on automatic, could throw out six hundred rounds a minute. Good for clearing out a room, but at any distance, accuracy suffered, and with a thirty-round magazine, you didn't make many hits on a single target on full automatic. So Sims carefully checked the selector switch, making certain it was on semiautomatic. Next, he made a small elevation adjustment to the rifle's rear sight, tapped the magazine with the heel of his hand to make certain it was fully seated and would feed bullets into the chamber. That done, he nestled the rifle butt into the hollow of his shoulder, and waited.

This time the Syrian fire came from two directions: from the airfield and from closer in, from the rise where the first three men had taken cover. This time, there was no high firing; the Syrians had the range down pat. The first rounds crashed into and among the boulders and Sims felt the air ripple with their passage. Instinctively, he winced from the intense fire. Eyes snapped shut, he dropped his head and wriggled his hips, as if he could burrow under the limestone hardpan beneath him. He felt the seductive tug of fear, and fought the urge to give in to it.

With a massive effort, Sims raised his head. It registered somewhere in part of his consciousness that none of the Israelis were returning the Syrians's fire and it registered, too, in yet another cell of recognition, that the eternity he had been fighting his own fear had been less than a second.

Two hundred yards away, three men broke from the airfield's sheltering rubble and, as though following Sims's script, sprinted directly for the boulders. They were not as well spaced as the first group had been. The first two men ran close together, almost touching, lifting their legs in high, kicking steps, firing their weapons on full automatic into the air. They reminded Sims of the TV clips of armed men in city crowds emptying their weapons into the air, celebrating with the noise, caring less where the bullets ultimately came down.

Yariv fired first, Jibril following so closely that the mechanical hammer of the machine gun and the hollow *blook* of the grenade launcher came almost simultaneously. The machine-gun slugs, traveling a flat trajectory at over three thousand feet per second, stitched the lead Syrian a millisecond before Jibril's pear-size grenade dropped just behind the man following him.

The two men collided. The first, hit from the front, staggered to a halt. The second man was thrown forward by the grenade concussion behind him. Both fell heavily to the ground.

Sims, in a swift crablike motion, shifted slightly to his right, bringing his sights on the third man. The firing from the airfield was now even heavier. Crackling, slicing sounds of death filled the air of the hilltop. But Sims's fear had vanished. In its place a manic joyousness . . . exulting rage . . . and Sims wanted nothing more in the world at that moment than the man in his sights. Almost automatically, Sims made a slight leading compensation for the man's running and began his trigger squeeze.

Stunned by the rapid killing of the two men, the guns of the Syrians and Jibril and Yariv and Ben-Ezra unaccountably hushed, like the random quiet that sometimes interrupts all conversations for a fleeting instant at a crowded party.

Sims's single shot punctuated the silence.

The third man, caught midstride, seemed suspended in midair, both feet off the ground, hands thrown overhead, still clutching his weapon. Suddenly, the weapon flew from his outstretched hands and he did a ragged arabesque, falling forward, crumpling in the dirt, his body, before so full of motion, now permanently still. The crashing echo of Sims's shot rolled down the hill and echoed in the rubble of the airfield.

Sims felt a torrential triumph, then an instant later, a wave of nausea. The man he'd shot hadn't been a sonofabitch like Schmar. He had been some guy who'd been told to wear his cheap uniform for his country and who went out to do dirty work for a bunk, three meals a day, and maybe cigarettes and twenty bucks a month.

Five minutes later, Sims searched the deepening shadows of the airfield down below. No movement among the buildings, the four empty trucks the only sign of the Syrian patrol—that and the three bodies, now dark shadows lying out in the open between the airfield and the boulders they'd never reach.

The ominous quiet taunted him. Another Syrian assault would have been better than sitting on this hilltop like a staked-out rabbit in a trap. Yariv had just gotten Aman operation center's transmission. The four men on the hill knew about the Syrian MiGs coming their way. And, Sims imagined, the Syrians down on the airfield knew too. Better to fight than wait passively for the winner of the race between the helicopters coming to pick them up, the MiGs hunting the helicopters, and the F-15s hunting the MiGs.

But the Syrians weren't going to make another run up the hill. The Syrians were betting on the MiGs.

Beside him, Ben-Ezra said nothing but searched the sky to the southwest. Realizing that the Syrians were content to hold them on top of the hill, Ben-Ezra had pulled Yariv and Jibril in closer to be ready for the helicopter. The helicopter—if it got here—would make one pass, slowing as it hovered a second or two. You threw yourself in or you were left behind.

Ben-Ezra punched Sims's arm. "There they are!"

Sims saw nothing in the closing darkness. Then he found them. At first, specks that danced in and out of sight, then, as they got nearer, steadying and taking on shape and size, two dark tadpoles skimming just above the valley floor.

As Sims watched, the helicopters banked left, turning away from Yaate. This was the start of a curving approach to come in on the hill from the northwest, to keep the mass of the hill between the helicopters and the Syrians at the airfield. About a mile northwest of the hill, the lead helicopter would begin its run in for pickup. The second helicopter would turn its arc into a complete circle and link up with the lead helicopter after pickup.

Just as it seemed both helicopters would pass by, the lead helicopter suddenly banked hard right and came toward them, boring in at over a hundred miles an hour, scant feet off the ground. Now Sims clearly heard the high-pitched whine of the turbine engine.

"Now!" Ben-Ezra shouted.

A hammering explosion beat on Sims's ears as Ben-Ezra opened fire—a burst of three rounds into the airfield. Sims had picked out his target as well, the rise where the Syrians' first assault element was holed up.

Soon all four men were firing, a measured sweeping of the airfield to discourage the Syrians from a last-minute assault as the helicopter came in for pickup. Tracers from Yariv's machine gun worked back and forth, fiery red fingers picking through the buildings and rubble.

The helicopter was now two hundred yards from the hill. Abruptly pitching nose-up, it slowed drastically, aiming for a spot just below the crest.

Still firing into the airfield, Sims twisted to catch a glimpse of Ben-Ezra. The Israeli colonel, coiled, tense, was watching the helicopter like a mongoose would watch the advance of a cobra.

The pickup point was fifty or so yards down the back side of the hill. When the helicopter was close enough, Ben-Ezra would give the word and Sims and Jibril would follow him to the pickup zone. Yariv, on the machine gun, would keep a covering fire on the airfield for a fast count of ten, then follow.

A cloud of gritty dust tore at Sims as the helicopter flared into a near-hover. The flat, smacking sound of the rotors beating the air made a counterpoint to Yariv's rhythmic machine-gun fire. The Syrians were firing back, their tracers floating lazily over the hilltop before disappearing into the purplish sky.

Sims twisted around. He saw that the helicopter was almost down.

Ben-Ezra started to rise, started to shout—to give the order to make it to the helicopter. But the explosions came and the words never got out.

A rapid *poom-poom-poom*. Blasts so closely spaced it seemed like the earth ripping apart. Everything happening at once: bright orange flashes on the hillside bracketing the helicopter . . . whining of steel fragments and limestone splinters . . . the helicopter shuddering . . . lurching drunkenly . . . then its bubble nose exploding as if smashed by an invisible hammer . . . churning rotor blades smashing at the boulders . . . stone and laminate shrapnel cartwheeling through the air with a deadly whispering sound like the passing of a scythe.

A heavy silence suddenly gripped the hilltop. Aftermath silence like the passing of a tornado. Then, a splitting, thundering shriek . . . a shuddering passage of black wings overhead.

Intuitively, Sims ducked, head swiveling, following the screaming noise. Several thousand feet above, in the direct rays of the setting sun, twin streaks of silver swooped and rolled, metal hawks pulling away into the dark blue sky.

Then Sims was up and running toward the burning

helicopter. Halfway there, he realized Ben-Ezra was with him, almost at his shoulder.

Broken and tilted on its side, the helicopter was a shapeless tangle of metal, flames from ruptured fuel and hydraulic lines licking at the smashed crew compartment. Reaching the crumpled left-side door, Sims wrapped his fingers around the twisted aluminum frame and wrenched it open.

The crew compartment was a meaty red smear. Like broken dolls, the pilot and copilot sagged, faces hidden by shattered flight helmets, chests torn open by the cannon shell that had exploded against the instrument panel inches away from them. Sims felt the heat of the flames and stepped back.

He saw Ben-Ezra, the Israeli's upper body hidden in the back passenger compartment. He was struggling to wrench something free from inside the helicopter.

"What the hell you doing?"

Sims stepped over to help, but Ben-Ezra's body filled the small opening. Sims pulled at Ben-Ezra's shoulder.

"Come on! This thing's going to blow!"

"They're coming back," Ben-Ezra screamed, as he wrenched back out of the helicopter. Chest high, he cradled the Stinger missile, a thick olive green tube about five-feet long. One third of the way down its length, a shoulder stock and a stubby optical sight.

The lead MiG, having thrown itself into a tight loop was already back over and descending toward the hilltop again. The pilot in the second MiG made a sloppier, wider loop and was trailing by almost a quarter mile.

At forty-three thousand feet, Flight Lieutenant Aryeh Redfa heeled his F-15 over into a near vertical dive, full afterburners. His wingman, less than a hundred feet away, followed. The remaining two F-15s would stay at altitude, flying cover in case more Syrians showed up.

Redfa caught the trailing MiG at eighteen thousand feet and by sixteen thousand feet, he had the Syrian in the heads-up sight display projected onto the windscreen before him. A floating off-white ring encircled the MiG. Redfa toggled the arm switch on the joystick grip. The ring around the MiG blinked red, then green, and simultaneously, Redfa heard a growling audio tone in his headset—the Syrian jet's heated exhaust was registering in the infrared seeker of Redfa's AIM-9L Sidewinder missile.

At fourteen thousand feet, Redfa squeezed the red trigger on the joystick and then pulled back hard and braced himself against the fist of gravity that would slam him into his seat with the weight of half a ton. His wingman, following closely, came out of the dive with him. Redfa cursed; they'd been able to get only one of the Syrians, the other they'd have to get next time around. If there is a next time, he thought, picturing the four men on the hilltop.

Sims heard Yariv cheer as the MiG disappeared, at first a silent flash, then a cloud, finally a roll of distant thunder as the sound came down to them.

"Goddamn it, get down!" Sims shouted to Ben-Ezra.

The Israeli colonel had sprinted thirty or so feet from the burning helicopter, and was standing upright, a lonely and vulnerable target in the boulder-strewn clearing. Seemingly oblivious to Sims, he struggled with the Stinger, swinging its sight over so he could fire from his left shoulder, using his good eye. Beyond Ben-Ezra, in the far distance, Sims saw the surviving MiG flattening out, coming in for its second run on the hilltop.

There was shouting as Jibril and Yariv realized what Ben-Ezra was up to, and Yariv muscled his machine gun around in a clumsy attempt to elevate the tripod on a boulder.

Sims slammed a fresh magazine into the Galil and flicked the selector switch to automatic, knowing that wouldn't do any good. You had to shoot one helluva lot of golden BBs to bring down a jet screaming in at you at six hundred miles an hour and he didn't think that the way things were going it would be that kind of day.

Ben-Ezra hoisted the Stinger to his shoulder. The MiG was growing larger and Sims was surprised the MiG hadn't started firing yet. "Get down!" Sims shouted again.

This time Ben-Ezra heard him. He swung his head toward

Sims. "It is *my* turn," he shouted back, then swung back to face the MiG.

The MiG's twin cannon began a malignant winking, and Ben-Ezra disappeared in a blinding bright flash.

His eyes recovering, Sims watched as Ben-Ezra lowered the empty launcher, and, already half a mile away, the tiny Stinger missile like a cosmic harpoon, streaked toward the incoming MiG, locking on the heat of the cannons in the incoming jet's nose.

Flight Lieutenant Redfa saw the light blossoming on the floor of the valley below. At the same time, the moving target indicator on his radar blinked out and he guessed that somehow the MiG wouldn't be coming back from its last run on the hill.

And at the operations center, Will Uhlmann sat back in his chair, drained of emotion as he watched the last red X disappear from the screen and the blue circle that was the chase helicopter swinging around to land on the hill at Yaate.

25

From the helicopter's open door, Sims looked down at the airfield several hundred feet below, rapidly slipping away as the helicopter picked up speed. It was hard to tear his eyes away, like breaking a hypnotic spell. He saw Ben-Ezra and the others also looking down at Yatte. Each had the rapt thousand-yard stare of combat veterans surveying the scarred terrain as they tried to piece together what had happened and to figure out why it was them who had survived. Ben-Ezra slowly turned to Sims as if from a dream. Sims saw that Ben-Ezra had a silly grin on his face and he realized he wore one too.

With Flight Lieutenant Aryeh Redfa's F-15s flying escorting orbits above, the tiny helicopter arrived at Aman headquarters in the outskirts of Jerusalem just over an hour later.

As the helicopter settled on a concrete pad surrounded by bright floodlights, ominous hooded figures looking like deep-sea divers emerged from the surrounding glare. The lead figure motioned toward a tent set up fifty yards away. Ben-Ezra led off, and Sims fell in beside the Israeli colonel. Behind him, he heard the helicopter turbine slow, then stop. He turned and saw that the pilot and copilot had left the aircraft and were following, accompanied by another hooded figure.

Inside the tent, the six men went through intensive

decontamination. At the first stations, they stripped, leaving clothing and equipment in self-sealing plastic bags. One of the hooded figures took the bag containing the rat from Sims's rucksack, sealed it in another bag, and disappeared.

Sims followed the rest of the men into the steaming showers, where for thirty minutes they scrubbed with a strong germicidal soap, rinsed, then repeated the procedure, while outside, pumper trucks washed down the helicopter with streams of harsh disinfectants. After the showers, the men sat naked on metal benches and dried under ultraviolet lights as blood, urine, and sputum samples were analyzed.

Half an hour later, the men emerged from the tent, dressed in surgeon's pale green scrub smocks and trousers. Will Uhlmann and General Reuven Eitan were waiting. Uhlmann gripped Sims's hand. "A plane's coming for you."

Eitan made a loud throat-clearing noise. "Meanwhile, I suppose you won't object, Mr. Sims, to telling us what you found at Yaate." Over meals brought in from the mess, the debriefing began, with a changing cast of specialists probing every aspect of the mission.

Shortly after one o'clock Wednesday morning, just as Sims was about to rebel, Uhlmann broke in. "We have a plane to catch and a schedule to meet, General," he said firmly.

Sour expression still on his face, Eitan muttered something about diminishing returns, perfunctorily shook hands with Sims and Uhlmann, then disappeared, followed by two anxious staff officers in smartly starched khakis.

Fifteen minutes later, Ben-Ezra, driving a dusty Peugeot staff car, pulled to a stop at the helicopter pad. Sims's luggage included a small insulated bag in which the rat from the crematorium had been safety-sealed and packed in dry ice.

On the pad, Sims saw a large Bell UH-1 helicopter with Israeli air force markings. The large rotor was slowly windmilling and the red and green running lights wavered and flickered in the hot turbine exhaust. The helicopter would fly Uhlmann and him to Sde Dov air base thirty-five miles away, where the Judge's plane waited. Nine or ten hours and he'd be back in the States.

Ben-Ezra walked with them to the waiting helicopter. There were the good-bye handshakes all around. When Sims stood back, to let Uhlmann board first, he felt a hand on his shoulder. He turned to face Ben-Ezra. The rotor downwash whipped the Israeli's hair and the glare of the floodlights made the black patch look all the more stark.

"*Shalom,* Bradford," Ben-Ezra said to Sims, shouting over the noise.

Sims squeezed Ben-Ezra's upper arm. "*Shalom,* Mordecai."

The Gulfstream took off from Sde Dov at two-fifteen Wednesday morning, February 17. Twenty minutes later, the plane topped out at forty thousand feet altitude on a westward heading at five hundred fifty miles an hour. Sims drafted an "eyes only" after-action report to the Judge. That took two hours. Then, exhausted and mentally numbed, he slept through much of the remainder of the ten-hour flight, waking only to stumble off the plane to stretch his legs during refueling at Lajes in the Azores. Landing at sunrise at Dulles, the Gulfstream rolled to a stop at a secluded ramp a half mile east of the commercial main terminal.

The Judge's sedan waited, Chuck Hunter, in a worn leather flight jacket, leaning against the front fender. As Sims descended the steps, he saw ten, maybe a dozen men, some in overcoats, others in orange ground crew coveralls, in a loose cordon surrounding the jet. Sims imagined the small arsenals concealed by the overcoats and coveralls.

"Big reception," he said to Hunter at the car.

Hunter shrugged as he opened the door for Sims. "They're government, just like you and me. They gotta be somewhere. Here's as good as any."

"The Judge?"

Hunter jerked a thumb to the east, in the direction of Langley. "Waiting."

Riddle, Alberich, and Alice Brenner had been waiting in the Judge's office when Sims arrived. All had read the after-action report, even so, it'd taken Sims another hour to fill in the details.

The Judge ducked his head slightly as he took off his glasses and put them on the side table next to his armchair. With his fingertips, he massaged his eyes, then brought the hands together as if praying. "So that's what happened at Yaate," he said to himself over his fingertips. Then looking at Sims: "Now, where does it leave us?"

"Zohdi was using the place to build a biological weapon," Sims answered. "There's the vacuum pump shipped from Bremerhaven, the crematorium with the rats, and the village—Boudaï."

"Boudaï?" the Judge asked.

"Zohdi—his people—screwed up the demolition at Yaate. That's what cut the crematorium off. The demo charges probably blew some stuff from the lab into the air and the wind did the rest. The Syrians had to contain it and so when they found out that Boudaï had been infected, they called in the air force."

"That's your conjecture, Bradford. You'll be hard pressed to convince Ralston Dean that his friends in Damascus would backstop Zohdi. Kill an entire village?"

Sims laughed in contempt. "Why not? They've been doing it for years. Hell, half the Syrian government's in on the Bekáa drug trade. And Zohdi's made himself untouchable. Dean's friends in Damascus are either scared shitless of Zohdi or they're on his payroll."

"Thin," the Judge worried. "Very thin."

"Look, Judge, I know we got a weak case. So we work on the evidence. We find Zohdi. We know he was messing around with something biological at Yaate. We don't know specifically what it was. We don't know if he failed or succeeded. But if he succeeded, it's damn sure not good news for anybody."

"How long will it take?"

Sims looked around to Alice Brenner, who cocked her head to one side in thought. "Workup on the rat? We could know everything this afternoon . . . or nothing a week from now."

"IDing the two corpses," Alberich entered in, "same thing. We could hit it lucky or we could miss it altogether."

Sims looked around. There was that suspended look that

people got when something wasn't finished between them, but there was nothing more that could be done. Before leaving, he slipped a hand inside his jacket to make sure he had the envelope that held the snapshot of two little blond girls.

The Navy Yard, a few blocks south of the U.S. Capitol near the juncture of the Anacostia and Potomac rivers, was built in the nineteenth century to service the Atlantic fleet. From the Civil War through World War II, the yard's foundries and machine shops turned out steam engines, gun barrels, even torpedoes. The lathes and forges shut down as the yard adapted itself to the Cold War.

In 1961, three seven-story buildings, windowless and surrounded by rows of chain link fence and triple coils of razor wire opened for business in the northwest corner of the yard. Yard blueprints collectively identified the complex as Building 213. Although there had been no ribbon-cutting ceremony, Building 213 soon became known through intelligence agencies around the world as NPIC, or CIA's national photographic interpretation center.

NPIC analysts, using the first photographs parachuted down from early satellite cameras, discovered the Soviet Union's growing fleet of intercontinental ballistic missiles. A year later, the same NPIC analysts provided President John Kennedy the proof he needed to back down Soviet leader Nikita Khrushchev in the Cuban Missile crisis.

By 1993 NPIC was the destination of an increasing flood of photography as newer imaging satellites broadcast digital pictures of the earth shot in complete darkness, through clouds and smoke, even images of manmade structures hidden below the earth's surface.

At 9:30 Thursday, February 18, a Marine guard checked Sims's Agency badge, waved him through the gate, and watched as Sims parked in the zebra-hatched portion of the parking lot reserved for visitors. At reception, a small room just off the entry lobby, another badge check by another Marine behind an armored glass window. As Sims retrieved his badge from the steel drawer below the window, he pressed his right hand on a plate set flush in the waist-high counter just to his right. In seconds, a computer in Building 213's cavernous basement matched Sims's handprint against the one on file and sent a confirming green light signal back to the Marine's console.

Stan Bleifeld, NPIC director, tilted back in his chair. His right hand held a pair of plastic film developing tongs. Gripped in the tongs, the snapshot Sims had found in Yaate.

"Cute kids." Bleifeld tilted the photograph, squinting at the glossy finish under the light from the overhead fluorescents. "Where'd you get this?"

"In an abandoned building in the Bekáa Valley. Day before yesterday."

For all the reaction Bleifeld showed, Sims could have said he'd found the snapshot in a family album.

"What can you tell me about it?" Sims asked.

Bleifeld, a wiry, dark-haired man, put the photograph and tongs down on his desktop. "I can tell you stuff you'd never need to know. Bury you. What do you need?"

Sims thought for a moment. "Who are those little girls? Where are they? When was the picture taken?"

Reaching for the tongs, Bleifeld picked up the photograph, again tilting it, then turning it over to examine the back. "Can I cut it?"

"Cut?"

"Just a nick off a corner. Lab test."

Sims nodded.

"Priority?" Bleifeld, still holding the photograph in the tongs, looked at Sims. He seemed to read the answer in Sims's face before Sims had to say anything. Bleifeld, shrugged, resigned. He got up, reaching for the phone as he said good-bye to Sims. "I'll call as soon as I get something."

As Sims stood to leave, the framed photographs on the wall behind Bleifeld caught Sims's eye, large black-and-white blowups, as well-known throughout the world's intelligence cloisters as the works of Karsh or Leibowitz or Ansel Adams in the universe outside the chain link fence and triple-coil razor wire.

301

From World War II, a British Mosquito reconnaissance plane's photo of Bergen-Belsen and the formations of inmates marching to the gas chambers with camp guards and accompanying dogs. A '60s-era *Corona* satellite photograph of Moscow's first SS-6 intercontinental ballistic missile on its pad, seconds before launch. U-2 shots of the Soviet missiles at San Cristobal, Cuba. The Vietnam War and low-flying drone photography of American POWs exercising in the courtyard of the Hanoi Hilton. Icons of war and devastation. And now, Sims thought, a snapshot from a cheap camera of two little girls standing on a riverbank.

It was well after six when he'd finished briefing Louis Vee at the Counterterrorism Center. Looking at his watch, he found it difficult to believe that twelve hours before, he had landed at Dulles. In spite of the long day, he wasn't tired. So he called Rollo Moss and two hours later the two of them sat in Rollo's season seats at the Cap Center, drinking beer and watching the Lakers pulverize the Bullets, with Rollo bitching all the time that it would have never happened back when Unseld had been playing.

Sims slept late the following morning, had a gargantuan breakfast at Kinney's, and passed through the Langley guard gate just after eleven.

The Judge's special assistant waved him down on the way to his office. "Bleifeld—seven-thirty," she said. "Grousy. Something about his analysts working their asses off while you got your beauty sleep."

Bleifeld came down to meet Sims at reception. Instead of returning to his office, he waved down a corridor behind the Marine guard.

"This way," he said, taking Sims through a maze of hallways. Walls and ceilings were painted the same shade of institutional buff and the air had a spiritless metallic smell to it. Toward the end of one corridor, Bleifeld stopped at a door marked only by a number. Punching a combination into the cipher lock mounted on the door frame, Bleifeld was rewarded with a rattling buzz.

Inside, a small room with several upholstered chairs, a

low table stacked with thumbed-through issues of *Jane's* and *Aviation Week,* and a large stainless steel institutional coffee urn. Beside the urn, a sink, and over the sink, a scattered assortment of coffee mugs hung on hooks set into a painted square of plywood. Bleifeld paused inquiringly by the coffee urn. Sims shook his head, and Bleifeld opened a door that led into a narrow passageway. The air was cooler and now the metallic smell was gone, replaced by a dry scent of electricity and ozone.

Through another door, and the passageway opened into a dimly lit room taken up by several swivel chairs, a wall-to-wall console, and banks of darkened projection screens, two columns of smaller screens flanking a larger screen that Sims estimated to be several feet square.

"Looks like a TV studio," Sims said.

"Grab a seat." Bleifeld took one of the chairs and pointed Sims to the one beside him. Bleifeld pulled a small envelope from inside his jacket and handed it to Sims. "First, the original."

Sims slid the photograph out of the envelope and examined it carefully. The two little girls, squinting into the sun, smiled into the camera. Sims turned the photograph over. It seemed intact.

"Thought you said you'd have to cut a piece off."

"Did—just a shaving." Bleifeld flipped several switches on the console. "That"—he motioned with a hand to the photo—"was taken in Russia."

"How do you know?"

"Paper analysis. Chemicals used to develop the film. Fixer and developer combinations the Russkies've used for years."

The large screen now glowed a ghostly bluish white. Bleifeld turned to the console and rapped a command into the keyboard. A blossoming—and from the high definition screen, the two little girls smiled at Sims.

"You know about pixels?"

"Dots."

Bleifeld nodded, "Look at a newspaper photo with a magnifying glass and you see the picture's made up of lots of those dots. Some black, some white, some gray. Smaller the dot—the pixel—the more shades of gray you have, the sharper the picture."

Bleifeld manipulated a tiny joystick, and a thin bright blue line appeared on the projection screen. He traced a path around the city skyline that formed a backdrop behind the little girls. "We took this portion of the photograph and put it into the computer. We broke it down into millions of pixels per square inch, over twelve hundred shades of gray. The computer manipulated each pixel, each shade of gray and . . ."

"Damn," Sims whispered as the screen twisted in a vertigo-producing swirl. As Sims got his bearings, he realized it was as if he had been launched into the sky above the girls, and was now streaking toward the distant city.

"Once we got the photo into the computer," Bleifeld was saying, "we could look at all the permutations of the skyline. We can even twist it around so we're looking down on it."

The dizzying sensation of rapid flight faded away. The city lay below, as if seen from a low-flying airplane.

"How do you know what's behind the buildings you can see in the original picture?"

"We don't," Bleifeld replied. "We do computer-generated fill-ins. But the structures we *can* see give us enough of an idea about the real city. See these towers?"

One of the smaller screens came to life. Again, the original photo. In the background, a luminous arrow pointed to a stand of fingerlike towers barely visible on the skyline.

"That gives us a relative position . . . here." The arrow jumped to the larger screen, coming to rest on the city's outskirts. "Using the real landmarks like the towers and the buildings we can see, we match this computer model against the files we have in our data base of real Russian cities."

"And?"

"We came up with two prospects. Only one, however, had a river this close. The city is Perm, the river's the Kama."

Sims placed the city on his mental map of Russia, just west of the Urals.

"Population a little over a million," Bleifeld recited. "The towers belong to the oil refineries. Perm also has lumber, metallurgy industry, agricultural machinery." He worked the console; the large screen split. The computer model jumped to the right, a photograph flashed on the left. "Left's a blowup of satellite photography."

"Yeah." The similarities were clearly evident.

Bleifeld did something else on the console. The screen flickered and the little girls reappeared. He looked at the picture for a moment or two. "Taken in early June 1990."

Sims guessed. "Sun angles?"

Bleifeld nodded. "You know the longitude and latitude, it's a piece of cake." He fiddled with the console and the screen went dark. He turned in the swivel chair and pointed to the envelope in front of Sims, the envelope that held the original photograph.

"One other thing. We found some partials on the front."

"Partials?"

"Fingerprints," Bleifeld said. "We checked personnel. They aren't yours."

"Matches the right thumb of Number Two," Alberich said. Number Two being the tag they'd put on the second corpse Sims had fingerprinted in the crematorium at Yaate.

Sims sat in Alberich's mezzanine office. A display panel showed two fingerprints side by side. It was early afternoon, and he had filled Alberich in on Stan Bleifeld's analysis of the photo taken at Perm.

"His kids," Sims said, opening a folder and looking at the photograph of the two little girls.

"You don't know that. All's we know is it's a picture Number Two touched."

"You're too damn literal. His kids. You run the prints to Moscow?"

"Isaacson's already got them."

"How about Okolovich? Has Isaacson tipped the Russians to the Latakia connection?"

Alberich nodded. NSA had traced telephone intercepts to the former KGB chief to the Meridien Hotel in Latakia.

NSA had even gotten Okolovich's room number. If the Russians couldn't find Okolovich now, they needed a Seeing Eye dog. He watched as Sims got up. "Where you going?"

"I wish I knew, Matthias."

It wasn't until the following afternoon that Alice Brenner finished the last of a series of over two hundred microbial identifications. She would call Sims in a moment. Now she would take time, if only a moment, for reflection.

She poured herself a cup of coffee and, feeling only slightly guilty, spooned in an extra helping of sugar. One hand jammed deep in the pocket of her lab coat, she perched on a tall lab stool and sipped the coffee, pulling her shoulders together as if chilled. She regarded the stack of computer printouts. On top of the printouts, a twelve-by-twelve, black-and-white photograph print from the scanning electron microscope, a spiky ball similar to a sandspur.

Alice Brenner raised her coffee cup in a mock toast to the vaguely malignant photograph. "To peace and brotherly love," she said, the fear in her voice breaking through the self-protective layer of sarcasm.

26

The eyes around the Judge's conference table focused on Alice Brenner. The faces reflected a mix of expectation and challenge. There was the Judge, of course, and Sims and Alberich. Across the table, the lineup Sims had come to think of as the usual suspects: Ralston Dean, high lord of the White House, Lars Nesbith, Famous But Incompetent, and Lewis Lindahl, the president's horse's ass science adviser.

Sims stared at Dean's face, wondering if the veneer of smooth assurance would still be there when the meeting was over, wondering if Dean, in turn, could read *his* face.

Sims was certain that the foreboding was there for anyone to see. Two days ago, he had sat patiently in Brenner's lab as she ran through the meaning of the computer printouts. Then she had worked backward from the printouts, laying out how it probably had come about.

The Judge had spent another day and a half, playing devil's advocate, framing opposing arguments, asking second- and third-level questions that had twice forced Brenner to raise her hands in temporary surrender. It had been back to the lab and the computers, with more follow-up sessions with the Judge. Then Alberich had gotten Isaacson's bundle of KGB documents which had arrived in the pouch via special courier. That had put enough together so that late last night, the Judge, sitting in the chair he was sitting in now, had reluctantly nodded his head and picked up the phone to call Ralston Dean.

"Zohdi's weapon." Brenner placed a slide on the projector. It was the ghostly sandspur from the scanning electron microscope. The slide had a depth that the photographic print had lacked: the spiky ball seemed almost three-dimensional, filling the screen, translucent and milky-white against a black background.

Around the table, heads cocked, lips parted, looks of curiosity. Except for Lindahl who sat there with a knowing smile, the light reflecting from the screen making silver mirrors of his round glasses.

"Anthrax," Lindahl murmured, the smile still on his face. He drew it out, "ANthrax-x-x," the teacher's pet smugly answering the question that had stumped the rest of the class.

"Anthrax," Brenner repeated. Sims noted the slightest flicker of irritation in her voice. Brenner slipped on half-frame reading glasses as she opened a gray clothbound laboratory journal to a paper-clipped page. Studying her notes for a moment, she looked up and addressed the room in a soft, coolly assertive voice.

"Anthrax is primarily a disease of sheep and cattle, but it can also infect humans. Natural human infection results from ingestion of contaminated meat or inhalation of anthrax spores. Both gastrointestinal and pulmonary anthrax are invariably fatal if not treated immediately with antibiotics. Initial signs of pulmonary anthrax are high fever, choking cough, and uncontrollable hemorrhaging. It is usually fatal within four days.

"Anthrax," Brenner continued in her dispassionate clinical voice, "is considered the prototypical biological-warfare agent. Besides its lethality, it is not contagious from one individual to another. As a result, anthrax would not spread far beyond the intended target or boomerang against the attacker's troops. And anthrax is rugged. Unlike other bioagents, anthrax spores can withstand delivery by missiles or bombs. The spores can be quite persistent. In World War Two, the British detonated experimental anthrax bombs on Gruinard Island off Scotland, and the spores remained active in the ground for more than forty years."

"Judge," Ralston Dean interrupted with a weary, put-upon note in his voice, "I see Zohdi and this . . . this hairy *golf ball*"—he waved dismissively at the photo of the anthrax spore—"but what's the con*nec*tion?"

The Judge studied Dean for a moment. With no expression other than a slight hooding of the eyes, he turned to Sims. Alice Brenner, catching the interplay, folded her lab journal and took her seat.

"Connection," Sims repeated, stepping back to the podium. "Next slide," he announced as he worked another slide onto the projector.

The L-shaped building appeared. Sims picked up a laser pointer. "This is a building in the Bekáa Valley. Six miles northwest of Baalbek at an airfield called Yaate. This photo was taken on December 17, 1991." A bright red arrow ticked along the building, then leaped to the interior of the L.

"This is a crematorium. Six days ago, in one of the ovens, we found two human bodies and a pallet of laboratory rats. Scorched, but not burned. We brought one of the rats back." He nodded to Brenner.

Brenner craned forward and peered down the table. "The rat died of pulmonary anthrax."

"You have witness-certified biopsy slides?" Lindahl asked.

"Certainly," Brenner replied, in a slightly offended tone.

"Abel Zohdi built this building," Sims picked up. "We have months of intercepts of the radio traffic during its construction and operation as well as human source reporting."

"Human source?" asked Dean. "From where?"

"From liaison."

"Liaison?"

"Liaison, Ralston," the Judge cut in to explain the Agency use of the term, "means another country's intelligence service. Here, the Israelis."

"The Israelis?" Dean sneered. "You'd trust *them*?"

"It was a prefabricated building," Alberich interrupted. "We have the shipping documents and transaction register from the German firm in Bremerhaven—"

"All *right*." Dean waved a hand, cutting Alberich off. "I don't have all *day*. Let's get on with this." He wagged an impatient index finger at Sims and the screen. "I will stipulate that *that*"—he pointed to the screen again—"was Zohdi's building and that a *rat* found there died of anthrax." He raised his hands dramatically in an empty-palm gesture. "But where does that get us? If Zohdi developed, or cultured—or whatever you do to get anthrax—if he did that, *how* did he do it? And more important, *why* did he do it?"

Sims sorted through the slides, found the one of the anthrax spore, and put it back on the projector.

"Zohdi got to this"—he pointed to the spore on the screen—"through a series of relationships that took shape in the early eighties. Zohdi wanted weapons; he had opium from his fields in the Bekáa. So first he went to the Sicilians, whose networks could handle everything Zohdi could grow. Cashing in on the opium, Zohdi then approached Josef Broz, head of Czech intelligence, with a deal. Zohdi would buy weapons through Broz, Broz would get rich and Czech intelligence would get a bonus: a window into the Middle East.

"This was too big an operation for the Czechs alone. So Broz got the backing of Sergei Okolovich, who was then the chief of the KGB's First Directorate. This fit neatly with the KGB, because Okolovich was looking for someone like Zohdi to run operations against us. Between the two of them, Broz and Okolovich set up a front in Bremerhaven, Germany. By 1984 the three-way trade of opium, weapons, and intelligence had settled into a regular pattern."

Ralston Dean raised a hand. "I assume there are facts to back up your story."

"The current Russian government has an interest in Zohdi too." Sims gestured to Alberich.

Alberich backed his chair away from his position beside the Judge and wheeled up to the head of the table, pulling in beside Sims. With the prosthetic arm, he reached down and pulled a thick three-ring binder from a shelf below his wheelchair seat. Setting the binder before him, he opened it to the title page and tilted the binder to show it around the table. Red, blue, and white flags framed a coat of arms over a line of ornate Cyrillic calligraphy.

"The title says: 'Eyes Only for the Chief of Staff of the President of Russia,'" Alberich translated. He tapped the binder with a metal finger. "This is one of two copies of an auditor's report of Sergei Okolovich. The other copy is in Boris Yeltsin's safe."

Alberich fanned through the pages. "The report traces Okolovich's personal financial dealings. It turns out that he and Broz were skimming the money Zohdi was paying for his little play toys. They built up accounts amounting to millions in Austria and Switzerland."

Alberich closed the binder, keeping his hand on the cover. "Other records from the old KGB files filled in the Okolovich-Broz-Zohdi relationship. That relationship changed dramatically during a meeting in Damascus in October '91. By then, Broz had been a private citizen for almost two years, and Okolovich no doubt knew that the Soviet Union wouldn't hold together much longer. Both men saw the gravy train coming to a stop. Zohdi put a lot of money on the table, enough to see Okolovich and Broz through several lifetimes.

"This time, Zohdi didn't want hardware, he wanted people." Alberich paused. "You might recognize the names, Dr. Lindahl—Eduard Ryzhkov and Mikhail Lushev."

Lindahl blinked and worked his mouth soundlessly, then, "Yes—both. I knew Eduard better, of course—"

Alberich cut him off. "They were the two bodies in the crematorium. We ID'd them through their fingerprints. KGB records show both men leaving the former Soviet Union toward the end of October '91. No record of their return. Ryzhkov was a bachelor; Lushev, married, two daughters."

Lindahl shook his head as if he hadn't heard right. "Eduard and Mikhail?"

"Zohdi said he wanted scientific help to protect herds in the Bekáa against anthrax. A real man of the people."

Ralston Dean, reflecting Lindahl's perplexity, looked toward the head of the table.

Alice Brenner spoke first. *"Our* records, Mr. Dean, show Ryzhkov and Lushev as the senior biologists at Military Compound Nineteen, in Sverdlovsk during the late sixties and through the seventies. Military Compound Nineteen was a secret biological warfare facility. Ryzhkov and Lushev's specialty was anthrax."

Brenner pursed her lips, then continued. "You might remember Sverdlovsk and anthrax, Mister Dean. In April 1979, an explosion in Military Compound Nineteen spread a cloud of anthrax spores over the city. Hundreds of people died. The Soviets denied there'd been any secret work going on. They claimed that only a handful of people had died from eating black market meat tainted with anthrax. Years later, Boris Yeltsin admitted that the meat story had been a lie. Sverdlovsk had indeed been done in by a militarized form of anthrax."

"The Russians also gave us copies of Ryzhkov's and Lushev's journals," Alberich put in.

Brenner nodded. "Ryzhkov was still working on anthrax derivatives when he left Russia. The spores we got from the Bekáa facility appear to have been modified in some way."

Lindahl cocked his head. "Modified?"

Another nod from Brenner. "DNA splicing. Records from the Bremerhaven front show shipments of endonuclease and DNA adapters and linkers." She looked around the table as if realizing they needed an explanation. "You cut a DNA chain—anthrax in this case—with an endonuclease. Then you modify the original by adding other DNA chunks. Finally, you paste it back together with the adapters or linkers."

She looked around again to see if the explanation took. Not completely satisfied, she continued, "I can tell that the Bekáa spore's been modified, but I won't know what it's been modified to do until I make up a similar culture and test it."

Dean was clearly unhappy. Hands clenched before him on the table, he interlaced his fingers, undid them, then locked them together again. "You mean to tell me that

Zohdi could put together a—a biological bomb—in a place like that?" Dean motioned to the building on the screen.

"It doesn't take much," Brenner said. "They do more sophisticated work refining heroin and making cocaine in the jungle labs in Colombia. And the choice of anthrax . . ." She shook her head, a worried look on her face. "And it doesn't take much anthrax, either. One ounce of anthrax spores can kill three hundred million people."

Sims watched shock, then disbelief ripple across Ralston Dean's face. Lindahl levered forward in his chair to protest.

"That's *alarmist!* It is *totally* unrealistic!"

"How so, Dr. Lindahl?" the Judge asked.

Lindahl's face was flushed and he had trouble breathing, as if he were laboring under a heavy load. "Why . . . why . . . this *woman* is *assuming* a perfect distribution of anthrax spores."

Sims caught Lindahl's exaggerated emphasis—"this *woman*"—and it seemed to carry the same contempt Sims had heard when people said nigger.

Brenner's voice sliced in. "I said 'theoretically,' Dr. Lindahl. Obviously, to kill that many people, the spores would have to be well-distributed. But a terrorist wouldn't have to be limited to a single ounce of spores."

"How do you mean?" the Judge asked, knowing the answer himself but anxious to cool down the confrontation.

"Take a small vial of freeze-dried seed culture, mix it in a fermenter with a nutrient like beef bouillon, keep it at constant temperature, and in four days you'll have several pounds of anthrax bacteria." Brenner paused. "And think what you could do with *pounds* of anthrax instead of ounces . . ." She looked at Lindahl as she let it trail off.

"Which," the Judge picked up, "leads us to a scenario that explains Yaate." And with that, he turned to Sims.

"Through Sergei Okolovich," Sims said, "Zohdi contracted for the services of the two Russian scientists, Ryzhkov and Lushev. Using equipment purchased through Karstens-Export in Bremerhaven, Zohdi set up the laboratory at Yaate. Construction began in October 1991. Over the next sixteen months, the Russians genetically engineered a new strain of anthrax. Now, Yaate was a lab, not a production facility. When Zohdi was finally satisfied, he freeze-dried the resulting seed stock, then executed the Russians. This was just over two weeks ago, on February 5. After killing the Russians, Zohdi had Yaate destroyed.

"But Zohdi's boys screwed up the demolition. The screwup not only left the crematorium intact, it released a cloud of anthrax spores that infected the village of Boudaï. The Syrians contained the anthrax the only way they could—with fire."

"And Damascus ordered the bombing of Boudaï?" Dean asked incredulously. "I know President Assad! He is tough because he has to be to survive in that atmosphere. But"— Dean spread his hands and shook his head as if putting down a drunk's barroom bluster—"to order the deaths—"

"In 1982," Sims cut in coldly, "Syrian president Hafiz al-Assad, faced with an uprising in the city of Hama, leveled the place, killing over twenty-thousand of his own citizens."

Dean was quick on the defense. "Hama was an armed insurrection, Mr. Sims. We killed far more in our own civil war."

Sims flared. "These were women and children—"

The Judge reached a restraining hand to Sims's shoulder. "This isn't about Hama, Bradford," he said quietly. Then, looking across the table at Dean, "or about the American Civil War."

Ralston Dean sat back in his chair, cupping his chin in the palm of one hand. "Is that it?"

Sims searched the man's face. The veneer of assurance was still intact. Part of Sims marveled, even as another part boiled with anger. He leaned toward Dean. "Only," Sims said, making his voice as sharp as he knew how, "that Zohdi's out there somewhere with the seed stock. And as Dr. Brenner said, all it takes is a couple of days in a fermentation vat."

Dean regarded Sims momentarily with a look of annoyance, as if a stranger in a crowd had elbowed him. With an air of dismissal, he turned to the Judge.

"We *don't* know," Dean said, with slow, lawyerly emphasis, "that Mr. Zohdi is *anywhere*. We *don't* know that his little operation in the Bekáa Valley was successful. We *don't* know that this squalid little village—Boudaï?—was infected with anything." Dean continued his litany: "We *don't* know that Zohdi has a supply of nasty bugs in his hip pocket."

"But—" Sims started to object.

"I *haven't* finished," Dean gritted at Sims.

Sims felt the Judge's knee give him a warning nudge beneath the table. He forced himself to take a deep breath and settle back in his chair. Even so, the anger burned hot in his guts.

"None of this," Dean was continuing, "is *rational.* It may be technically possible to build some kind of bioweapon as you suggest. But terrorism depends on symbolic killing, not megadeath."

"On the contrary, Mr. Dean," Alice Brenner interrupted. "Terrorists have already used bioweapons."

Dean threw a challenging look at Alice Brenner.

"United States, 1972," Brenner began. "An outfit called the Order of the Rising Sun was caught with eighty pounds of typhoid cultures that they intended to inject into water supplies of major Midwest cities.

"In 1974," she continued, "German intelligence agents broke into an apartment in Paris. They killed two members of the Baader-Meinhof gang. They found a *Clostridium botulinum* culture. The apartment had been set up as a sophisticated biological laboratory.

"And in 1986, the Rajneesh cult in Oregon allegedly used *Salmonella thphi* to contaminate salad bars in local restaurants in order to influence the outcome of a local election."

Dean, with a pained look, heard Brenner through, then shook his head as if shaking off what she'd said. "But this—what you describe—such an enterprise would entail the complicity of the Syrian government . . . and President Assad *himself.* Now, Assad may not be the ACLU's poster child, but he *is* a pragmatist. He clearly sees what is best for Syria's long-term interests."

"Ralston," the Judge said, softly, but firmly. "Kamāl Zohdi is a killer."

Dean nodded. "Of course. Zohdi's a bad, bad boy. But there're a lot of bad boys in the world today"—he cut a glance toward Alice Brenner, and nodded at her with a nineties-guy unctuous grin—*"and* girls." Returning to the Judge, he went on. "And we have to get on this fellow's trail just as we watch for all the bad boys—*and* girls."

Riddle drained the last of the *turska kava* and set the small cup on the Pembroke gaming table.

"I will make some more," he offered.

Sims, sitting across from Riddle, shook his head. The bookstore was quiet, with only the occasional muted sound of late night traffic out on K Street. Sims stared at the chessboard. Riddle had worked his knight into a forked attack, checking Sims's king and queen. Sims could rescue his king by sacrificing the queen, but in the end, the queen's loss would mean the game.

Sims sighed and got up, coffee cup in hand, and followed Riddle into the kitchen alcove. "Changed my mind."

Riddle fussed with grinding the dark coffee beans. "At least Mr. Dean allowed that Zohdi was something more than a petty shoplifter."

"Oh, yeah," Sims said cynically. "Dean's willing to have the Center for Disease Control issue a watch advisory for anthrax outbreaks and said the Bureau'd put Zohdi at the top of their list."

"Lars Nesbith?"

"Just nodded. Didn't say squat. Sat there the whole time with his nose up Dean's ass."

"And the Agency?"

"Oh," Sims said with heavy irony, "we get to keep doing what we've been doing. As long as we do it quietly and not in America."

"No joint task force with the Bureau?"

Sims gave a small bitter laugh. "Hell, Riddle. Don't want to do *that*—don't want to screw up Dean's chances to snag a Nobel peace prize."

27

At his office the next morning, Sims found a call slip taped to the back of his chair: Roy Cantrell. Using the scrambler, he got Cantrell's office on the second ring. Cantrell came on immediately.

"Neptune's checked in."

Neptune . . . Neptune, Sims thought wearily, rummaging through his memory, dredging up long ago code names; code names that once learned, were impossible to erase. There'd been Saturn; but that had been '83—setting up the escape from Leningrad of a Soviet mathematician with his wife, a poodle, and hundreds of pounds of design notes for a break-proof cipher system. And ERPLUTO—an agent he'd run in East Berlin until Pluto had fallen victim to too much booze and too little caution. *What—who—the hell is Neptune?* Then he opened the right mental drawer: Neptune— the Jersey City police source. Cantrell gave directions and a time.

Half an hour later, Roy Cantrell took the first photo from a worn attaché case at his elbow and slid it across a glass-topped dining room table to Sims. "Ramzi Ahmed Yousef."

It was an eight-by-ten print, black and white. Shooting across a busy city street, the photographer had caught the tail end of a dump truck rumbling out of the picture to the left. On the far side of the street and roughly centered, a slender, dark-haired man in jeans and leather jacket, opening the door of a pickup truck. In the background, set back from the street and reached by a long driveway that was almost an alley, a ratty-looking frame and brick two story house. On the sidewalk, one of those cheap plastic bigwheel tricycles.

"Ninety-three Toyota," Cantrell supplied.

Sims looked up from the first photo. Over Cantrell's shoulder, a glass door opened onto the balcony. Off in the distance, Hains Point, and, across the Potomac, National Airport. A Boeing 737 was taking off. The wind must be coming from the south, Sims thought as he watched the plane climb over the rooftops of Old Town Alexandria. In a few seconds it would be over Mount Vernon, several miles farther downriver.

Cantrell had given Sims the address of an apartment in southwest Washington, not far from Fort McNair, and only a few minutes from Building 213. It was one of Cantrell's safe houses used for stowing witnesses and for meetings where it wouldn't be smart to be seen walking into the Arlington police department across the river in Virginia.

"Blowup," Cantrell announced, sailing the second photograph across the glass.

The enlargement showed Yousef from midchest up. Thick dark hair, black short-cropped beard, blacker deep-set eyes glaring out from under heavy eyebrows. Sims held the first photo alongside the second. Looking over the top of the opened door, a large bag cradled in his arms, Yousef seemed to be scanning the street around him.

Another photograph followed, this one inside, taken by a flash camera. Three bearded men at a stable strewn with dishes, sitting stiffly and smiling reluctantly for the camera. One of the men was thickset with red hair and beard. The other was black. Sims spotted Yousef as the man on the right.

The first two photographs, Sims knew, were surveillance shots, probably taken from behind the one-way glass of a van parked across the street from Yousef's car.

"This?" He held up the third photograph.

"Neptune took it—a restaurant near the mosque."

"When?"

"The surveillance shots, last week, Thursday. The restaurant, Saturday night."

"Who're the other guys at the table?"

Cantrell consulted his notebook. "Two a Yousef's friends. Yousef's the newcomer. The others've lived in Newark or Jersey City for some time. All three hang out at the al-Salam mosque."

Checking his notebook, Cantrell leaned across to tap a finger on the heads of the men at the table: "Redhead's Mahmud Abouhalima. Black guy's Clement Hampton-El." Cantrell looked up. "Abouhalima is an 'Afghani' too. Reportedly left Afghanistan July '90."

Sims started to pass the photographs back. Cantrell held up a hand. "Your copies." Cantrell leafed through his wirebound notebook. "Yousef told Neptune that he was born in Iraq. Neptune estimates Yousef's age as twenty-six, seven. Under thirty anyway."

"Young," said Sims, realizing he was ten, eleven years older and still thought of himself as young.

Cantrell continued. "Yousef showed Neptune an Iraqi passport. Said that was how he got into the States." Cantrell paged through his notebook, scanning the pages. "That's about it—full report's here." He took a large manila envelope from the attaché case at his elbow and handed it to Sims. Cantrell went back into the attaché case and came out with a small tape player.

"More?"

"They body-wired Neptune for the restaurant scene." Cantrell made a head motion toward the photograph. At the same time, Cantrell flicked on the recorder. "There's a bunch a shit conversation. It's all on here, but here's some a the good parts." Cantrell pressed the forward button.

A clanking sound that Sims identified as silverware on china, then a muffled voice in American English came from the recorder. Indistinct at first, Cantrell rewound the tape for a brief instant, then turned up the volume. "The first voice's Hampton-El. The conversation's between him and Yousef."

"The target is important. Just any will not do."

"Obviously. There is a symbolic importance and a technical importance." Yousef's voice carried what Sims identified as a Palestinian accent.

"I understand symbols," Hampton-El said. "With regard to symbols, it must represent the Great Satan. But I do not understand the technical importance. How is that meant? Is the target a person? Or a place?"

"It is decided, but it is not revealed. Not yet."

"Decided? Who decided?"

"He who makes such decisions. The leader of the Jihad. Read about death and about Jihad. What is said about death and Jihad?"

It sounded to Sims like someone working through a catechism.

"Seek death and you shall find life in the hereafter," Hampton-El answered.

Sims imagined Yousef nodding approval at Hampton-El. Hampton-El, Sims decided, was a suck-up.

Yousef's voice came oily with righteousness. "Whosoever dies and does not invade the enemy of God and his soul does not tell him to fight, he is unfaithful. Abaddon is among the most faithful."

Cantrell pressed stop. "Next voice's Abouhalima," he injected, then hit the start button. A deeper, more accented voice came on.

"Did you talk with the sheik about this?"

"No, no, no," Yousef was saying. "Sheik doesn't know anything about this subject at all."

Sims raised his hand. "Sheik?"

Cantrell hit the stop button again. "The head guy at the mosque."

"The imam?"

"Yeah, if that's what you call the head guy at a mosque." Cantrell started the tape again.

"He doesn't interfere."

"No, no, he doesn't interfere and he has no relation with it. You simply ask him a general question, that's all. I don't make a step unless I check with the law of our religion from the sheik."

The recorder fell silent, and all Sims heard was the internal turning of the tape reels. Cantrell pressed the stop button, then rewind.

"Target?" Sims asked.

"Who knows?" Cantrell shrugged. "Arabs exaggerate. Could be a bunch a guys really up to something. Could be a bunch a guys just jacking off."

"You passed that on to the Bureau?" As he asked the question, Sims imagined how carefully Cantrell would have to play it so that he wouldn't tip his own hand, how he'd pressed the Jersey City police to do a job the FBI wouldn't do for itself.

"Yeah. The whole ball of wax. Day before yesterday."

And Lars Nesbith knew this yesterday, when he sat across from me at the table, Sims thought. He asked Cantrell: "And?"

Cantrell opened the recorder. "Your copy." He handed the black plastic cassette to Sims. He saw the question was still on Sims's face. "And?" He shrugged again. "And B-B-H. That's why I called you."

"B-B-H?"

Cantrell got a cynical grin. "Bureau's black hole," he explained. "The word's out. Arab terrorists don't exist until Lars thinks it safe for them to."

Leaving Cantrell, Sims returned to the Agency, driving up the George Washington Parkway through a softly falling afternoon snow. He stopped to pick up Alberich and together they made their way to Louis Vee's office in the Counterterrorism Center.

This gray winter afternoon, Louis Vee was wearing a mango-colored shirt with a wide, green checked tie. The effect was wildly tropical. Tilting dangerously back in his swivel chair, the CTC chief pulled an unlit but well-chewed cigar from his mouth and used it to point to a file folder lying closed on the desk between him and Sims and Alberich.

"DESIST file on two a the assholes your Arlington buddy fingered up in Jersey."

Sims reached for the file and pulled it into his lap. He glanced at the file header.

"Yousef and Abouhalima—nothing on Hampton-El?"

Louis Vee shook his head. "Nothing international."

Sims didn't open the file. Louis Vee was a raconteur of the twisted personalities that peopled the Charles Addams world of terrorism. The DESIST computer program held the substance of the biographies, the hard fact, the whispered innuendo, but Louis Vee supplied a certain panache that the computer could never match.

"Ramzi Ahmed Yousef, born 20 May '67, Baghdad, Iraq." Louis Vee wagged the slobbery-end of the cigar at the file now in Sims's lap. "Alias Ramzi Yousef Ahmad, Rasheed Yousef, Muhammud Azan, Rashid Rashid, Khurram Khan—shit!—the fucker probably couldn't give you his real name if it was tattooed on his dick."

Louis paused to smile at his own joke, then continued. "According to Pakistan International Airlines, Yousef, carrying the Muhammud passport, had the proper U.S. visa when he boarded a flight from Karachi to New York in September '92. He didn't have it when he landed."

"Counterfeit?" Alberich guessed.

"Prob-ly. Standard MO's to get a good-enough visa to fool the airline ticket agents when you board, then flush the visa down the toilet before you get to New York so immigration won't arrest you for carrying bogus. You claim political asylum in New York and after a little bit a shit from immigration, they turn you loose on your own recognizance and you're on your way."

"So Yousef's on the loose in New York five months ago."

Louis Vee nodded to Sims. "That mosque where he showed up? Run by Sheik Omar Abdel Rahman. Remember the rabbi that was shot?—Kahane?" Louis Vee looked toward the ceiling as if checking his facts up there.

Sims shook his head.

"Kahane," Alberich cut in, "a militant rabbi. New York. Jewish Defense League. Hard-nosed guy."

"Yeah," Louis Vee nodded, jamming the cigar back into the corner of his mouth and launching backward into a precarious tilt of his chair. "Rahman made the Jersey City mosque the center of the fundamentalists who supported Kahane's killer. Anyway, the mosque and Rahman got the reputation from that. Now this guy, Abouhalima, the other guy in the restaurant picture, he's a New York cabbie. Doubles as Rahman's driver."

"Driver?" Alberich asked.

"Rahman's blind," Louis Vee explained. "Anyway, the Neptune source was right; Abouhalima had been in Afghanistan." He consulted a note on his desk. "The Pakistani intelligence records show him in training in Peshawar, November, December '88. Pakistani evaluation was that he was, quote: 'a very good commander who fought in various provinces of Afghanistan.' Yousef met Abouhalima in Afghanistan, and met Zohdi there too." Louis Vee pointed to the file. "It's all in there."

"All in there?" Sims asked. "Like where's Zohdi?"

Louis Vee took the cigar from his mouth, held it out and looked at it in sudden distaste, then sailed it toward a nearby wastebasket. He watched in disgust as the cigar missed, hit the side of the container, and dropped to the floor. He turned to Sims with an angry, disappointed look. "No. I guess we don't have it all."

Motionless as they listened, Sims, Riddle, and the Judge stared at the small recorder on the Judge's desk. The Judge, his face gray and stonelike, heard the tape end, then motioned for Sims to start it over.

". . . Is the target a person? Or a place?"

"It is decided, but it is not revealed. Not yet."

The Judge reached across and punched the stop button. "Not yet," he repeated. Apprehension tightened his face, making him look worn and older.

"The Bureau had that tape two days ago," Sims said with anger, pointing to the recorder. "And yesterday, Lars Nesbith didn't say shit about it."

"He might not have known. It might not have gotten to him."

"Well, Judge, if he wasn't holding out on us, he was

goddamn incompetent," Sims retorted. He pinned the Judge with a look. "Suppose we said nothing about it now? Suppose we just sit and wait? How long do you think it'd be before Nesbith would bring that Neptune stuff to us?—ever?"

Sims read the answer in the Judge's eyes. Riddle, impassive, hands folded across his paunch, sat Buddha-like in the Queen Anne chair off to the Judge's right.

"Nesbith knows his job's on the line with the new people in the White House," the Judge went on, trying to explain. "I don't agree with his tack, but I understand it."

Sims angrily punched the air with a fist. "He's aiding and abetting stupid shits like Ralston Dean. They call it foreign policy, but all it is is denial. They don't want to see because it's inconvenient."

"Do you think the Bureau's sitting on this?" the Judge countered. "Do you think they're doing nothing?"

Sims, about to say yes, paused for a moment, then shook his head. "Nesbith's been inside the Beltway too long not to cover his ass. I'm sure that if—when—Zohdi pulls something off, Nesbith'll be able to say that the Bureau's been doing its job. They may not be able to shoot good, but they're fast as hell on the spin. No, Judge, the Bureau's doing *some*thing, but it's damn sure in slow motion."

The Judge looked at the recorder then picked up the surveillance photo of Ramzi Yousef. "And you?" He looked at Sims across the top of the photo.

"I was thinking about a couple of days in Jersey City."

"Doing?"

"Check out Yousef. See what he's up to. He's one of Zohdi's baddest boys and the only connection to Zohdi we got. He didn't come here for the climate."

A silence, then the Judge asked cautiously, "Will you need any help?"

Sims read the Judge: he'd asked because he had to, but he didn't really want to ask because he was afraid of what he'd get into if Sims said yes. And so Sims shook his head. "I'll talk to Cantrell," Sims said. "He'll work an introduction to the Jersey City cops."

* * *

Riddle listened without commenting, his hazel eyes never leaving Sims. After Sims finished, Riddle asked, "So you're going alone?"

Sims shrugged. "Comes down to that, doesn't it? Everybody's got their head in the sand or up their ass."

"A moment."

Riddle disappeared into the back of the shop, into his apartment. Minutes later, he returned, carrying his battered Gladstone bag in one hand, and in the other, his shoulder holster with a huge Webley revolver.

"What the hell do you think you're doing?"

"Why, I'm going with you." Unperturbed, Riddle strapped on the shoulder holster. He looked up from the task to flash Sims a mischievous smile. "Young man, I am terminally *bored* sitting on the sidelines. At my age, I don't have too many turns around the paddock left in me, and as your H. L. Mencken put it, every normal man comes to a time when he wants to spit on his hands, hoist the black flag, and begin slitting throats. This," Riddle proclaimed, "is *my* time. I think a few throats beg slitting."

An hour later, Sims, driving north on I-95, cleared the Fort McHenry tunnel under Baltimore harbor. Following Cantrell's instructions, Sims's destination was a Howard Johnson's motel in Secaucus, several miles west of Jersey City proper. In the morning, Cantrell's Jersey City counterpart, a man named Higgins, would work a meeting with Neptune.

Turning on the radio, he found an all-night jazz station, and adjusted the volume so it wouldn't disturb Riddle, now noisily dozing in the passenger's seat. He hadn't fought Riddle's coming too hard. It was, as he secretly admitted to himself, good to have the older man along, even if Riddle's throat-slitting days were far behind him. Wynton Marsalis's sweetly elegant trumpet spilled into the car, and Sims felt a snug security in the dark and the warmth and the music. Tomorrow morning, he and Riddle would see if they could pick up a puzzle piece or two in Jersey City.

One of those pieces, Sims was certain, was Ramzi Yousef. Sims mentally replayed the Neptune tape, the part where

Yousef was saying, *"Whosoever dies and does not invade the enemy of God and his soul does not tell him to fight, he is unfaithful. Abaddon is among the most faithful."*

Yeah, great—Abaddon is among the most faithful. The question from there, Sims told himself, was how Yousef fit with Kamāl Zohdi—or Abaddon, as he called himself, the angel of Hell.

28

Kamāl Zohdi's suite looked north across Central Park, snow-covered and grayly empty in the cold light that precedes winter sunrise. Zohdi, dressed in a Givenchy silk bathrobe, stood at the French doors opening onto the covered terrace, sipping a glass of orange juice and staring at Donald Trump's ice skating rink.

Zohdi's journey from Yaate in the Bekáa Valley had been anything but straightforward. First, there'd been Damascus, where he'd had to stiffen the spines of President Assad's small army of corrupt sycophants who had gotten a severe case of the wobblies because of the cleanup at Boudaï. Boudaï had been an accident, of course, but an instructive one. It was yet another validation of the Russians' work—the new spores retained their lethality after being carried a great distance by the force of an explosion.

From Damascus, Zohdi flew to Algiers, where he'd gotten the Algerian passport that he'd used for the Paris leg. Another identity change in Paris, and Zohdi entered Montreal on a French passport. At the post office in Montreal, he picked up the envelope with yet another identity, a driver's license that made him a resident of Bloomfield, New Jersey. A voter's registration made him an American citizen. A fashionable sporting goods shop yielded the parka, stretch pants, and duffel bag that allowed him to melt into the crowd of skiers returning to the States on Amtrak's Montrealer after a weekend at Mont Tremblant.

Just to his right, on an elegant Philadelphia chest-on-chest, a telephone chirped discreetly. It was the desk, announcing a visitor, using Yousef's alias. Zohdi murmured an acknowledgment. Moments later, the door chimes sounded. Right hand thrust into his robe pocket and curled around a compact .380 Beretta, he squinted through the judas hole.

Yousef stood in the corridor, well away from the door. He carried a small attaché case. His other hand was deep in his overcoat.

Zohdi allowed himself a small ironic smile. Two men on either side of a door, both ready to draw and shoot. America and High Noon at the Plaza Hotel. He swung the door open and in the next second, the two men embraced, kissing each other on the cheek in greeting. Zohdi led the younger man into the living room.

Yousef swung his head with the wariness of a panther, taking in the opulent suite.

"Orange juice?" Zohdi pointed to a silver pitcher on the antique Sheraton end table. Yousef shook his head in a tight, wired motion, and stood, tense and coiled, both hands holding the attaché case in front of himself.

The two men faced each other, Yousef attentive and waiting, Zohdi inspecting the man before him as if seeking for evidence of fault lines that might have emerged since their last meeting.

Apparently satisfied, Zohdi relaxed, a microscopic easing of the hard lines and planes that made up his face. He cocked his head to the side. "The two parts . . . ?"

". . . are ready," Yousef finished. "There is a television? With recorder?"

Zohdi pointed to a Chinese lacquered cabinet. Yousef strode across the room, opened the cabinet doors. Squatting before the television set, he reached into his attaché case and came up with a cassette that he fed into the VCR. Then he stood and punched buttons on the remote. As he did so, Zohdi came up beside him and the two of them stood shoulder to shoulder, watching the screen.

A large green plastic tub abruptly materialized, bright under off-camera floodlights. The background was deep in shadow, but Zohdi could see electric power cables like dark snakes, working their way between the dim shapes of other, similar tubs set out along the floor.

Suddenly, the camera pulls back slightly and Zohdi saw a dusty, granular solid pouring into the tub.

Another shift of the camera—the frame now shows a man, shot from the back. He bends over the tub, cradling a large bag. The man's legs are spread and it is apparent that he is struggling with the heavy weight of the bag. Another man stands close by, watching. Both men have kerchiefs over their mouth and nose.

"Fertilizer," Yousef explained.

The screen blackened for an instant, then, from a different angle, the green tub. The fertilizer is clearly visible. Heavily gloved hands appear, holding a large glass beaker. The hands tilt the beaker and a clear, steaming liquid spills into the fertilizer.

"Melted paraffin," Yousef said. "One can use motor oil, but the wax makes the charge less susceptible to moisture."

As the last of the paraffin drips from the beaker, a large wooden paddle resembling what it was, a cut-off oar, enters the picture to stir the wax and fertilizer together. Another flicker of the screen and the two kerchief-masked men pour the mixture from the green plastic tub into a series of open cardboard cartons.

Zohdi noticed a logo on the sides of the cartons.

"That . . . on the boxes."

Yousef flicked the stop control on the remote, and craned his head toward the screen. "Oh. That. The rental company for the van. They also provide packing materials." He smiled. "Very professional. Very neat." He flicked the control again and the tape moved on.

"And it works?"

Yousef manipulated the remote. The screen jerked and pulsated.

A hand scrapes the insulation off a set of wires. Fast forward again. Outdoors, now. An open field surrounded by low scrub brush and stunted trees. The unidentifiable figure of a man places the box inside a clunker automobile.

The camera focuses on the automobile for several seconds, then follows an insulated pair of wires from the car to a blasting machine, a square box with an upright T-shaped handle.

The camera pans back to the car. Pause. A bright flash of light fills the screen. The camera shakes from the shock wave, then recovers to capture a huge pillar of smoke and dust. The camera pans and—parts of the car arcing through the air.

"That was a demonstration using but one box," Yousef explained. "We will be using fifteen boxes—over a half a ton of explosive. And the blast will be enhanced by cylinders of compressed hydrogen."

"And the second part of the operation?"

Yousef produced another cassette from the attaché case and fed it into the VCR. A moment of squirrelly on-screen flashing, small dark object against a white background. The camera zooms in.

Zohdi recognized the object as a fountain pen. *His* pen, a Mont Blanc President. The pen he'd carried from Damascus to Paris and to Montréal and into the United States. Suddenly, Zohdi imagined the pen as an arrow, one aimed into the very heart of Satan. The pen and its contents now waited only for his command to bring death to Satan.

A latex-gloved hand enters the picture and picks up the pen. The camera backs away, revealing the white background to be a sheet draped over a chair. The camera swings to the figure standing beside the chair, a hooded figure in coveralls holding the pen out toward the camera.

"That is Ali." Yousef motioned to the screen.

"From Yaate?"

"From Yaate," Yousef confirmed. "He is wearing a rubberized suit, and under the hood, a mask of high filtration."

The scene shifts. A closeup of Ali's latex gloved hand unscrewing the Mont Blanc's top. Another scene shift: two petri dishes, two flat-bottomed glass saucers set against a black background, the hand tapping the Mont Blanc barrel.

A fine dust gathers on top of the clear liquid in the petri dishes.

Zohdi watched, hypnotized. The time, the effort that had gone into developing that small pinch of seed stock. The cosmic promise of it—it was like watching a motion picture of a sperm fertilizing an ovum; the minute act that would have such gargantuan consequences. He felt his heart pound in his chest and his breath grow short.

"Four days ago," Yousef narrated.

"And now?"

As if to answer him, a new scene flashed on the screen: a long shot of a windowless room, apparently a basement, judging from the small windows set high up against the ceiling. Two long benches separated by a walkway between. On each bench, Zohdi counted ten round metal containers, each thickly wrapped, an electric cord running from each wrapping to a heavier cable lying on the floor along the middle of the walkway.

"Electric blankets, set to a constant temperature of fifty degrees Celsius."

"We will have—how much?"

"Ali estimates at least three kilos. That is the weight in fermentation. We will have a more accurate weight when Ali transfers the product to the container."

"We will be ready?"

Yousef nodded.

"Everything?"

Yousef nodded again, drawing himself up in pride. Zohdi gave one of his rare smiles, embraced Yousef, then stepped back, signifying their meeting was over.

With a few words of encouragement at the door, Zohdi saw Yousef out. He stood for a moment, looking at the now-blank television screen exposed within the Chinese cabinet. Yousef had left the two cassettes for him should he want to view them later. He stared at Yousef's cassettes, then went into the bedroom to reappear seconds later with his own video cassette. He slipped the black plastic box into the VCR slot and sat back on the love seat to watch.

The screen flared, then settled.

A black-and-white surveillance camera frames through the bars in a cell, four men. In the screen's upper right-hand corner, a digital clock rolling off seconds, minutes, hours.

The cell is brightly lit. There is no furniture. The four men, all fairly young, are barefoot and dressed only in shorts and T-shirts. Two are sitting on the floor, their backs against the wall, another is lying on the floor on his back, forearm thrown across his eyes as if attempting to shut out the strong overhead light. The last man stands. He grips the cell bars above his head with both hands, and lifts slowly, methodically chinning himself.

The screen's digital clock, Zohdi noted, showed that almost two hours had elapsed. This was Yaate and the four men are Israeli soldiers kidnapped in Lebanon the year before.

Zohdi had wanted healthy specimens and had paid premium prices. The payoffs had gone directly to President Hafez Assad's brother, Rifaat, the Assad family's treasurer, who was charged with building the clan's fortunes. Rifaat, also Syria's vice president, was an imaginative entrepreneur with his hand in every money exchange in Lebanon and Syria from shaking down the pornography smugglers of Marseilles to outright complicity in the thriving drug trade out of the Bekáa.

The clock now showed 2:01:37.56.

Zohdi had lost count of the number of times he'd viewed the video—enough times so that he knew each unfolding event. And now, knowing what would happen in the next second, his heart began a rippling, throbbing beat and, unconsciously, he leaned forward slightly toward the screen so he could capture and savor each moment of the wonder that was about to unfold.

2:01:39.02—just over two hours after the anthrax spores had been blown into the cell.

"Yes!" Zohdi whispered, his lips parted in feverish anticipation, "yes!"

The tape was silent. The sound, Zohdi had found, distracted from his fullest enjoyment.

The exercising man stops midway on the upstroke toward another chin-up. He hangs from the bars for a fraction of a second, then drops to the rough concrete floor. He lands with a gymnast's balanced poise, toes first, lower legs flexing to take up the shock. He stands stock-still in his landing pose. A puzzled look contorts his face.

"Now!" Zohdi breathed out, half-command, half-plea.

2:02:05.63—the man jerks forward at the waist, his head thrusts outward, the hands fly up to clutch at his midsection. He stands bent over and frozen, muscles locked in a rock-hard spasm.

The two men sitting against the wall look up. The man lying on his back has moved his arm off his eyes and is in a partial sit-up position. All three stare at the exercising man.

He straightens—it is now 2:02:53.29—the pain of the act draws his face into a grimace of clenched teeth. A moment—the pain seems to have passed—the man throws his head back in relief. Tension visibly departs, his body relaxes. Then the pain strikes again. He throws his hands up to pull at an invisible dagger thrust into his chest. He doubles over at the waist. His body racks with a deep cough. A massive gout of dark blood erupts from his mouth, splashing on the dirty concrete floor.

One of the sitting men rushes to the bleeding man's side, throws an arm over his shoulder, tries to hold him while standing awkwardly away from the splattering torrent of blood. The other sitting man watches, the alarm plain on his face. The man previously lying on the floor has scrambled to his feet.

"Ohhh," murmured Zohdi, his every fiber of consciousness totally absorbed in the drama before him. His hands moved slowly back and forth, stroking his knees and the tops of his thighs.

2:03:17.44—the man who had been on the floor takes a lurching, staggering step. Falling, he grabs for the bars. He connects, but he cannot hold on and sags to the floor. Doubling over fetallike, he vomits.

2:04:35.11—all four men writhe on the floor which is now awash with a sea of blackish blood. Arms and legs flail and kick in frantic, uncontrollable spasms. And there is the blood . . . always more . . . now issuing from every bodily orifice.

"Where is your god, now, Jews?" The scream came full-throated, Zohdi stood, every muscle locked in a paralyzing fanaticism of hate.

Zohdi's thoughts flickered at the speed of light. A kaleidoscope of erotic horror, a horror complete and thorough . . . a horror and ecstasy capturing every cell of his being, locking him within it. He was slave and master . . . victim and aggressor . . . sadist and masochist. But, one thing, one thing of certainty . . . an elevating rapture rising through the swirling ambiguities. He was Death. He was Abaddon, the keeper of the Pit. He was the Destroyer.

Abruptly, Zohdi stood and, as if in a trance, walked toward the French doors leading to the covered terrace. On the screen four bodies lay crumpled in a sea of blood. Throwing open the doors, Zohdi stepped out onto the terrace.

After the enfolding warmth of the suite, the frigid February air touched Zohdi's face and hands like the clean stroke of a cold steel blade. He walked to the parapet and stared to the west where the sky was still dark with the night.

Later in the morning, a cold front would sweep down from Canada, bringing with it a northeast wind. So much the better! Looking across Manhattan and into the depths of the continent that Satan called home and the millions of infidels who did Satan's bidding, he saw the terrible strength of the evil that was the ultimate enemy of Islam. In his gut, like a cold worm, he felt a twist of fear. Then he conjured up the reassuring images from the television, of the four men in the cell, and he muttered the holy passage aloud.

"The unbelievers declare: 'The Hour of Doom will never come.' Say: 'By the Lord, it is surely coming!' " He faced to the east. The sun was now coming up over the towers of Manhattan. "Tomorrow," he promised America the Great Satan. "Tomorrow."

And then Zohdi fell to his knees for *al-fajr*, the dawn prayer.

29

Three hours after Kamāl Zohdi had finished his dawn prayers, Francis X. Higgins, a short, bald-headed man with nicotine-stained fingers and a creasing scar over his right eye rapped on Sims's door at the Howard Johnson's motel in Secaucus. Higgins faced the door with his overcoat pulled open enough to show his badge hooked into a leather carrier in the breast pocket of his sport coat.

Higgins stayed less than fifteen minutes. After he left, Sims went down the passageway to Riddle's room. Riddle opened the door, his face half lathered, half shaved. He waved Sims into the room with a hand that held a glistening Sheffield straight razor. The huge Webley revolver rode in its shoulder holster under Riddle's left arm.

"We've got a meeting with Neptune this morning at ten. Docks near the Bayonne Terminal," Sims announced, taking a seat on the foot of the bed, watching Riddle go back to his shaving.

Riddle lifted his neck and poised the blade at the base of his throat. "I suppose Neptune has a history?" Riddle asked into the mirror.

Sims consulted a small pocket notebook. "Neptune's last name is Khalid, first name Munzhir. Higgins—that's his handler—says Khalid's story checks out with immigration. Egyptian, left Cairo in September '87. Former Egyptian

army officer. Valid green card, no trouble with the law."
Sims held up a color photo. "Here's a recent picture."

Riddle craned toward the photo, studied it, then went
back to the mirror. "Livelihood?"

"Taxi driver."

With a roll of his wrist, Riddle swept a wide path through
the lather with the razor, then turned to Sims. "This man
Higgins. The handler. Where is he?"

"He's not coming with us."

Riddle's eyes widened. "No?"

"Said Neptune wanted to meet alone."

"Without a handler? Meet with us? Two strangers? Unusual."

"Higgins said Neptune insisted." Sims paused. "There's
another unusual."

Riddle worked his upper lip with four deft strokes, then
ran water over the shiny steel blade and then wiped the
razor carefully with a towel. He looked questioningly at
Sims. "Another unusual?"

Sims got up off the bed and stretched. "Higgins said that
Neptune was a walk-in."

"So?"

"So before he came to work for the Jersey City PD,
Neptune had worked for the Bureau."

A mile west of Manhattan, across the Hudson River,
fifteen miles of New Jersey waterfront and port cities are
patched together under the Hudson County government.
The northernmost of these is the small town of Guttenberg,
population slightly over ten thousand. Then there is
Weehawken, where Alexander Hamilton and Aaron Burr
met to duel, and Hamilton to die. Working south, one runs
into the larger places like Hoboken and Jersey City. Below
Jersey City, Bayonne points across the Kill Van Kull chan-
nel into Staten Island.

Like Manhattan across the river, Jersey City began as a
real estate deal between Peter Stuyvesant and the native
Americans. Stuyvesant, continuing his sharp trading, got
what is now Jersey City for forty yards of cloth, a dozen

brass kettles, several muskets, and a half-barrel of strong beer.

Intrigue winds its way beneath the surface of Jersey City's respectable if prosaic history, like a maiden aunt's secret affair with a young bullfighter one long ago summer in Grenada. It was in Jersey City that Benedict Arnold's espionage tradecraft slipped, guaranteeing him a place in history as America's most famous traitor. In the run-up to the Civil War, Jersey City had been a major way station in the Underground Railroad, and in 1916, German saboteurs engineered the Black Tom explosion, blowing up a munitions plant and causing property damage of over twenty million dollars.

Jersey City, population two hundred thousand plus, a major port in its own right, is a gateway to Manhattan. Each morning, hundreds of thousand of commuters fight their way into the Holland Tunnel in order to fight their way back again in the crush of late afternoon traffic. Perhaps as an irony of geography, the Statue of Liberty, the icon of America and New York City, is far closer to Jersey City than to Manhattan.

Following a sketch map Higgins had given him, Sims pulled the Pontiac to a stop just opposite a busy Jersey City dock. It was just before ten, and across the Hudson, the morning sun, cutting through the thickening clouds, fired silver and gold laser reflections from the towers of Manhattan. At one end of the dock, dump trucks arrived, backed up onto a ramp, and tilted their cargos of used tires into a huge open steel container that looked like an open railroad freight car minus the wheels. At the other end of the container, a crane dropped its scoop, clawed up a load of tires, swung them over, and released them into a waiting barge, filling the air with the laboring sounds of the crane's donkey engine and the deep thudding noises of the tires dropping into the barge.

Sims and Riddle sat without talking, each lost in his thoughts. The crane, lifting out a claw full of tires, dropped several onto the dock between the container and the barge. The tires bounced high in the air; one rolled drunkenly off the edge of the dock and splashed into the black water. Finally, Sims fidgeted with impatience. He looked at his watch. Neptune was fifteen minutes late.

"I think our man's here," Riddle said, eyeing the sideview mirror.

Sims glanced up into the rearview. A bright yellow cab made its way slowly toward them along the dockside frontage road and pulled up against the curb several car lengths behind Sims's car. He could see the driver was alone. The driver sat for a moment, then got out. Brown leather jacket, khaki corduroy trousers. No hat. Heavyset. Not quite six feet, forty, maybe forty-five years old, Sims estimated. Dark complexion, dark hair. Round, vaguely friendly looking face, clean shaven.

Sims eased the Llama automatic from his shoulder holster and slipped it under the *New York Times* on the seat between Riddle and himself. He rolled his window down and watched the man approach.

Neptune walked with the assured stride of a soldier or an athlete, erect carriage, slight rolling of the hips to keep his feet under himself at all times. Hands empty and, it seemed to Sims, held deliberately away from his body.

The man came to Sims's side of the car and bent to look in.

"You are friends of Higgins?" The voice was a rich baritone, Mediterranean-accented American English with a trace of Brit thrown in.

Sims nodded and reached back to unlatch the back door. The man looked back up the street past his cab, then got in. Sims smelled a not unpleasant hint of tobacco and coffee. Sims and Riddle twisted in their seats to face the newcomer.

"I am Neptune," the man announced. "Higgins said I should talk with you. You aren't Jersey City police—who are you?"

"Isn't it enough that Higgins okayed us?"

"Maybe for Higgins. You know how Higgins and me . . . ?"

"He said you were a walk-in," Sims answered. "He said you used to work for the Bureau."

Neptune searched Sims's face as if considering whether to

go further. Then, apparently satisfied, said, "He inherited me." .

"In*her*ited?"

"Yah. I was a little or-fun."

Sims said nothing.

Neptune shifted in his seat. "You Agency?"

Sims shrugged. "If I was, I could still say no. If I wasn't and wanted to be I could say yes."

"You're Agency," Neptune said with finality, as if the decision had been handed down and was not subject to debate.

"You said you were an orphan. The Bureau cut you loose?"

Neptune laughed. "Nah. *I* quit. *I* deliver, but *they* do nothing with it. Just want me to keep on, keep me on the string. Those Bureau boys do nothing but sit on their ass."

"How'd you come to work for the Bureau?"

"I drive cab in New York when I first come to America. I met many other Muslim. I hear of mosque here in Jersey City. Very active. So I come here with my friends to pray. A year ago, maybe a little more, I meet some at the mosque who talk about a war against the Great Satan. I get to know these men, then I go to FBI."

"How much'd they pay you?"

"Five hundred."

"A month?"

"A week."

"When'd they start paying you?"

"Last of March."

"Last year?"

"Yes."

"When'd you quit?"

"Three weeks ago. They weren't doing anything with it. That's when I go to Mr. Higgins."

"What were you delivering to the Bureau?"

"Deliver?"

"What information were you giving them?"

"Plans."

Irritated, Sims snapped. "Come on, don't dribble it out a word at a time. If you're going to talk, talk."

"Ramzi Yousef . . . Abouhalima. They have plans."

"And a guy named Hampton-el?"

"Yes. Black American." Neptune studied Sims. "You Muslim?"

"No."

Neptune kept looking at Sims. "What, then?"

"What do you mean?"

"If not Muslim, what are you?"

"AME—African Methodist Episcopal." Sims watched Neptune take that in. "What were Ramzi's plans?"

"I record them."

"I heard some of your recordings. Targets. What targets?"

"Mubarak."

"Hosni Mubarak? The Egyptian president?" Riddle asked.

Neptune nodded. "And Alfonse D'Amato—the senator. They talk about killing—assassinations—that kind of thing. But Bureau doesn't do anything. Doesn't do shit." Neptune's voice rose in indignation. "I risk my life to get these recordings, but they do nothing. *Nothing!*"

"You ever see this man?" Sims slipped a photograph of Kamāl Zohdi from his inside jacket pocket and stretched over the back of his seat to hand it to Neptune.

Neptune took the photo, gave it the briefest of glances, shook his head, and returned it to Sims. "No," Neptune said. "Who is he?"

"A friend of Ramzi Yousef."

"Ah, yes, Ramzi. I try to tell the Bureau about him. 'Put on watch' I say. 'Tap the telephone' I say." Neptune got a disgusted look. "They do *no*-thing. Ab*s*olutely *no*-thing. That's why I quit." Neptune's voice was climbing toward a self-righteous rage. "That's why I leave! I—"

Riddle made a smooth and calming interruption. "Ramzi . . . what is he up to now?"

Neptune, halted in midflight, looked mouth-open at Riddle, then threw up his hands in a helpless gesture. "I don't know what he does, specifically. Yousef has circles inside of circles. I was in one of the outer circles. Others were closer in. That is why the Bureau should have—"

"Well, the Bureau didn't," Sims said, blocking Neptune from taking off again. "Where does Ramzi live?"

"Kensington Avenue. Number thirty-four."

Sims thought for a moment. Then, "Could you stake it out?"

Neptune jerked a thumb over his shoulder toward his cab.

Sims reached into his pocket, pulled out a roll, and peeled off five fifties. "Rent something with a cellular phone." He handed the bills to Neptune. "Nothing flashy."

"I know how to sit and watch," Neptune said somewhat stiffly. "I need help," he added. "Watching is a two-person job." He saw Sims's question coming and answered it before it got out. "I have a friend who . . ." Neptune let it trail off, while rubbing his thumb against his forefinger in a more-money gesture. Sims peeled off two more bills. The fifties disappeared inside the leather jacket.

"Yousef scratches his balls," Sims said, "I want to know."

Neptune gave Sims a lazy, confident grin. "I tell you left or right. How do I contact you?"

Sims gave him the control number. "You get your car phone number, call it in to here."

Neptune recited the control number several times to himself, then nodded. "I work for the Agency, now?" He grinned some more.

"You work for me," Sims said.

Sims and Riddle watched as Neptune drove off. Both sat without speaking until Sims broke the silence.

"What do you think of that?"

"We started the morning with 'unusual,'" Riddle replied. "And it has gotten more unusual."

The yellow cab, a bright splash of color against the dockside drabness, turned a corner and disappeared between a row of warehouses.

"Hard to find walk-ins getting five hundred a week who walk out because their cash-cows aren't performing."

"Yes, he wanted action more than money," agreed Riddle. "And his manner—"

"Yeah. A man with a plan." Sims reached into the

envelope for the print of Kamāl Zohdi. "You hand a picture of a stranger to somebody, they study it because they *are* looking at a stranger. You hand them a picture of somebody they know, they recognize it right away—"

"—and they hand the photograph back right away," Riddle finished. "You think Neptune knows Zohdi?"

Sims tilted the photograph. He saw Neptune's prints on the glossy finish. "Yeah, I think he knows Zohdi, and I think we ought to get to know Neptune a little better."

Sims slid the photo back into the envelope and started the car.

"Where to, now?"

"Find a Fed-Ex office somewhere. Get Neptune's prints down to Louis Vee, then scope out Thirty-four Kensington Avenue."

Sims and Riddle drove slowly down Kensington Avenue. Sims typed the street immediately: an ethnic working class neighborhood, he decided, where in the summer the kids would play stickball in the street. Cars along both sides were well-preserved veterans of pregas shortage 70's Detroit: huge machines with long hoods, massive grills, and thick bumpers with stickers boosting Honduran soccer teams, demanding a free Eritrea, and damning apartheid. Nothing about whales or nuclear power, Sims noted. People here drank beer, not chardonnay.

Sims spotted Yousef's pickup truck. "'Ninety-three Toyota," he grunted. Neptune could park down the block and cover the pickup without being seen himself. And there were two restaurants and a bar fronting Kensington opposite Yousef's apartment for alternate observation posts and piss calls.

Sims slowed to a near stop and pulled out the surveillance photo of Yousef, the one with Yousef standing beside his pickup. No. 34 Kensington Avenue was a 1920s three-story brick block with a center flight of steps running up from the sidewalk. Sims pictured a center hallway and stairs going to the apartments on the second and third floors. Two apartments front, two back.

Without comment, he passed the photo to Riddle, who

looked at the photograph, at the street outside, then back at the photograph. "They caught Mr. Yousef somewhere else," Riddle said, handing the photo back to Sims. The Kensington apartment building bore no resemblance to the free-standing house in the background of the surveillance photograph.

At the end of the block, Sims turned left.

"Looking for real estate, are we?" Riddle guessed.

A shirt-sleeved Francis X. Higgins sat at a scarred wooden desk, both hands holding the Yousef photograph. Off to the side, half-eaten, a brown-bag lunch consisting of an apple, a Hires root beer, and an egg salad on rye. Lips pursed, Higgins squinted at the photograph. He turned the photo over, glanced at the back, then turned it over to Yousef again.

Higgins flicked an index finger against the edge of the photograph. "We make a lotta these," he said to Sims and Riddle, who had drawn up two straight wood chairs around Higgins's desk. Higgins's office was a tiny glass-walled cubicle looking out on the larger squad room of the Special Investigations Section where Higgins's detectives worked elbow to elbow at desks crammed together in rows that reminded Sims of a newspaper city room. Half the desks were empty, and at the others, tired-looking men—and a single woman—worked the incessantly ringing telephones or typed reports. It had been, Sims realized, a long time since he'd seen anyone use a typewriter. Over it all the stale odor of so many people mingled with the sour smell of burned coffee and the chemical sweetness of institutional disinfectant.

"Yeah," Higgins repeated, handing the photograph back to Sims, "we make a lotta those."

"Can we find out where this one was made?"

Higgins's face pulled into weary resignation. "Yeah. I guess." He thought for a moment, then consulted a ledger book covered in a pale green cloth. "Watch list," he said to no one in particular as he turned to the day's page, marked with a red plastic paper clip. The bald-headed man ran his finger down the list of names. Sims noticed that the purplish scar over Higgins's right eye was wide and wandering—not a blade, Sims decided, more likely a broken bottle.

Higgins looked up from the watch list. "Panyard's our camera guy. He comes on at one."

Panyard actually came on several minutes early. A stocky sandy-haired man Sims estimated to be in his late twenties, Panyard nodded to Sims and Riddle during Higgins's introduction. After the shift briefing, Panyard led Sims and Riddle down a narrow back corridor with cracked linoleum flooring and clanking steam radiators to a small windowless office.

Compared to the gritty slovenliness of Higgins's office and the squad room, Panyard kept a neat shop. A Formica counter ran around three walls, and above and below the counter, rows of cabinets and drawers, each labeled with neatly typed cards in shiny brass holders. Fluorescent lights hidden beneath the cabinets lit the office with a cool antiseptic glow. A small desk had been set into the counter-top, and the workspace was marked with a Macintosh computer, a jar of pencils and felt-tip markers, a light-box for viewing negatives, and several framed photographs that Sims figured were of Panyard's wife and child. On the wall space facing the desk, a New York Giants banner. Above an interior door, a sign with a do-not-enter message and beside it a red warning light. The darkroom, Sims guessed.

Panyard, the Yousef photo in hand, sat down in a rolling chair and scooted himself over to the desk, flicked on the Mac, and rapped in the alphanumeric code printed in the lower right-hand corner of the photograph.

"Funny thing," Panyard said, eyes on the screen, "you think you'll remember every picture when you shoot it, but you shoot so many . . . give yourself a couple of weeks and you wonder if you ever shot it at all."

"It doesn't get any better," Riddle muttered to himself. Then to Panyard and pointing to the computer, "How is this catalogued?"

An hourglass blinked on the screen; the computer was still searching.

"Requestor," Panyard replied, "date, time, and location. Subject name if there is one."

"Location?"

Panyard reached into an overhead bookshelf and came down with a thick black three-ring binder. Opening to a tabbed section, he unfolded a map of the city. "I divided the city into a grid with squares designated by a letter and a number—W-Nine, C-Seven, that kind of thing. I cross-referenced the squares to streets. It took me three years to—" He stopped, the computer screen having attracted his attention. "Here we are."

Panyard checked the print's code number against that on the screen, then turned to Sims. "I took that one a week ago—that was a Thursday. Afternoon—two thirty-seven, to be exact. And the address is 40 Pamrapo."

It was two-thirty in the afternoon when Sims and Riddle slowed to a stop opposite 40 Pamrapo. It didn't have the feel of a neighborhood the way Kensington Avenue had. Instead of apartments and row houses there were service stations and outlet storefronts. The house, set back from the street, was the only residential building on the block. A cheap two-story frame, four smallish windows on the upper floor looked out over a two car garage that took up the entire ground floor. The paint, a bland industrial beige, ran black with fingers of rain-carried soot from a nearby paper plant.

"Depressing looking place," Riddle murmured.

Sims watched for a moment. Isolated tufts of grass in the smallish yard. No hedges, no sign that humans had exerted any care of the outside. No cars in front. He leaned forward to get his back away from the seat and rolled his shoulders to work out the stiffness at the base of his neck.

"Okay," he said, thinking aloud and looking at the house, "Yousef is Zohdi's advance man. Yousef comes to the States to put together an organization to pull off the operation. If Brenner's right, Zohdi's little bioboutique in the Bekáa cranks out a thimbleful of freeze-dried anthrax—seed stock. Zohdi smuggles the anthrax into the States and ferments it into a lethal batch in a lab Yousef has—"

"Set up in a depressing house in Jersey City," Riddle finished.

Higgins's voice came over the phone rusty and weary. "The owner?" A pause, then, "City tax rolls."

"Can you make a call?" Sims asked, picturing Higgins slouched in his chair at the battle-worn desk. There was a silence and Sims imagined Higgins sitting there, measuring just how far his friendship with Cantrell ran and how many miles had already been run off.

"Yeah," Higgins said finally.

"I'll tell Cantrell he owes you."

Higgins laughed. A harsh, humorless bark. "Don't worry. I'll tell him myself."

Jersey City's Department of Taxation was a large bull pen of an office, the long length of it divided by a waist-high barrier. On the city's side, dozens of government clerks sat shoulder to shoulder, consulting files, working keyboards, and looking morosely into computer screens. The other side of the barrier, the public waiting area, a single row of folding metal chairs lined up, backs against the wall. The wall itself, a pale green, bore a dark grease stain six or so inches above the row of chair backs, a witness to countless taxpayer heads that had watched the clerks feed appeals into the computer terminals, then come back to stand behind the protective barrier and deny the appeal, flashing a bureaucrat's smug smile of satisfaction and condescension: No, the computer said . . .

"Francis Higgins said to help you." Sims faced an imposingly large middle-aged black woman with a head of tightly wound silver curled hair.

"Whatever you have on this address," Sims said.

The woman glanced at the slip of paper Sims had handed her, nodded, and went off to two clerks standing by a water fountain. Five minutes later, she brought a printout to the counter and spread it out in front of Sims and Riddle.

"It says here"—she pointed with a yellow pencil—"that 40 Pamrapo is owned now by Sterling Investments, Incorporated."

"Now? You said 'owned now'?"

She nodded and ran the pencil point down the printout. "They just bought it. See this date?"

"October?"

"October twenty-first. That was the settlement date."

Sims scanned the printout. "Previous owner?"

The pencil darted to another section.

"Harders and Garven?"

"That's the realtors. I guess Archie was selling it for himself."

"Archie?"

"Archie Harders. The senior partner."

Back in the car, Sims called Higgins on the cellular phone. "I'd appreciate one more phone call."

Fifteen minutes later, Archie Harders, a pleasant-faced middle-aged man with thick brown hair, closed the door to his office and waved Sims and Riddle to two matching Chippendale smoking chairs. Harders and Garven occupied the ground floor of a new high-rise office building, and, if you judged from the antiques, carpet thickness, and the Klee original behind Harders's desk, real estate was the business to be in, in Jersey City.

"I don't often get calls from the Jersey City police," Harders said, as he casually perched on the corner of the large partner's desk, and swung one expensively shod foot back and forth.

Sims handed Harders the printout. Harders reached across the desk and came up with a pair of tortoiseshell reading glasses. He glanced at the printout, then back to Sims. Harders's mouth turned down in a worried frown.

"Shit, 40 Pamrapo." He shook his head.

"Something wrong?" Sims asked.

Harders rolled his eyes heavenward. "Ahh—I should have known—that property was a dog. I picked it up on a foreclosure. Thought I could turn a quick profit. Got stuck with that sonofabitch for five damn years. I was even thinking of deeding it over to the city for a tax break when I got a bite." Harders got a resigned look. "Just my luck. I should have known it was too easy." He looked inquiringly at Sims. "Let me guess—you're DEA? And they're pushing kilo batches out of 40 Pamrapo?"

Sims held up a hand. "We don't know that anything's going on there. What was too easy about it?"

Harders threw both hands open. "No haggling. Full price. Bam! One minute I had a dog, next minute, a fat profit and more capital gains for the I-fucking R-S."

"Who is Sterling Investments?"

A shrug. "No faces. A local lawyer closed for them. Full power of attorney, the works. Check drawn on Sterling account."

"Might we examine the records of the transaction?" Riddle suggested gently.

"And a layout of the house?" Sims added.

Harders nodded and reached for the intercom button.

Half an hour later, Harders accompanied Sims and Riddle through the now-closed outer offices. Stopping at the entrance, Sims noticed a stack of large metal FOR SALE signs on sharpened stakes. He stopped, thought for a second, gazing at the signs, then turned to Harders.

"Mind if we borrow one of those?"

Harders eyebrows arched. He nodded. "Have I got another salesman?"

Sims bent to pick out a sign. "Depends," he said, "on the commission."

At six-thirty Thursday afternoon, the fax in Alberich's office signaled incoming. He took ten minutes to review Archie Harders's files, then wheeled up to South Cafeteria where he got a carryout of lasagna, spinach salad, and almost fresh sesame seed rolls. Back at his computer keyboard, he started on the lasagna and punched the first key as he began what he suspected would be a long night tracking down Sterling Investments.

At seven, Sims and Riddle drove down Kensington Avenue. A dark blue Ford Escort, Neptune had said when Sims had called. The Escort was parked across the street from 34 Kensington and down about fifty yards. Sims went by without stopping or slowing. Through the car's darkened glass, he could see only the dimmest outline of what he assumed to be Neptune's head and shoulders.

"All quiet," Sims said to Riddle. "How about dinner?"

Riddle, staring intently at 34 Kensington, turned from the window with a look of approval. "How *about* dinner?" he asked back.

At the same time that Sims and Riddle were sitting down to thick cuts of rare prime rib at Ruth's Chris in Weehawken, a huge red-haired man in chambray shirt and dirty blue jeans stood in a garage and supervised the packing of a van. Leaning in through the vehicle's open side cargo door, he counted the cardboard cartons already in the van—eleven. Four more to go. Eighty pounds each, total of twelve hundred pounds. The fifteen cartons had to be fitted tightly against each other, Yousef had warned. Three rows of five, with detonators in each alternating box, their wires carefully spliced and taped into three parallel circuits with two timers per circuit for reliability. After the boxes, the six cylinders of compressed hydrogen.

He carefully checked his watch. Now five after seven. As Yousef had directed, he had set his watch precisely from the recorded time announcement on the phone. It was now just under seventeen hours until, until . . . his mind reeled with the prospect. He had been into battle before, so many times it should have become commonplace. But each time, the night before, he felt his blood surging through his veins. Tonight was no exception. If anything, his heart beat even more strongly than ever before. For tomorrow would be the deciding battle—God and his chosen angel, Kamāl Zohdi, would at last strike down the Great Satan and he, Mahmoud Abouhalima, would gain Paradise because he had helped bring about the final judgment.

30

Temperatures in the Hudson Valley the following morning had dropped toward freezing and a chill northeast wind carried a damp scent that told Sims snow was on the way. Even so, he stepped outside his motel room just after six in watch cap, gloves, and nylon running suit and started out at a slow pace east on Paterson Plank Road. At Mill Creek Drive, he turned into the wind, looped the massive convention center at the Meadowlands, and then, the wind now at his back, started to work up a heavy sweat in a full-out run back toward the motel.

While Sims was still five minutes away from the motel, Mahmoud Abouhalima locked the van doors and pocketed the keys. A few paces from the van, he stopped, turned, and looked back at the vehicle, going over once more his mental checklist of last minute details. The six timers had been set. He had removed the shorting shunts from the detonating circuits that had prevented a premature explosion from a police radar or nearby two-way radio transmissions. The six hydrogen containers had been lashed firmly on top of the cartons of explosives and a jumble of blankets and boxes of household goods had been laid over the whole thing for camouflage. And the last touch: just before locking the van, Abouhalima connected the mercury switch booby trap that would set off everything if someone pried with the van.

Abouhalima noted the position of the van beneath the maze of overhead ducting, vents, and blowers. It was the right place, no doubt about it.

With that, the big redheaded man turned and walked toward the exit ramp. After months and weeks, the day was finally here. There was a powerful sense of finality—no more decisions to be made, no more problems to overcome. Everything was done that could be done, and with that a wave of serenity swept over him. It was in the hands of God . . . and Kamāl Zohdi. For the first time that he could remember, Mahmoud Abouhalima felt at peace.

Sims got in from his run and he dialed Neptune's cellular phone. Neptune answered on the second ring.

"It was very cold last night." Neptune didn't sound as if he were complaining.

"All quiet?" Sims asked.

"Hah." Neptune laughed. "Nobody out here except us crazy people."

Fifteen minutes later, Sims was drying off from a long hot shower when Alberich called.

"Sleep well last night?" Alberich asked.

"You didn't?"

"Good guess," Alberich replied sarcastically. "Sterling Investments took a lot of looking. But some old friends turned up."

"Oh?" Sims recognized the tremor in Alberich's voice that usually signaled excitement and victory.

"Sterling's a shell. Incorporated last October in Delaware with a P.O. box as an address and a phony list of officers somebody lifted out of a Wilmington phone book. Anyway, Sterling's corporate bank account showed only two transactions, a withdrawal—the check written to Archie Harders's real estate firm—and a deposit the week before from the Habsburgerbank, Vienna."

"Habsburgerbank?" Sims remembered it vaguely but couldn't place it.

"Un-uh."

"Vienna? Familiar . . . what—"

"Karstens-Export, Bremerhaven? Their bank was Deutchesbank, Frankfurt. Karstens transferred payments each month to a numbered account in—"

"Habsburgerbank, Vienna," Sims finished. "The payments to Broz." He paused, then asked, "A coincidence?"

Alberich hung up with a low, cynical laugh.

Ten minutes later, Sims sat on the foot of Riddle's bed. Again, he'd caught Riddle in the middle of shaving. Riddle listened without interrupting, the razor making its swift, whispering passes through the thick lather.

Bending to splash cold water on his face, Riddle sputtered, then, face emerging from a towel, looked questioningly at Sims.

"Do we wish to engage our friend Higgins in our morning adventure?"

"Adventure?" Sims asked in mock innocence. "What adventure?"

Riddle eyed the canvas kit bag on the floor at Sims's feet as he folded and hung the towel on the rack beside the basin, then tugged on the straps across his chest to readjust his shoulder holster. "Why," he answered as innocently, "our exploration of the house at 40 Pamrapo."

Sims shook his head. He'd already thought about bringing in Higgins. It'd mean search warrants and probable cause. "Let's just keep it between the two of us."

He and Riddle were on Kennedy Boulevard, heading south to Jersey City and 40 Pamrapo when the cellular phone buzzed.

"Our friend is still here," Neptune's voice came clearly over the phone, and Sims got a mental image of the Egyptian's round face and white, even teeth.

"You sure he's still inside. Hasn't slipped out?"

"Nah. He still here."

Sims looked at his watch. A few minutes before ten. He was thinking about getting into the Pamrapo house and he didn't want Yousef and his buddies showing up.

"You see him, you call me right away."

"I follow him—"

"Goddamnit," Sims interrupted, "you *call* when he moves. You're not in this by yourself. You understand?" Sims waited until Neptune said yes, then hung up.

"A bit testy, Mr. Sims," Riddle gently chided.

"Too much of the cowboy in that guy," Sims countered, wiping the inside of the windshield with the back of his glove to remove a thin film of frost. Outside, the snow was beginning to come down more heavily.

Half an hour later, Sims turned left off Kennedy Boulevard onto Pamrapo. Aside from a few cars parked scattered along both curbs, the street was empty.

"Snow usually improves appearances," Riddle observed as they drove by the house. He shook his head. "Same degree of dreariness as yesterday. No cars, no lights, no smoke from the chimney."

"Let's see if we can get a temperature reading."

Riddle had been cradling the infrared scope in his lap. He brought what looked like one half of a pair of binoculars up to his right eye and aimed it at the house as Sims slowed to a crawl.

"No sign of warmth," Riddle announced. "A temperature just below fifty degrees Fahrenheit." He swung the scope to the house on either side. "Seventy-five degrees." He nodded at the comparison. He brought the scope back to his lap, giving it an appreciative pat and a smile.

Sims circled the block, and on the next pass, pulled into the driveway at 40 Pamrapo. They faced one of the two garage doors. To the left of the garage doors, a sheltered entryway. Inside that doorway, Sims recalled from Harders's floor plan, a mudroom with an entry into the garages and another door leading to a flight of steps up into the house proper. Switching off the ignition, Sims and Riddle sat for a moment, watching the lifeless house. Sims reached inside his jacket and loosened the Llama automatic in its shoulder holster.

He and Riddle locked eyes. Riddle gave a terse nod and both men got out of the car. Sims went around back, opened the trunk, and came out with one of Archie Harders's FOR SALE signs, which he leaned against the back bumper. He would leave the sign there while he and Riddle were inside. It was the kind of neighborhood, Sims bet himself, that satisfied itself with the thinnest of answers. Next out of the trunk, the canvas bag with the gloves, masks, and his burglar kit.

The lock at the entry door gave Sims no trouble, and in less than thirty seconds, he and Riddle stepped into the small vestibule. To their left, a coat rack built into the wall; to the right, a solid panel door that according to the real estate folder, led into the garage. To their front was another door that should open onto a stairway to the house above.

Both men stood motionless, alert to the slightest hint of what lay in the house behind the doors. Sims heard nothing except the sound of his own heart beating and the slight rasping of Riddle's breath. A faint odor in the cold air vaguely reminded Sims of apples and tickled at the inside of his nose. As he shifted his weight, his shoes made a small grating sound over the linoleum tile floor. He slipped the shoulder strap of the canvas bag off his shoulder, worked the zipper open, and withdrew a stethoscope which he hooked into his ears and bent forward to place the wide listening probe against the door. After long seconds with no sound from upstairs, he straightened up, shook his head to Riddle, and put the stethoscope away.

Hand still in the bag, he felt around for the two protective masks. He wordlessly passed Riddle one, then fitted his own over his mouth and nose, tugging at the elastic straps to ensure a tight fit against his face. The double layer of fibrous anhydride and activated charcoal filters, Brenner had assured him, would trap any anthrax spores before they could be pulled into his lungs. Next, he snapped on the latex gloves. Slinging the canvas bag over his shoulder, he slipped the Llama from its shoulder holster. Riddle already had the big Webley revolver out, muzzle pointed ceilingward, his thumb resting on the hammer.

Sims nodded toward the door that would lead them upstairs into the living area of the house. With his left hand, Sims reached for the knob, grasping it with his fingertips. The cold of the metal penetrated the latex glove as he gently turned the knob a fraction of an inch. He forced himself to stop breathing as he strained to detect a strange tension, a different sound—anything that shouldn't be a part of opening a door. Keeping the lightest touch on the knob, he slowly twisted. The tightness in his chest made it hard to breathe. Finally, the doorknob came to its stop.

He glanced back at Riddle, who gave him an I'm-ready nod.

He cracked the door open. Searching the door edges, he saw no threads, no wires or tapes, and so pushed the door wide. A flight of stairs led up to the living room. The stairwell was dirty, the drywall sides scraped and scarred, and the stale flatness of the air put Sims in mind of the calm mirrored surface of a forest pond.

Every grain of his intuition screamed that the house was empty. Still, he hesitated for a moment before taking the first step up the stairs.

The stairs opened onto a small living room. From this, a hallway led to two box-size bedrooms, a bath, and a kitchen—all as shown on the real estate diagram. No furniture. Bare wood floors. The bath and kitchen showed the only evidence of human passage, a hole kicked in the drywall near the bathtub, a stack of institutional paper towels on the toilet tank. In the refrigerator, an orange, a half-empty bottle of Evian water, and a dried-up slice of cantaloupe.

Standing in the kitchen, Sims pointed to a wall phone, and Riddle carefully picked the handset out of the cradle, listened, then pointed the instrument toward Sims. Sims nodded as he heard the dial tone. Riddle hung the phone up and jotted the number on one of his pale blue index cards. When Riddle had finished, Sims pointed to the floor, to the garage below.

Back down the stairs, standing in the vestibule, Sims tried the door into the garage. He felt none of the apprehension that had spooked him before going up the stairs. The house was empty with a finality that said that Yousef or whoever else had been here, wouldn't be coming back.

The door was locked with an interior lock meant to ensure privacy more than security. Sims took a straight pick from his case and, inserting it in the hole in the center of the doorknob, pressed until the lock sprang with a loud clicking sound.

He pushed the door open. Two wooden steps led down to the large two car garage. As he stood in the vestibule, the tubs caught Sims's eye first. Two large green plastic industrial tubs, each capable, Sims estimated, of holding fifty or so gallons, took up the nearby garage bay. A huge stack of cardboard boxes and large white paper sacks filled the farther bay, and the throat-drying clutch of ammonia filled the air. None of Brenner's laboratory glassware. No fermentation tanks. No biohazard cabinets. No dryers. Sims reached up and pulled down the mask, letting it hang around his neck. His relief mixed with disappointment.

"So much for anthrax."

He stepped down from the vestibule. He almost missed the extra give in the step and the barely perceptible metallic clockwork click.

The meaning of the slack step and the noise came together before he stepped down to the next step . . . before he lifted his weight from the first step.

He froze in place, stopping so abruptly that he felt Riddle nudge him from behind. A huge knot of fear twisted in his gut and he suppressed a convulsive shudder.

"What is it?" Riddle whispered, sensing Sims's tension.

"The . . . fuc-*king* . . . *step.*" Sims had to force the words from his throat.

"Step?"

"There's something under—"

"Your picks?"

"What?"

"Your *picks,*" Riddle demanded, his voice hoarse with urgency.

"In the bag."

Sims felt Riddle's hand in the kit bag.

"Don't move."

Sims breathed deeply. "Like I'm even thinking about it, Riddle."

"I'll be right back."

And Riddle was gone.

Poised as he was, one foot on the stair, the back foot still in the vestibule, the calf of his forward leg tightened under the strain. Would he feel it, Sims wondered, if he lifted his foot off the stair? Would there be a cosmic instant of consciousness before you turned into ash and blood spray? And in that instant, could you live another lifetime? He'd read a science fiction story once about whole universes inside an atom—why not entire lifetimes inside a flash of lightning?

He heard a metal-to-metal scratching, then the lock of the garage door clacked open and the big door rolled up and back on its greased track as Riddle, stowing away Sims's lock-pick kit, came through the opening, then rolled the door back down again.

"No sense alarming the neighbors," Riddle said, coming over to Sims. "It'd only drive down property values. Can you give me your kit bag without disturbing the step?"

Sims slowly handed the bag to Riddle, taking care not to shift his weight.

Riddle found a flashlight in the bag, then, setting the bag on the floor to the side of the wooden steps, he eased himself to the floor, groaning softly as his knees creaked and popped. Flat on his stomach, he aimed the flashlight under the open steps.

"Ah, yes."

"What the hell is it?" Sims asked in a hoarse whisper.

Riddle continued to play the flashlight back and forth. "Ummnh," a doctor's sound of examination. He rolled on one elbow and looked up to Sims. "A pressure-plate device. European origin. German, maybe Russian. Your weight down snapped the safety; removing the weight will allow the firing pin to—"

"God, Riddle, I *know* how it works!" Part of Sims was embarrassed that his voice had almost cracked. His enemy now, he told himself, was himself. He beat back a tendril of hysteria and willed his heart to stop its furious pounding. "What's it hooked to?"

"Looks like *plastique,*" Riddle said calmly. "A block about the size of a deck of cards."

"So if I'm lucky, all I lose's a leg?"

Flat on the floor, Riddle looked up at Sims with a frown of disapproval. "All you are going to lose, young man, is the price of dinner tonight."

Taking off his jacket, Riddle rolled up his sleeves, unfastened his wristwatch, put it in his trousers pocket, then, flashlight in hand, bellied down on the floor to study the booby trap.

The bright glare of the flashlight revealed two bricks under the step. On top of the bricks, the pressure-plate. It was like looking at a seesaw from the side. Sims's weight kept one side of the lever pressed down. Lift the weight and a spring would drive the other side down.

Sims saw Riddle set his face in concentration. "What is it, Riddle?"

Riddle said nothing for a moment, then, in the measured, careful way a doctor breaks the bad news about a suspicious lump, he made a small clearing of his throat. "If you lift your foot, the other end drops down."

"Yeah? I know that, Riddle. It makes contact, completes the electrical circuit, and *blooey*. So cut the wire—"

"This one's different."

"Different?"

"There are two wires leading out, one from the bottom and one from the top. It could be that if you release your weight—"

"It breaks a circuit that's holding off the detonator," Sims finished, seeing in his mind how it'd work.

"Precisely. Snipping wires won't do it. We have to keep the bloody seesaw from tilting." Riddle set the steel pick aside and reached into his jacket and came up with one of his blue index cards.

"Making a wedge?"

"Exactly," Riddle replied, flashing the light under the stair, judging the distance between the pressure-plate's open contacts. He doubled the index card, folding it in the middle, then slowly slid it into the gap. "A bit more," he said, carefully removing the folded card. He added another card.

Sims watched as Riddle's arm disappeared beneath the

stair, and imagined the unknown bomb maker wiring the pressure-plate to a pull-switch. Move the pressure-plate and you close the pull-switch connection. Booby-trapping the booby trap. His imagination, having gotten wound up, began yet another gloomy excursion. Take the pull-switch, and hook it to—

"That's it," Riddle said, the cool English accent cut into Sims's deadly fantasy.

Sims gazed down into Riddle's hazel eyes.

"You sure?"

Riddle, eyes grave, looked up from the floor, his face but inches from the plastic explosive. "Step down."

Sims started to, then stopped.

"What's the matter?"

"You get out." Sims jerked a thumb toward the outside.

Riddle shook his head with great deliberateness. "You asked if I were confident."

"Yeah?"

"I *am* confident. Step down."

Sims took a deep breath and stepped down.

The explosion didn't come and in the silence of the nonevent, Sims's knees nearly buckled, and he felt a trembling start in his hands and work its way into the core of his body. The shakes passed as quickly as they'd come and by the time Riddle had gotten to his feet, Sims felt weak, but steady again.

Riddle held the pressure-plate in his hand. He turned the mud-colored device over. "Russian, I think." Putting the palm-size booby trap down on the concrete floor, he joined Sims, who by now had walked over to the pile of debris and pulled out one of the large sacks.

"Ammonium nitrate fertilizer," he said, tossing the bag back on the heap. He pointed to the green tubs. "We found a goddamn bomb factory, Riddle."

Riddle nodded. "It would so appear." He scanned the garage like a ship's captain searching the horizon. "And there's another thing."

"What's that?"

"Whatever they built here—they've finished it. They've taken it away, and they aren't coming back."

Sims was reaching for his cellular phone to call Francis Higgins when the phone buzzed insistently. Startled, Sims answered.

"It is Yousef," Neptune's voice came, the excitement carrying through a slight fuzz of static.

"He's leaving?"

"He left twenty minutes ago. I have followed. Pier D. Port Jersey. They are in warehouse. I think—"

"Goddamnit, Neptune, I told you to call me first."

"I did try!" Neptune cried. "The damn circuits, they busy, and he has him with him!"

"Him?"

"Zohdi—Yousef has Zohdi with him."

31

While from a proud tower in the town
Death looks gigantically down.
                    —Edgar Allen Poe *The City in the Sea*

Alice Brenner pressed the large red button set into the wall. A few inches away, a door telescoped into the ceiling with a hydraulic hiss, and she stepped into a low-ceilinged chamber. In front of her, the double entrance doors of the air lock, to her right, a row of blue plastic pressure suits hanging from wall hooks. The suits resembled outsize pajamas with feet and yellow rubber gloves. Each had a clear visor hood with a metal air valve on the side.

Once sealed inside her suit, she reached overhead to a coiled red air hose hanging from the ceiling. Attaching it to the valve on the visor, she felt the suit inflate slightly. Now the air pressure inside the suit was higher than that outside, and keeping that differential meant keeping bad bugs out. With the suit pressurized, she disconnected the air hose and pressed through the air lock. The suit was designed to hold enough air to go three minutes without hooking up to another hose. Inside the lab itself, more hoses dangled every few feet.

Tiled in white, the lab was completely soundless. She had designed the lab and managed its construction, had worked in it for over ten years. Even so, Brenner never got over the strange feeling that she was working underwater. To her right, a five-foot-high square vault for storing culture vials in liquid nitrogen. Beyond that, two laminar flow biohazard cabinets. Inside each glass-fronted cabinet, a slight vacuum so that air could come in, but contaminants couldn't get out. Brenner walked to an air hose in front of a bank of plastic cages on her left and reconnected her pressure suit.

Brenner's interest this morning was four stacked rows of clear plastic boxes, five boxes to a row, numbered one to twenty.

Boxes one through four were empty, the rest were occupied, each with a single white laboratory rat. Each box had a pair of remotely operated mechanical hands that could be operated from a central control panel, and behind the boxes, Brenner knew, a network of tubing that permitted her to mix the air supply from any box with that of any other box.

She stopped in front of box five. Fifteen minutes before, she had introduced a millionth of a gram of anthrax spores into the air supply, the amount that would cover less than one-tenth the head of a pin. This was the cloned anthrax, a duplicate of the DNA-engineered bacillus that Sims had brought back from Yaate.

Rat five was, of course, dead. As though sensing this, rat six next door huddled in the corner most distant from its neighbor. For the past five minutes, box five had been purged by hundreds of cubic feet of compressed air sweeping through and venting, and Brenner was certain that none of the anthrax spores remained free in the box. She would now turn down the airflow and begin the painstaking autopsy of rat five.

Brenner reached for the airflow controls at the base of the stacked boxes. Depressing a lever, she watched as the tiny red plastic ribbons stopped their wild fluttering at box five's air inlet.

Whether it was Brenner's fatigue or the clumsiness of the pressure suit, her hand hit the airflow override lever and she watched in shocked horror as plastic ribbons in the remaining nineteen boxes trembled and came to life. All twenty boxes now had a common, interconnected air supply.

"Shit!" Brenner flipped the override back into lock position and stood shaken, and angry at herself. She hadn't fully recovered when rat six began to die. Ten minutes later, all the rats lay dead in their plastic boxes, surrounded by pools of their own dark blood.

"Take Garfield to Broadway," Riddle read from the map, "then left on East Forty-Ninth which leads into the Port Authority."

Sims wheeled south on Garfield. Just after eleven, the morning rush had died down and the lunch traffic hadn't yet picked up. Though impatient, Sims kept his speed down to just five miles an hour over the limit. Even with Higgins's help, a stop for speeding and—and *what?* What would happen? What would Zohdi do? None of it made sense. Is this what San Gimignano and Rosslyn, Schmar and Okolovich, Bremerhaven and Yaate had come down to—Zohdi and Yousef meeting up with some asshole who made fertilizer bombs in garages? At a pier in Jersey City?

"What?"

"Your phone," Riddle repeated. The car phone buzzed insistently.

Sims pressed the speaker button.

"Bradford?" Alice Brenner's voice came over the speaker, brittle with an electric urgency. "Have you found them?"

"No, but we think—"

"God, Bradford, you've got to find them!"

Sims and Riddle looked at each other, both struck by Brenner's outburst and obvious desperation.

"Alice—"

Brenner interrupted, sharp and decisive. "Get this, Bradford. Your Mr. Zohdi has created a goddamned monster!" There was a pause and Sims imagined Brenner mentally translating the science into everyday English.

"Remember I said that the Yaate anthrax showed signs of modification?"

"Yeah. Genetic engineering. DNA, that kind of stuff."

"Okay, here's what that bastard has done. Normal anthrax can be treated with antibiotics. The Yaate strain was cultured with an antibiotic mix in the nutrients."

"So the Yaate strain—"

"Is immune to any antibiotics I know about. Even with a lot of luck, it'd take us months to develop something."

"Mother of God," Riddle murmured.

"But that's not the worst of it," Brenner continued.

Sims took a deep breath. He didn't want to know. "What?" he finally asked.

Brenner's tone dropped, "Normal pulmonary anthrax has another characteristic—it isn't contagious. To catch it, you have to breathe in the spores. You can't catch it from someone who is already infected."

There was a dead space for a moment, then Brenner returned, coming over the speaker, hollow and sepulchral, as if reading out a death sentence. "That's the normal anthrax. Yaate anthrax, Bradford, is contagious."

"Contagious? One person to another?"

"Yes." There was a long silence and Brenner and Sims and Riddle knew there was nothing more to be said. A click and Brenner hung up.

Sims had only half asked the question. He knew what the answer would be. His brain raced ahead, part of him coolly plotting the unfolding progression of Zohdi's plan, the other part recoiling in revulsion from the consequences.

"The wind," he talked it out as if in a trance, "carries the original spores as far south as Baltimore, Washington. Maybe Richmond. In hours, hospitals jammed. No treatment. People begin dying everywhere—on the streets, in their homes, cars. Corpses all over the place. No burials. Electricity and water go out, transportation stops. Law and order falls apart. A couple of hours of looting, killing, riots. Three, four days—the whole goddamn eastern seaboard would be dead or dying. Then, to keep it from spreading . . ."

Riddle picked up. "What remains of government tries to stop it the way the Syrians stopped it in Boudaï—with fire and the sword. Americans using nuclear weapons on other Americans." Riddle shuddered as if his soul had been contaminated. "This isn't terrorism."

"No," Sims said. "It's extinction."

"But this could sweep the world. There's nothing to keep it confined to this continent. Zohdi's followers could die as well."

"You think that matters to Zohdi?"

"Irrational," Riddle said pulling up from his reservoir of there'll-always-be-an-England stiff-upper-lip.

"No," Sims disagreed. The speedometer needle climbed. Half a mile ahead, Audrey Zapp drive, the docks of Jersey City's waterfront, and, he hoped, Zohdi. "Not irrational. Not to Zohdi. He probably thinks he's got his shit together. The way Zohdi probably sees it, he'll have it all. He's killed Satan and now has paradise.

"We wanted so badly to believe our brand of rationality was Zohdi's. It wasn't. His kind have always been around, people who would bring it all down, people who want it all their way or nothing at all. You saw that kind at Wannsee. Zohdi would have fit right in there, planning the Holocaust with Heydrich and Eichmann. But now he can do them one better. Now he can bring the Holocaust to the whole world."

Three minutes later, Sims turned into the Port Authority Marine Terminal. Port Jersey Boulevard, the backbone of the terminal, ran straight as a string for two miles until ending in Upper New York Bay. The Port Authority itself was a massive array of roads and rail spurs from which trucks and trains loaded and off-loaded ocean freight.

"Bremerhaven, *deja vu* all over again," Sims muttered, as they sped by a sea-land container ship, a dockside crane effortlessly plucking a huge pallet out of a hold and swinging it to a waiting semitrailer cab.

Riddle peered ahead. "Pier D should be next." Sims turned the windshield wipers on to clear away the snow. Visibility had closed in and Manhattan, three miles across the bay, was now hidden by a gray veil.

Pier D, Sims estimated, jutted about three hundred yards into the bay. Six flat-roofed brick warehouses lined up along the pier, three on either side of the main access roadway. Cars of dockworkers lined both sides of the roadway. Beyond the warehouses, the choppy black waters of the bay. He slowed to a crawl.

"There he is." Riddle pointed to the left side of the road. Ahead, by the second warehouse, Sims saw Neptune's Escort, parked between a raggedy pickup truck and a bright red Buick.

He found an open spot on the right side, pulled in, and waited for a moment. A thin layer of snow quickly covered the windshield. Sims worked his hands into his gloves, and then reached into the backseat for his mask, which he slung around his neck, nestling it below his chin, tucking it in the thick folds of his jacket. That done, he reached into his shoulder holster for the Llama automatic. Jacking the slide back, he fed a cartridge into the chamber, thumbed the safety on, then looked at Riddle.

"Ready?"

Riddle had the big Webley out. "As ready as I'll ever be," he answered, opening his door into the falling snow.

As if by silent agreement, Sims and Riddle separated as they walked toward the Escort, Sims taking the curbside sidewalk, Riddle the roadway along the right side of the row of parallel parked cars.

With the tip of his tongue, Sims captured a snowflake that had fallen on his lower lip. A minute burst of clear coldness and it was gone.

Behind the sensation, like a sudden thunder clap on a clear summer day, alarm bells shrilled in Sims's mind. He and Riddle were now just feet from the rear of Neptune's Escort. A subconscious tripwire had been tripped, and now Sims worked furiously to bring it out, to give it form.

"Windshield." Sims thought it was his own voice inside himself and then realized Riddle had come on it at the same time. The Escort's windshield was covered with snow, as were the windows on Sims's side of the car. He tightened his grip on the pistol and from the corner of his eye saw that Riddle had the Webley waist high, holding it in against his hip.

Both men stopped. Riddle looked over to Sims. Sims nodded toward his side of the Escort. Riddle nodded back, then dropped behind the Escort where he could cover Sims's approach.

Standing beside the car, Sims saw that the snow hitting the hood was still melting. Bringing his pistol up, Sims reached with his left hand to the side window and swept the snow from it.

Neptune smiled at Sims through the window. His round-faced grin showed the even teeth, startling white against his olive skin. Neptune's head rested back on the headrest, his eyes locked with Sims's and there was an expression of surprise and question behind the grin.

Sims saw both bullet holes at once—the one in the car window and the one in Neptune's forehead, just above his right eye. Sims tried the door. As he'd expected, it was locked. He bashed the window with the barrel of his pistol. Already cracked and crazed from the bullet hole, the window disintegrated into hundreds of small greenish blue pellets.

There was another body in the car, a man slumped in the passenger's seat—Neptune's helper, whoever that was. Sims saw that the back of the man's head had been blown away and that the window on the passenger side had a hole that matched the other.

Sims stripped off a glove to feel Neptune's throat for the pulse he knew wouldn't be there. Neptune's skin was still warm. He ran his hand up and, with his two fingers, closed Neptune's eyes. "Sorry, cowboy," he muttered.

Sims glanced around the Escort and a foot away, a small dimple pockmarked the snow. He bent and came up with a shiny brass cartridge case. Nine millimeter, the same caliber as the Llama he was carrying. He knew that there was another cartridge case somewhere on the other side of the car, somewhere out there in the street. Leave it for Higgins and his colleagues in homicide, he told himself.

Sims searched the direction from which he and Riddle had come, the direction from which the killers had come. He saw the other sets of footprints, not as sharp or distinct as those Riddle and he had made. He looked ahead. Both pair of footprints led to the last warehouse on the right at the end of the pier about a hundred yards away.

"Zohdi must have had a rear-guard security," Riddle observed quietly, also eyeing the footprints leading to the warehouse. "Neptune followed Zohdi and they followed Neptune."

Sims looked back into Neptune's face, then to Riddle.

"Whatever Zohdi's up to, he's up to it now." Sims grabbed for the cellular phone. "He wouldn't have left them here if he was planning on staying here long." Sims was already punching numbers into the phone, at the same time, starting toward the warehouse.

Riddle fell in beside him. "You're calling Higgins?"

"Yeah." Sims picked up the pace, telephone in one hand, pistol in the other. The two men were now at a slow trot through the snow, ducking to keep some half-assed cover behind the rows of parked cars between them and the warehouse. Sims saw Riddle's face flush with the effort, but the older man managed to keep up.

Over the sounds of heavy breathing and the noise of running, Sims heard Higgins answer. In short rasping bursts, Sims told the police officer about Neptune, the warehouse, and the house at 40 Pamrapo.

"Goddamnit, you stay put!" Higgins's voice rose. "I'll have cars there in—"

For an instant, Sims thought about telling Higgins about the anthrax and Brenner's call, but then gave up on it. It was too long and too involved for here and now. "I don't think we have time," Sims cut him off. He and Riddle were now less than twenty yards from the warehouse. "Just get here quick," he told Higgins, and stuffed the phone in his jacket pocket.

Across the roadway from the warehouse, Sims and Riddle came to a stop, crouching behind a parked car. Sims eyed the warehouse. The trail of footprints led to the smaller door to the left of the large, sliding double doors. The far end of the warehouse opened onto a large square section of the dock that ended on the harbor.

Sims and Riddle took only seconds to cross the roadway, and then they stood on either side of the warehouse door. Sims reached for the heavy steel handle, twisted, then pushed gently. The door opened a crack. Tensed, Sims pushed farther, waiting for a rattle of gunfire, the slamming impact of the door splintered by a hail of bullets.

Nothing.

Sims slipped inside the door. He was in a dark hallway,

perhaps ten feet long. It opened into the major storage area of the warehouse. He could make out the dim shapes of stacked crates and containers. Far away, at the back of the warehouse, a dim light broke the inky blackness, and in the glow he saw shadows shifting against the ceiling beams. Men's voices came from a distance, muffled and indistinct.

Keeping his back against the wall, Sims edged down the hallway. A few feet behind, Riddle followed, both men moving soundlessly across the concrete floor. Sims realized the warehouse was very warm and the air carried with it a brownish leafy odor of rotting vegetation with an overlay of kerosene fumes.

At the end of the hallway, an open space of perhaps ten to fifteen feet, then the bays of the storage area. The center lane angled slightly out of Sims's line of sight. He pictured it running down the long axis of the warehouse, down toward the light and the shadows and the voices.

Crossing the open space quickly and quietly, Sims flattened himself against a large wooden crate. He searched the center lane. Able for the first time to see down its entire length, he froze in surprise.

Fifty feet away, all the way down at the end of the warehouse, a huge translucent cocoon pulsed and billowed, lit from within.

Then Sims realized the cocoon was heavy-gauge clear plastic sheeting covering a massive frame, creating a room within the warehouse. It had to be, Sims estimated, thirty feet long and almost as wide. The dim light outlined low work counters made of sawhorses and planking. Tangles of tubing and wiring led into three large glass-fronted boxes— biohazard cabinets! *Here,* not the house on Pamrapo, was where Zohdi was building doomsday.

But what was Pamrapo and what did Pamrapo have to do with . . . with *this?* Sims felt a slight touch at his shoulder. It was Riddle, staring past Sims at the makeshift laboratory. Riddle prayerfully mouthed a "Mother of God," then nodded toward the end of the warehouse.

As if materialized from nowhere, Kamāl Zohdi, a respirator mask slung around his neck, stood at the corner of the laboratory, just a few feet from the warehouse door leading out onto the dock. It was a dramatic presence—full red lips, skin pale against the black, well-trimmed beard—the leading character spotlighted on an otherwise dark stage.

A wiry, somewhat shabbier man, also wearing a mask, came out of the laboratory to Zohdi's side. The man turned toward Zohdi to say something, and Sims recognized him as Ramzi Yousef. Zohdi, dressed in a black nylon jumpsuit and wool watch cap, wore a holster beneath his left arm. Yousef, similarly outfitted, carried a shiny metal canister about two feet long and a foot in diameter slung by a web strap over his right shoulder.

Zohdi must have asked the time, Sims guessed. Ramzi had thrust out his wrist to glance at his watch.

And then it all came apart.

Zohdi cocked his head toward the rafters as if listening for a signal from heaven. It came—distant, at first, then rapidly louder, the beat of helicopter rotors.

At the same time, more distant, the warbling of sirens.

Yousef threw the door open and Sims saw the dark shape of a hovering helicopter flaring in for a landing on the dock outside. The sirens were now louder, but in an eternity of trying, an infinity of opportunities, the sirens would always lose out to the helicopter on the dock, now settling on its skids.

Sims covered the first ten yards toward Zohdi in less than two seconds.

In those two seconds, Zohdi saw Sims and shouted. As Ramzi Yousef went for his pistol, Zohdi swung the canister from Yousef's shoulder to his own.

Running hard, Sims passed the laboratory, part of him registering the rows of round containers on the workbenches and the moldy odor of rotting vegetation.

A rapid motion out of the corner of his eye, momentarily distracted him. A man stood on top of a sea-land container crate. The man had an Uzi, and Sims realized that he had seen the man too late. He swung his pistol but he knew, like he knew about the sirens, that he'd never make it in time.

The man with the Uzi swung his stubby submachine gun

to line up on Sims, at the same time, his finger tightened around the trigger.

Two rapid explosions filled the warehouse and from behind Sims, bolts of orange light flashed through the darkness.

The man on the container flew off his feet as if hit by an invisible locomotive. Spasming in death, his finger closed around the trigger of the Uzi. The weapon stuttered angrily, and Sims heard the slugs dinging into containers, slamming wooden crates, and smashing glass along the workbenches in the laboratory.

A third heavy explosion. To Sims's right, a second man, also armed with an Uzi, jerked wildly again as a half-inch lead slug tore through his sternum, the exit wound making a fist-size hole through his spine.

Sims quickly glanced over his shoulder. Riddle stood in the middle of the floor, both arms extended, both hands cupping the heavy Webley, a wild, killing smile splitting his face.

Sims ran at the speed of light, focusing only on Zohdi and Yousef and the door and the helicopter on the dock.

Zohdi had ducked out the door. Yousef, following behind, fired twice in Sims's direction, the shots high and harmless. Yousef stopped at the door, grabbed the lifting handle of a kerosene space heater, and, heaving underhanded, lofted the heater toward Sims.

The heater sailed in a high arc, its leaking fuel tracing a path of flame through the air. Crashing on the concrete floor, the flame billowed up and spread rapidly into a lake of fire between Sims and the doorway.

The sudden ferocity of the flames slowed Sims for a fraction of a second, and then he was through the door, rolling in the snow, snuffing out the flames on his jacket and trousers. He smelled the sweetness of seared flesh and knew his hands had been burned, but he felt no pain as he scrambled to his feet.

A beating roar filled Sims's ears as the helicopter charged him, coming toward him nose down, skids just feet off the dock, surrounded by a whirlwind of stinging snow and ice.

"Zohdi!" Sims screamed at the helicopter, at the evil within, screaming in frustration and at his own helplessness, so mismatched against Zohdi's power and invulnerability. Anger driving him forward, Sims threw away his pistol to leap high and grab the skids of the helicopter as it passed overhead.

The jolt nearly wrenched Sims's arms from their sockets as the massive momentum of the helicopter hurled him up and backward. A hurried glance down revealed that he was already several hundred feet above the docks and headed out over the bay. He heard Klaxons and saw the flashing blue and red strobe lights of three Jersey City squad cars now just a block or two from Pier D. From the warehouse, a black plume of smoke rose as flames broke through the roof, and Sims felt a wash of helplessness as he imagined Riddle trapped in the fire.

A freezing gale force wind buffeted Sims as the helicopter gained speed and altitude. He swung his legs up in an attempt to wrap them around the skids and relieve the terrible strain on his arms. His hands, he saw, had been burned badly enough to blister. The first attempt to scissor lock the skid failed and the pain in his arms and shoulders caused his hands to start losing their grip on the skid's slick metal surface.

He felt himself slipping. The wind tore at him, trying to peel him from his perch. Twisting his body so the wind hit him squarely in the back, he tried again, mustering all his strength to lever up. Aided by the wind, he felt his right heel hook itself over the skid. Using the additional leverage, he got his left leg around the skid and gasped in relief as the pressure dropped from his arms and shoulders.

Snow and ice pelted his face, freezing in his eyelashes. Nearly blinded, he lost all sense of direction. With great effort, he managed to rub his right eye into his shoulder. Regaining his sight only momentarily, he caught a flashing glimpse of a giant bronze-green arm and realized they had just whipped by the Statue of Liberty.

Eyes now frozen shut again, Sims conjured up a mental map. They had to be almost above Ellis Island, heading for

Manhattan. Needles of pain pierced the exposed skin of his face and hands and he realized that he'd lost all feeling in his ears and nose. With an air speed of at least eighty miles an hour, Sims knew the wind chill had to be well below zero. A few more seconds and he'd lose his grip, and for the second time that morning, he previewed his death. This time, no instantaneous explosion. This time, a long fall . . . tens of seconds . . . body reaching a velocity of one hundred twenty miles an hour . . . slamming into the bay, a street, the corner of a building . . .

The noise around him changed character with a hint of a deepening pitch, at first so subtle Sims wondered if he had imagined it, then more pronounced as he felt the helicopter slow, then tilt tail downward. The rush of air by Sims became a downward draft as the rotor blades sliced more deeply into the cold air and the steady roar became a rapid *whopping* noise.

Again, he rubbed his eye against his shoulder. As his vision cleared, he saw the fuzzy outlines of a large square. The helicopter was coming in for a landing on the top of a building.

Sims scanned the horizon—nothing. No other skyscrapers, no bridge tops, nothing except gray sky and the snow.

Below, a small white square centered in the middle of the rooftop. In the middle of the square, a red circle around the number fifteen. They were rapidly approaching a rooftop helipad. The pad itself rose perhaps ten feet above the roof. Passengers got to and from the pad by one of two metal grate stairs leading up from the roof. The rest of the roof was the usual maze of Manhattan skyscraper hardware— white-fronted microwave dishes on industrial scaffolding, conduits and piping for electrical power and cooling and heating, and in each of the corners of the rooftop, a massive ventilation tower.

They would land in seconds, Sims thought. And if he stayed where he was, he'd be crushed between the helicopter skid and the elevated concrete pad. The helicopter was now about thirty feet from the pad . . . fifteen feet above it . . . closing fast, Sims estimated. He flexed his arms, said a prayer for the strength for one last effort, then unlocked his legs from their scissor grip on the skid to hang only by his hands. He held for another second, then let go.

Sims landed, as he'd intended, well short of the elevated helipad. However, his legs, numb from clinging to the helicopter, crumbled as his forward momentum tumbled him viciously along the roof and slammed him against the supporting wall of the helipad.

Stunned, Sims struggled to clear his head. He felt a gone-to-sleep sensation in his left arm. Sitting up, he saw the arm hanging at a crazy angle. Unzipping his jacket midway, he reached across with his right hand, carefully lifted the broken arm, bringing it across his chest and placing the hand and wrist inside the jacket, forming an improvised sling. Above him on the helipad, the engine noise had subsided to the whine of a jet turbine at idle.

Using the helipad wall as a support, Sims managed to get himself upright into a standing crouch, immobilizing the left arm as best he could by clutching it against his chest with his right hand. Standing and resting his back against the wall, he heard only the helicopter turbine and the singing of the wind through the structures jutting from the rooftop. Then came a mutter of voices, then footsteps grating on the metal stairs just around the corner—one set of footsteps. As the footsteps receded, he carefully edged closer to the corner.

Alone, with the canister slung over his shoulder, Kamāl Zohdi walked away from the pad, toward the far corner of the rooftop.

Sims waited, listening for a following set of footsteps. Nothing. Zohdi by himself. Zohdi wouldn't want help. God alone created the earth; Zohdi alone could destroy it.

Peering around the corner again, Sims watched Zohdi disappear behind a small blockhouse that probably housed the giant pulleys and electric motors for the elevators.

Sims stretched and looked up. Above him, the helicopter's tail rotor. That meant that Yousef and whoever else was sitting in the helicopter was facing away from Sims. They were probably up there watching the spot where Zohdi had disappeared, waiting for him to come back after—after what?

Ducking low to stay in the helicopter's blind spot, Sims sprinted across the roof toward the concealment of an elevated observation walkway that paralleled the four sides of the helipad. With every step, his cramped thigh muscles protested, and shafts of electrifying pain shot through his left arm.

Under the walkway, Sims paused to orient himself. Forcing down the pain, he pictured the top of the skyscraper as a clock face. The helicopter, in the center of the clock, pointed to noon. Zohdi had taken off for the corner at two o'clock, and he, Sims, was under the walkway at six o'clock.

Keeping under the walkway, Sims worked his way counterclockwise until he came near the housing for the elevator machinery. He cleared the gap between the walkway and the elevator building in two running steps, coming to a stop with his back against the concrete wall. Inside, he could hear the busy working of the elevator motors and cables.

Sims scanned the rooftop for anything he could use as a weapon, a length of pipe, a workman's abandoned tool, anything that he could hold in his one good hand and use to throw, cut, or thrust. He gave up. Whoever took care of the roof did too good a job. Nothing loose lay around to be caught by the wind or the downdraft from the helipad.

Edging along the elevator building, he came to the corner, froze, and listened. The wind carried small indistinct metal-on-metal sounds. He lowered himself to his belly, wincing at the pain in his arm. Pulling himself forward with his right elbow, he peered around the corner of the building.

Zohdi, back to Sims, was at the ventilator shaft. To his right, at his feet, the aluminum canister. Zohdi appeared to be working on something on the shaft itself, then Sims saw that he was unlatching a waist-high maintenance hatch into the shaft.

Oh my God! The elegant simplicity of Zohdi's plan stunned Sims. Like some cosmic collision, the bits and pieces came together, fusing into an incandescent nova, bright and deadly.

The bomb and the anthrax worked together. Somewhere down below, Sims was certain, was a bomb. The bomb goes, part of the explosive force rushes up the ventilator shaft. The massive gust carries the tiny anthrax spores thousands of feet into the air where the wind . . .

Zohdi swung the hatch open and bent to pick up the canister.

Rising to a crouch, Sims sprang forward. Picking up speed across the rooftop, he aimed for the middle of Zohdi's back, just below the shoulder blades.

Sims was still twenty feet away when Zohdi turned. He had a look of cool deliberateness, as though he'd known all along Sims was there. The sensual red lips parted in a half-smile. Zohdi had the arrogant self-satisfied smirk of a man who was about to enjoy himself tremendously as he switched the canister to his left hand and with his right, reached almost casually for his shoulder holster.

Zohdi took a fraction of a second to bring the automatic up and fire.

Sims ducked lower, jink-faked slightly to Zohdi's left, then cut right.

As with most right-handed shooters, Zohdi overcompensated, swinging his aim point high and too far left.

Sims felt a skidding blow to the right side of his head as he threw himself feetfirst in a flying mare at Zohdi. In an unconscious reflex from his football years, he shouted in rage and victory as he connected, reveling in the solid sensation of his body slamming into another.

Zohdi's second shot fired skyward as he crumpled under Sims's weight. At the same time, the pistol recoil and Sims's attack threw the automatic out of Zohdi's hand. The weapon caromed across the rooftop, ending up out of sight behind the ventilator shaft.

Falling with Zohdi, Sims hit on his left shoulder, then rolled onto the broken arm. Wicked fireworks of pain exploded behind Sims's eyes. He twisted, freeing himself from the tangle with Zohdi, and tried to get to his feet while snugging down the broken arm inside his partially unzipped jacket.

Zohdi got to his feet first. Sims, who'd pulled himself up

to one knee, saw Zohdi swing his foot, and threw up his right arm in an attempt to ward off the kick. Zohdi's booted foot brushed by Sims's arm, catching him in the midsection, lifting him up and over, and throwing him sprawling onto his back.

Get up! Get up! A voice screamed inside Sims coming to him through the pain. Yet he lay helpless, suffocating, trying to breathe against the deep piercing agony deep in his chest that told him Zohdi's boot had collapsed a lung.

Zohdi's face suddenly filled his view. At the same time, Sims felt his fingers, like steel claws around his neck. Zohdi, standing astride Sims, bent forward, tightening his grip. His face came even closer.

Oddly detached, somehow watching a film where none of this was really happening to him, Sims clinically studied the face: almost a perfect oval, the white skin and red lips and black pointed beard. Sims felt in Zohdi's eyes the hypnotic pull you feel when standing on the edge of a high place. The look of death was in the eyes, absolute black, absolute cold.

Zohdi's breath came heavier and the muscles in his face tightened as he closed his hands around Sims's throat.

Sims felt no pain, only an increasing lightness, a euphoric weightlessness, as the sharp outlines of Zohdi's face began to fade. Like someone had thrown a switch, Sims's detachment vanished and he realized he was dying. In a concentrated burst that summoned up his remaining strength, Sims kicked upward.

Zohdi's eyes suddenly flattened. His mouth jerked open in a spasm of surprise and question as a preview message raced through his nervous system, up the spinal cord, and into his brain. In that thousandth of a second, he learned what was coming, but even knowing, he was helpless, waiting for the inevitable.

In the next thousandth of a second, the explosive neural response hit, telling Zohdi that his testicles had disintegrated. The primal, hollowing pain overloaded every nerve in his body with an intensity that obliterated everything else in the universe. Zohdi's hands flew from Sims's throat to clutch himself.

Sims head-butted Zohdi in the chest, throwing him

reeling backward. Breath coming in ragged gasps, Sims staggered to his feet. The snow pelted his face and his legs felt close to collapse and his lungs burned and he heard the *whop-whop-whop* of the helicopter and someone shouting in Arabic to Zohdi.

Lurching forward, Sims swung a sloppy undercut. Zohdi, still doubled over, was able to shift ever so slightly and the blow skidded off to the right, Sims's knuckles opening a wide cut on the man's left cheek.

Zohdi stumbled backward, stopping his fall with a hand that grasped the edge of the ventilator shaft. To his left, lying glistening in the snow on the rooftop, the anthrax canister. Zohdi bent swiftly and in a quick, scooping motion, grabbed the canister by its webbed carrying strap.

Sims, still recovering from the effort of swinging at Zohdi, staggered toward the man, each step sending jabbing pain through his chest and his broken left arm. In nightmare slow motion, he saw Zohdi twist, carrying the canister toward the big black mouth that was the maintenance hatch. In the background, the shouting in Arabic had become more shrill, its urgency overlaid with a high treble of panic.

A wailing voice inside him screamed . . . *too late!* . . . *too late!* . . . Sims dove, his good right arm hooking Zohdi around the shoulder, pinning the man's upper arm to his side, the momentum crashing the two of them against the heavy gauge steel of the ventilator shaft.

Sims felt the toe of his boot nudge something round and hard, and he kicked at it, hoping it was the canister, and hoping he wouldn't hit a release that would cause it to pop open.

Zohdi twisted violently to his left, the motion breaking Sims's one-armed grip, carrying Sims around, pinning Sims's back against the ventilator shaft. The two men were now belly to belly, with Zohdi pressing against Sims, one hand on Sims's neck, the other on Sims's left shoulder.

Sims felt his right shoulder being pushed back into the open maintenance hatch. He flailed with his right arm at Zohdi, but his fist beat helplessly on Zohdi's back.

Zohdi twisted at Sims's broken arm.

Sims's pain brought him to the edge of unconsciousness. Zohdi had him squarely in front of the open hatch, the edge of the hatch cutting across Sims's lower back.

Zohdi pressed harder, and now Sims's upper body was fully into the opening. In a rapid motion, Zohdi brought both hands up to Sims's throat.

Again, Sims felt the steel fingers closing . . . total vulnerability, inescapable and complete . . . again Zohdi's face filling his world . . . Zohdi, choking him, bending him farther into the ventilator shaft.

Sims brought his right hand around, trying to get a counter grip on Zohdi's throat, but the man easily elbowed away Sims's feeble attempt. Zohdi's face blurred as Sims pulled vainly for breath.

Dropping his right hand to Zohdi's chest, Sims found an opening in Zohdi's jumpsuit. Sims's frantic fingers closed around a long cigar-shaped object in an inner pocket.

Sims jerked the thing free, and with a desperation swing, stabbed at Zohdi's face, once, twice, then a third time.

The scream came from the depths of Zohdi's chest, a high-pitched aria of pain. Zohdi stiffened and jerked away from Sims as if he'd been hit with high voltage.

Sims levered forward, his throat free of the killing fingers. Zohdi's scream filled his ears and as his vision cleared, he saw Zohdi stagger toward him.

Zohdi's hands, both of them, frantically worked around his face, the fingers writhing around the black casing of a Mont Blanc pen jutting from Zohdi's left eye.

Sims twisted and hit Zohdi with his right shoulder. Zohdi's momentum and Sims's weight carried both men forward.

The lower ledge of the maintenance hatch caught Zohdi just below his waist, and, hands still clutching at the pen and his destroyed eye, Zohdi fell through the opening.

Barely able to stand, Sims felt the beating of rotor blades just above him as the helicopter lifted off, disappearing into the driving snow.

At his feet, the aluminum canister with its payload of death glinted dully. Sims dropped to his knees, then fell forward, wrapping himself protectively around the canister.

As he did so, the entire rooftop swayed as if struck by a giant fist.

On level B-2 in the World Trade Center parking garage, Mahmoud Abouhalima's timers had worked flawlessly. On detonation, the fireball cut into the central ventilation system, directly above the van, creating a gigantic chimney effect, just as Zohdi had planned. Roaring through the shafts at speeds approaching the velocity of sound, the fireball pushed a huge plug of cooler air before it.

Falling down the huge ventilator shaft, Kamāl Zohdi gained speed each second. Zohdi focused on the cauldron of pain that had been his eye. A small fragment of his consciousness, however, sensed a momentary, almost cushionlike resistance at the ninety-seventh floor when he met the compressed air that was to have blown the anthrax high above New York. Then, speeding ever faster into the pit of blackness, Zohdi plunged into the rising fireball.

Clutching the canister, Sims lay on the roof as a column of black smoke shot skyward from the ventilation shaft. The justice of it suddenly struck him—the smoke carried Zohdi's ashes, the last remains of Abaddon, the angel of Hell.

EPILOGUE

From some other world, a voice said, "Good morning, young man, you're coming around."

Wrapped in a warm, comforting darkness, Sims didn't care who was talking or who was coming around.

He tried to ignore the voice by struggling to sink deeper into the darkness, but he felt the warmth escaping, as if evaporating from the pores in his skin. A pinpoint of light flickered in the center of the darkness. The pinpoint steadied and expanded and he felt as if he were rushing out of a long tunnel into the daylight. A shape before him took form, a round white arm with brown fingers.

He was trying to figure it out when the voice said, "They've got your arm in traction."

He willed his left hand to move. The fingers at the end of the suspended cast wiggled slightly.

He turned to the voice and Riddle came into focus. Riddle in a loose gown. Gauze bandages covered the left side of his face. Forcing his mind to work, he retrieved the last image of Riddle, the cannonlike revolver in both hands, standing in the burning warehouse.

"How're you, Riddle?"

Riddle touched the side of his face with a hand also wrapped in gauze. "Slightly singed, young man, just slightly singed," Riddle said softly.

"Head, chest hurt," Sims said drowsily. "What . . . ?"

"You've been out two days." Riddle put a hand on Sims's right shoulder. "You have a minor scalp wound. Burns on your hands. An operation on the arm. They had to remove your spleen and repair your left lung."

"Lung?"

"A broken rib puncture."

Sims lay completely still. Playing ball, he'd learned to take a quick body inventory after he'd been creamed. No doubt about it, he'd been creamed again. His body was a new definition of bad.

"Where the hell was I? What happened after . . ."

He listened as Riddle put it in a capsule: Zohdi and Ramzi Yousef's hijacking of a commercial helicopter from Newark, the van in the basement of the World Trade Center.

"How many?"

"Many?" Riddle asked back.

There was something about the way Riddle said it that told Sims that Riddle knew what Sims was asking about but didn't want to talk about it.

"Dead—how many dead, Riddle?" insisted Sims.

"Six. There could have been many more. Millions."

"Six," Sims repeated. Better than millions, but still too many. Then he looked at Riddle. "Add one—Zohdi."

Riddle looked surprised. "We thought he escaped with Ramzi Yousef."

Sims told Riddle how Zohdi had died.

For a moment, Riddle sat and thought about it, then shook his head wonderingly. "Fitting."

Sims started slipping. Zohdi, the tower, none of it mattered. "Hurts," was all he could muster. His head was pounding and the pain from his chest and abdomen was now rampaging through his body. Over Riddle's shoulder, he saw the door open and a nurse come in, carrying a tray.

Though part of him fought the bite of the nurse's needle, another part welcomed it, and the room and Riddle and the light closed back down to a pinpoint. He sank gratefully into the warmth and darkness again.

* * *
382

As Sims slipped into unconsciousness, night had already come to Lebanon, and in Latakia, the manager of the Meridien Hotel called police headquarters, his voice skirting the edge of hysteria.

Forty minutes later, Detective Lieutenant Samih Farsoûn stood in the master bedroom of the plush oceanfront suite that had belonged to Sergei Okolovich.

Okolovich, quite dead, lay sprawled on the floor, his blood a dark stain on the burgundy carpeting. The stain, Farsoûn noted, was almost perfectly circular, having spread evenly almost a foot all the way around Okolovich's head.

Farsoûn had known of Okolovich's true identity the day the former KGB officer had sought sanctuary in Latakia. And Farsoûn had known, too, of Okolovich's relationship with Kamāl Zohdi, and of Zohdi's connections in Damascus. Zohdi had mysteriously disappeared, and with that disappearance had gone the protective mantle he had cast around Okolovich.

Good riddance to both, Farsoûn thought to himself. The detective noted the single entry wound in the back of the head. None of the hotel help reported the sound of a gunshot, so they'd probably used a silencer. No weapon, no spent cartridge case. Yesterday, one of Farsoûn's informants had reported the arrival of two Russians in Latakia. Farsoûn imagined they'd now be gone, leaving behind their false names in the register of one of the cheaper waterfront hotels.

Farsoûn lit a cigarette, savoring the rich smell of the strong tobacco. He turned to the hotel manager, standing in the middle of the room, wringing his hands, sweating profusely.

"An unfortunate case of suicide," Farsoûn said, exhaling a plume of blue-gray smoke. "A truly unfortunate case."

Over the next thirty-six hours, Sims's periods of consciousness increased. He regained his sense of time as he registered the feedings, calls for bedpans, the nurses and doctors coming and going, quietly taking blood, urine, examining, checking, probing, doing everything it seemed, but talking.

"It's Tuesday, March second," the nurse finally answered Sims as she took his blood in the predawn quiet of the hospital. As she labeled the sample, she answered his second question: "You're getting out of here when the doctor *says* you're getting out of here."

A few minutes later, Sims tried several spoonfuls of bran cereal, pushed aside the soft-boiled egg, and drifted off to sleep.

"How you doin', Bradford?"

Lying on his side, Sims opened his eyes to a fuzzy out-of-kilter world. The first thing his eyes focused on were the remains of breakfast still on the bedside table.

Then he saw Rollo Moss, like a huge black genie, standing by the side of the bed. Through his grogginess, Sims felt a rush of warmth.

"How you doin'?" Rollo repeated to Sims.

Sims heard the words from a great distance. He wiggled his fingers in the cast. "Can't play piano," he mumbled. He heard Rollo's laughter like faraway thunder on a summer afternoon.

"Hell, Bradford," he heard Rollo say, "you couldn't play before."

Laughter came from somewhere and then Rollo disappeared.

Late that afternoon, Riddle knocked softly and entered followed by the Judge and Alberich. With them, a tall olive-skinned man in a pin-striped double-breasted suit. Before the door closed, Sims got a glimpse of the hallway outside. Two men stood watch, one by his door, another across the hall. The one across the hall had an earphone in his left ear with the flesh-colored spiral cord snaking down and disappearing under his collar.

"I am Khalid Riad," the visitor said after the door closed and before the Judge could perform the introduction. Riad extended a hand. Sims took it and felt the hard horn of callous running along the blade edge of Riad's hand.

"Mr. Riad is the deputy political counselor of the Egyptian Embassy here," the Judge said in way of explanation. "And, I should add, chief of Mukhabarat el-Aam's liaison branch for North America."

"Neptune," Sims guessed.

Riad nodded. "He was one of ours," the Egyptian intelligence officer said. "One of our best."

Not knowing what to say, Sims said simply, "I'm sorry."

Riad shook his head philosophically. "He had been tracking Zohdi too long. He lost his patience."

"Long?" Sims asked. "How long?"

"Several years. Long before he came to America. You see, Zohdi and those like him—his fundamentalist co-believers—may believe the United States is the Great Satan, but they also consider Arab moderates the enemy as well. Islam is a tolerant religion. The Koran tells us that he who kills an innocent has killed everyone. But the fundamentalists"—Riad searched for the words—"regard any deviation from their thinking as evidence of Western infection."

Riad's sad face grew even sadder. "For many of us, scholars, artists, politicians, this has become the dark age of the Arab. Remember Anwar Sadat, who made peace with the Israelis, was assassinated by fundamentalists like Zohdi, and even now, they are waging war within the Islamic world against their Muslim brothers."

Sims felt his face flush. "Six of those innocents were killed at the World Trade Center, and a lot more before. And if Zohdi'd had his way, he'd have killed millions more. Why the hell didn't you people hammer him in Egypt? Why'd you wait until he got here?"

Riad shrugged apologetically, showing his empty palms to Sims. "Because we could not attack Zohdi and his followers in Egypt or Syria or anywhere in the Middle East, not openly, or we'd have a civil war on our hands."

The pieces fell into place for Sims as he remembered Neptune's smiling eagerness. "So you sent Neptune here to help us bag Zohdi."

Riad pressed his lips together. "We—I—thought that with a little quiet assistance, you would, as you say, roll Zohdi up."

"And Neptune became a walk-in source for the Bureau," Sims said. "But no one listened."

Riad drew a deep breath. "Oh, there was interest at the working levels, but when the case got higher, I guess we fell into the category of politically inconvenient . . ." He shrugged and let it trail off.

The Egyptian intelligence officer stepped closer to Sims's bed. "I came to thank you," he said, brightening. "I regret we cannot acknowledge your contribution publicly, but I'm afraid if we did, neither one of us would ever be able to come out of hiding."

Riad gave Sims a smile, shook hands with Riddle, the Judge, and Alberich, and was gone.

For several moments, no one spoke.

"How about our friends in the White House?" Sims asked the Judge.

The Judge pursed his lips in thought, as if he were about to testify in court. "Ralston Dean reports that he 'had words' with the Syrian ambassador."

"And—"

"And the Syrian ambassador told the president's national security adviser that the government of Syria was shocked at the allegations."

"Shocked?" Sims got a sick feeling.

"I believe that was the word."

"So Dean's not going to do shit . . ."

"Ralston believes, as he said in his own words, 'it is better to engage the Syrians in a constructive dialog than to make them into outlaws.' But"—the Judge's voice picked up an ironic tone—"he is going to take *some* action."

Sims shot him a questioning look.

"The talk is that Dean has convinced the president to fire Lars Nesbith—a sacrificial lamb."

Sims frowned, remembering how Lars Nesbith had turned his back on Neptune. "Deserving asshole," he muttered.

"There are a few more matters," said Riddle. He and the

386

Judge pulled chairs up around Sims's bed, leaving a space between the two of them. Alberich scooted his chair in.

"More?" Sims asked.

"More," said the Judge, nodding to Alberich. "Matthias has mined a few nuggets out of the KGB files our friend Aristov opened for us."

"The *files!*" Alberich shook his head. "You wouldn't believe it! Miles and miles of files. The commies couldn't make washing machines, but they sure could make files. Anyway,"—Alberich got a sly look—"Zohdi and Okolovich killed Gribbins and Felton and tried to kill you because they thought one of you or maybe all three of you were trying to blackmail them."

Sims stiffened. "What the hell're you talking about?"

Alberich ignored the question. "Let's go back to the defection of Miloslav Valek. You picked him up in the Rosslyn metro just after Christmas, 1991."

"Two days after Christmas. A Friday," Sims supplied.

"You were the case officer, but the Russians—Okolovich's boys—whacked him before you could get him to open up. That was when?"

"When they killed Valek? January—the last of January '92."

Alberich straightened out several notes in his lap. "Aristov had part of the picture right. Valek found Zohdi and introduced him to Okolovich and Broz. What Aristov didn't know was that Valek was up to his ass in the drug deals and the money laundering."

"In what way?"

"Valek set them up. He was Okolovich and Broz's leg man. It was all in Valek's case files. The Mafia guys—the Porta Nuova clan?" Alberich looked questioningly at Sims.

Sims nodded, remembering the two men he'd killed in San Gimignano.

"Valek helped Zohdi furnish the Sicilians with raw opium that Zohdi's people had grown in the Bekáa. And it was Valek who recruited Spiedel and helped put together Karstens-Export."

"Busy man. But if he was in so tight with Broz and Okolovich, why'd he run?"

Alberich shrugged. "May never know for sure. Maybe he thought Okolovich and Broz were going to retire him without a pension."

"Pair of concrete overshoes?"

"Remember, Bradford, Okolovich did get rid of Broz," Riddle pointed out. "About the same time his people killed Valek."

"Anyway," Alberich continued, "Valek went on the run. But he took along some insurance."

"Copies of the files," Sims put in. "A golden parachute."

Alberich continued. "After Okolovich's people assassinated Valek, Okolovich thought he was safe."

"How about the copies of the files Valek had?"

Alberich shrugged. "Okolovich must have decided that he was safer with Valek dead than with Valek alive. Okolovich probably figured that Valek had hidden the files well enough that they'd stay hidden. And even if the files were found, they'd mean little without Valek's knowledge of the context."

"And?"

"And you can imagine the look on Okolovich's face when, six weeks ago, someone demanded five million dollars for the files."

"That's what happened?"

Alberich nodded. Reaching in the folder, he came out with two photocopied pages stapled together. He pushed the pages across the polished tabletop to Sims. The first page bore no heading or signature, just the date: January 14, 1993. The page was typed in English.

This is a sample of the files Miloslav Valek brought out with him. Valek photographed the files with a Minox Model B, resulting in four 50-exposure cassettes of quality microfilm.

The entire collection of files is for sale. The price is five million U.S. dollars. Nonnegotiable. Instructions follow.

The second page, typed in German, described arrangements for a forthcoming arms shipment from Bremerhaven to Latakia: diversionary stops in Rabat and Tunis, false end-user certificates, phoney bills of lading.

"Where'd you get this?" Sims asked.

"Felton's safe deposit box, along with these." Alberich reached into a pouch on the side of his wheelchair. He handed Sims four tiny cylindrical plastic cassettes.

"Microfilm."

"The Valek files."

"How'd you find them?"

Alberich shrugged. "Not too hard. Felton was a shrink, he wasn't operational. He never got the five million, of course, but he set up a numbered account in the Caymans to handle it when it came. Strictly amateur job, his fingerprints all over it. Then I went back to Valek's polygraph exams. Felton had run three. Each printout has a sequenced serial number. Felton had doctored the numbers on the second and third exam printouts. I figure he broke Valek, and the two of them cut a deal—he and Valek would become partners. He reran the polygraph exams with innocuous questions and substituted those printouts for the originals. We tossed Felton's house and . . ." Alberich gestured to the cassettes.

Sims stared at the cassettes, then up at Alberich. "But how did Zohdi and Okolovich home in on Gribbins, Felton, and me?"

"You, Felton, and Gribbins," Alberich said, "virtually controlled Valek until his death. Okolovich must have reasoned that one of you—"

"Or maybe all three of us—"

"Or maybe all three of you—sweated the files from Valek and went into business on your own."

"But how'd Okolovich get our names in the first place?"

"You, no problem. You were in Okolovich's face from the start. Gribbins? He was Valek's baby-sitter. They didn't stay in the safe house. Gribbins took Valek out to eat, to the movies. Hell, Gribbins was there when Valek was killed in that men's store. The Russians had surveillance on Valek before they killed him. They could have spotted Gribbins easily."

"And Felton?"

"Surveillance again. Felton came to the safe house three, four times to put Valek on the box."

Sims flexed his hand, rolling the cassettes about in his open palm. In them, the beginnings of what had almost happened. Seeds of evil, he thought. He closed his hand around them as if he could stop them from taking root. Then he opened his hand and gave them back to Alberich.

The Judge stood, followed by Riddle. On their way out, Riddle stopped by Sims's bedside and gripped Sims's shoulder.

"Get your rest, Bradford. It's over."

Riddle, Alberich, and the Judge had just left when the phone rang. Annoyed, Sims muttered a mild curse and picked up the receiver.

"Hello," came the smoky voice.

He felt a sensuous warmth and realized that the voice no longer reminded him of Lourdes.

"Hello, control," said Sims, a grin beginning.